Books by Timothy James Beck

IT HAD TO BE YOU

HE'S THE ONE

Published by Kensington Publishing Corporation

HE'S THE ONE

Timothy James Beck

KENSINGTON BOOKS
http://www.kensingtonbooks.com

KENSINGTON BOOKS are published by

Kensington Publishing Corp.
850 Third Avenue
New York, NY 10022

All Kensington titles, imprints and distributed lines are available at special quantity discounts for bulk purchases for sales promotion, premiums, fund-raising, educational or institutional use.

Special book excerpts or customized printings can also be created to fit specific needs. For details, write or phone the office of the Kensington Special Sales Manager: Kensington Publishing Corp., 850 Third Avenue, New York, NY 10022, Attn. Special Sales Department. Phone: 1-800-221-2647.

Kensington and the K logo Reg. U.S. Pat. & TM Off.

ISBN 0-7582-0324-1

First Hardcover Printing: January 2003
First Trade Paperback Printing: December 2003
10 9 8 7 6 5 4 3 2 1

Printed in the United States of America

To the great city of New York—
a love letter from TJB.

Acknowledgments

With deepest gratitude to Alison Picard, John Scognamiglio, Michael Vicencia, and Tom Wocken.

Special thanks to Jean-Marc Chazy, Dorothy Cochrane, Steve Code, James McCain Jr., Steve Nordwick, Erin Swan, and Bill Thomas.

Additional thanks to Christine Bradley, Jim Carter, the Carter family, Joyce Cavalier, Colin Chase, Becky Cochrane-Wocken, the Cochrane family, Andre Coffa, Darren Connell, Jason Crawford, Jennifer Damiano, Carlton Davis and Veronique Gambier, Caroline De La Rosa, Jonathan De Michael, Lynne Demarest, Kim Duva, Ghalib El-Khalidi, Paul Enea, Jeffrey Fischer, Timothy Forry, the Forry family, the Garber family, Amy and Richard Ghiselin, Lowry Greeley, Terri Griffin, Jennifer Hackett, Will Hatheway, Larry Henderson, Henry Hershkowitz and the Screening Room, Jim Hitchcock, Anthony Johnson, Alan Josoff, Julian's Restaurant, Christine and John Kovach, John and Nancy Lambert, Theodore J. Lambert, Timothy J. Lambert, Marla McDaniel, Robin McElfresh, the Miller family, Debbie Milton, Helen C. Morris, Steven Parkhurst, Jay Peabody, Ron Pratt, the Rambo family, Leah Rappaport for not evicting Tim when she had so many chances, Lori Redfearn and Bob Corrigan, the Rose family, Carmela Roth, Mary Russo, Terry and Allen Shull, Laurie and Marty Smith, Denece Thibodeaux, Dana Thomas, Aubry Vance, Steve Vargas, Tim Wade, Jeffrey Wallen, Ellen Ward and Pat Crosby, Don Whittaker, Carissa Williams, Tracy Wilson, the Wocken family, Casper Yaqoub, Yojo, AOL, the Big Cup, the folks at Crossroads and Lobo, the Renaissance Diner for always delivering, and the supportive and funny gang from G&L.

For unconditional love, thanks Arthur, Guinness, Lazlo, Margot, Merc, and Striker.

ONE

In my opinion, the best part of sex was the feeling of elation I always experienced afterward. The rush of endorphins, mixed with the thrill of release, always left me light-headed and giddy. I never felt tired afterward. For me, sex was like a double espresso, something I sought when I needed a pick-me-up to boost my spirits as a reward after a long day.

Usually, my sexual partners would get caught up in the after-rush of excitement with me. I'd grip them in a bear hug and surrender to the joy that coursed its way through my body, which I generally expressed by a huge, goofy grin, since I often found it difficult to put into words how much I enjoyed sharing that moment with another man in my arms.

Sam69wu was no exception, but he also made me aware of a feeling that had been lurking inside me. When his invitation to meet him had popped up on my computer screen while I was researching an artist on the Web, it awakened a craving I'd been only dimly aware of.

Computers were my livelihood as well as part of my off time. If I wasn't teaching, running my Web consulting business, or spending time with friends on a ball field, I was relaxing in front of my computer, chatting with acquaintances online. I had never used the Internet to hook up with a guy before. I usually regarded everyone I met online as faceless entities or players in an imaginary theater who improvised their roles as they went along. But I didn't see the point of lying to someone about yourself on the Internet if you were going to meet him face to face. Why would you set up yourself—and someone else—for a big letdown? Sam69wu described himself to me, sent me a picture that matched, and asked me to do the same. I reciprocated, and we agreed on a meeting place. It wasn't that different from picking up someone at a bar, other than that in real life you didn't have to download your date.

Apparently, Sam69wu felt the same way. He was every inch the six-foot, sandy-haired devil in the blue shirt he'd described in the online messages that led me to meet him at Scooters. I agreed to follow him to his house, where he showed me the meaning of his screen name.

Hours later, he said, "That was amazing. Uh, what's your name again?"

"Adam," I answered as the post-sex excitement slowly wound down like a blender after its power is cut off. I had hoped our two hours together would inscribe my name in his memory like the bite mark I left on his right butt cheek.

"Oh, yeah." He grinned. "That was great, Adam. It's so hard to find someone as hot as you online. Most guys in Eau Claire look like Fred Flintstone. Or Barney Rubble, for that matter, since most of us are blond. Do you want something to drink? A towel?"

The shift from raw sex to a Saturday morning cartoon forum was a bit jarring. He was hot on the outside but had the energy and attention span of a puppy. Still, sex with Sam was exceptional, and his enthusiasm had me longing for more.

"I gave up drinking towels a long time ago. It was becoming a problem," I wisecracked. "Since you brought it up, what cartoon character do I remind you of?"

"Superman." He blushed.

"Do you have a thing for the Man of Steel?"

"Yeah, I do," he admitted. "Do you have a boyfriend?"

Sam had a way of asking out-of-the-blue questions, which could quickly become a turnoff. He'd brought up the very subject I tried to put out of my head whenever I had sex with a guy. At least until the ride home, when I could fantasize about another meeting with Mr. Right. Or thank my lucky stars I got out unscathed, if he turned out to be Mr. Right-Out-the-Door.

The guys I'd tricked with in the past usually proved to be bad choices. Either they only wanted to fulfill a jock fantasy for a couple of hours, or they wanted to spend the rest of their lives with me. Which, as much as I didn't want to admit it to myself, was becoming an idea that appealed to me—finding someone permanent. However, the guys I met often turned out to have criminal records, bankruptcy histories, personality disorders, or wives.

"No. I don't have a boyfriend," I said. Thinking about my dating history and lack of boyfriends had made the Man of Steel quickly deflate into Gumby, as I lost every urge to continue to round two.

"Good," Sam said. "I don't like guys who cheat on their partners."

"I've never really had one," I said.

"Had one what?" Sam's mind had obviously wandered elsewhere in the span of five seconds.

I shifted my body so I could put my arm under him to draw his head to my chest as I lay back on the pillows.

"A partner," I answered. "Boyfriend, lover, or whatever you want to call him. I mean, I've had a couple of relationships, but they didn't last longer than three months. It's hard to meet good guys, I guess. Or good gay guys. The guys on my softball team are all straight. I teach at UW-Stout, but I would never date a student. And I run my own business, so I don't even have the opportunity to dip my pen in the company ink. You're the first guy I've ever hooked up with online, which is odd, since I've been online for years."

"It's hard," Sam said.

"It is?" I quipped, lifting the covers to peek at his body.

"That's not what I meant." He laughed. "I meant it's hard to meet guys. You're the first guy I met online who's normal."

"I know what you mean. My friends and my parents are always trying to fix me up with every guy they meet who's gay. You know, he's gay, so he must be perfect because I'm gay, too. As if that's all that matters."

"I don't see why you'd have to be fixed up," Sam mused. "You've got the bluest eyes I've ever seen, Alex."

"Adam," I corrected.

Sam blushed again.

"I'm sorry, Adam. I love blue eyes and dark hair on a guy. And you've got a strong jaw, just like Superman. You're so handsome. And tall. How tall are you?"

"Six foot two," I said absently.

"And you obviously work out a lot," he said, tracing his finger over my abs.

"Yeah, two or three times a week. I have a home gym, too."

Sam wore his jock fantasy like a brightly colored football jersey, and his eyes lit up like a scoreboard when the Man of Steel returned at his touch. Putting all thoughts of relationships, fix-ups, and mixed emotions out of my head, I rolled Sam onto his back and kissed him hard.

"I like it rough," Sam said.

"I like it silent," I said, covering his mouth with mine again.

Okay, maybe he was scatterbrained. Maybe he wasn't a rocket scientist. But sex with Sam was gratifying.

I could get used to this, I thought, as I rolled on my second condom that night. He might be fun to come home to after a day at the university. During the semesters when I didn't teach and worked at my home-based office full time, I could draw from Sam's limitless reserves of energy. And with his fervor, he must be successful at whatever he did.

His enthusiasm for sex seemed to know no bounds. We both came a second time and I collapsed, sated, alongside him once again.

"Incredible," Sam panted. I bit my lip and tried not to smile too broadly but couldn't help it. Sam looked too cute as he nuzzled against me, burrowing his face in my neck.

We'd connected online shortly past midnight, then met at the bar an hour later. After hours of marathon sex, it was no wonder the sun was starting to rise. Slivers of dim light pushed their way through the blinds and crawled across the walls of Sam's bedroom. It was then that I took in my surroundings for the first time. The top of his dresser was littered with mail, papers, and miscellaneous clutter. Clothes draped over chairs and the floor looked like clocks in a Salvador Dali painting. Not only were posters of rock stars and pictures cut from magazines taped to the walls, but a large, framed poster of Superman faced me from the wall opposite the bed. This wasn't the bedroom of a man who would provide stability and the kind of future I was beginning to yearn for.

"Um, Sam, what do you do?" I asked.

"Do?" he sleepily parroted.

"Yeah, you know, for a living? A career? Job? Hobbies? Do you have any hobbies?" I grilled.

"I work at Subway," he mumbled.

I reminded myself that it was okay if everybody wasn't as driven as I was. Besides, maybe Sam was working his way up to a management position and would someday take over the company. Or maybe this was a job he worked while he got his degree in astrophysics.

"Are you going to school?" I asked hopefully, despite my reservations about college students. Hopefully, he wasn't enrolled at my school.

"Nope. I dropped out." I felt panic set in. "But maybe I'll go back once I'm further along in my steps."

Somehow I knew he wasn't talking about aerobics. Or tap dancing.

"I assume there are twelve of them," I prodded, but he'd fallen asleep. I was just about to ease him aside and race home to change my screen name, when the door creaked open and a person stuck her head inside.

"Oh, hi there," an older woman with brown, feathered hair said. Since only her head protruded through, I had no idea what the rest of her looked like. She was grinning like the Cheshire Cat in *Alice in Wonderland* and hardly seemed perturbed at the sight of two naked men in bed together. "You must be one of Sam's little friends. Sorry to bother you, but I was just checking on him. He said he was going to a bar. Did you meet him there?"

"Yes," I answered, pulling the covers up to my neck.

"Was he drinking?" She let out a nervous peal of laughter, like a hyena at a comedy club.

"No. I mean, he wasn't when I met him. I don't think he did. Are you his mother?" As soon as I asked, I knew she was by the beatific smile that spread from ear to ear.

"He's my little angel," she beamed. I wondered if it occurred to her that I had just fucked her little angel three ways to Sunday. She'd have to be Helen Keller not to know, I supposed, but if she did, she didn't say anything. Instead she asked, "Would you like some pancakes, dear? Waffles? A towel? I could throw your clothes in the laundry while you eat."

"That's okay. I'm fine, and I have to get going. Could you toss me my jeans? No, those on the floor are his. Mine are the ones folded on the—thank you," I said as she threw my jeans to me. I caught them, causing the sheets to slide down to my waist. I swore I saw her complacent smile falter as she caught a glimpse of my chest. Another burst of hyenalike laughter followed as she backed through the door and shut it behind her.

Sam didn't stir at all as I slipped out of bed and into my clothes. I crept out of his room, down the hall, and past what I assumed, from the smells of bacon and tinny humming, to be the kitchen, where Sam's mother was obviously cooking breakfast. I raced from the house to my pickup truck and peeled out of the driveway.

I drove without direction, cursing myself for succumbing to lust with an imperfect stranger. What bothered me most wasn't the disappointment of learning that Sam was a flawed human being. It was realizing that I had been lying to myself. I didn't want to be single anymore. I wasn't dating for fun and recreational sex. I was trying to find someone to share my life.

And that wasn't even the scary part. I was comfortable with the idea of sharing myself, flaws and all, with another man. The awakening idea of staying with one man for the rest of my life was oddly satisfying. Having someone by my side to share my fears and dreams would give me even more strength to face every new day we spent together. The alarming thought in the back of my mind was that maybe I had exhausted the limited supply of gay men in Eau Claire, Wisconsin. All the men I met were too young, too coupled, too incompatible, or too wrapped up in being dysfunctional. I knew everyone had problems, and I wasn't going to find anyone around my age, which was thirty-one, who didn't have some baggage. But instead of sticking it in the attic like an old Samsonite, they displayed it like Louis Vuitton.

It was too grim to think about. I knew I should go home and sleep, but finding myself near my gym, I decided to sweat out last night's remorse and tomorrow's anxiety. Besides, my gym bag was always in my truck with a change of clothes. I could shower after my workout, then go to my parents' house squeaky clean. Which I would have to be unless I wanted my all-too-perceptive mother to hammer me with questions. Not that she'd be dismayed if I wandered in with the contented look of a man who'd had a night of great sex. On the contrary, she'd call Dayton's and register a china pattern for me and my "lucky young man."

The baying of Sadie and Marnie, my parents' two spoiled weimaraners, let me know they were protecting an empty house. Usually, they couldn't be bothered to leave whatever comfortable spot they'd chosen for the second most important part of their lives, sleep. After I let myself in the kitchen door, I had to fend off their joyful welcome and resist their frantic attempts to persuade me that the most important part of their lives, food, had been neglected. I knew my parents had not only fed them first thing that morning, but would have also shared bits of their own breakfast with them. As I ate the sandwich I made for myself, they cast mournful, injured looks my way. Finally, they stretched themselves across the sun-dappled linoleum, with only an occasional groan to remind me that death by starvation was imminent.

After I cleaned up after myself—my older brother Mike and I had been much better trained by my parents than their two dogs—I stretched out on the sofa in the den, idly flipping through channels to find something nap-worthy. But before I could doze off, frenzied barks let me know someone was home. I went into the kitchen just as my mother came in with her arms full of groceries.

"Down, Sadie, Marnie," she commanded and cast a glance my way. "I'm glad you're here. Your father and Mike are fixing a leak in Mike's roof. Can you get the rest of the groceries?"

After I brought the bags from her car, I helped her put everything away, the two of us moving easily around each other. I hadn't lived at home for more than a dozen years, but everything there remained familiar.

"What have you been doing today?" I asked, noticing that she was wearing her rainbow T-shirt.

I grinned as my mother talked about the activities she and "the gals" from PFLAG—the organization for parents, friends, and families of lesbians, gays, bisexuals, transgenders, transexuals, pansexuals (all were welcome)—were planning during Gay Pride. When I'd come out to my parents as a college freshman, it had propelled my mother into a new life. She took the zeal that deposited her in cold stadiums watching Mike and me play high school football, or drove her to organize bake sales and car washes for our sports teams, and transferred it to supporting this new facet of her younger son's life. But long after rallies, meetings, and parades stopped being part of my activities, she continued her efforts on behalf of other gay kids and their families. Everyone knew that

Agnes—Aggie to her friends—Wilson was a force to be reckoned with in the face of discrimination, and she was always ready to lend a sympathetic ear to troubled parents and their gay children. After college, when I'd been busy starting my career, she'd had no shame about goading me into writing checks for her causes in place of giving my time.

At five feet two, with a husband and boys who towered over her, she ruled our house. I was certain that, given the chance, she could rule the world with equal aplomb.

As she opened a box of dog biscuits for the expectant Sadie and Marnie, she remembered to ask, "Are you hungry?"

"That's not my brand," I said. When she gave me her exasperated-mother look, I added, "I had a sandwich. But I'll be hungry by dinnertime."

"Good. Julie is at a class in Stevens Point this weekend, so Mike and the boys will be here, too."

"What kind of class?" I asked, thinking how Mike's wife was a younger version of my mother. An indefatigable high school teacher, she nonetheless gave her two sons as much energy and devotion as my mother had given us. Normally, her weekends with her family were sacrosanct.

"I'm not sure, just one of those continuing education things for her teaching credential," my mother said. "The boys are playing softball. If you pick them up, it'll give your father and Mike enough time to finish, clean up, and get home in time for dinner."

I let Sadie and Marnie ride in the back of my pickup truck as I drove to Carson Park to find my nephews, Kit and Cody—so named because my brother was an Old West history buff. As the dogs romped ahead of me through the park, I came upon a group of my buddies playing a game of touch football and stopped to watch. It was a perfect Wisconsin June day, temperature in the mid-seventies, with only the whitest clouds drifting across the brilliant blue sky above me. As I tossed sticks for the dogs, my cell phone rang.

"Hey, Adam, it's Tracy," my assistant said. "I'm at your place."

"You shouldn't be working on a Saturday," I scolded her.

"I'm not working," she assured me. "My printer is screwed up again. I'm using yours to print my church bulletin for tomorrow."

"Go ahead and use our copier if you need to," I said. I never minded being generous with Tracy, who often went way beyond the call of duty as my assistant. "And get J. B. to load that printer in your car. I'll be glad to look at it on Monday."

"Thanks, Adam," she said. "I noticed a fax still on the machine from yesterday. Some guy in New York wants you to speak at a convention there. It sounds like he needs a fast answer. I wasn't sure if you were out of town or something."

I heard the curious tone in her voice. I should have realized I wouldn't be able to spend a night away from home without someone's knowing.

"No, I'm at Carson Park to pick up my nephews," I said. "I'll deal with the fax when I get home tonight. I'm having dinner with my folks."

"Carson Park? I'm driving right by there. I'll bring you the fax."

I knew if I refused Tracy's offer, she'd be sure I was hiding something, so I told her to look for the dogs and she'd find me. As I sat on the grass, watching the football game and occasionally trading banter with the guys while they played, I thought of how much I'd come to savor the slower pace of life in Eau Claire, among people I'd known all my life, and how odd it was that the high-tech world of computers had brought me home.

I was introduced to my first computer when I was in the sixth grade. Our school purchased five Texas Instruments computers, and one was in my classroom. Our teacher tried to get us excited about its limitless possibilities, but our enthusiasm didn't meet his expectations when the computer froze and had to be rebooted every fifteen minutes.

By the time I graduated from high school, however, computers had taken over my life. Despite being a football letterman and all-around jock, I was also the editor of our school newspaper. I was constantly glued to a Mac Plus, reconstructing page layouts, re-touching photos, and spell-checking articles. By my high school years, computers had come a long way from the Texas Instruments model I first used in elementary school.

I turned down an athletic scholarship to college, deciding I'd rather use my brain than end up with a battered body and little hope of getting into pro ball. I majored in business and minored in graphic arts. Throughout my years at the University of Wisconsin, I worked hard at a variety of odd jobs to earn money so I could buy my own computer and any software I wanted. I bought a Mac Plus just like the one I'd used in high school and named it Mathilda.

At the end of four years, Mathilda and I both graduated to a Mac II. I secured a position in the accounting department of a law firm in Stevens Point, but I found my job unchallenging. I started attending night classes to receive an associate degree in computer programming. I learned all about the latest platforms and programs for PCs and used my new skills to secure a job in Madison as a systems manager for a marketing research firm. I made sure all of their computers were up and running at all times. It was a big job, but I loved it. I felt like the company couldn't operate without me, and in a way, I was right. I had my own office on the tenth floor of their building, but I was rarely in it. I was constantly being paged because of a computer that wouldn't start up, a file that was lost, or a bug in the system.

As technology advanced, I set up an interoffice e-mail system and received a huge bonus for my efforts. The president of the company said that I'd saved his employees time and energy as a result of my work. He put the word out to some of his colleagues, and I found myself doing the same job for five other companies in the city. Within a year, I was working for myself.

Unfortunately, being a slave to corporate America grew to be extremely boring. I had minored in graphic arts in college because I genuinely loved art. As a child I was constantly drawing and continued to sketch everything in sight as I got older. I hid this talent once I became a jock in high school. It didn't seem to be a "manly" thing to do, and I was afraid my friends would think I was as geeky as the boys we antagonized on a daily basis for similar interests. Computers were considered a skill, and my years in journalism fulfilled course requirements needed to graduate, so my friends overlooked my participation in those areas.

But I loved feeling creative, and working for corporations was stifling that urge. The World Wide Web was gaining popularity and the Internet was a wide-open field for business and personal expression. I studied HTML and Java and learned how to build Web sites. Finally, I could use my creativity, business degree, and computer expertise to create my own personal business.

I didn't eschew corporations right away. They were the bread and butter of my start-up business, Adam AdVentures. As Web access spread to in-home use, opening new markets, I was one of the first to create Web sites for businesses in Madison, Milwaukee, and other major cities in Wisconsin. Setting up my own Web site, I branched out to receive work from companies in Minneapolis–St. Paul, Detroit, and Chicago. By the mid-nineties, I was one of many young entrepreneurs reaping the benefits of high tech.

When I was twenty-eight, I had a sizable nest egg, corporate stocks, and a huge apartment in Madison. This time when I started growing tired of what I was doing, I took a long, hard look at myself. I'd gone from accountant to systems employee to self-employed wonder boy, but I still felt something was missing. As news of friends filtered in from home, I realized that what I lacked was a personal life. Everyone was getting married, having babies, and buying houses. I lived alone in an apartment I rarely saw. I decided it was time to downsize my business and cut the cord from corporate America. I wanted the simplicity I'd grown up with as a child in Eau Claire. I was never a suit-and-tie kind of guy. It always felt like a costume. I sold my fancy car, subleased my apartment, and sent out letters to my clients, referring them to Web designers who would maintain their Web sites with the same consideration and care that I had provided. I packed my belongings and moved to a farmhouse that I purchased on several acres of land outside Eau Claire.

I took a vacation from my life and spent a whole summer renovating the farmhouse. The exterior remained vintage clapboard white, but inside I blended rustic country with high-tech touches. Since I didn't have a family of my own, I turned the family room and den into a separate working office. Six phone lines, three PCs, two Power Macs, a laser printer, three scanners, a network server, and three employees later, I had my new business set up within the comforts of home. I donated my suits and ties to Goodwill and worked in jeans and flannel shirts.

I was still creating Web sites, but from then on, I worked almost exclusively for artists and small businesses rather than faceless organizations. I wired up musicians, visual artists, novelists, and even a few dance clubs. I also donated my time to help several local schools design sites. This brought me to the attention of the University of Wisconsin, who contracted me to help develop their Web site.

My stint with the university put me in touch with a sideline job, teaching. Once a week during spring and summer semesters, I commuted to Menomonie to teach electronic publishing and fundamentals of computer design classes at the University of Wisconsin–

Stout's College of Arts and Sciences. Stout's B.S. degree in technical communications was a new program, and despite the chancellor and the rest of the collegiate hierarchy overseeing my every move, I had freedom to create my own lessons. I subtitled my electronic publishing class "We Are the Web" and wrote those words on the blackboard on the first day. This prompted my students to start singing the words to the tune of "We Are the World," which I didn't mind, since I wanted my classes to be fun. I figured if I had fun, so would the students, and they just might learn something.

My teaching job and Adam's AdVentures were mixed blessings. I had two comfortable careers, both creative and productive outlets, and the respect of my parents, who'd worried that I was going to be a corporate competitor with no personal life until I died young of a heart attack. Of course, leaving that frantic life behind didn't mean I worked less. Running my own business required even more stamina and dedication. But at least now I could manage my own schedule and be only as busy as I wanted to be, which left me free to watch for the man who hadn't shown up yet.

"Hey, sissy boy," Lars Ziegler said as he ran by me with the ball. "Why don't you join the game?"

I smiled and shook my head as he kept running, holding the football over his head in a victory dance. Rather than being offended by his comment, I watched Lars with a mixture of pity and nostalgia. He and I had been quite the pair in high school. I'd been running back to his quarterback. We'd continued the winning tradition started by my brother, Mike, and his quarterback, Ted Tucker, who'd gone on to play for the Vikings.

Lars had been hot in those days, but over the years, he'd shed his appeal as he packed on the pounds. I was probably the only one of our group of friends who knew that Lars was gay, if such a word could be applied to someone as fiercely closeted as he was. I'd given up trying to convince him that if he started living honestly, he'd be a happier, healthier person. He owned a local insurance office, so I figured that to protect his business reputation he went to the Twin Cities or Madison for whatever sexual encounters he had.

A whoop drew my eyes to Jake Meyers. Just as Ted and Mike had been the dynamic duo five years older than Lars and me, Jake and his running back, Blaine Dunhill, were five years behind us. They'd been the pair whose stats surpassed Lars's and mine, turning in three amazing championship seasons. Like me, Blaine had stopped playing after high school. He'd gone away to college and never moved back to Eau Claire. Jake got a football scholarship to Notre Dame, where his career was derailed by injuries. He'd finished college in Eau Claire and worked in some kind of forestry job for the state. Jake was every bit the glorious specimen he'd been as a young quarterback. He was one of those tall, Nordic types who managed to look better every year. Too bad he was straight.

The barking dogs snapped me out of my reverie, and I looked up. Apparently everyone was converging on me at once. I saw my nephews, led by Sadie and Marnie, coming my way from one direction, and Tracy coming from the opposite direction, fax in hand. The football game had also ended, and a few of the players fell to the grass next to me. I declined a bottle of Gatorade, nodded that Kit and Cody could take one each, and stood as Tracy reached our group.

"Here you go," she said, handing me the fax before she bent to scratch Marnie's ears.

I read it over as everyone made small talk around me. It was a letter from an organizer of *WebTek: PlugN2theFuture,* a Manhattan expo and conference about the Web, new technologies, and how they affect society. They wanted me to give a lecture based on my class, suggesting the title "We Are the Web: Yesterday, Today and Tomorrow." The producers of the WebTek exposition had been watching my career for years. This wasn't the first invitation I'd received from them, but their schedule had never fit into mine. I took out my PalmPilot and checked the dates, which for once fell during a time I had nothing planned.

"What's that?" Cody asked, and I told him as the others listened.

"New York City," one of the guys drawled, mimicking a popular commercial for picante sauce.

"In *July?*" I wondered aloud with distaste. "Isn't the concrete city supposed to be unbearable then?"

"You should go," Tracy said.

"I want a Yankees cap," Kit said.

"Me, too!" Cody demanded.

"I could order those on the Internet," I said.

"It's not the same as one from there," Kit said.

"It'll do you good to get away," Tracy added.

Lars Ziegler was even bold enough to say, "Isn't Manhattan supposed to have the hottest guys in the country?"

"Have you been talking to my mother?" I asked.

"You haven't had a date in months," Tracy said. "At least that *I* know about. What's a little hot weather?"

Jake took my nephews' empty Gatorade bottles and said, "Hey, my little sister lives in Manhattan. She loves it. We couldn't drag her home with a John Deere tractor. In fact, she's sharing a place with my best friend, Blaine Dunhill."

This remark was followed by attentive silence. Blaine's family owned Dunhill Electrical, a company I often contracted to rewire homes and businesses for more powerful computer systems. Blaine had been married to Sydney Kepler, daughter of Eau Claire's wealthiest and most prominent citizen, Jonas Kepler. Their divorce had been a scandal among Eau Claire's society crowd. No one was sure what had happened, but rumors of another woman seemed to be confirmed by what Jake had just said.

The tension was broken when Sadie plowed through our group in a game of chase with Marnie. As everyone laughed and began dispersing, I turned to Jake and said, "You know, Blaine is the player who broke all my football records."

"All the more reason for you to look up him and Sheila. You can kick his ass," Jake said. We were often on opposing softball teams, so Jake knew just how competitive I was.

As I gathered up dogs and nephews and said my goodbyes, I folded the fax and put it in my pocket. If I decided to accept the invitation, the last thing I wanted was to be stuck in New York with some straight couple from Eau Claire. Instead, it was what Lars had said that rang in my ears: *the hottest guys in the country.* After the previous night with Sam, that sounded awfully tempting.

Later that evening, as Mike and I competed with the boys to see who could scarf down more of my mother's feast of chicken, potato salad, and freshly baked yeast rolls, Cody brought up the WebTek invitation.

"Uncle Adam's going to New York and buying us Yankee caps."

"New York?" my dad asked, pushing back from the table with a satisfied look before looking at Kit's plate. "Are you going to finish that roll?"

"Hank, you don't need another roll," my mother reproached him.

"He wants it for the dog," Mike said. "I can't believe you'd take food out of my son's mouth for one of those mongrels."

"I can't believe getting you boys grown and out of the house wasn't the end of sibling rivalry," my mother said.

Mike and I exchanged a confused look, and I said, "We shared the last of the potato salad."

"Not rivalry with each other, with the girls," my mother explained, pulling off a piece of chicken to give Marnie.

"I can't believe you think of those two shit machines as my sisters," Mike said, ignoring my mother's disapproving glance over his language in front of the boys.

"And they don't even have to do chores," I complained as I began picking up plates to rinse and put in the dishwasher.

"They like to do dishes," Cody said, cracking himself up as he held his plate under Sadie's nose so she could lick it.

When my mother simply took the plate as she walked past Cody, Mike gave me a dumbfounded look.

"If I'd done that as a kid, I'd have gotten a swipe to the back of my head," he said.

"Dogs and grandkids get special treatment," I reminded him.

"Yes, you two had it so rough," my mother said. "Everyone get out of my kitchen. Except you, Adam. You can help me do the strawberry shortcake. We'll eat it on the deck."

As the others wandered out, I continued to load the dishwasher while she fussed over dessert.

"What's this about New York?"

I explained the WebTek invitation to her, and she nodded. When my father took early retirement from the dairy plant, their friends had urged them to buy a Winnebago and see the country. Instead, they'd followed me down the information superhighway. They couldn't set the clock on their VCR, but because they always took an interest in whatever I did, they knew as much about computers as they did about field goals. Which was saying a lot, since my mother had been the assistant coach of my Little League football team.

"While I'm thinking about it, your father forgot his AOL password again."

"All he has to do is call, and they'll give him another one."

"I already did that. I'm just telling you in case he tells you. Don't be so quick to explain it to him. It's been a relief to me to have him off the computer."

"Is he going in those sports chat rooms again?"

"I can't get any time online," she complained. "I have PFLAG work to do."

"Aggie," I said, taking a parental tone with her, "the last few times I saw you online, you were talking in some crafts chat room."

"Cyber-spy," she said accusingly, without a trace of guilt. "Before you run off to New York, I want you to help me buy another computer so your father and I can get online at the same time."

"If you want to be on AOL at the same time, you'll need a second account."

"It will be worth it."

"Anyway, who said I'm going to New York?" I asked.

"You mean you're not?"

"I haven't decided."

Her expression showed she was holding back something, so I prodded, "Go ahead. Tell me what you're thinking."

"Adam, you're stuck in a rut. You came back to Eau Claire so you wouldn't work all the time."

"I don't work all the time," I argued. "I work *out*. I play ball. I hang out with my buddies."

She set the whipped cream on the counter and turned to face me, asking, "Are you happy?"

"Sure I'm happy. I don't seem happy?"

"You're getting boring. What's the use of having a gay son if I have no outrageous stories to tell the gals?"

"I see where I get my competitive urge. You just want your gay-son stories to be better than their gay-son stories."

But she refused to be teased, saying, "I like having you live near home again. I'm glad you're happy with what you're doing. And it's wonderful that your oldest friends like you for the man you are."

"But?"

"But you *are* like me; it's true. I have my old friends, too. And I have plenty to keep me busy. But there's something special about me, and it's because of you." When I waited, she went on a little slowly, as if she was thinking while she talked. "Being the mother of a gay child opened up another world for me. I notice things now that I never saw before. I hear things that would have gone right by me. And I'm involved with people with whom I sometimes have nothing else in common except that we have gay children. We have a bond based on that, and it's different from what I share with my other friends. Adam, don't you ever wish for people around you that you don't have to explain things to? They just *know*, because they're like you in some unique way, even while they may be different in other ways."

I nodded, thinking how she had put into words some of the vague dissatisfaction I'd been feeling.

"But you know, that isn't going to change just because I spend a few days at some convention in New York."

"It's also not going to change if you stay in the same rut, day after day, and . . . *settle*, Adam. I don't want any child of mine to settle. Look at Mike. I guess on the surface his life seems very average. Nice home, good job, strong family. But he and Julie have fun together. And you never know what odd thing they'll think of to do next. Remember the time they got Willard Scott to wish Mr. Gunderson's cow Gertie happy birthday on *The Today Show?*"

"They still shouldn't have won that bet, because Willard didn't show a picture of the cow," I grumbled. "Anyway, Mom, if you believe what you read and hear, what they have isn't average at all. It's kind of rare and wonderful."

"That's exactly what I mean. I want you to have something rare and wonderful, Adam. I think you want that, too. Sometimes you have to go out and look for it."

"Dessert?" Kit asked hopefully, sticking his head in the door.

"Almost," my mother said. She turned to me again. "Just don't let too many opportunities slip by, honey."

Later that night, looking around the beautiful old house I'd made into a comfortable place to live and work, I recognized the truth of my mother's words. The reason something became a rut was because it was a safe and familiar place to be. I envied some of the guys I talked to online who lived in cities where there were large, thriving communities of gay men. I didn't want to live in what some people called a gay ghetto. Nor would I change Eau Claire, even if I could. But gay life in Eau Claire seemed to be either about bars or political groups of one sort or another. I didn't want to look like some of the desperate men I saw in bars. And I'd had my share of queer politics in college, even if those days had given me the sense of gay community I was missing now.

Building my various careers had kept me too busy to take advantage of opportunities to develop lasting friendships with gay men. But it would be nice, as my mother had said, to feel close to some people who just *knew* me. Not as the high school jock. Not as the ambitious computer geek. As something else, something I hadn't given myself the time and space to be. Was there such a thing as being too grounded, too stable, too *settled?*

Once again, it seemed like time to make a few changes. I picked up the fax and logged on to the computer to send an e-mail accepting the invitation to speak at WebTek.

TWO

"Would you like me to check that in the baggage hold for you, sir?" a flight attendant asked me, her plastic smile fastened in place just like the Mr. Potato Head I had when I was five.

I'd packed carefully for my trip to New York City. I carried my PowerBook in my padded briefcase, which also held my PalmPilot and several pens that I hardly ever used. My Gateway laptop, external CD-ROM drive, portable printer, technical manuals, software, and backup storage disks were in a special carry-on bag, which I tried in vain to ease under the seat in front of me.

"My very existence is in this bag, ma'am," I replied. "It can't leave my sight. I'll buy a ticket for it to ride in the seat next to me if I have to."

"Sir, it's obviously not going to fit under the seat. Let's see if we can stow it in the overhead—"

"No! I have equipment in this bag that is very delicate," I objected.

"The overhead compartments are much safer than the baggage hold, sir," the flight attendant said in a calm tone that was obviously masking her impatience with me.

"I've flown enough to know that when we land, you'll say, 'Please use caution when opening the overhead compartments, as their contents may have shifted during our flight.' Am I correct?"

"Yes, but—" she stammered.

"If the luggage in the overhead compartments can be damaged, then obviously what's inside the luggage can be damaged. Do you want that on your conscience? All because you have to follow some stupid procedure? Huh? Do you?"

The flight attendant burst into tears.

"I'm just trying to do my job!" she wailed. "It's my first week and I have to follow the rules. I'm sorry. I was just trying to . . ." She trailed off into a fit of sobs and sank to my seat as another flight attendant rushed up the aisle to her aid.

"What the hell is going on here?" Flight Attendant Two hissed.

"He wouldn't check his bag or put it overhead, and I tried to—to . . ." the first attendant blubbered.

"Sir, give me your bag right now, or I'll have you taken off this plane," Flight Attendant Two demanded.

"Are you crazy?"

"Apparently, sir, you're the mayor of Looneyville, and the town's not big enough for the two of us. Now hand me that bag, or I call Security."

There was a pause as we glared at each other. Finally, I begrudgingly handed my bag to Flight Attendant Two.

"Thank you," she said. "Now apologize to Wendy."

Wendy, Flight Attendant One, wiped her eyes and looked up at me expectantly.

"I'm sorry, Wendy. I'm not a good flyer. I'm nervous and stressed out about going to Manhattan, and I guess I took it out on you," I said.

"It's okay," Wendy sniffled. "I understand. I'm not a good flyer either."

"But you're a flight attendant." I laughed, as did Wendy and everyone around us.

"Wendy, finish the rounds so we can take off," Flight Attendant Two ordered. "Sir, sit down and fasten your seat belt."

"What are you going to do with my bag?" I asked as I sat down.

She reached across me to set my bag on the empty seat beside me as the plane began to taxi slowly to the runway.

"You're lucky that whoever was supposed to sit here missed his flight," she said with a wink and wove the seat belt through the handles of my bags, fastened the buckle, and secured it in place.

"Thank you," I sighed.

"You're also lucky that you're cute," she said. "Have a nice flight, and try not to torment poor Wendy anymore."

I felt ashamed of my previous actions and put several claw marks in the armrests as I personally steered our jet to the runway and lifted it from the ground. I had almost forgotten my lunacy until Wendy rolled the drink cart up the aisle. With a forgiving smile, she gave me the vodka and cranberry juice I ordered.

I looked up from my laptop, where I'd been typing an account of my first trip to Manhattan a couple of months before. Of course

I'd exaggerated. We hadn't argued about my luggage, though Wendy *had* told me she was a bad flyer, too. But I was writing only to entertain myself and to look like I belonged among the rest of the patrons of Café Pick Me Up, the artist-friendly coffee shop I'd discovered in the East Village across from Tompkins Square Park. If voyeurs peeked over my shoulder, I'd rather they thought I was a writer than a computer geek.

I returned my attention to my laptop autobiography.

I passed the time on my flight playing computer games until the captain's voice alerted me that it was time for me to help land the jet. Once again my skillful control of the armrests, as well as my ability to make my body weightless, got us safely on the ground. I felt that I should be allowed to fly for free, it was such exhausting work for me. As the plane taxied to the terminal, Wendy began her spiel.

"Ladies and gentlemen, it's a warm eighty-five degrees in New York City tonight, and we thank you for flying with us. For your safety, we ask that you please remain seated until the plane stops moving. When we stop, please use caution when opening the overhea—he—heehee—"

Wendy caught my eye and dissolved into a hysterical laughing fit, collapsing to an empty seat, with Flight Attendant Two standing over her and frowning.

We landed, and I found a line of drivers standing in a sort of receiving line outside baggage claim. One of them held a sign that read "Wilson," so I stopped.

"Hi," I said to the driver. He was a short, balding man with a wide grin.

"Are you Adam Wilson?" he asked in a thick New York accent.

"Yes, I am. I didn't know anyone was picking me up."

"I'm just the driver; I ain't takin' ya for a night on the town," he said, punching me in the arm and laughing loudly. "Let's get your bags."

We found my bag with my clothes in it, and he carried it to a black Lincoln Town Car. I tried to help, but he wouldn't hear of it, so I got into the backseat. He started the car and took off like a bat out of hell for Manhattan.

"So you're in town for business?" he asked.

"Yes. I'm speaking at a Web convention."

"What's that? A meeting of Spider-Man fans?" he joked, slapping the wheel and guffawing.

"No. It's a convention about Internet technology," I explained, wondering why I bothered.

"Oh. Computers. That Internet's just a vehicle to get porn into your house without having to go to the newsstand. But that's just my opinion."

"Can't argue with that," I mumbled.

I watched the skyscrapers grow closer as we crossed a huge bridge. Then I got angry. How dare some stranger negate my livelihood?

"Wait, I will argue with that. I spent most of my life in a small suburb not knowing anything about the world around me, except for what other people told me. Kids today don't have to be as ignorant as I was. With the click of a button, they can know anything. They can talk to anyone."

The driver looked at me in the rearview mirror and said, "You take this very seriously."

"It's my life," I said. "It's what I do."

His eyes darted back to the road as a yellow cab cut him off. He glanced quickly back up to the rearview mirror and asked, "Do you have a family? Any kids?"

"No. I'm a teacher. My students are the only kids I have."

"Let me tell you a little something about kids," the driver said with a chuckle. "Long before the Internet, there were libraries. Kids that wanted to learn would go there to do just that, my friend. And the kids who wanted to goof off and look at porn would be searching through their fathers' sock drawers. It's not up to kids to decide if they want to be ignorant or not. It's up to parents."

"You're right," I agreed. I paused in thought, then asked him, "So which kid were you?"

"Which kid, what? Whattaya talkin' about?"

"Were you at the library or the sock drawer?"

He whipped the Town Car around the corner and pulled up in front of a hotel that occupied half the block. We got out of the car, and he opened the trunk.

"I was in the library during the week," he said, handing me my bag. "On the weekends, my buddies and I spent our fair share of time in and out of sock drawers. If you get my meaning."

"I think I do," I said, wincing as the driver punched me jovially on the arm again. "You're saying we should take life seriously but also enjoy it while we can."

"Something like that. Oh, no, no tip required. Your little convention's already paid me in advance, and I gave myself a nice tip," he explained when I tried to palm him a twenty-dollar bill. "Ya gotta relax, Mac. Look around at what your life has brought you."

He stepped back and did a Vanna White sweep of his arms to indicate the massive hotel. I looked up at what had to be fifty stories of glass and *steel, decorated with flashing neon lights that added their heat to the July night.*

"Life's bigger than the Internet, Mac," the driver said as he started to get back in the car. "Sometimes it's better to get there and learn in person."

"Do you have a family?" I asked him.

"Yeah," he said with a laugh, "and I got a Ph.D., too, but you didn't ask about that. Don't judge a book by its cover. I learned that in the library."

He sped off, and I carried my bags inside the hotel to check in. The woman at the front desk gave me a key card to suite 30A.

The producers of the convention had outdone themselves. My suite had a main room furnished with small sofas, a desk, modem connections, a television inside an armoire, and a minibar in a walnut fridge. Off the main room was my bedroom, with a queen-sized bed, two chairs on either side of a bookcase, another television in another armoire, and an antique dresser. I sat on the bed and opened a folder that had been left for me with the itinerary for the WebTek convention. It was a three-day affair consisting of demonstrations and lectures, which concluded with an exposition of new technology, new software, and new ideas.

"Whatever," I said aloud to myself and started to unpack. When I took my toiletry bag into the bathroom, I stopped, staring at my reflection.

My short, black hair was doing an Alfalfa thing in the back, so I smoothed it down, then surveyed my appearance again. A lot of people complained about the effects of air travel on their skin, but I didn't think I looked too bad. I splashed some water over my face and looked into the blue eyes of my reflection.

"You're an all-right guy, Adam. So why are you on a trip all alone? Maybe because you're talking to yourself like a big old computer geek."

I was full of restless energy and, ever the jock, decided to expend a little of it in a productive manner. I phoned the desk and found out there was a gym on the nineteenth floor. I threw on shorts, a T-shirt, and sneakers and jogged down to the gym. The only fee was five dollars to rent a locker for when I showered.

I hit a treadmill right off and jogged for twenty minutes to get my heart rate up. After that, I used the machines to work on my arms, chest, and back. The ache from my exertion was washed out of me by a wave of relief just as my endorphins kicked in, and I stepped away from the biceps curl machine so I could sit on the floor and enjoy the rush. I chugged some water and leaned against a wall to take in the sight of men straining against machines in quest of the perfect body.

Everywhere I looked, I could see all types of male bodies: tall men, short men, toned men, and muscle-bound men pressed, lifted, and power-

walked their way to perfection. I thought back to my days in high school, when exercise wasn't about the perfect body. Winning a game was more important. But now, as we neared the millennium, it appeared that our only competitor was Father Time. We pumped, lifted, and exercised away the demons of aging. Everyone wanted to look younger and more beautiful than the man on the machine next to him, and nobody would ever admit it.

After doing my crunches, I went to the locker room, threw my sweaty clothes into a small locker, wrapped a towel around my waist, and found the sauna. I walked to a raised wooden bench in the corner and sat down to relax in the heat. I kneaded my arms and soothed my triceps.

The door creaked open, and a man entered. He sat opposite me and flashed me a polite smile. He looked about my age but had light-brown hair that reached his shoulders. He was very handsome. His tanned skin made him appear golden, as if he was a main character in a movie. My mental camera panned across a field, where he carried a bale of hay on his shoulders, his shirt open and flapping in the breeze. I shook the image from my mind as I realized I was enjoying the fantasy a little too much. I could feel my enjoyment starting to take form beneath my towel.

I glanced at him and realized he was smiling at me.

"Hi," I politely said.

"Hi," he said back and smiled at me again.

Neither of us broke eye contact as he got up and stepped across the sauna to where I sat. He didn't bother to hold up his towel, but kept it in his hand as it fell away from his body. I reached out and put my hands on his hips, and he leaned in and kissed me. His lips were full and soft, but our kiss was hard. His teeth hit mine when we opened our mouths and tasted each other's tongues. I kissed my way down his neck, tasting his soft golden skin. He gently pulled my head up by my hair and pushed me back against the wall of the sauna. My eyes closed and my mouth fell open as he started giving me head. Sweat was running out of my pores and down my body as I gasped for air.

"Wait, I'm gonna—"

"Don't hold back," he said, rising up and kneeling over my hips on the bench. "We gotta do this quick so we don't get caught."

Golden Boy suddenly grabbed my shoulder as his body shuddered. I tried to hold on to his hard back, but my hand kept sliding off of him. So I hooked my left arm around his shoulders and drew our faces very close together. With our foreheads pressed firmly against each other, intently looking into each other's wild eyes, we came together, and I tried not to moan too loudly. The force of orgasm combined with the stifling heat of the sauna made me feel lethargic and weak. Golden Boy rolled off me and wobbled as he tried to stand.

"If I don't get out of here, I think I might pass out," he said with a sly smile. "Thanks."

I didn't say anything in return. I simply smiled and waved briefly as he opened the door and let it shut behind him.

"Mmmm, porn in Café Pick Me Up," a distinctly feminine voice spoke from behind me.

I felt my face turn scarlet, and I reached to close my laptop. A hand came over my shoulder to stop me.

"You didn't save," she warned.

I saved the document, then turned to see the face of the person who now thought I was a sauna slut.

Her hair was a shade of pink not found in nature, as frizzy as a very synthetic Beatles wig my uncle had once thought made him cool. She had several earrings in each ear but no other visible piercings. Her face was clear of makeup except for lipstick so red it was almost black. Her eyes were hidden behind a pair of black glasses that made me think of the singer Lisa Loeb. She looked utterly adorable and about fifteen years old.

"You're not old enough to be reading this without a parent or guardian," I said.

She laughed and said, "I'm twenty-one. Did that really happen or are you writing fiction?"

"A guy *did* cruise me in the steam room," I said.

"So, instead of following the advice of your driver with a doctorate, you're still living through your computer?"

Though I'd extended no invitation, she came around to sit across from me, offering me a cigarette from a crumpled pack of Marlboro Lights.

"No, thanks, I don't smoke," I said.

She shrugged and lit one for herself.

"I'm Blythe Mayfield," she said.

"Adam Wilson," I said. "How much of that did you read?"

"From the end of the flight, when Wendy got all hysterical. What was that about?"

I turned the laptop around to face her and watched her as she read it from the beginning. It made me feel good when her smile showed that she was entertained by what I'd written.

"So are you really a jock-slash-computer geek?" she asked, lighting another cigarette.

"You smoke too much."

"I don't inhale," she said. "It's just part of the image."

"What image is that?"

"Artist-slash-whatever-pays-the-rent," she said. "So tell me the rest of it. You came to New York in July for some Web Trek convention and you stayed?"

"WebTek," I said. *"Tek.* Well, I met this guy."

"Not the guy in the sauna?"

"No, like I said, that was fiction. I met a guy through the convention. He was impressed with my speech, we talked about my background, and he made me an offer. He owns a chain of discount stores in New York and New Jersey. I had to finish up a college class I was teaching; then I came back to New York in August to do this job for him. He wanted his own computer network to link all his stores, a Web site, all kinds of boring stuff," I said, noticing, in spite of the glasses, that her eyes were glazing over. "You don't really want to hear all of this."

"Not the computer stuff, but life stuff. That's more interesting."

"I don't see how my life could interest you," I said, thinking that anyone with her shade of hair must have a more fascinating life than mine.

"Just tell me. I need something to keep me from my art."

"Why?"

"Because that's what artists do. We find reasons not to work. Go on," she urged.

"What kind of artist are you?"

"A lazy one," she said and gave me a big grin. "We're talking about you. I never monopolize a conversation until I've given the other person a chance to talk first. Then they feel obligated to listen."

"Okay, like I said, I met this guy, Ray Patel. He offered me an obscene amount of money for my computer expertise. Since I can work for my other clients long-distance, and my employees back home can run the rest of my business, I decided to take his offer. Manhattan on somebody else's dime sounded like the chance of a lifetime."

"But now you don't think so? Are you homesick? Where's home?"

"Eau Claire."

"Where's that, Minnesota?"

"Wisconsin," I sighed. "Kids learn nothing in school these days."

She laughed good-naturedly and said, "I confess. I've never been out of the Northeast."

"No, I'm not homesick. I see this as a great opportunity. But I've spent most of my time working. I had to adjust to running my business in Eau Claire remotely, and Ray's work has kept me busy. I've just recently been able to enjoy leisure time. But," I added in my own defense, feeling like I was talking to my mother, "I haven't been sitting around being lonely. I work out. And I've done some exploring. Especially the museums."

"Really? Which ones?"

"The Met. MoMA. The Statue of Liberty Museum and Ellis Island Museum. Let's see. . . . The Museum for African Art. The Cloisters. And the Frick Collection. I'm sure there are others that I'm forgetting."

"Trying to fit them all in while you're here?" Blythe asked curiously.

"Not at all. I'm not one of those see-Europe-in-three-days kind of guys. I'll probably never see everything I want to, especially if I keep going back to my favorite paintings at the places I've already been."

She nodded as if she understood, then asked, "Where are you staying in Manhattan?"

"That's another perk. A buyer who works for Ray is back in India for a while, so I have her apartment just a few blocks from here. Hey, you're an artist. I should show you her collection."

"She has art?"

I laughed, unable to keep a straight face, and said, "Okay, neither one of us is old enough to remember this, but back in the sixties there were these artists who—"

"Not the dogs playing poker," she interrupted.

"Worse. She collects these prints of myopic children. I looked them up on the Web. Apparently, there were all these artists—"

"I know the kind you're talking about," Blythe said with a little whimper. "They look like they're all suffering from advanced thyroid disease?"

"Yes! I call the place 'The Waifs Land.' "

"Oh god, no wonder you hang out here."

"It gets worse. Part of the deal for me staying there is that I'm supposed to take care of her plants. I'm thinking of titling my autobiography *The Homicidal Horticulturist*. She'll be lucky to have a single brown vine left when she gets home. Hopefully, by then I'll have been paid and can live as a fugitive in Wisconsin."

"Good plan. Maybe New York can't extradite from there."

"Now, let's talk about you. To start with, where's your nanny?"

"I really am twenty-one," she insisted. "Do you want to see my license?"

She whipped it out of a tiny purse, and I took it. Blythe M. Mayfield, born March 12, 1977, brown hair—in the picture, it *was* brown—and brown eyes.

"What does the M stand for?" I asked.

"Mason. My mother's maiden name. Now yours."

I removed my license from my wallet, and she read it aloud.

"Adam F. Wilson, May thirtieth, nineteen sixty-seven—that makes you, what, thirty-one? Ancient, poor thing. Black hair, blue eyes. Great blue eyes, I might add. I don't understand why you haven't been snapped up by some record producer with a Central Park view and a houseboy named Kim."

"I'd *be* the houseboy named Kim if it would get me out of The Waifs Land."

"You don't look like the houseboy type. Could be the flannel. I bet you're a hit with lesbians."

I laughed and said, "I like to keep things simple. I also have to keep the apartment cold because of all my computer equipment."

"It may actually work for you. Most jaded New Yorkers would love to snag a guy fresh off the farm in Eau Claire, Wisconsin."

I glared at her and said, "I do live in a farmhouse, as a matter of fact, and it's infinitely more pleasant than waking up every morning to astigmatic foundlings."

She had a really fat laugh for such a small girl.

"You're funny, Adam F. Wilson," she said. "And the *F* is for?"

"Not even for a woman who knows my sauna fantasies will I reveal my middle name," I said.

"May thirtieth," she mused. "Gemini, sign of the twins. So one is the jock and one is the computer geek?"

"Sometimes the boundaries blur," I confessed. "Athletics developed my competitive side; I can be just as aggressive in business. Enough about me. Are you a dreamy, impractical Pisces woman? It's your turn to tell me about you."

She gave me a long look and finally said, "Okay. Why not? Do you have some free time?"

"Sure," I answered.

She powered off my computer and closed it, saying, "Come with me."

She walked like a New Yorker, full of such purpose that I could barely keep up with her. As we covered several blocks, I realized what an odd pair we must seem, if anyone bothered to notice. She barely came above my waist and was dressed in black from head to toe, which made her magenta hair all the more striking. And I looked exactly as she said—a farm boy new to the city. Unless I looked like her baby-sitter. It was impossible to believe she was really twenty-one.

She used her key to open a nondescript door next to a deli; then we climbed about a thousand stairs until she opened another door and led me into a huge loft with skylights. The few pieces of furniture were undistinguished, probably left over from a variety of prior tenants. I could see an unmade bed behind a screen. But what I really noticed were the canvases stacked against the walls, and, more particularly, the one that was on an easel in the middle of the room.

"Geez," I finally said, unable to stop gazing at the painting. "This is yours?"

"Yes."

I finally tore my eyes away to see that she looked even tinier as she watched me, perhaps waiting for a more specific reaction than *geez*.

"You probably think I don't know anything, being from the outer reaches of civilization and all, but I do Web sites for artists and I—oh, who cares about the art I studied in college? This is great!"

She exhaled, and I turned back to the canvas. The vivid colors and swirls rushed out at me, but the longer I stared, the more I saw the subtleties beneath. It was like Susan Sontag dressed as Cyndi Lauper.

"Believe me, a lot of people don't get me," she said. "Droves of people. Hordes. Multitudes."

"It's because you're not like everybody else," I said. "Which is the best way to be. Unique. Okay, I no longer think you're fifteen. I don't even think you're twenty-one. Your painting is too wise. Where does this come from? Where do *you* come from?"

"Vermont," she said. "A little town that probably isn't so different from where you grew up. As for this, both of my parents are artists. They fled from Manhattan years ago because they said they couldn't work here. Too many distractions. That's why it appealed to me. So here I am, with their blessing and enough money from them to keep me in art supplies. Which is lucky, because that's more than my rent. I got this place for nearly nothing because it has no heat and it's not much to look at. But it's got light, and that's more important."

"Well, you know, it's not The Waifs Land, but it'll do."

"I couldn't have everything," she sighed. "I wonder if I know anyone who's good with plants, though. I feel sorry for your victims."

"Forget the plants. Do you know a good photographer?"

"A photographer? For what?"

"To shoot your paintings. I could build a Web site for your work." The look she gave me was pure panic. "What?" I asked.

"I don't think I'm ready to put myself out there."

Having dealt with artists before, I understood her fear and said, "Okay, why don't we take it slowly? We'll find someone to photograph your work, and I'll design a site. When it meets your approval, and not until you're ready, we'll actually activate a domain name for you."

"I'll think about it," Blythe said. "And thank you."

"For offering to design a Web site? Piece of cake."

"Well, that, but for not—hmmm, how do I say this? For not explaining my work to me, or saying why you like it. Most people feel compelled to do that. It's very annoying."

"I just figure until you can do something as good as big-eyed children . . ."

She exploded into that fat laugh again and hit my arm.

"Okay, Adam F. Wilson, now you have a friend in Manhattan. Next step, a boyfriend."

"Did I say I was looking for a boyfriend? Don't forget, when this job ends, I'll be going back to Eau Claire. What's the point of finding a guy only to divorce him?"

"Did I say you were looking for a husband?" she mimicked me.

"Other than fictitious sauna liaisons, has your life in Manhattan been chaste?"

"Regrettably. Like I said, I've been focused on work. Now that I have leisure time, men are not, oddly enough, beating a path to my door."

"You have to let them know you're available." She eyed me thoughtfully. "It's time for a Blythe Mayfield makeover."

"I hope that doesn't involve coloring my hair."

She laughed and said, "No. You're too handsome to tamper with. Manhattan is about appearances. If you want to keep it simple, the jeans are fine. Just add a T-shirt and buy yourself a couple of nice jackets for social wear."

"I've got no social life," I reminded her.

"I can fix that. I have lots of friends. Of all ages and interests."

"More distractions?" I asked. Her smile was a confession. "Anyway," I confided, "in spite of my sauna fantasy, I'm not usually into anonymous public trysts. But I can't imagine inviting a guy back to The Waifs Land."

"That bad?"

"Did you ever see those cartoons of Nancy Reagan gazing adorably up at her Ronnie?" She nodded. "I call the girl over my bed 'Nancy.' It's that bad. I feel like I'm doing time in an orphanage before I get to be a real boy back in Eau Claire."

Blythe shuddered and said, "That's awful. We have to get you out of there to experience the charm of Manhattan. It's time you looked at something other than tourist attractions and art. Most of all, it's time to get *you* looked at."

"Why don't we have dinner tonight and talk about it some more," I suggested.

She looked a little uncomfortable and said, "Actually, I'm short on funds right now."

I'd figured as much, which was why I'd asked.

"Not a problem," I said. "I told you Ray is paying me well, and I have almost no living expenses. If you're going to bring color to my drab existence, feeding you is the least I can do."

That became the pattern of our new friendship. During the days, when I worked for Ray and talked on the phone to my clients in the Midwest, Blythe painted. No matter what she said about distractions, I came to realize that she could be very disciplined about her work. She didn't have a phone, so I'd wait until the light was fading before I showed up at her loft. I almost always took something with me, and while she cleaned her brushes or just stared at what she was working on, I gradually stocked her shelves and small refrigerator with food.

She'd scrub her hands, change out of her work clothes, and we'd spend the late afternoons and early evenings exploring. Blythe showed me things tourists would never find on their own. Little out-of-the-way galleries featuring artists and photographers who she believed would one day be successful. Shops that offered unusual merchandise: everything from essential oils—Blythe blended her own perfumes and skin care products—to great designer clothes at resale prices. Bookstores where I could buy interesting postcards or find used hardbacks by good writers. Wonderful restaurants tucked in hidden places where there was never a wait and the food was inexpensive and good.

I slowly came to realize that Manhattan wasn't all about frenzy and money. It was possible to meander through a vast array of places and characters if one was willing to look through Blythe's funny little cat-eyed glasses. Taking care of some of her creature comforts seemed too small a price to pay for the way she was taking care of me.

Just how pointedly she was doing that was brought home to me one night after dinner when, instead of letting me walk her to her door as usual, she looked me over and said, "Okay, you're ready."

"For?"

"I feel like coffee. In a different place. If you would be so good as to spring for a cab."

I flagged down a taxi and she gave the driver a Chelsea address. We stopped in front of the Big Cup, a place I'd shunned since my one visit, when I'd been overwhelmed by too many men with too much attitude.

"Are you trying to pimp for me?" I asked accusingly.

"Nope. You're not here to connect with a guy. You're here to *absorb,*" she said. *"Observe. Listen."*

"Hmmm," was all I said, focusing on giving the driver his fare with a good tip.

I felt a familiar crisping of the nerves in my neck and back as we walked into the coffee shop. Dozens of eyes stared, evaluated, moved on, or lingered. Blythe, even with her shocking pink hair, could have been invisible. This was all about sex, or its potential, and I was the candidate.

I let her order for both of us while I purposefully avoided eye contact with anyone. I hated feeling like I was on display. I was relieved when I could follow her through the crowd to a sofa. Once we sat down, the eyes moved on, waiting for the next fresh arrival.

"Breathe," Blythe commanded, and I did. "You are so gorgeous, Adam. I doubt there's a guy here who doesn't think so. Why does this make you so tense?"

"It's dehumanizing," I said. "And shallow. I'm more than just a body."

She picked up a discarded copy of *HX* and said, "The way I figure it, if what you want is sex, then looks are all you have to go by. Yours or theirs."

She became preoccupied by the magazine as I stared at her, disgruntled. She might as well have said, *Ah ha!* I felt like I'd been caught. As much as I grumbled to her about my celibate life, I knew it was self-imposed. Some days it seemed like the entire city was in heat. The gyms I went to, the subway, the sidewalks, were all packed with men who evaluated me as I evaluated them. I saw approval in their eyes and knew that with only a little effort, I could have whatever I wanted: a half-hour, a night, a weekend.

What stopped me was the dread of what came later, when everyone zipped up and moved on. I wanted conversation. Some intimacy. As my mother had said, and I agreed, I wanted someone to *know* me. Someone to get past the layer of jock, then past the layer of geek, to find *me* and like what he found. Maybe not a boyfriend, which would only complicate things, since New York was only an interlude. But—

"Jeremy, my *god*, how *are* you? It's been *forever* since I saw you. You look *fabulous*," came an intrusive squeal from a nearby table.

I glanced over to see a somewhat chunky man enthusiastically embrace a real beauty.

"Andy," the beauty breathed, extricating himself, "it's only been a few weeks. I saw you at Ken's memorial service."

Their next words were lost as I contemplated—what had his friend shrieked? *Jeremy?* He was the kind of man who would always get a second look. Blond hair, brown eyes, beautiful skin, slim but good body, but it was something more that made him so striking. A certain confidence. He looked like a celebrity. For all I knew, judging by the other glances directed his way, he *was* a celebrity. He seemed very much at ease with the attention he drew, accepting it as his due without making too much of it.

By now they were both sitting down. I stared into my latte while I eavesdropped.

". . . even *see* Daniel," the squealer was saying, "and as for poor Martin—"

"Poor Martin? Hardly, Andy. Not after inheriting Ken's money," the beautiful Jeremy said in a caustic tone.

"Yes, dear, but didn't you *hear?* Ken put it in some kind of trust. Martin can only get wee bits out at a time."

"Which was really smart of Ken," Jeremy answered, seeming bored by the whole topic.

"No doubt Martin would have just run through all that money," Andy agreed with a sigh. "I mean, *I'd* have put it right back into Club Chaos, had Ken left it to *me.* The place that made him famous!"

"According to Daniel, that's exactly why Ken left it in a trust. So people wouldn't take advantage of what Daniel sees as Martin's generous nature."

"Do you mean *me?*" Andy demanded. "I would consider using it for the club as an *investment* for Martin if he gave me any of the money."

"Moot point," Jeremy said, sounding as if, for him, the subject was closed.

"So how *is* Daniel?" Andy asked. "Do you see him often? Are you still carrying a *torch* for him?"

"We're friends, Andy," Jeremy said. "He has a boyfriend. I'm seeing someone, too."

Figures, I thought. Anyone with Jeremy's looks couldn't be single.

I glanced at Blythe to see if she was listening, too.

"What a dreadful little man," she said. "I gather he owns Club Chaos. Have you ever been there?"

"No," I said. "It's a nightclub?"

"It's wonderful," she said. "They have the best drag shows there. And the drinks are good. Not watered down. All the bartenders are beautiful. We should go sometime." She flipped through her copy of *HX,* then handed it to me so I could see the ad for Club Chaos.

"Looks like fun," I said.

As she opened her mouth to say something else, I shook my head, trying to hear why Andy was squealing again.

"... can't *believe* you would go to his party! You *know* how I feel about him."

"I'm not going because it's *his* party," Jeremy said. "I'm going because a friend invited me. Do you always have to see everything as if it affects you in some way?"

"Wade Van Atterson is the most vile creature who ever slithered out from under a rock," Andy snapped. "You *know* he's been trying to destroy me for twenty—er, ten years."

"Since you were practically in kindergarten, right?" Jeremy asked, his eyes dancing at Andy's attempt to shave years off his age.

Before Andy could reply, they were joined by a guy who stared at Jeremy with open adoration. My first thought was that he was too young to be Jeremy's boyfriend; then I realized he was timidly handing Jeremy a napkin and a pen.

"I'm sorry to interrupt, but I was wondering. Could I have your autograph?"

Andy rolled his eyes and turned his head away, but Jeremy's expression was friendly as he said, "Of course. What's your name?"

"Eric. I love your work. I think you're great."

"Thank you," Jeremy said, giving him a glacier-melting smile. "What is it that you do, Eric?"

"I'm just a student. At NYU."

"What's your major?"

"Anthropology. I know that sounds boring," Eric said apologetically.

"It's not boring if you love it," Jeremy said. "Do you love it?"

"Yeah."

"Then you're exactly where you should be," Jeremy said with another smile as he handed Eric his pen and the signed napkin. As Eric backed away, Jeremy turned to Andy and said, "Sorry to cut this short, but I have to run."

He stood and headed toward the door, with a still-complaining Andy and the wistful gazes of a few dozen men trailing in his wake. I watched with regret as he disappeared into the embrace of the night—and probably a waiting date. When I looked back at Blythe, I realized she was staring after them, too, an odd expression on her face.

"What is it?" I asked.

"I know him," she said absently.

"Jeremy?" I asked hopefully.

"No, Wade Van Atterson," she said, then suddenly snapped out of her reverie, as if she'd said more than she meant to.

"You know the guy whose party Jeremy is going to?" I asked.

"Jeremy? Oh. The beautiful one?"

"Right. Do you know this Wade guy well enough to get an invitation to his party?"

"He's not really part of my social circle," Blythe said in a tone of dismissal. When I kept staring at her, she said, "Wade Van Atterson is a businessman who happens to be a heavy hitter in the art world. As a patron. He gives money to museums, backs gallery showings, stuff like that. Way out of my league."

It occurred to me that a connection like Wade was exactly what Blythe needed. Maybe this was just another case of her insecurity, like the Web site. I'd already realized she couldn't be pushed. But simply going with me to a party so I could try to see Jeremy again . . .

"You didn't by any chance recognize Jeremy?" I asked.

"No. He's probably in a band. Or an actor. Almost everybody's an actor."

"I could find out for myself if I went to Wade Van Atterson's party," I said, giving her my most beguiling look.

She sighed as she said, "Okay. If it's the blond beauty you want, I'll see what I can do about getting us to the party. I knew there was no such thing as a free meal."

"At least we don't want to eat the same entree."

Men turned to stare as her huge laugh exploded out of her.

THREE

I decided, finally, that I should call Jake Meyers' sister, Sheila. It was a warm afternoon. I poured myself a big glass of water and flopped down on the sofa under the gaze of a starving child before picking up the phone and dialing the number Jake had given me before I left Eau Claire.

"Hello?"

"Sheila?" I asked.

"Yes?" Her voice dragged out the vowel as if, given extra time, she could figure out who was on the other end of the phone.

"Hi. This is Adam Wilson. I'm a friend of your brother Jake's."

"Hey! Jake's asked me a couple of times whether you'd called me. You went to school with him or played ball together or something?"

"No, Jake was a few years behind me in school. We play in the same softball league now. I don't think you and I have ever met."

"Probably not. Jake's three years older than me, so I don't know a lot of his friends. How good to hear from you."

"You don't have to be polite," I assured her. "I figure we both know he wanted me to check up on you. Just tell me that you're not being held hostage or about to become homeless, and I'll let him know you're okay."

Sheila laughed and said, "Really, I am glad you called. It's always nice to know someone in a big city. You are still in New York, right?"

"Yeah. I've been here for a while. I probably should have called you sooner, but if you don't tell Jake, I won't. If you're up for it, maybe we can get together some time. Lunch, dinner, whatever fits into your schedule. I'm pretty flexible."

"Jake can be relentless, can't he?" Sheila asked with a laugh. "Lunch sounds great. What about tomorrow? Or is that too soon for you? What did you have in mind?"

"Tomorrow's fine," I said. "Do you know a place?"

"Only my new favorite restaurant!" Sheila gushed. I could almost hear her say *"m-m-m-m-m"* as she thought about it. "Julian's on Ninth Avenue, between Fifty-third and Fifty-fourth. I hope you like Italian. Who doesn't, right?"

"I love it. It sounds great to me. I'm looking forward to seeing you."

"Me, too. Why don't we meet around one?" Sheila suggested.

"Julian's on Ninth at one tomorrow. I'll see you then."

After we hung up, I wondered what must be going through her mind. Was it possible she thought I was asking her out? That Jake was fixing her up? Having been the victim of a few bad fix-ups myself, the thought made me snicker. I wouldn't hesitate to set her straight, so to speak. She'd either feel relieved—after all, how many fix-ups were ever a success—or uncomfortable. If so, after an hour we could go our separate ways, no harm done. I could tell Jake his sister was fine, and she could tell him why blind dates were a terrible idea.

I picked up the phone as it rang.

"Adam AdVentures."

"What are you doing?" Blythe asked, sounding a little out of breath.

"Are you okay? What are you doing?"

"My friend Jennifer is over here. I'm on her cell phone. We're dyeing our hair, and I just ran up from the deli."

"Where you got cigarettes."

"How did you know?"

"Lucky guess. What color are you today?"

"Frivolous Fuchsia."

"I can't wait to see that one."

"You already have. I was fuchsia when we met."

"Ah, yes, I remember it well," I said. We'd watched *Gigi* a few nights before.

"Okay, Maurice Chevalier. Jennifer wants to know what's better, a Mac or a PC?"

"What's she using it for?"

"E-mail, mostly."

"Doesn't matter. If she's into graphics or music, a Mac. If she wants to program—"

"Don't get all technical on me. Thanks, I'll tell her. I have to go. My grilled cheese is done."

"That reminds me. I'm trying out a new restaurant tomorrow. Would you like to join me for lunch?" I asked, trying to remember how long it had been since I restocked her groceries.

"Depends. Where are we going?"

"This great Italian place uptown called Julian's."

"Sounds fine to me. I was wondering how to put off working tomorrow. I think I have today under control."

"Great. What are you doing tonight?"

"Hanging out with Jennifer. It's our day of beauty. Manicures, pedicures, the works. And we rented movies just in case we run out of ways to make ourselves look glamorous."

"At least you're up front with your procrastination," I said, pretending to believe the myth Blythe projected about herself. If she was taking time away from her canvases, it was a well-deserved break. "I'll swing by your place with a cab around twelve-thirty tomorrow. We're supposed to be there at one, and I don't want to get stuck in traffic and be late."

"Why do I have the feeling there's more to this lunch than you're telling me? It's not just you and me, is it? What have you got going on, Adam F. Wilson?"

"Okay, I confess. I'm meeting the sister of a friend from home. She lives here now."

"Hmmm."

"Don't make that noise. It won't be that bad. At least, if you're there."

"Sweet talker," Blythe sighed, unconvinced.

"C'mon. She's probably only a couple of years older than you. It'll be fun."

"All right. But if you start talking about 'home on the range,' I'm leaving."

I laughed at the thought of Sheila and me crooning at the table, with Blythe sprinting to the door to get away from us.

After we hung up, I realized I hadn't asked her if she'd managed to get us invited to Wade Van Atterson's party. I hoped the date hadn't passed. I took a drink of water and dialed the phone again.

"Hello?" my mother answered in a bright tone.

"It's Adam," I said, knowing she could never tell the difference between my brother and me on the phone. "New computer still working okay? I saw you in metaphysical chat last night. What were you doing there?"

"I met the nicest lady online," she said. "She lost a son to AIDS, but I've never known anyone who gives off such positive energy. That's the chat room she likes best. I go in there to talk to her. She and her husband live in San Diego. They're both active in PFLAG, too. Your father and I are thinking of meeting them some time. In person, I mean."

"Be careful about that," I said, thinking of Sam69wu. "People online can sometimes be different in real life. Or worse."

"Give us some credit. Your father and I are pretty hard to fool."

"You two are amazing," I agreed.

"Thank you, Adam. Your brother thinks we're nuts."

"That's just an act. He and Julie are trying to be exactly like you. That should tell you something."

"I loved your last e-mail," my mother said. "Blythe sounds so interesting. But you didn't say much about you. Are you working all the time?"

"Not at all. This is the most incredible city, Mom. I'd really like to come back some time with you and Dad. We'd have a blast. Tomorrow Blythe and I are having lunch with Sheila Meyers, Jake's little sister."

"That ought to be fun," she said. "So is Blythe involved in most of what you do socially?"

Here it comes, I thought. *What about men, Adam?*

"I hope so," I said. "She's trying to get us an invitation to a party that I really want to go to."

"Lots of potential business contacts?"

"Nope. We were at a coffee place one night, and I shamelessly eavesdropped on the best-looking guy. He's going to this party. Blythe knows the man who's hosting it. It's a long shot, but if I can get in the party, I may have the chance to meet Jeremy."

"Tell me about him," my mother said, her voice excited.

"He's blond, a few inches shorter than I am, swimmer's build. Brown eyes. The funny thing is, it wasn't really the way he looked that caught my eye. It was something about the way he carried himself. Really confident. And he was so obviously not there to cruise, although everybody was looking at him. I think he may be dating someone, but I got the idea it's not really at the boyfriend stage. And if I meet him . . ."

"You plan to be a contender," my mother finished.

"Exactly. I'll keep you posted."

"You'd better."

We talked a bit more about news from home before we hung up. I watered the plants, trying to convince myself that they looked a little better than the week before. I'd already decided to spend a quiet evening in, eating a light dinner at the computer while I caught up on personal e-mails. Finally I turned in early, Nancy's woebegone eyes watching over me as I read myself to sleep.

New York offered up the most glorious morning the next day. I opened all the windows to let in the sun-drenched September air, with its hint of coolness. I dressed in jeans and, deferring to Blythe's displeasure with flannel, a black sweater. A final glance at the mirror assured me that Sheila would have no reason to feel ashamed of her lunch date.

Then again, I had to wonder about Blythe as she clambered into the cab next to me. Her newly dyed hair was vivid in the sunlight. Wrapped in a sheer black scarf with a bell-sleeved, black cotton dress underneath, she looked like a cross between Lydia from *Beetlejuice* and Stevie Nicks. Blythe, her neck adorned by a choker with a cameo attached, her feet clad in combat boots, looked as if she were ready for a funeral in Victorian England.

"Do you even know this person?" she asked.

"I don't think I've ever seen her," I admitted.

"How will you recognize her?"

"She'll be a young version of Edie McClurg."

"What's that?"

"She played the school secretary in *Ferris Bueller's Day Off,*" I said.

"Oh. I thought you were clearing your throat."

"I love Edie McClurg. She reminds me of some of my friends' mothers. In fact, she could be a twin to Betty Hamilton."

"You've already started down memory lane. You are the only person I would do this for."

I paid the cab driver and joined Blythe on the sidewalk in front of the restaurant, waiting while she puffed on a Marlboro. "See?

You have me so stressed out, I'm inhaling." As she spoke, smoke blew alternately out of her nostrils and mouth.

"I know, honey," I answered in my Agador from *The Bird Cage* voice. "C'mon, let's go."

We stepped into Julian's together and scanned the tables separately. What Blythe was looking for, I had no idea. Possibly Edie McClurg. I looked around for Sheila and saw only couples or trios at the tables.

Finally, I noticed a man tap the arm of the woman sitting across from him, and she craned her neck to look at us. I recognized her immediately. Sheila was gorgeous, like her brother, a tall Nordic blonde without a visible flaw. Even the slightest of overbites looked perfect on her, and when her smile broadened her face, it brightened the room. She and her companion got to their feet as I directed Blythe toward their table. The man, too, had an open, friendly smile. Like me, he was dressed in jeans and a black sweater, and his brown, slightly curly hair fell messily a couple of inches below his collar.

"Adam?" Sheila asked, and I nodded. "How are you?"

"Hey, Sheila, nice to meet you," I answered. "I'm Adam Wilson," I said as I extended my hand to the man who was standing with Sheila.

"Josh Clinton." He shook my hand.

"This is my friend, Blythe Mayfield."

I couldn't help but notice Josh and Sheila exchange a glance after giving Blythe the once-over as we sat down. In all fairness to them, it wasn't a glance with malice or condescension, but a look that could have easily been followed by a shrug of the shoulders.

"What brings you all the way to New York?" Josh asked.

I launched into my spiel about Ray Patel, the work I was doing for him, and how I was thinking of finding more clients on the East Coast. I could tell Blythe was desperate for another cigarette as she sat through this again, fidgeting and looking at other people in the restaurant.

"Yes," Sheila said. "You must get more New York clients."

Josh laughed at my surprised look and said, "Sheila is not Eau Claire's biggest fan."

"You're not?" I asked.

"New York is where I'd rather stay," she answered in an Eva Gabor accent. "Though I don't exactly have a penthouse view. Yet."

"What about you? What do you both do?" I asked.

"I'm a photographer," Josh said.

"Really?" Blythe asked, Josh's mention of a visual art piquing her interest. "Portrait? Landscape? Black and white? Still life?"

"Fashion. The artistic stuff is more of a hobby. I take pictures, and Sheila has them taken."

"He makes it sound like I'm constantly being burglarized," Sheila said, then explained, "I'm a model."

"What about you, Blythe?" Josh asked.

"I'm a professional freeloader."

Josh and Sheila laughed uneasily as Blythe looked at them deadpan. Then one corner of her mouth turned up. "Actually, I'm an artist. But it comes out to about the same thing."

"What medium?" Josh asked.

"Oils. That's why I live in squalor."

Sheila's laugh was a little nervous.

"Her work is really great," I said, wondering if Blythe would be on bad behavior our entire lunch. "You guys should see it. In fact, I'm about to start working on a Web site for her. It'll be a great way for her to get some exposure."

"My gosh, what a great team you two are!" Sheila exclaimed. "How did you meet?"

As Blythe opened her mouth with an evil gleam in her eye, I kicked her under the table and said, "In a coffee shop. We started talking about art."

"Art? Was that Sauna Guy's name?" Blythe asked.

Fortunately, the waiter chose that moment to take our orders. When he left, Sheila broached the subject of Blythe's hair color, commenting first on how good it looked on her, then saying she'd never have the nerve to change her hair so dramatically.

"Rest easy. I don't think the world's ready for two of us, anyway," Blythe said, and they both laughed.

"I don't know; I think it would be really sexy," Josh said.

"How long have you two been together?" Blythe inquired.

"Almost a year," Josh said with a smile.

"That's great. You seem so in sync with each other. I hope Adam finds a guy like you."

"Me, too," I agreed. "Hey, what about Blaine Dunhill?"

Sheila's eyes widened as she repeated, "What about Blaine Dunhill?"

"I do a lot of work for his family back home. Jake told me he's your roommate. How's he doing?"

"He's doing really well."

She seemed a little relieved. Maybe she'd heard about the gossip in Eau Claire and was glad I knew that Blaine was just her roommate.

"I wouldn't mind seeing him while I'm here."

"He's so busy with work," Sheila said. "Even I hardly see him. He travels a lot, and when he's not on the road or at the office, he's at the gym."

"Yeah?" I said. "I wish I could find a good gym."

"I'm not sure where he goes," Sheila said. "You've got our number. Call him some time. I'm sure he'd give you the name."

I intercepted a sideways glance from Josh to Sheila as the waiter returned to our table. While we ate, Sheila took another stab at conversation with Blythe.

"I'll bet you have a really hard time being taken seriously."

Blythe gave her a surprised, slightly insulted look and asked, "Why do you say that?"

"Because people can be very shallow," Sheila said. "I mean, you're so small. Do you find that people treat you like a child? Or a doll?"

"All the time," Blythe said, her face growing warmer. "It infuriates me."

"I know what you mean," Sheila said. "People look at me and see a dumb blond model. They act surprised that I can carry on a conversation. I don't mean to complain; after all, I wouldn't have my career without looking the way I do. But it's tiresome never to be taken seriously."

"It must be great to be tall, though," Blythe said. "Half the time, people don't even see me."

"But I was the gawkiest kid," Sheila said. "I was taller than all the boys and flat-chested. I'm okay with it now, but kids can be such assholes. They called me Amazon Woman, Stilts—oh, I hated it."

"I got Shorty, Midget, and Runt," Blythe agreed.

"With me it was Four-eyes," Josh chimed in. "I was so glad when I got contacts."

"What did they call you?" Sheila asked, looking at me.

"Um," I said, dismayed that I had no childhood traumas to relate.

"Oh, him," Blythe said dismissively, "he was born perfect and only got better."

"Don't hate me because I'm beautiful," I whined, and everyone laughed.

"Other than work, what have you been doing while you're here?" Josh asked me.

"I did the tourist sites first. Statue of Liberty, Empire State Building, that kind of stuff. But it's the museums I like best."

"I did all that, too," Sheila said. "In fact, I told Blaine I wanted to move into the Metropolitan Museum of Art."

"That would be creepy," Blythe said in a tone that made it sound delicious. "All that Egyptian stuff."

Sheila's expression brightened as she said, "Exactly! The idea of being in there alone late at night. Thrilling in a scary, wonderful way."

"The one thing I haven't done yet is a show," I said.

"I love Broadway," Sheila said. "I have some friends who are actors, so I've even gotten to go backstage after a hit show."

"You know," Josh said, "that's something we could all do together some time. If you're interested."

I felt a rush of gratitude in response to their warmth, especially for the way Josh had included Blythe in his invitation.

"That would be fun," Blythe said, letting me know she'd bestowed her approval on our new acquaintances.

When the waiter brought our check, Josh and I argued over who would pay until Sheila settled the matter by slapping down her platinum Amex. Then we all walked outside, and Blythe lit a cigarette. She inhaled deeply, exhaling a plume of smoke that covered Sheila and Josh.

"We must have a new pope," I said, and Blythe rolled her eyes.

There were hardly any pedestrians on the sidewalk, because it was early afternoon. However, a dog walker advanced toward us, leading a small pack of various breeds. We sidestepped out of the way as they drew closer. One errant poodle managed to tangle its lead around Blythe's leg.

Sheila began to giggle as she helped free Blythe, saying, "Look, I think this one's been in your hair dye!"

She held the poodle up, comparing colors, and Blythe let out her first real laugh, one of her trademark bellows. As the two of them bent over the dogs and talked to the dog walker, I nudged Josh away from them.

"I didn't want to ask this in front of Blythe," I said in a low tone. "I've been looking for a photographer to get some shots of her artwork for her Web site. Could you recommend someone? Or do you do freelance?"

"I could do it," Josh said, matching his tone to mine.

"Do you have a card? I'll call you to work out the details. She doesn't need to know I'm paying you."

"I understand," Josh said, discreetly handing me his business card.

As we said our goodbyes, Sheila surprised me with a hug. We all turned at the sound of a bus. Sheila's image, blown up many times, grinned at us from the side of the bus, her blond mane flipped over one shoulder and her teeth sparkling like Tony Curtis's in *The Great Race*. She was silently imploring us to buy Autumn Dusk, for "Freshness That Stays With You."

"I feel fresher already," Blythe declared.

We all laughed, said goodbye again, and Blythe and I watched Sheila and Josh walk down the street arm in arm.

"What was that all about?" Blythe asked me after they were gone.

"What was what all about?" I asked with surprise. I'd thought lunch went rather well, all things considered.

"You mentioned that guy. What was his name? Blaine? And they had a strange reaction."

"I don't know. I don't really know much about him, except that he broke all my football records from high school. He's Sheila's brother Jake's best friend. I heard he went through a messy divorce."

"What were you and Josh whispering about?"

"He wanted to know the name of your hair color. I meant to ask, have you gotten us an invitation to Wade Van Atterson's party yet?"

Blythe sighed, as if Madonna had phoned inviting us to her party instead, suddenly making Wade's party seem passé by comparison.

"No, not yet," she answered. "But I think I know a good place to start."

She strode into the street and threw up one of her arms. Just as I lunged to drag her out of the way of an oncoming bus, a cab swooped to the curb to pick us up. We climbed in the back, and Blythe gave the driver an address that sounded fairly close to her apartment.

"Are we going to your place?" I asked.

"No, we're going to Disorient XPress. It's a bar that Wade owns."

"It's in the East Village?"

Blythe answered, staring out the window of the cab in a distracted way, "Their slogan is 'Where East Meets West.' How original, right? Gay boys, lushes that you all are, rarely dedicate themselves to one bar. And before you interrupt me with your *Cheers*-like story about your dear little hometown bar, let me add that if New York boys are dedicated to one bar, it's because it happens to be the hot spot of the moment. Or it's cool to be there on a Wednesday night. Something inane like that, which will all be different when the next *HX* hits the newsstand."

"I was going to say that where I'm from, we only have a handful of gay bars. But I like straight bars better," I said.

"Really?" Blythe asked, turning to me with an incredulous look. "Why?"

"Because the gay bars back home have pool tables that are always available, but nobody knows how to play," I explained. Blythe pondered that in silence for a minute, so I added, "That was a bit of local humor."

"I wish you had forgotten to pack it," Blythe said, rolling her eyes. "Anyway, Disorient XPress is a theme bar. Their bartenders, cocktail servers, and performers are all Asian drag queens."

"What about the bar-backs?" I asked.

"Sumo wrestlers," Blythe wisecracked. "I'm kidding. I don't know. I never paid attention. It's all extremely visual; you'll see. Here we are."

I paid the driver, we disembarked from the cab, and I found myself in front of a nondescript building featuring bright red doors with ornate gold handles. A fabric sign designed to look like rice paper hung from the building's facade. Characters, possibly Japanese or Chinese—I was no expert—ran down the side, and next to those was a red-painted dragon breathing the words *Disorient XPress* in fire.

"How . . ." I trailed off, at a loss for words.

"Exactly," Blythe agreed. "Wait until we get inside."

I followed her through the doors and into a small lobby. Before me stood a sexless figure in a flowing kimono, a tall black wig pinned up with chopsticks, and what looked like two blocks of wood strapped to its feet.

"Welcome to Disorient XPress," he said. Despite the heavily painted face, the voice belied a man in Kabuki garb. "May I check your bag or coats?"

"No, we're fine," Blythe replied and breezed by him through an open doorway.

"Thanks all the same," I said and smiled. He gave a low bow and shuffled off into the cloakroom.

I followed Blythe into the bar, which represented every Asian stereotype imaginable. A long jade bar sprawled its way across the room, a huge tapestry depicting scenes from the *Kama Sutra* hanging behind it. Statues of the Buddha, red dragons, fans, and gongs were scattered about the room. Rice paper screens and large ferns stood in nearly every corner. Tall, cylindrical lamps made of scrunched-up rice paper cast a soft glow over everything. At the far end of the room was a low platform, which I assumed to be a staging area, perhaps for Kabuki Theater or hara-kiri ceremonies. Rugs with intricate patterns were laid haphazardly on the floor between low tables made of oddly shaped glass balanced atop just as strangely shaped wood.

"Are the tables and lamps real Noguchis?" I asked Blythe.

"You're asking me? You're the design maven," Blythe answered. "I don't even know what that is."

"He's a famous artist. I'm surprised you've never heard of him. Let's grab a table."

Grabbing was hardly necessary, because it was much too early for the bar to have more than a few scattered patrons. We sat at one of the tables, which were surrounded by round, firm black leather pillows. I examined the table and said with awe, "Holy shit, it *is* a Noguchi. I think it's authentic."

Blythe, disinterested, lit a cigarette and proceeded to flick ashes all over the antique table as she spoke. "Is this hunk of glass and wood expensive?"

"Yeah, I guess. I mean, I'm no art dealer, but these things were made in the nineteen-forties. Noguchi designed them for Herman Miller and I don't think they made too many of them." I stopped because I couldn't tell if Blythe was looking around the room with boredom, or if she was looking for a cocktail waiter. "Noguchi was primarily a sculptor but also did interior design, furniture, gardens, and playgrounds—and he even painted."

Blythe turned back to me and stubbed her cigarette out on the table. "Sounds fascinating. I'll have to look him up at the library. You'd think, with all Wade Van Atterson's money, he could get a Noluchi ashtray."

"Noguchi," I corrected.

"Bless you," Blythe said, and I laughed.

A drag queen swooped down on us to take our drink orders. She was tall to begin with, but in her wooden platform sandals, she was easily a half-foot taller than I was and had to crouch down to hear us. Her skin was flawless, like fine porcelain, and she needed very little makeup. Her features were accented with color: pink cheeks, with orange streaks, and thick, dark lashes around oval eyes. Her lips, dark and full, parted to make way for a voice that sounded like Brenda Vaccaro staying up all night to smoke a carton of Marlboro Reds.

"Hi, my name's Brenda Li," she wheezed.

"Brenda Lee?" I queried. "Like the country singer?"

"No. Li," she repeated and spelled it for me. Blythe shrugged apologetically at Brenda, as if she knew all along how to spell it and had no idea what she was doing with a lumphead like me. "Now, what can I getcha, doll?"

"Do you have Budweiser?" I asked.

"I wasn't talkin' to you, hot stuff. I was talkin' to the lady," she said, her voice rising to Harvey Fierstein register as she jabbed the air around me with her pen. But then she let her eyes wander from my groin up to my eyes and said, "I always save the best for last. Now, what can I getcha, dollface?"

"I'd love a dirty martini," Blythe said, suppressing a fit of giggles as I crossed my eyes and feigned death while the drag queen's back was turned. I recovered before she turned back to me so I could order my Budweiser.

"I'll bring it cold in the bottle, hon," she rasped, "but what's the point? 'Cuz the second it gets near that bod of yours, it's just gonna get all hot and bothered. And I should know."

"Brenda Li." I giggled as she walked away to get our drinks.

"Hey, don't knock it," Blythe said, lighting another cigarette. "I hear Brenda Lee's big in Japan."

"Don't give me that. You don't even know who Brenda Lee is," I said.

"My parents own every Brenda Lee record in existence," Blythe stated, daring me with her eyes to question her further on the subject.

"Okay. Name one Brenda Lee song."

Blythe giggled and said, " 'The Crying Game.' "

" 'Rock-a-Bye Geisha Blues,' " I offered.

" 'Noguchi, Won't You Please Come Home,' " Blythe screeched, and we both rocked back and forth on our pillows with laughter.

Brenda Li returned with our drinks but didn't have time to flirt, because a small crowd had entered the bar.

"Do you see Wade Van Atterson anywhere?" I asked Blythe.

"No, I don't," Blythe said, scanning the room again. The patrons in the bar seemed mostly a mixed crowd of college students, single men, and older couples. It was a strange group. Blythe seemed to read my mind and said, "NYU is nearby, so a lot of students come here. And tourists stop in to gawk at the drag queens. Tonight won't be a big gay night, even though it's a gay bar, because it's Dunk-a-Diva Night at Club Chaos."

"What the hell is Dunk-a-Diva Night?"

"Business is faltering there, so I hear the owner—what was his name? Andy?—cooked this night up as a once-a-month event to bring in business, and half the proceeds of the evening go to Gay Men's Health Crisis," Blythe explained.

"You don't mean to tell me—"

"Yup." Blythe nodded. "There's a dunking tank onstage; a diva comes out, sits in the booth, and sings a song while a patron pays for three chances to dunk her before she finishes singing."

"That's kind of degrading," I stated.

"Yeah, but it's for charity," Blythe said. "What's worse is that when they do it, every performer at Club Chaos has to be on hand. Nobody gets the night off."

"Why not?"

"Think about it," Blythe began and gestured toward a cocktail server in the vicinity of our table. "Look at her, for example. The glamorous dress, the heels, the stockings, the padded chest, and the nails. That would take a half-hour to get into. Then there's the wig. That alone would take forever to style. And all that makeup. Imagine all that being plunged into a tub of water."

"I think I see your point," I said.

"The end result would look like a painting by Jackson Pollock,"

Blythe established. "So when the diva gets dunked, she has to hurry backstage, put it all back together, and wait her turn for the next time. But who wouldn't pay to see that? Tons of people go, so the club makes lots of money, lots of money is donated, and word of mouth gets around about what a great place it is. At least that's the theory. It's not like I see their books or anything."

"That's why it's so slow here, honey," Brenda Li wheezed in my ear from behind me, and I nearly jumped out of my skin. She laughed and placed a gentle yet large hand on my shoulder. "Can I getcha guys somethin' else?"

"Is Wade here tonight?" I asked, trying to sound casual, as if I had known Wade all my life. Blythe visibly cringed, horrified, I was sure, by my namedropping.

"Oh, no, hon. He ain't here," Brenda gasped. "You know how Wade is."

"Right," Blythe agreed, shrugging her shoulders at me once Brenda had turned toward me again.

"He's gettin' ready for his big party tomorrow night. Anyways, he probably won't show his mug in here for another week. Hey, you goin' to the party, big guy?"

"Are you?" I asked.

"I gotta work, of course, so's I won't be there until after midnight. But you oughta go. I'd love to see ya there," Brenda panted.

"Well," I faltered, pretending to be nonchalant, "we were going to go, but I lost the invitation. And, geez, this is embarrassing, I can't remember Wade's address."

Blythe looked as if she would kick me under the table had our legs not been visible through the glass.

"Oh, honey, that's nothin'. Here ya go," Brenda said, scribbling the address on her notepad and ripping off the sheet. "I'm gonna be really miffed if ya don't wait for me to get there."

"I can't wait," I said, taking the address from her and putting it in my pocket.

"Adam F-is-for-Falsehood Wilson, that was terrible," Blythe snapped when Brenda clacked away. "I can't believe you lied like that."

"I didn't lie," I said, downing the rest of my beer. "I've been looking forward to this party, and I can't wait to see Jeremy again."

FOUR

Jeremy was all I could think about the next evening as I got ready for the party. I wasn't sure what it was about him that held me so spellbound. He was good-looking, but Manhattan was full of handsome men. His conversation with Andy hadn't been that riveting. He hadn't noticed me; our eyes had never met.

Even if Jeremy was someone enjoying his fifteen minutes of fame, I'd never been dazzled by celebrity. Of course, I hadn't had much opportunity to be dazzled in the heartland—John Mellencamp wasn't exactly a gay heartthrob—but I'd never been one of those guys who swooned over Cher's newest tattoo or could recite every line of *Mommie Dearest*. This wasn't to say that I hadn't seen *Top Gun, A Few Good Men,* and *Born on the Fourth of July* a few dozen times, but that could mean I just appreciated a good military movie.

What stayed with me was the way Jeremy had treated Eric. He'd been gracious when asked for an autograph. He'd put Eric at ease about being a student with a "boring" major. He'd handled the whole interchange without flirting or acting superior in any way, which I found admirable, even a little sexy.

Blythe and I had agreed that since I couldn't call her, she would come to my apartment, and we'd cab together to the Upper East Side. She arrived precisely a half hour late, as I'd expected, wearing her trademark fiercely red lipstick and an oddly mature black dress that hung perfectly on her small frame.

"You look so sophisticated," I said, smiling my approval.

"Ann Taylor. Thrift store. Fifteen dollars. Mistakenly put into the children's section," she said.

I turned to give her a better look at me and said, "No idea. Christmas present. Mom's credit card."

"American Express looks good on you," Blythe said.

It was a balmy September night, so we kept the windows down in the cab. The streets were full, and our driver wove in and out of lanes in a way that no longer alarmed me. As much as I wanted to pretend I was a worldly New Yorker, though, I was still enthralled by the tall buildings, the lights, and the pulse of the city. We stopped in front of a large old building with a black awning that extended to the curb, held up by two regal-looking brass poles.

A doorman in an absolutely ridiculous outfit opened the door and said, "Good evening. May I ask who you're calling on, please?"

"Yes," Blythe answered. "Wade Van Atterson."

"Thank you, miss."

The doorman shut the cab door and nodded to another doorman stationed inside the lobby, who pulled a heavy glass door inward to let us enter. It all reeked of money, and I felt a momentary qualm.

"I feel like an impostor," I murmured to Blythe.

"What?" she asked, her eyes big.

I repeated myself and she exhaled a long "Oh." After a pause, she added, "I misunderstood what you said."

It suddenly occurred to me that Blythe was acting a little strange, almost nervous, but before I could evaluate or question that, the elevator doors noiselessly opened onto a foyer with a door directly in front of us and a hall that extended in either direction with doors at both ends. I looked at Blythe.

"Let's go," I intoned and started enthusiastically down the hall to my right.

"Adam?" Blythe's voice stopped me. I turned to look at her.

"Yes?"

"This way," she said, and went in the other direction. I realized she must know that we should be going left because the door at that end was partly ajar, something I'd missed on my first scan of the hallway.

We entered a large formal living room with overstuffed sofas and chairs that, although new, were designed to look as though they were from the thirties and forties. People were comfortably sitting and standing about the room, holding cocktails or glasses of wine. Blythe plucked a glass of white wine from a silver tray that a server presented to us as we entered the room; I declined the offer.

"Look who's here!" A handsome man wove his way through the twenty or thirty people in the room. "Hello, kitten!" He put his arms around Blythe, giving her a peck on each cheek and glancing at me.

"Hello," Blythe said, seeming to avoid my curious gaze. "Wade, this is Adam F. Wilson. Adam, Wade Van Atterson."

"Nice to meet you," I said, shaking our host's hand even as I concealed my shock that Blythe and Wade obviously knew each other much better than she'd led me to believe.

"Nice to meet *you*," he replied. "The *F* must be for *fabulous*. Blythe told me you were quite handsome. She didn't lie."

I darted another questioning glance Blythe's way, but she was looking over the room like a cheetah scanning the Serengeti plain for a wildebeest calf.

"Excuse me!" she said, then dashed toward some prey only she could see.

"Such an impetuous young lady," Wade said, staring after her. "Do you know her well?"

He seemed to recollect himself, cast a guarded glance at me, and said, "Not as well as I'd like to get to know you."

"This is quite a place you have," I said hastily, realizing Blythe wasn't the only predator in the room.

"Thank you. I'm happy to have you as my guest. The bar's in the next room. Maybe later you'd like a tour?" Wade rested his hand on my arm.

"Sure, that sounds great. I'll just get a drink," I said, relieved to have a reason to escape him.

I looked for Blythe, determined to find out why she'd lied about not knowing Wade. When I couldn't spot her, I made my way to the next room. The bar was set up in a corner, tended by an older woman who looked like she would have quite a story to tell. She was the kind of woman my mother would call "weathered." I was tempted to drag Blythe in and illustrate the perils of cigarette smoke to the skin.

"What'll it be?" the bartender asked while wiping out a glass with a white towel.

"Do you have any beer?" I asked, not sure what I'd get.

"Only MGD. Not much of a beer crowd here."

"That's fine, actually. Light, if you have it."

"Ya get whatcha get, honey," she said, cocking her head to one side as she twisted off the cap. "Glass?"

"No, thanks."

I stuffed a couple of singles into the tip snifter on the bar. As I turned to make my way back to the front room, I bumped into a man behind me. He was tall and slim, with long brown hair. His eyes might well have been black, they were so dark.

"Oh," I said, startled that someone was standing so close to me and I hadn't known it, "excuse me!"

"My pleasure." He smiled back at me with dazzlingly white teeth in a picture-perfect smile.

I smiled at the quickness of this unexpected comeback and brushed past him. Looking into the front room, I could see my host, who was now talking with someone else. He glanced away from his conversation to wink at me, then turned his focus back to his companion. I scanned the room, looking for Blythe's pink hair and didn't find it. I wondered if she was avoiding me.

There appeared to be quite a mix of people at the party. Men and women, from ages twenty to seventy, in various shapes, sizes, and styles of attire, drifted comfortably from room to room. A piano was being played somewhere, providing background music, and glasses clinked while people laughed.

The apartment was huge. From where I stood, it seemed to go on forever. I surveyed the space. It was elegant without stuffiness, with a relaxing quality that seemed to encourage the guests to enjoy themselves.

"And what do *you* do?" a brunette asked, resting one hand on my arm as she bent to adjust a strap on her shoe. "Television? Have I seen you in something? That *Lifetime* movie with Valerie Bertinelli?"

"I'm in computers," I said.

"Really? Like Bill Gates?"

"Not quite on that scale," I admitted.

"Ah," she said, her eyes going past me. "Oh, there's Betsy Pelham!"

She was gone in a flurry of perfumed purpose as I stood gazing after her. In a way, it made me happy to be treated somewhat as if I were another piece of furniture. I might not have the cachet of a celebrity or a mogul, but blending in was better than looking awkwardly out of place.

I'd always enjoyed watching people without drawing attention to myself, so I did that for a while, noticing the way many guests seemed to be participating in a formal, highly ritualized dance. Approach, touch, turn, step away, eyes looking toward the next partner. Before I knew it, it was time for another drink.

I went to the bar, and before I could open my mouth, the bartender had a beer sitting on the counter for me. She winked and turned her gaze to the person standing behind me, nodding her head back as if to say, "Next?" I stuffed a five into the glass on the counter and heard her say, "Thanks, honey," as I turned back to the party.

I surveyed the room with a different eye. It was time to find my partner in the dance, but I saw no one who even resembled Jeremy. Nor had Blythe reappeared. I took a long drink from my beer. The room had become more crowded. There had to be at least sixty people standing in pairs or groups, talking, drinking, laughing, then scanning the room with radarlike precision for the next dance—a reel? A waltz? A minuet? Certainly, with this crowd, it would not be a polka. I grinned, picturing some of the more sophisticated women in the throes of the chicken dance.

I made my way back to the front room, locking eyes with several good-looking men. Many men in the fifty-and-over age bracket were looking at me, but I wasn't interested. I only wanted to find Jeremy. I smiled politely and continued to allow my gaze to wander the room. I noticed the man I'd bumped into at the bar. He was talking to a tall, thin woman dressed in something like a body turban. She had feathers in her hair and wore silver jewelry on anything that could be considered an appendage. He glanced at me, smiled again, and kept his focus on me, although his conversation partner seemed oblivious. I smiled back at him, raising my beer in his general direction as a form of toast. His eyes went past me for a moment; then he gave a little nod, as if warning me to look behind me. I did and saw an Eva Perón look-alike bearing down on me.

"Excuse me," she said, baring her teeth. "I'm Betsy Pelham. Are you the computer person?"

"Yes, I am," I said with a smile. "Adam Wilson."

"Please tell me you're what I'm looking for," she said, which sounded a little scary, but I inclined my head, waiting. "My broker keeps talking to me about dot-coms and E-commerce. It's all such a mystery. And he makes it sound so dreary that I don't care how it turns out. I was desperately hoping you could help unravel it for me."

"Yes, you're just handsome enough to hold her attention," said a middle-aged man as he joined us, introducing himself as Carl Nash. "I have to admit, I'd like to understand this whole Internet thing better, too."

Within a few minutes, as I found myself surrounded by party guests who hammered me with questions about venture capital, IPOs, and infrastructure, the detached part of me was reminded of a Gary Larson cartoon about circling sharks. But I understood their dilemma. I'd been lucky when I made my own investments. I not only had a sound financial background, but I had a grasp of new technology. Though their ages indicated that they were seasoned investors, they were being advised to put their money into something foreign to them—online stores that were for the most part intangible, unlike their brick-and-mortar investments of the past. They didn't want me to tell them whether the risk was worth it. It was obvious they were willing to be pioneers, or at least to bankroll pioneers. Some simply wanted a better understanding of the terminology they were hearing. Others wanted to prove how much they already knew.

I suppressed my competitive streak—this was a party, after all; I didn't have to prove I was an expert—and focused my attention on the questioners. I answered them as best I could, measuring my success by the level of comprehension in Betsy Pelham's eyes. Just as I could see that it was getting beyond her, her gaze went past me and she said, "Isn't that, uh, what *is* his name?"

I turned to look behind me, barely aware when Betsy hurried off to catch up with whoever she'd spotted, because my eyes met Jeremy's. He was less than five feet from me and returned my instant smile automatically and with warmth, as if he thought he might know me.

"Is she running to find a balcony?" he asked.

It took me only a split second to remember that I, too, had thought Betsy looked like Eva Perón, and I used the first *Evita* lyric that came to mind, grateful for the times my sister-in-law, Julie, had insisted on playing the CD.

"I guess I wasn't surprisingly good for her."

"Her loss. I feel like I'm in some Disney Animatronics nightmare," Jeremy said.

"Because?"

"The younger version of George Hamilton is bearing down on us."

"Jeremy, Adam," Wade spoke from behind me, and I half turned, reluctant to share my Jeremy moment with my host. "Are you ready for that tour now?"

"Sure," I said, grateful that his invitation included Jeremy.

"Actually, I'm waiting for my date to bring me a drink," Jeremy said. "I wouldn't want him to think I ditched him."

There was no way I could get out of the tour without being rude. Jeremy and I exchanged another smile before I allowed Wade to lead me away. As we moved among the little group I'd been talking to earlier, about a dozen business cards were thrust at me by people suggesting I call them so we could talk more. I nodded and carefully tucked the cards into my inside jacket pocket.

"Perhaps you should give a seminar," Wade commented. "I wouldn't mind attending it. In fact, I wouldn't mind hosting it. But right now, I felt I should be a different kind of host and rescue you from them. Were you overwhelmed?"

"Not at all," I said, covering my annoyance that he'd rescued me from the single person I'd wanted to see. "They remind me of my college students. Eager to learn new things that will make them money."

"And do you make money?" he asked a little too casually.

"I do all right," I said, thinking how horrified my parents would be by his question. In fact, most of the people I knew were more likely to talk about anything—even sex, religion, or politics—than money.

Wade showed me the rooms I'd already seen, then led me through a door that separated the rest of the apartment from the living quarters. The apartment was immense, taking up half the floor of the building. It was very open, and I was sure that during the day natural light flowed freely. He had a sunroom loaded with plants. Outside the sunroom was a terrace with a table and chairs. His kitchen was full of stainless steel, flush with enough amenities to make a four-star chef's mouth water. He also had a private gym, complete with a whirlpool, small steam room, and sauna.

As we circled back toward the door we'd entered, Wade opened another door to a small gallery, which was kept cooler than the rest of the apartment. Paintings filled the walls, seemingly without rhyme or reason. A Renoir hung next to a Warhol, which was next to a Hopper. There wasn't a myopic child in sight. It was certainly obvious that *he* had money, as I was sure I was meant to understand, especially when he hurried me to the next room.

"This is my bedroom," Wade said, opening a door to a palatial master suite. The furniture was all genuine Shaker.

Wade stood motionless, watching me as I glanced around. I was beginning to feel as if he were waiting for me to make a move, or waiting to gauge my reaction if he were to make a move. While I thought he was a handsome man, I had no desire to know him more intimately.

"Should we get back to the party?" I asked.

A disappointed look washed quickly over his face, then gave way to a cheery smile.

"Yes, I suppose people will start to talk if we're gone too long."

I laughed, then asked, "What is it that you do? If you don't mind me asking."

"Not at all. Most of what you see was inherited. My family did rather well in the Second World War building machinery and artillery for the government." Surprised as I was by yet another reference to money, I kept my face blank. "I moved from Concord to New York and worked as a stockbroker for a few years. I'd graduated from Harvard without a clue as to what I wanted to be. Most of my chums from school got their Series Sevens, and I followed suit. Now I work primarily with artists, helping them establish their names. I also own a nightclub downtown. I hope I'm not boring you."

"No, I'm the one who asked. In fact, you sound a lot like me. I went into accounting, then computers, and now I, too, work with artists."

"We have so much in common," he said in a tone that I found distastefully suggestive.

I was happy to reenter the party, until I spied Jeremy across the room. He was with the dark-eyed man from the bar. In fact, Dark Eyes had an arm casually resting across Jeremy's shoulders. It was obvious this was the date Jeremy had mentioned to Wade.

He *did* tell Andy he was seeing someone, I reminded myself, thinking of the night I'd eavesdropped at the Big Cup. But how typical was it that the two best-looking guys at the party turned out to be together?

"I thought I recognized you," a woman said, and I turned to see Sheila Meyers giving me her brilliant smile.

"Sheila," I said with real pleasure, having been abandoned by the mysterious Blythe and disappointed by the ineligible Jeremy.

"It's so lucky you're here, Adam. I seem to have lost the girl I came with, and I don't know another soul."

"Funny, the same thing happened to me," I said. "Sheila Meyers, Wade Van Atterson."

"This is your place," Sheila said, extending her hand to him.

I was embarrassed that my cell phone chose that moment to ring. I thought I'd turned it off.

"I'm so sorry," I said. "I have to take this in case it's a client with a problem."

They both made gestures to let me know it was fine and continued to talk to each other while I put the phone to my ear.

"Adam AdVentures."

"Adam, it's Blythe."

"Where are you?"

"I'm sorry, a group of my friends whisked me away. I looked for you to tell you, but I didn't see you anywhere. We're at Club Chaos. I didn't want you to worry when you couldn't find me." Before I could say anything, she finished, "Oh, we're going in now. Have a great time at the party! I hope you get to meet Jeremy."

She hung up, and I stared at the phone a second before I closed it and put it back in my pocket.

"Anything wrong?" Wade asked.

"Blythe ditched me for an outing to Club Chaos."

"I love Club Chaos!" Sheila said, missing the odd look Wade cast her way. "Are you supposed to join her there?"

"Yes," I lied, relieved that I had an excuse to escape from Wade Van Atterson. I was convinced that Blythe was avoiding me, but sooner or later she would have to answer my questions. And if she knew Wade, and Wade knew Jeremy, the evening wasn't a total loss. One way or the other, I'd find a way to see Jeremy again.

"Adam, would it be terrible of me to invite myself along?" Sheila asked.

"Not at all," I answered, realizing she wanted to leave as much as

I did. I could explain to her outside that I wasn't really going to Club Chaos.

"So nice to meet you, Wade," Sheila said, turning her radiant smile on him.

"It was lovely to meet you, Sheila. Thank you so much for coming, Adam," Wade said.

"Thank you for having me."

"Oh, but I haven't yet," Wade said flirtatiously.

Once we were in the elevator, Sheila exhaled and said, "I could kill Christy for stranding me like that. Thank you so much for rescuing me, Adam. You don't really have to let me go with you to the club. I just had to get out of there. Some man actually called me the 'douche girl'!"

"Ew," I said. "I'm sorry."

"That product will haunt me until the end of time," she said. "You know how big stars always have grainy little porn movies or nude photo layouts to come back and bite them in the ass? Autumn Dusk is my albatross."

"Albeit freshly scented," I reminded her, and she giggled. "I have a confession to make. Blythe didn't really invite me to join her and her friends at Club Chaos."

"Damn, I was hoping you'd let me go with you," Sheila said. "I love that place. Have you ever been?"

"Nope. But the night's young. We don't have to tag along with Blythe's group. If you really want to go, I'd love to. Escorting me there is the least you can do for a hometown boy."

"Yay!" Sheila said. "Let's do it."

I hailed a cab, and we settled in.

"Who is Wade, anyway?" Sheila asked. "I was only there because Christy dragged me along. What crime did you commit that had you doing time there?"

"I take it you weren't impressed with our host?"

"I didn't talk to him long enough to form an opinion," Sheila admitted. "I'm still reacting to his rude guest. I suppose I shouldn't blame Wade for that."

"I wanted to go to the party," I said. "A man was involved. But he was with someone else, so I was ready to leave."

"Too bad," Sheila said in a sympathetic tone. "You'll get plenty of eye candy at Club Chaos, though. Josh will be jealous when he finds out we went without him."

"He likes the eye candy?"

She laughed and said, "He likes the shows. Oh, I forgot to tell you. I called Jake and told him about our lunch."

"How's he doing?"

"He's fine. He's so funny. His take on things is that he didn't want you to feel alone in the Big Apple. As if I didn't know he really wanted you to check up on me."

"Has your family met Josh?"

She gave me a guilty look and stretched out her, "Nooooo."

"Do they *know* about Josh?"

"They don't know how serious it is."

"How serious is it?" I asked in a big-brother tone.

"I don't ever want to wake up with anyone else," Sheila confessed. "I know when they meet him they'll like him, too."

"So what's the problem?"

"My parents have convinced themselves living in New York is something I have to get out of my system. They think I'll go back home. They want me to. I don't want them to think I'm staying here because of Josh."

"What about your career?" I asked.

"They don't take modeling seriously."

I thought about that as I stared from my window at the buildings and traffic. My family had always been supportive of whatever I did. Even Blythe's parents sent her money so she could paint in New York.

"We're here," Sheila interrupted my thoughts.

We had stopped in front of an old stone structure on the corner of an intersection. I got out, then Sheila extended a high-heeled foot to the pavement and stepped out of the cab, one black satin pant leg at a time. She wore a thin black camisole top under her black leather jacket, which created a striking contrast to her fine features and glowing hair. Her expression exuded confidence as we walked arm in arm to the doorman, who acknowledged Sheila with a nod. We walked in without paying the cover.

"They know me here," Sheila murmured as she led me through the lobby.

I gazed in awe at the opulence of the club's interior. The walls were painted a deep scarlet. Framed pictures and paintings hung from the chair rail to the high ceiling. Two bars lined the walls on either side of the room, drawing people forward from the entry into what appeared to be a larger room on the other side of a wide doorway with curtained drapes held back by thick, black cords.

If Disorient XPress looked like Charlie Chan's estate sale, Club Chaos could be a set for *Phantom of the Opera*.

"This used to be a theater," Sheila said, obviously pleased to be in the know about the building's history. "It was a vaudeville house, then a burlesque house; then it was rebuilt and enlarged into a theater for dramatic purposes. You know, real plays. But everyone went uptown to Broadway for real theater, so it was turned into a movie theater, then was closed down for a long time. Andy bought it for a song before it could be demolished and made it into a club. Isn't it great?"

I had to agree that yes, it was great. There were a lot of people packed into the bar, drinking, laughing, and talking. I noticed there were cocktail waiters working the floor and taking trays of drinks through the doorway into the other room. Sheila saw me looking in that direction and began pulling me that way.

"Come on, let's see the show," she urged.

We quickly ordered drinks, then made our way through the crowd to the back of the bar toward the doorway, where I got sidetracked by one of the pictures on the wall. It was a large black-and-white photograph of Princess Diana and Judy Garland standing arm in arm in the same room we were in. At first I was confused, because I was certain Judy Garland had died long before Diana even met Prince Charles. As I got closer to the picture, I realized it was a photograph of two men in drag, and I laughed. Their resemblance to the two icons was staggering.

"Those are my friends," Sheila's voice spoke from behind my shoulder.

"They look lovely," I said, meaning it.

"They both used to perform here, but I never saw them onstage. They were supposedly *the* acts to see here, too. It's a shame." Sheila's voice trailed off as she stared wistfully at the picture, and I wondered if there was more to the story than she was telling me. She snapped out of her reverie and said, "But my other friend still performs here. We should go in before his act starts."

We went into the performance hall, and I was once again struck by the elegance of the interior. There was a stage at the other end of a large space that obviously had once held hundreds of seats in its days as a theater. The floor was now leveled and covered with bistro tables and chairs, except for the area under the mezzanine, which was a standing area. Most of the tables were occupied. I tried to search the room for Blythe's electric hair, but couldn't find her, since the lighting was quite dim. There were a lot of people in the standing area, talking in low whispers and laughing at the show, but I followed Sheila to the front of the crowd.

"Oh, good," she said softly, "my friend's not on yet."

Sheila scanned the area for a vacant table, and I looked at the club's high ceiling. Through the lighting grid above us, I could see a large mural of comedy and tragedy masks. One large mask smiled maniacally down at me, while the other frowned in gloom and despair. I turned my gaze behind me to the mezzanine. The ornate railing was still there, but the area where seats had probably once been was now a wall, with a window and two large holes for spotlights to follow the performers.

"Quick! Grab that table," Sheila said, spinning me around and pointing at a table being vacated by two men who looked more interested in each other than the next show.

"Ladies, gentlemen, and queens, Club Chaos is proud to present our final act for the evening: Sister Mary Amanda Prophet!"

As we took over the table, a nun strode onto the stage and stood before a large microphone to thunderous applause. She took a few little bows and withdrew her hands from beneath her habit to gesture piously that she was not worthy. She attempted to bless herself, but poked herself in the eye. While the audience laughed, a piano was rolled onstage by two stagehands, who promptly exited.

"Lord, please heal me in my minute of embarrassing pain," Sister Mary said, rubbing her eye. "Man, that smarts."

"That's my friend, Martin," Sheila whispered to me as she wriggled out of her leather blazer and hung it on the back of her chair. Even though Blythe had told me about the Club Chaos drag shows and I'd seen the photos on the way in, it hadn't occurred to me that the nun was a man until that moment.

"Today's sermon: 'Confession Cleanses the Soul!' Sister Agatha, can you give it to me in G major?"

Sister Mary pointed, without looking, at the piano behind her and waited for a chord that wouldn't be played, because nobody was there. The audience tittered and giggled, and Sister Mary looked aghast at the vacant piano, then turned to the audience.

"Um, excuse me," she said and walked into the wings. After a brief pause, she returned, angrily rolling a chair on which sat a tiny, ancient sleeping "nun." The audience roared with laughter as Sister Mary deposited the chair in front of the piano, then banged on the keys to awaken her.

"You'll have to excuse Sister Agatha," Sister Mary said to us. "She's with us by divine Providence, and I don't mean a miracle. She served in a convent in Rhode Island for seventy years, and they shipped her to us by mistake when they were sending some stuff to the Salvation Army. We were gonna ship her back, but we found out she's a good piano player. Although she snores in church and has a memory like a sieve." Sister Mary clasped her hands over her mouth and gasped, "I can't believe I said that. But then again, confession cleanses the soul! Agatha, a G major?"

Sister Agatha played a chord, and Sister Mary planted her feet and started a low, ominous chant.

Dominae Christae, what the hey
I know you all have things to say
You could tell your problems to a priest
But I'd rather you tell them all to me
This sister's lips will remain sealed
If you confess, you will be healed
I know about Lewinsky's trysts
But even I can't spill that dish
Madonna confides about her guy
Kato told me the real alibi
I've heard every story
From people rich and poor
I've heard lots of confessions
Now it's time for yours . . .

Sister Mary Amanda Prophet stepped from the stage and made her way into the seating area. She picked people seemingly at random and provoked them into telling her their secrets, which she then made light of, to everyone's delight. It could have come across as a mean act, but Sister Mary had the confessors laughing at their own misfortunes and foibles.

"And what would you like to confess?" Sister Mary asked a table of hunky men in tank tops and crew cuts.

"We don't like this table," one of them laughed.

"That hardly bears confessing. Still, I want my parishioners to be happy. Do you want a table in front?"

I was still laughing as Sister Mary Amanda Prophet managed to rearrange the seating area. I was so busy checking out the hunky guys that I didn't notice when she came my way.

"Well, well, this is a table of beautiful people," she said, gesturing to Sheila and me. "I know this one; she confessed a rather bawdy story to me on the phone last night. It seems there is this photographer she's dating, and they did something under the table at a restaurant that would—"

"Okay, that's quite enough," Sheila yelped, and the room erupted in laughter.

"How about you, child," Sister Mary said to me. "Care to give a confession?"

"I'm afraid I have nothing to confess," I said.

"Oh, now, that can't be true," Sister Mary responded, clucking her tongue.

"He writes porn on his laptop!" someone yelled. I followed the voice to the other side of the room and spotted Blythe at a table with four young men.

"Pornography!" Sister Mary gasped. "I don't know what to say. Yeah, I do. Can you print that out and get it to Sheila?" Even from across the room, I heard Blythe braying. "This reminds me of a story." Sister Mary gave me a reproving glare, then returned to the stage. "One evening, I went out to minister to the people. I found myself in a dungeon of filth. Depravity. Sodom and Gomorrah. And you know what?"

She paused for effect, staring raptly toward the heavens with her arms up. She glanced down at the audience with a frown.

"What?" someone yelled.

"Well, thank you. I was beginning to think I was alone in here. Can we try that again with feeling? *And you know what?*"

"What?" everyone in the room yelled at once.

"I liked it!" she yelled. "I looked around at all those boys in their tight T-shirts, tight jeans, hot bodies, writhing, dancing, sweating, lusting, and I liked it! It was a celebration. The music was pumping a joyful noise to the heavens. Every day should be like that moment. We should *all* celebrate life! That is *my* confession!"

Sister Agatha struck a few chords on the piano as a music track began to play on the club's sound system, moving into a raucous version of "Ballroom Blitz" by Sweet, complete with a backing gospel choir of bewigged drag queens. The audience was up on its feet, clapping and singing along.

At the end of the act, Sister Mary Amanda Prophet crossed herself, high-fived Sister Agatha, and left the stage, twirling the cross tied around her waist while doing a penguin walk.

"He's great," I enthused to Sheila. "I've been to a couple of drag shows back home, but they were nothing like this."

Blythe suddenly threw her arms around me with that fat laugh.

"You bad, bad boy. Sister Mary didn't give you your penance, so I will. I decree that you must dance with this one," she said, letting go of me long enough to shove me toward one of her companions. All I saw was a flash of white teeth in a face that made my mind go lightning fast through the words *tanned-beautiful-swimmer's build-surfer-hot.*

Before I could speak, he laughed and pulled me to the dance floor, where we were absorbed into dozens of hot, gyrating men while lights flashed and music blared.

"Steve!" my partner yelled at me.

I laughed as I shouted back, "Adam!" I couldn't help but think of the bigots' mantra, *God made Adam and Eve, not Adam and Steve!* I wouldn't be able to keep a garden of rocks alive, but right now I did feel like I'd wandered into Eden.

I decided to let the secretive Blythe and stunning Sheila take care of themselves while I surrendered myself to the night's pleasures.

FIVE

At ten the next morning, I stumbled over my threshold into The Waifs Land, bleary-eyed from lack of sleep, reeking of cigarette smoke, and thoroughly sated after a few hours at Steve's apartment. I had no idea what Steve's last name was, what he did, or even how to call him. Which was fine. A friend in Eau Claire called this a "just-one-of-those-things date" from the Cole Porter song in which a love affair is too hot not to burn out quickly. It was a nice way not to say "trick."

I mentally inventoried my night, ignoring little Anorexia's hollow-eyed gaze as I made myself a huge breakfast of pancakes, eggs, and sausage. I was ravenous. I'd been mildly propositioned by a millionaire, seen my first professional drag show, been manhandled by lots of gleaming, gorgeous men, and was now fully and truly initiated into one of the most elite groups in the world, the gays of Gotham. Life was good, but all I wanted was sleep. Desperately.

I'd showered at Steve's, so once I was out of my pungent clothes, I slid between the sheets with a groan of pleasure. I drifted to sleep, thinking of Steve's large hands gripping my back, and his large—

Riiiiiinnnnng.

"That is not the phone," I said aloud. "Your ears are still ringing from the music."

Riiiiiiiiiinnnnnng.

I burrowed deeper into my pillow.

Rrrrrrrrrriiiiiiiinnnnnnngggggg.

The machine clicked and I heard, "Hi, this is Adam. Leave a message."

"Adam, this is Ray Patel. Something is wrong with the system, and four of the stores in New Jersey—"

I grabbed a pen and wrote down his answers to the questions I fired at him after I picked up the phone. Ray was my bread and butter, and I had to take care of him no matter how exhausted I was.

Ten hours later, dumb from fatigue, I crawled into my bed a chastened person. Man and machine had done battle. Man had finally won. And now man was going to collapse if he didn't—

I whimpered as the phone rang again, picking it up in case Ray had more bad news.

"What happened to you last night?" Blythe trilled, obviously none the worse for wear.

"Can't . . . talk," I mumbled. "Must . . . sleep."

I woke up Monday morning to find the phone still in my hand. Poor Blythe. I wondered when she'd realized that I was unconscious and she was stuck at some pay phone talking to thin air.

The waif Nancy watched reproachfully from above the bed as I dressed after my shower.

"That's right, Mrs. Reagan, I fucked a man," I said smugly. "Without regret. It was *my* turn."

I dialed in to make sure everything was still running smoothly with Patel, Inc., thinking about how playful Ray had been the day before when we were working. He'd obviously understood that in spite of being able to handle his crisis, I was suffering the effects of too much alcohol and no sleep.

"Burning the candle at both ends," he'd said in his melodious accent, lighting a stick of the Nag Champa incense that always perfumed his office. "You are lucky to be a boy. When you get old, these nights with the ladies—"

"You know I'm thirty-one," I reminded him. "And I spend my nights out with *guys.*"

"Miss Blythe is no guy," Ray scolded.

"It wasn't Miss Blythe who kept me awake all night," I answered with a leer.

He shook his head, but I saw him smile as he turned away. Like my straight friends back home, he understood perfectly well that I was gay, but seemed to derive satisfaction out of ribbing me about women. Maybe it was just his way of goading me into revealing details about my personal life, which I would never have done on my own.

Ray could have had an auspicious position in India in genetic research. He was well educated, with a gifted intellect. But he'd come to the States during a time when the economy was bad, and hostility toward anyone who looked Middle Eastern was high. The best position he'd ever been offered was as a lab tech. Instead, he became a successful retailer. In America, commerce still ruled and was open to anyone with an entrepreneurial spirit. He and I had that in common.

Everything was fine with Patel, Inc., so I made a call to Tracy in Eau Claire and caught up on news about other clients and the rest of the staff. After a light lunch, my impatience to see Blythe got the best of me. I wanted to find out why she'd misled me about knowing Wade. Her actions at the party alluded to a story she hadn't told, and I wanted to see the bigger picture. I showed up at her loft with a bag of groceries and a bunch of slightly wilted daisies.

"Give me those fast," she said, grabbing the bouquet after I walked in. "Leaving flowers in your possession is like asking Rush Limbaugh to stand guard over a bowl of jellybeans."

"I think it was Ronald Reagan who ate jellybeans," I said.

"Okay, then it's like asking Bill Clinton to hold your Big Mac. What happened to you Saturday night?" I merely smiled, thinking of Surfer Steve, and she shook her head and said, "You were supposed to be doing penance, not research."

She took the daisies to the sink, unwrapped them, and began snipping off the ends with an oversized pair of shears that were presumably designed to cut canvas. She wore overalls spattered with paint of every hue. From her white T-shirt, *Hello Kitty* peered over the bib of the overalls. There was a daub of cerulean blue paint on her cheek, and I wondered if she knew it was there. It looked as natural on her as a mole.

"What about you?" I asked her. "What did you do?"

She rolled her eyes and said, "I'm not the one who looks like the cat who ate the canary."

"Maybe I'm not the kind of boy who likes to kiss and tell," I said smugly.

Blythe looked at me through her glasses as if they had microscopic lenses.

"Doesn't matter. You've told me all I need to know," Blythe said cryptically, as if she were Mata Hari. She pointed to the daisies, which she deposited in a glass vase with beige water. "What do you think?"

"I think I'm going to run down to the deli and buy you a jug of real water."

"No, the flowers. What do you think?"

"Like I'm any judge of flower arrangements," I said, eyeing the vase with indifference.

"Are you sure you're gay?" she asked. I gave her another smug smile. "Spare me the details, you slut. What did you think of your first New York party?"

"It was pretty overwhelming," I confessed. "I like to consider myself a worldly kind of guy, but all that money on the walls and on everyone's back was a lot to take in."

"All that ostentatious behavior that goes along with being rich is like a trap, I guess," Blythe mused as she set the vase on a windowsill and assessed its effect on the room. "It consumes you."

"I'm so glad I got out of all that," I agreed.

Blythe looked over her cat glasses at me and said, "There's money to be made in what you do?"

"Oh, hell, yeah," I said, wondering what parallel universe Blythe had been living in. I looked around us at her loft and realized that the modern world and all its trappings seemed to have passed her by. The reason she had a TV and VCR was because she'd found them on some curb. The only way to turn off the TV was to unplug it, and the VCR often stuck in fast-forward mode unless she pounded the top of it. "I could've gone on building Web sites for corporations and all the technologists developing new ideas and made far more than I already had. But I wanted to feel like what I was doing really meant something. I wanted to work with people who would appreciate the energy and knowledge that I had to give."

"Which is why you work with artists," Blythe finished for me.

"Yes," I agreed. "And because I love art. Is that why you shy away from technology, Blythe? Are you afraid of success? That the end result won't justify the means?"

"Adam, I may live in squalor in the East Village," Blythe laughed, "and I may have pink hair, but I've never been a cliché. I'd love to be successful. I'd love to be taken seriously by the 'art world,' whatever the hell that is these days. But if it means having my art: my thoughts, my emotions—hell, my soul—hanging on the walls of someone like Wade Van Atterson's gilded showcase of an apartment, then no, thank you."

"I don't get it. I mean, the guy seemed fairly slimy to me, but what's so bad about the art he had? He owns some really nice pieces."

"It has nothing to do with that," Blythe said, then paused as if to collect her thoughts. She turned back to the vase of daisies and snatched it off the windowsill as if it offended her. "We'll get back to that. Tell me about the other people you met."

I told her about Carl Nash, Betsy Pelham, and the impromptu oration I gave on E-commerce. But thinking about the party made me remember Jeremy. He was the one I would rather have talked to, laughed with, or woken up with in the morning. Blythe, making a face at yet another reference to technology—or at how the daisies looked next to her hot plate; I couldn't tell—brightened when I described Betsy and Carl.

"That's so sweet of you to take the time to talk about that with them," she beamed. "Especially when you were there to have fun."

"It was fun," I protested. "I love to teach."

"You were there to meet guys."

"I did meet guys," I said.

"Yeah, but not until later, when I practically threw one in your lap," Blythe said. "And what happened to Jeremy? I went through all that trouble to get us to the party—"

"You? I got the address. What the hell are you talking about?"

"I was the one who knew where to find Wade," Blythe countered.

"But he wasn't there," I parried.

"Yes, but I led us to Disorient XPress," Blythe insisted, "where we got the information we needed. *And* the invitation from Brenda Li."

"Good work, Nancy Drew. Let's go get an ice-cream sundae."

Blythe threw back her head and laughed. Then she moved the daisies to an empty corner of the room and set them on the floor.

"Jeremy was there, but with a date. We only spoke briefly. I hope Sheila wasn't mad that I ditched her at Club Chaos."

"*Sheila?* What about me?" Blythe demanded.

"You ditched me at Wade's party!"

"Oh, yeah. Well, I didn't really ditch you. I was doing reconnaissance."

"Is that some new designer drug?"

She giggled and said, "Anyway, you and Steve hit it off, huh?"

"In that see-ya-around-sometime kind of way," I agreed. "Yesterday I had to work all day on Ray's system. By the time you called, I was delirious."

"What did you think of Wade?" Blythe asked nonchalantly. "What did you call him? Slimy?"

"He kind of made a move on me. Not blatantly, but the feeling was there."

"He's not your type," she said.

"I'm not sure I have a type," I protested. "But speaking of Wade—"

"I think the daisies work here," Blythe interrupted.

"Good," I encouraged, "now sit down on the sofa with me. You're making me nervous with all that indecision."

Blythe curled up next to me on her tattered sofa. Instead of looking at me, she gazed toward the canvas on her easel. I was definitely getting the idea that she wanted to shelve the topic of Wade. I decided to try a different approach and kill two birds with one stone.

"At the party, there was this one guy . . ."

"Describe," Blythe said.

"Tall, really long brown-black hair, dark eyes; he looked like he could be Italian or—"

She was already shaking her head, so I broke off.

"He's Indian. As in Native American. And no, no, no. Don't go there."

"Why? Who is he?"

She thought a moment then said, "You saw that Wade is comfortable. Financially."

"I'd say that's an understatement."

"He collects things. Mostly as investments. Like his art. Did you notice anything? You can almost see him ticking them off on his fingers. *Now I have a Van Gogh; now I have a Picasso,*" she said. "Just accumulating things for their financial worth, not because he admires them or can't live without them, or even because they go with his furniture." She paused, and I held my breath, not wanting to distract her now that she was talking about Wade. "I find his collection of people interesting. Sometimes, even though he's really only thinking ahead to some bottom line no one else has quite figured out, he stumbles on a treasure. The guy you're talking about, Ethan Whitecrow? I'm not sure about him yet. I don't know who's using whom."

"Okay," I said. Even though I was disappointed that she was straying from the topic of Wade, at least I might find out more about Ethan, my competitor for Jeremy's affections.

"Ethan is supposed to be this really spiritual guy. He latched on to Bonnie Seaforth-Wilkes at some retreat."

"That name seems familiar," I said.

"It should. I think the family used to own a couple of railroads and the entire states of Indiana and Illinois."

"They sound like a Monopoly game," I said.

"Exactly. They still own a lot of companies in the Midwest. She's older than God—and richer—and has devoted herself to any number of spiritual pursuits in her lifetime to make up for it. She was at the party—"

"The woman in the mummy dress?"

Blythe giggled and said, "That was her. She and Wade may be bankrolling Ethan. He's some kind of motivational speaker. I think he's even written a book. Wade is probably trying to incorporate him and start some movement that will make lots of money. Maybe he wants his own Crystal Palace like that guy in California—"

"Crystal Cathedral," I said, laughing at her.

"Whatever. There's a lot of money to be made scaring the devil out of people. Maybe Wade wants Ethan to be a spiritual leader to millions. That stuff gives me the creeps."

"I just thought he was hot," I commented.

"Out, demons of the flesh!" she yelled, laying a hand on my forehead.

"Oh, stop it," I said, dodging her. "But remember, if you see me on television manning the phones for some gay religious cult, you have only yourself to blame. You took me to that party."

"No," she said. "*You* got the address, remember? I wash my hands of any consequences."

"How biblical," I said. "See, our lives are already being transformed."

She shuddered and said, "Let's change the subject."

I made a quick decision. I had maneuvered Blythe into going to the party, not realizing there was some reason that Wade made her uncomfortable. Now that I knew, it was obvious she didn't want to get into it. Since she was my friend, I would stop badgering her. I could find another means to meet or get information about Jeremy.

"Back to Sheila," I said. "How did you and she get along?"

"She's a lot of fun. For a girly-girl glamazon, she can really knock back the hooch. We ended up closing Club Chaos and going on to a lesbian bar in the meat-packing district," Blythe said. "Oh! That reminds me. Sheila told me that you talked to Josh about taking pictures of my paintings for a Web site. Aren't you sneaky? When I explained that I'm a not-starving-but-impoverished artist, she reminded me that I have a means of paying him."

"Is it immoral?"

Blythe slapped my arm and said, "A painting! I can trade a painting for photographs."

"Of course! And one day, when Wade looks at a finger"—here I held up my middle finger and Blythe laughed—"and says, 'I must have a Mayfield,' he can give Josh thousands of dollars for your painting and everyone will be happy."

Blythe frowned at me and said, "Like Josh would give it up for less than a million."

"That Josh drives a hard bargain."

"Doesn't he?"

I nodded and said, "I'm glad you're going to cooperate with me about the Web site. If nothing else, it's good to own your own name on the Internet. Otherwise, when you get famous, someone else will either make you buy it for some outrageous price, or they'll use it to write scurrilous stories about you."

"Or stick my head on somebody else's body and claim they have nude pictures of me."

"Wow, you could end up with Pamela Anderson's body."

"She's not short enough. They'd probably use Billy Barty."

"I love Billy Barty. Let's rent *Foul Play* and go to my place. While we're there, we'll register your domain name."

"Stop! You're moving too fast again," she wailed.

"There won't be anything on the site; it just reserves your name. One small step for art's sake. Trust me. You won't feel a thing."

"All right." She glanced at the daisies. "I need to check on the plants, anyway. I told Sheila about your herbicidal tendencies. She has a friend who may be able to help you."

"That Sheila is so useful," I said.

The next day, I woke up at The Waifs Land and logged on to my business site through the laptop. I clicked to the About Adam AdVentures page, where there was a picture of my house and front lawn. The image was provided by a live Webcam, wired from my server and posted in a weather-protected box on a tree in my front yard. I watched as the image reloaded itself every thirty seconds.

I mused about how different Sheila's opinion of Eau Claire was from mine. What would be exile to her was home to me. But as much as I missed my farmhouse and the countryside that surrounded it, developing and maintaining ties in Manhattan seemed like a good decision.

I'd slowly been developing the idea that I'd mentioned to Blythe, Josh, and Sheila during our lunch. Expanding Adam AdVentures' client base might be profitable enough to enable me to rent my own place in Manhattan, as a location for conducting business as well as a place to live while I was in New York—much like the borrowed apartment I was now in. I wondered who owned Blythe's loft and if there might be space in her building that I could lease. Of course, my space would have to be air-conditioned. Not only did I like my creature comforts, but my computer equipment would make summer living unbearable without air-conditioning.

I decided to close up shop for the time being, made some calls, and watered the plants, wondering why they responded no better to attention than they did to neglect. It was too bad it hadn't been a cat or dog that Prajna had left behind in her apartment. I always had better luck with animals than plants. I'd warned Ray that the plants were not doing well, but he didn't seem to realize the gravity of the situation. It was only a matter of time until last rites would be required.

Feeling bored, I signed back online to check my e-mail, but most of it was junk except for a note from my mother. I answered to let her know that I was fine, then stared at the computer for a moment, thinking about my conversation with Blythe the day before. I went to Amazon.com and typed in *Ethan Whitecrow*. Sure enough, it came up with two book titles, *Shamanic Energy* and *Shamanic Dance*. Then I did an Internet search on his name. There were reviews for both books, articles on lectures or workshops he'd been part of, and even a Web page for one of the books.

Ethan was my best link to finding Jeremy again. Maybe I could set up a meeting, where I could pump him for information. I smiled as I found what I was looking for and hit the hyperlink to send him an e-mail.

Hi, my name is Adam. I tried to spill my beer on you at Wade's party last weekend. Don't know if this is still your e-mail address, but if it is, how would you like to meet in person? Not really a hookup, just to talk somewhere public. Let me know.

I hesitated before I hit "send." What if Jeremy and Ethan were a couple? Did I want to be a home-wrecker? Once upon a time, I had briefly dated a man who turned out to be married. I had quickly dumped him, not wanting to end up in some Springer-like talk-show/nightmare situation. When I'd needed a shoulder and confided in Lars, he started singing Peter Gabriel's "Sledgehammer," much to the delight of our friends. For a year, I was nicknamed "Sledge" or "Sister Sledge." My stint as "the other woman" was an accident, however, and I'd learned to laugh about it. But I would never intentionally break up a relationship. It wasn't my style. I decided not to send the e-mail.

Then again, although Jeremy and Ethan were obviously together at the party, they didn't have the familiarity of a couple who had been dating seriously for a long time. I'd seen them independently of each other before I saw them together. And Ethan had definitely flirted with me. I wasn't sure if it was only wishful thinking that made me believe Jeremy had flirted with me, too.

Also, Jeremy had told Andy he was going to the party with "a friend," and had merely referred to Ethan as his "date" when Wade offered to take us on the tour. Later, the way Ethan had stood with his arm around Jeremy seemed casual. Fraternal. Especially when compared to the intimacy I had witnessed between Sheila and Josh. I returned my cursor to the *send* button.

Jeremy was the epitome of temptation or desire. He was like chocolate to someone on a diet. Beer to an alcoholic. An intern to Bill Clinton. Despite my natural tendency as a Gemini to jump right in, I decided to be rational. It wouldn't hurt to meet Ethan. I could find out how serious their relationship was, and whether they were living together. Even if they weren't living together but were still in a committed relationship, I'd let it go and find something equivalent to Jeremy Anonymous to beat my addiction.

Nothing ventured, nothing gained, after all. I hit *send*. Then I began composing an e-mail to my brother. I'd written only a couple of sentences when I heard my mail chime and checked my "in" box.

Hi, my name is Ethan. If you promise not to spill anything on me, I will be in Central Park in a couple of hours. Could meet you at Bethesda Fountain. If, however, you are a stalker, I should warn you that I will be accompanied by a large bodyguard with a quick temper. Just kidding. Hope to see you there.

No, no, no, Blythe's voice was saying in my head.

"Sounds great," I said out loud, snubbing Blythe.

I felt giddy as I jumped up to take a shower and change clothes. I knew I was being goofy, but I couldn't help feeling that Jeremy was almost within my grasp.

I took a cab to Central Park. I would be really early, but that would give me time to walk through the park and do a bit of people watching. I wandered until I came to Bethesda Fountain, where I sat down and looked around. Mothers and nannies pushed babies and toddlers in strollers. People with all breeds of dog, large and small, were out exercising their pets, while still others took the time to exercise themselves. In the distance I could see a group of people performing the slow, methodical movements of tai chi. In-line skaters and runners observed an invisible track. Occasionally a good-looking, T-shirtless runner would turn his head to glance at me, but for the most part, people minded their own business.

As warm as the weather was in the early fall, I still sensed a familiar charge in the air. Autumn had always felt like a time of expectation to me. Things seemed to move faster and toward something. Maybe I still connected the season to those days in high school when a new briskness in the air meant new classes, new experiences, and new chances to outperform myself and everyone else on the football field.

"See anything you like?" A voice behind me made me jump. I turned to see Ethan Whitecrow watching me with amusement. "I'm sorry; I didn't mean to startle you. What were you thinking so hard about?"

"High school," I said.

"I would swear your thoughts were on something else," he

replied with a brief nod toward the bridge, where a pack of men was running by wearing nothing but shorts and sneakers.

"They were down here, but I started singing 'My Heart Will Go On' and they took off running," I quipped.

Ethan let out a hearty laugh, then said, "That song is enough to make the Dalai Lama strangle Céline Dion."

Which let me know he had a sense of humor. Damn. I had hoped he would turn out to be duller than Ben Stein and Ted Koppel discussing the finer points of applied genetics, which could only make me look better by comparison in Jeremy's eyes. But I shrugged it off and smiled at him, holding out my hand.

"Adam Wilson."

"Ethan Whitecrow," he said, shaking my hand. "Thanks for coming on such short notice. I'm part of a group that does tai chi nearby on Friday afternoons, so I thought this was as good a place as any. I'm glad you e-mailed. I wanted to get a proper introduction to you at Wade's party, but by the time I was free, you were gone."

"Yeah, I was called away earlier than I thought I'd be," I said and wondered what he meant. When he was free from Jeremy? Did he think I had requested this meeting to follow up on his advances at the party? Or had I misread him that night?

Ethan and I sat on a bench, both of us seeming to experience a sudden attack of shyness. I wasn't sure what was going through his head, but I was bothered because I found myself liking him more than I wanted to. Especially since I was using him as a link to Jeremy. Maybe it was because he'd just finished doing tai chi, but the energy he put off was calming. His eyes had a certain wisdom that made me want to get to the point. I wondered why he couldn't have *looked* like Yoda.

"I hope you don't mind my asking, but how old are you?" I asked, then offered, "I'm thirty-one."

"Twenty-nine."

"With two books to your credit already? Impressive."

"You've read my books?" Ethan asked, looking surprised but also a little self-satisfied.

"Actually, no. Someone at Wade's party told me your name. I thought Whitecrow was unusual, so I searched it on the Internet. That's when I saw your book titles and your e-mail address."

"It's nice to know you're not a deranged fan," he said, in just the right tone to let me know he didn't care that I hadn't read his books. Apparently, we were going to do a little ego parry-and-thrust, which I actually found enjoyable. It put us back on an equal playing field. "So tell me about yourself, Adam."

As I gave him a brief summary of where I was from and what I did, he seemed to connect to the news that I taught.

"College level?" he asked.

"Yes. Why, do you teach, too?"

"No. My background is in adolescent counseling. Interacting with kids is some of the most gratifying work I've done."

"Me, too," I agreed. "It really bugs me when people act like teenagers are so out of control. I think the kids I teach are much smarter and nicer than my friends and I were at that age." He nodded in agreement, and I said, "Tell me more about you. Where are you from?"

"Yellow Springs, Ohio. I'll bet you've never heard of it."

"Nope."

"It's close to Dayton. This little granola town settled by liberals, artists, and former hippies. In other words, my parents. It's been a few years since I lived there, though."

"Then you've been in New York a long time?" I asked.

"No, I've moved around. Eugene, Oregon. Mendocino, California. Small towns in the Southwest. I've only been in New York a couple of months."

"Me, too. You seem to have made friends with some prominent people, though. That's quite a place Wade has, huh?" I asked, looking for a reason to talk about the party and, hopefully, Jeremy.

"Yes, it's quite the place." He looked down for a moment, then unexpectedly asked, "Are you hungry?"

"Me? I can always eat something. I just have to work harder at making sure it gets sent to the right place," I said with a grin, grabbing what I perceived to be a love handle.

"Seems to me like your hard work is paying off," he countered. "There's a restaurant just over there. Would you like to grab a bite?"

"Sure."

We skirted the edge of the small lake on a winding path, going around large boulders littered with the bodies of lazy sunbathers taking advantage of the pleasant weather. I could hear the laughter of people in the gondolas dotting the lake. It seemed everyone had begun the weekend early, and I had a comfortable sense of lethargy, both from the scene around me and the calm man next to me. The restaurant Ethan led us to had tables going right up to the water's edge. It looked packed, but I wouldn't mind a wait, it was such a beautiful day.

"Have you been here before?" Ethan asked. When I shook my head, he continued, "The Boathouse Café is Central Park's less expensive restaurant, but it's nearly as famous as its expensive older kin, Tavern on the Green."

As we went through the entrance, the host seemed to recognize Ethan right away and asked, "Would you like outdoor seating today, sir?"

"Yes, please," Ethan responded.

We were quickly seated, even though I hadn't seen an open spot before. I was reminded of my smooth entrance into Club Chaos with Sheila. Apparently, I'd found an inside track to the social clime of Manhattan very quickly. People I'd gone to college with had moved to New York City only to come running back to the Midwest with their tails between their legs. They would say how tough it was, how after a year they'd met only one person who actually called them back or didn't flake on them at every turn. I felt lucky, since I was considering making Manhattan a second home, that my experiences were so different from theirs.

A tall, willowy man approached, handed us menus, took our drink order, then quickly disappeared. I peeked over my menu to lock gazes with Ethan.

"Anything catch your eye?"

Whether or not he was involved with Jeremy, Ethan was definitely flirting with me. There had to be a way I could use that to my advantage. As my coaches always said, *Play with strength and always wear a cup.* The latter didn't apply, so I decided charm was definitely a strength I could use.

"You did," I answered.

"I should go. I'm a terrible distraction for you." He began to stand as if to leave, all the while keeping our gazes locked.

"No, you're a wonderful distraction. Now, sit down."

"Don't worry; I'm only going to the rest room."

"Hurry back. The waiters look ready to clear the table before we've even ordered."

I began concentrating on the menu in Ethan's absence. Nearly all of the entrees were some sort of fish. I'd never liked seafood. I kept scanning the menu and decided that I would order either a salad or one of the three choices that didn't contain fish.

Ethan returned with that gleaming white smile plastered on his face. He must have noticed my somewhat frustrated expression.

"What's wrong? Nothing on the menu interests you?"

"Well . . ."

"You don't like seafood, do you?"

I shook my head. The waiter returned with the drinks. He set them down and immediately readied his pad and pen.

"Have you decided?" he asked, as if demanding that we order that instant.

I ordered a salad, not wanting to feel weighed down by a heavier dish. Ethan ordered the red snapper and sipped his iced tea, savoring it as if it were gold.

"Maybe I should do tai chi with you," I commented. Ethan remained silent, content to wait until I explained myself. "It could be the energy of the city, but since I've been here, I always feel like I'm rushing from one place to the next."

"What's your sun sign?"

"I'm a Gemini."

"A twin," Ethan said happily. "I've always found Gemini's multiple personalities very stimulating."

I didn't miss his slight emphasis on the word "stimulating."

"What do you do here in New York?" I asked, determined to find an opening to talk about his personal life.

"Right now I'm putting together a healing retreat. Wade is funding a portion of it."

I pondered that for a nanosecond and jumped to a hopeful conclusion.

"That sounds great. Are you and Wade involved, if you don't mind my asking?"

"Yes, we're involved, but not in the way you mean. It's strictly business and friendship."

Damn. That was awful news. I was hoping he was a duplicitous slut, sleeping with Wade for funding.

"That's good news." Ethan's eyebrows lifted, and I quickly said, "I mean, I get the idea Wade isn't exactly . . . I don't know what I mean."

"Wade isn't a bad guy. He's got a good heart, even if he is ruthless when it comes to business. He's got as many enemies as he does friends, but even his enemies pretend to be his friends, and he knows it. He's smart. He didn't graduate with honors from Harvard for nothing."

Ethan's tone had changed as he talked, as if he understood that I hadn't liked Wade very much. In an attempt to make the mood more congenial, I said, "I've heard he helps artists. That's a nice thing to do."

"Don't get me wrong; he does have his motives. When he sees people with talent and good ideas, he helps them, but not without helping himself as well. After all, he has to make money somehow. His inheritance will only carry him so far, I suppose. But I don't want to bore you with Wade's life."

"It's interesting, really. I like hearing two sides of the story."

"He *has* done some things that don't make him all that popular. Most people only see that cutthroat side of him. Some of his artist 'friends' think he collects art only because it has monetary value. He appreciates it more than they think, though. He's a complicated guy."

"How did you two meet?"

"Maybe that's a dinner story rather than a lunch story."

Suddenly "Can-Can" began to play. I groaned and pulled my cell phone from my pocket.

"Impeccable timing, as always," I commented.

I looked down at the screen but didn't recognize the phone number. I decided to let my voice mail pick it up. I put the cell phone back in my pocket and smiled at Ethan as he slid a piece of tender fish into his mouth. As soon as he began chewing, the strains of a midi waltz emanated from somewhere near his lap.

Ethan wiped his mouth with his napkin and said, "Excuse me," extracting his own cell phone from his pants pocket. He swiftly opened it, saying, "I have to take this call," and placed it to his ear to greet the caller as he stepped away from our table.

I began stabbing at my salad with a vengeance.

How rude of him to take a call during our meal, I thought, thinking of the call I had just ignored for his sake.

I stopped assaulting my salad and took my cell phone from my pocket to see if my caller had left a message. The number displayed still didn't ring any bells. It wasn't one of Ray Patel's numbers, but since it was Manhattan's area code, it couldn't be any of my other clients. I glanced around the dining area and saw Ethan deeply engrossed with his phone call in an out-of-the-way corner. My display showed one message, but I decided to retrieve it later. I didn't want Ethan to see me making calls in his absence. I preferred to be a paragon of good taste and the perfect date.

Ethan shortly returned to our table and sat down.

"I'm sorry about that, Adam," he apologized.

"It must've been important," I observed, not quite accepting his apology and letting him know I was a little annoyed.

"Kind of," he said. "It was Wade, actually, speak of the devil, wanting to discuss the details of the retreat. In fact, I'm afraid I have to leave to meet with him and his financial advisors. Or his lawyer. Something like that. Anyway, I'm sorry to cut our meal short."

"I see," was all I could think to say.

"Please stay and finish your salad. It's on me," Ethan insisted, and stood to leave.

I stood with him, not knowing what to do. Ethan stepped toward me and clasped my hand in a half handshake, put his other hand on my shoulder, drew me toward him, and kissed my cheek. It was a formal yet somewhat intimate goodbye.

"I'll be out of town next week, but I'd love to meet for dinner. How about tomorrow night?" Ethan offered tentatively.

"Actually, Ethan, I have plans tomorrow," I said, though I was happy he made it easy to meet again, so I could continue my fact-finding mission. And if he'd meant it as a date, it was more proof that he and Jeremy were not a couple. "I promised my friend Blythe that I'd work on a project with her, and I'm not sure how long it will take. But we could exchange cell phone numbers and call each other to get together at some point. If not tomorrow night, then definitely another."

As we exchanged business cards, Ethan asked, "Blythe Mayfield? What sort of project are you working on with her?"

It hadn't occurred to me that he might know Blythe. There was something almost too casual about his tone that put me on my guard. Regardless of what Blythe had or hadn't told me, my loyalty was to her, so I decided to be evasive.

"I'd tell you about it, but you should be on your way to Wade's right now," I reminded him.

When Ethan left to pay the bill, I sat down again and picked at my salad, not really hungry but brooding over our conversation. I was annoyed that I had found out nothing about Jeremy. I still didn't know if they were just friends, casually dating, or, worst-case scenario, having a commitment ceremony next spring. And why was Ethan interested in Blythe? Furthermore, why had she warned me to stay away from him? He seemed like a levelheaded guy.

I waited five minutes, then turned around in my chair to make sure Ethan was gone. There was no sign of his presence, so I wiped my mouth on my napkin and left the restaurant.

Outside, I quickly scanned the park and saw Ethan walking in the distance, heading east, presumably to Wade's apartment. I briefly courted the idea of following him, but stalking was definitely not my style. Nor was it like me to assume someone was lying to me. I decided it was all Blythe's fault. Her warnings about Ethan had caused me to distrust him.

I paused to check my voice mail.

"Adam F. Wilson, it's Blythe M. Mayfield. I've been thinking about this Web site thing since our little talk about technology the other day. I have to say, I'm getting excited about it. Now I'm all wired up, and everything I paint looks like poodles on speed. I need somebody else's art to calm me. I think I'm going to walk to the Museum of Modern Art. It's open later on Friday and admission is by donation. Even I can afford to make a donation! If you find yourself with some time, come and help me gawk at the Pollocks. Actually the Pollocks may not be available. Did I already tell you they're mounting a Pollock retrospective at the end of October? I love this city. Anyway, maybe I'll see you there. My quarter's gonna run out. Bye!"

I smiled ruefully. After watching beautiful men run in the park and enjoying that brief interlude with Ethan, once again I would be spending a Friday night with Blythe. Too bad I wasn't straight. It would make my social calendar a lot easier. Blythe and I could spend all our nights together. For variety, we could double date with Sheila and Josh.

As a group of four guys walked past me, one of them gave me a look of approval and winked at me, and I laughed. Why on earth would I ever want to be straight when I was living in a city filled with incredible men?

And besides, I realized later that night as I watched Blythe look at paintings, it wasn't exactly a burden to spend an evening in her company. We'd developed a system for looking at art together. Blythe liked to react instinctively, whereas I had a habit of putting everything into the context of what I'd studied. I was allowed a minimum amount of pontification as long as I didn't demand that she explain her immediate responses. I'd found that if I behaved and didn't question her, after a few hours or a few days, she would dazzle me with some brilliant gem of insight.

This night, however, the missing Pollock canvases reminded her of the upcoming exhibit, which would take up the entire third floor of the museum and feature the artist's paintings from collections throughout the world. She was so jazzed up about it that she barely spoke of anything else. It made it easier for me not to confess about my meeting with Ethan. I wanted to wait until I knew if anything would come of it before telling her that I'd ignored her advice.

We made an early evening of it. I could tell by the way her energy seemed to bunch up just beneath the skin of her small body that the next few days would probably be very productive for her. Since I knew it would be better for me to stay away and let her work, I decided that I'd spend the following week connecting with some of the people who'd given me their business cards at Wade's party. Some of them might turn into new clients for me, or lead me to new clients.

With that in mind, a few days later I met Carl Nash for lunch at Café Baptisto. He was the older man who'd joined Betsy Pelham when she approached me at Wade's party. He explained that he was a buyer for Martemare, an upscale Parisian store that sold jewelry purchased from estate sales and individual collectors. Their first U.S. store, recently opened on Madison Avenue, sold finely crafted reproductions of French furniture and vintage jewelry cases as well as jewelry.

Carl was himself a collector of antique jewelry, on a smaller scale than Martemare. He wanted his own personal Web site to feature some of his pieces and put him in touch with like-minded collectors, with the intention of possibly turning that into a start-up company for buyers and sellers of rare and antique jewelry. He'd brought copies of his insurance photos with him. As I looked at the pictures and listened to his stories about the pieces—their history and how he'd acquired them—I caught his enthusiasm and gave him some off-the-cuff ideas for a site. It was obvious that his pride in his collection had very little to do with its monetary value. I thought I could convey that excitement in a Web site. He agreed to lend me the pictures so I could do a mock-up for him, with the understanding that if he liked it, I would want higher-quality, more artistic photographs. He didn't blink at the price estimate I quoted him, which probably said less about how well paid he was by Martemare than about how devoted he was to his collection.

I was in a good mood when we parted outside the restaurant. Since I was so near the southeast entrance of Central Park, I decided to return to Bethesda Fountain. There were fewer people milling about the sun-warmed concrete of the vastly ornate terrace than on the previous Friday. I walked to the fountain and sat on the rim of the basin, thinking about Carl's Web site, then about Ethan. Since he'd told me he would be out of town this week, I hadn't expected a call, nor had I tried to call him. It appeared that there would be no information about the ever-elusive Jeremy in the immediate future.

I remembered Jeremy's bright eyes and charming laugh at the party. I let my mind wander forward in time to when we would wake up together in bed. The sun would shine through the window and over his face and awaken him. His eyes would squint in the light, crinkling the skin around them, but he'd look over at me and smile, so happy to be next to me. We'd reluctantly get up, and I'd sit at the table in the kitchen and watch as he made breakfast. Jeremy wouldn't be the best cook in the world, but if anyone were to ask me, I would testify that eggshell was the perfect seasoning, and I'd crunch into my scrambled eggs with gusto because Jeremy had made them for me.

Later, we'd shower together, lathering each other's backs and sharing soapy kisses. We'd dry each other off and have to get dressed quickly, before our sexual appetites took over and we were late for work.

But I didn't even know what Jeremy did. What kind of person was asked for autographs? Actor? Rock star? Newscaster? Gossip columnist? Movie director? Chef with his own TV show? Member of the mayor's staff? Writer?

The Jeremy in my fantasy stood in front of the closet, not knowing what to wear, because I knew nothing about him. Other than the fact that he was hot.

"Oh, Adam, how shallow are you?" I asked myself aloud.

A woman who had been sitting on the rim of the fountain next to me turned, gave me an odd look, then slowly walked away as if any sudden movements might cause me to attack like a wild beast.

I turned to look at the statue in the water's center and noticed there was a lip inside the rim of the fountain just wide enough to place my feet on. I spun my body around and rested my feet on the rim, balancing my elbows on my knees so I could gaze up at the statue. It was quite tall and depicted an angel with flowing robes who pointed over the water in the fountain with one hand. Her face radiated a calming serenity, and she seemed to beckon her visitors forward, inviting them to relax.

Rather than spend all my time in a fantasy world, I tried to recall the story about the Angel of Bethesda that I'd learned in Sunday school many years ago. Our teacher had told us about how the angel touched a pool in Jerusalem and gave the waters healing powers. I'd been quite young when I heard the story, but somehow the generalities had stuck with me. I'd been fond of biblical angels, at least the ones who helped people, healing them or teaching them valuable lessons. As a child, I was always looking over my shoulder, hoping to catch a glimpse of a beautiful angel watching over me.

I gazed dreamily at the angel sculpture and wondered, if I were to dip my hand into the waters of the fountain, whether I could be healed. Healed of what, though? I was as healthy as a horse and hadn't had a need to see a doctor in months, other than my yearly physical and HIV test at a Madison clinic. But still, I felt as if there were something hollow deep inside me, a small cavity in my midsection longing to be filled.

Was it possible that Jeremy was the one who would help me fill in the absent parts of myself? How could that be, when I didn't even know his last name?

My eye was caught by a runner heading my way. He was fair-skinned with blond hair. His body was slim but well toned. There was something familiar about him that made me keep staring. He looked a little like a guy I remembered from high school. What was that guy's name, anyway?

Whether this was him or not, he was hot. Pretty blond hair, blue-blue-blue eyes. I could swear he was scrutinizing me, too.

The runner broke eye contact and passed me without a word. I turned, sure he was slowing down. What had that kid's name been?

He always sat in the back of class and never talked to anyone. Davie? Donnie?

He circled back and stopped running once he hit the terrace. He walked swiftly, breathing heavily, around the vast fountain, perhaps three or four times, obviously cooling down from a long run.

I couldn't take my eyes off him. He stopped in place and bent down to grab his ankles, breathing deeply as he stretched his back. He put one foot on the rim of the fountain and bent into it, stretching his leg muscles, then repeated with the other leg. Finally, he stretched his arms with an air of finality and settled into place on the rim of the fountain, about twenty feet from me, in the exact same position as I was seated.

I stared at him as he ran his hands over his forehead to wipe away the sweat, then through his hair, until he finally slapped them down on his knees with what appeared to be nervous energy. Endorphins, I decided.

He turned his head in my direction and caught me looking at him. I didn't avert my gaze. Instead, I looked as deeply into his blue eyes as I could across the distance. He quickly turned his head back to the statue and tried to look passive, but a brief appearance of lines on his forehead told me that my lingering stare had troubled him.

Apparently, it was my day to disturb people in Central Park. First I'd sent that woman scurrying away, and now Blond Runner was bothered by me. Maybe I should walk away before he did. The statue stared down at me as if to say, *There you go. Fuggeddabowdit!*

The idea of this glorious statue having a De Niro accent sent me into a quick giggle fit. I glanced over and caught the runner looking briefly my way again. Then he turned his head and stared at the angel, as I had been, and suddenly I sensed some kind of hostility surrounding him. He did remind me of that boy from high school, who'd had the same nervous energy and lost look. *What* had his name been? Sammy? Stanley?

Spaniel Daniel, a voice in my head chanted, and I laughed out loud again, then stopped, catching myself at the ugly memory. My friends and I had thrown those words at him in the hallways of school between classes, trying to knock his books out of his arms or throwing paper balls after him while he desperately tried to walk away as quickly as possible without breaking eye contact with the floor. I wasn't such an asshole all the time, but if my football buddies were around, I would give in to peer pressure and join their ruthless antics.

Spaniel Daniel. Danny Stephenson. The runner certainly did look like him. Actually, I'd never thought he looked like a spaniel. If there were a canine comparison to be made, I would have said he resembled a golden retriever: glowing blond hair, noble intelligence—a graceful, beautiful creature, indeed.

Though I'd never seen a golden retriever look as nervous as this runner did. He kept looking back and forth from the statue to where I sat. I supposed I was doing the same thing, which might be making him uncomfortable, so I decided to stop looking at him. I let my eyes glaze over and listened to the sound of water running off the statue and into the pool below. Somewhere deep in the park, I could hear tribal drums beating and soft voices chanting along. The warmth of the Indian-summer sun on the back of my neck felt comforting.

I made a quick decision and stood, crossing the distance between the runner and me. His face lost all expression as I approached him.

"I feel like I—Spaniel Daniel?" I blurted before I allowed myself to think better of it.

It had to be him. His eyes grew wide and his lips parted in an expression of disbelief, perhaps even horror. He squinted at me, as if looking at me through a microscope, and made his hypothesis.

"Adam Wilson?"

"I thought it was you," I said with excitement. "What are the odds of seeing you here? Wow."

"Yeah," he said slowly, "what *are* the odds?"

"I can't get over it. How many years has it been? How the hell are you?"

I made a move to lightly slap him on the back in a fraternal gesture. But he visibly cringed and ducked, like I was swinging a two-by-four at him, which made me stop and realize he might not be so happy to see me.

"Hey, easy, Danny. I'm not gonna tackle you or anything," I said nervously. He didn't look so certain, so I added, "I guess you never were one of my fans."

There was an awkward moment of silence as we looked at each other. What I thought would be a nice reunion was quickly turning sour. We both looked nervously around us, perhaps hoping Oprah would burst onto the scene to mediate any further conversation with gentleness, honesty, and understanding. Unfortunately, it was just us and a few dozen tourists.

"I have to admit," he said slowly, looking up at the statue and not at me, "I was never fond of your work when we were growing up. Or your circle of friends."

"Bill Hamilton was part of that circle," I reminded him, trying to find something mutual to get us past this awkward moment. Bill had been Danny's best friend, since Bill and Danny had acted in school plays and sung in the choir together, as well as living close to each other.

"Bill Hamilton was everyone's friend," Danny reminded me, which was true; Bill's affable personality knew no social boundaries.

"You're right," I agreed. "He was rather like a whore that way." His mouth hung open, as if he wasn't sure what to say. I realized he didn't know I was kidding. "Come on, Danny, was I really that bad way back then?" I asked, knowing I was.

He turned to look me right in the eye, saying, "You used to call me 'faggot' in the hallways and hurl red rubber balls at my head in gym class!"

"Oh, that," I said dismissively. "We were just kids. It didn't mean anything."

"Maybe not to you," he argued, turning his gaze back to the fountain. "And don't call me Danny. My name is Daniel."

"Was I really that awful?" I asked again.

"Yes," he said adamantly, swinging his gaze back in my direction. I could see the emotion boiling its way to the surface in his eyes. "I was terrified of you and your jock friends. I don't know why I'm even talking to you. I have nothing to say."

"Come on, Daniel."

"Nope. I don't know what you're doing here, but this city's big enough for both of us to live here without encountering each other again. I'm pretty sure we can live the rest of our lives without affecting each other at all." It was my turn to stare at him, astonished and unsure how to defend myself. "It's a good thing I have my running shoes on," was the last thing he said before turning around and jogging away.

I turned back to the fountain and caught two small children staring at me, with a woman who could've been either their nanny or their mother. They had obviously overheard the entire conversation between Daniel and me, because her mouth was open in disgust and she gathered them to her as if to protect them from me.

"What the fuck are you staring at?" I growled, finally starting to feel like a stereotypical New Yorker.

SIX

The phone snapped me out of a daydream. Jeremy had been kneading my shoulders in my office back home, while I worked diligently at my computer. Tracy was there, too, and laughed at another of Jeremy's witty remarks. Just as she commented on what an attractive couple we made, the phone rang.

In the daydream, just as in real life, I jumped at the sound, which caused Jeremy and Tracy to fade into oblivion, leaving me alone once again in The Waifs Land.

The call was from one of the guests I had met at Wade's party, who offered me an interview for an Information Systems manager position that was available with his company. I politely declined, referring him to a former colleague of mine in Madison, Wisconsin. I was not interested in a permanent position in Manhattan, especially not in the dog-eat-dog business I'd left behind. I was busy enough with my existing accounts. Patel, Inc. was maturing at a rapid pace. Ray was excited about the increase in sales, which he credited to the Web site and network I'd set up for him. Although he was thinking about opening another store and going public with his company, he still operated his business with a mom-and-pop feel, which was why I enjoyed working for him.

In addition, I had connected with a few people from Wade's soiree who met my client criteria. A woman who sought up-and-coming jewelry designers to feature in her shop, a man who ran an off-Broadway theater, and a woman who'd recently finished a jazz vocal CD were now in my roster of New York clients culled from Wade's party.

I tried to get back into my Jeremy fantasy world after I hung up the phone, but I couldn't, since the handsome Jeremy in my home office kept morphing into the choleric Daniel I had encountered in Central Park. I'd been dwelling on Daniel for an entire week, mentally replaying our encounter at Bethesda Fountain, each time revising it so I explained myself better and we were friends by the end.

But that was not how it had ended. Daniel's accusations and version of our history had left me stupefied, unable to defend myself. The problem was, I knew he was right. I was everything he claimed when we were in high school. My friends and I had called him terrible names, thrown things at him, and taunted him when we could. Some of us were worse than others. I may have thrown wadded-up balls of paper at him, but I knew that no matter what Daniel said, I'd never used the word "faggot," because I hated that word even then. I may have called him "pussy" or "wimp," but never "queer" or "fag," which were part of my friends' vernacular. I could see Daniel's point of view though. I was guilty by association.

Which was why Daniel left me shaken and angry. I *was* guilty. Even as a boy in high school, I knew deep down inside what I was. I was textbook Freud. A living, breathing after-school special. The insecure boy trapped in his role as an overcompensating high school jock, afraid his friends would see him looking into Spaniel Daniel's eyes as if they were a mirror. Fearing my buddies would turn on me, too, I had done little to stop them as they made Daniel's life miserable. Running into him had opened a path to uncomfortable memories more than a decade old. I found myself wishing I could show Daniel there was more of a bond between us than he knew.

I'd never acted on my desire to have sex with another guy until the last day of high school, when I went to a party straight out of the movie *Dazed and Confused*. Back in the days before school-sponsored events that kept graduating seniors from drinking and driving, practically the whole senior class met at the Monroe family's camp on Altoona Lake for a graduation party. Rachel "Daddy's Little Girl" Monroe had managed to get permission to use the family's rustic summer cottage to throw what she promised would be the "most awesome unchaperoned event of the year." And Rachel delivered.

After our graduation ceremony, I had to endure a two-hour photo session with my family, dinner at Fischer's White House, and more photos and tears with Mom, until I was finally picked up by Lars Ziegler in his Camaro.

The Monroe cottage was a two-story, three-bedroom log cabin with no indoor plumbing. We could hear Motley Crue screeching from inside as we parked the Camaro on the lawn, which already looked like a used-car lot. I couldn't believe how many kids from school were crammed into that little cabin; many of them ended up hanging out in the backyard or on the boat dock. There was a full bar set up in the main room downstairs, two kegs in the kitchen, and three coolers packed with ice cubes. The cabin was littered with pretzels, plastic cups, and bad hair. It was 1985.

Lars and I found our buddies and were swept into their current drinking game. Every time someone said, "Hi," we had to take a drink. Since we were popular and everybody we knew was at Rachel's party, Lars and I were drunk in less than an hour. By midnight, I was in deep conversation with a floor lamp, and Lars was giggling on a hassock in the corner.

Rachel found us, took away our car keys, and gave us one of the upstairs bedrooms. She could easily have driven us home or found someone else to drive us. However, it was my belief that she wanted a readily available clean-up crew the next morning.

We were deposited in a room with bunk beds. We were too drunk to crawl in the bottom bed, let alone climb the ladder, so we lay on the floor laughing for a good hour. We talked about graduation and retold highlights of the party that night.

"Did you see Peter and Sharon sneaking off into the woods?" Lars asked.

"Yeah, where was his girlfriend?"

"Passed out in the outhouse," Lars answered, and we both laughed until our sides hurt.

"I think I'm gonna barf," I said.

"No, man, don't do that," Lars pleaded.

"Okay," I said, and the nausea passed.

I sat up and looked down at Lars. He was a lean, sinewy-muscled boy who had the body of a Greek god and the face of a one-hit wonder pop star. He lay on the floor with his arm under his head, which caused his T-shirt to rise up. He kicked off his sneakers and slowly stroked his stomach.

I took off my shoes, rose to a standing position, and started re-moving my clothes. Lars looked up at me from the floor and started clapping.

"Woohoo! Take it off, baby!"

My pants were around my knees, but I fell to the floor and grabbed Lars's wrists to stop him from clapping.

"Shut up," I whispered. "You'll wake up the whole cabin, you idiot."

"Who you calling an idiot?"

"You, you idiot."

It was the opening to our usual one-up contests. Whether it was who could throw a football the farthest or who could come up with the worst insult, on or off the field, Lars and I were always in com-petition. It usually ended up with us wrestling until one of us was pinned.

In one fluid motion, Lars had his hand free of my grasp and lightly slapped my face. Stunned, I laughed, then the match began. We rolled in and out of half nelsons, crab vices, and scissor holds. My jeans came off, as did Lars's T-shirt. I quickly sobered up as we grunted and sweated, each trying his hardest to be the victor.

Lars maneuvered me into a hammerlock, and I said, "Illegal hold; no fair. I win."

"This isn't a ring," Lars laughed. "No holds barred."

"Fine, then you won't mind if I do this," I said, swinging my legs in the direction of the hold so I wouldn't dislocate my shoulder, and neatly sweeping Lars off his feet. He hit the floor with a loud thud, and I pinned him by sitting on his chest, my knees on his shoulders.

He tried to pry me off of him by swinging his feet around my shoulders, but I grabbed hold of his foot and held it, rendering him helpless.

"I win." I laughed. He grunted and struggled but wouldn't admit defeat, so I started counting. "One," I said, then reached behind me with my free hand and undid his jeans. His eyes widened. "Two," I said and unzipped them. Which was difficult since he was bent like a pretzel. "Three," I continued and let go of his foot, grabbed his pant legs, and neatly shucked off his jeans.

"Okay, you win," Lars conceded, and we both started laughing. Unlike me, Lars was never a sore loser. He stopped struggling, but I stayed where I was. "Now what?" Lars asked, ready to accept whatever punishment I proposed. I saw a gleam in his eyes and wondered how far I could push him. I rolled off of him, lying beside him on the floor.

"I'm too tired to think of anything humiliating for you to do," I said and swept my hair off of my sweaty forehead. "Why don't you just shut up and kiss me?"

"What?"

"You know you want to. Go ahead."

Lars leaned over and kissed my lips with far more tenderness than I would have expected. I had thought kissing another man would be hard and forceful, but Lars was tender with his passion. Even later, after we moved to the bottom bunk, he continued to be a gentle lover.

Inevitably, Rachel Monroe found us in bed together the next morning. My leg was wrapped around Lars and my head was on his chest when I opened my eyes and found her peering through the door with her mouth open. She was gone in a flash. I quickly dressed and went downstairs, where I found Rachel and five of our friends cleaning up and cooking pancakes.

"Good morning, Adam," Rachel said in a saccharine voice, not looking up as she violently threw plastic cups into a Hefty bag. "Did you sleep okay?"

"Yeah," I said, rubbing my head and wondering what to say. I didn't have to wonder long.

"Where's your—ah, here he is," she said as Lars thumped down the stairs. "Can I see you boys outside?"

"If she makes us clean the outhouse, I'm out of here," Lars mumbled, and we followed Rachel outside.

Rachel whirled around amid the clutter of empty beer bottles, plastic cups, and litter on the front lawn and asked, "Do you have everything?"

"We didn't bring anything but ourselves," I said.

"Good," she hissed. "Get the fuck out of here."

"Geez, Rachel. Next time we'll bring a six-pack or something," a confused Lars said.

"Rachel, calm down," I said.

"I am calm, Adam. I could be yelling. Do you want me to start yelling and tell the others that our friends are a couple of faggots?"

"Whoa," Lars said, as if Rachel were a team of horses. The way her nostrils flared, I wasn't entirely convinced he was wrong.

"I can't believe you two *did* that. In my cabin," she sneered "That's so gross! My little sisters sleep in that room. Yuck!"

Lars looked like a boy being scolded by his parents. Staring at his shoes or at the sky, anywhere but at Rachel or me, he looked like he was searching for an explanation or some way out of the situation.

My initial wave of panic faded quickly when it struck me that we were out of high school. I wouldn't have to face Rachel or any of our friends if I didn't want to. Anyway, what did I care if they knew? I remembered how it felt to hold Lars as we climaxed together. I felt like I'd scored a winning touchdown. Everything about myself that had seemed blurry was suddenly brought into focus. Never wanting a girlfriend or thinking about a future with a wife and kids—it all made perfect sense now.

"Rachel, you're being immature about this," I said.

"Fuck you, Adam. Immature would be if I went in there and told everyone what I saw," Rachel snarled. "Just get the hell out of my sight, both of you. I think you're disgusting. I can't believe I was friends with two faggots."

She stepped past us, twisting her shoulders to avoid any physical contact, and walked with great strides back to the cabin. She turned around one more time and said, "You're going to hell, you know," and slammed the cabin door behind her.

That was the last I ever saw of Rachel Monroe. Despite her animosity, she was true to her word and never said anything about Lars and me to our friends. Months later, when I came out to them, they were surprised but took the news in stride. Most of them were just happy to have new material for when they ribbed me during parties, softball games, or pool tournaments. And my parents practically gave me a cotillion.

I never realized how easy I had it until my past and Daniel caught up with me in Central Park. I sat at my desk and wondered how it must have felt for Daniel when we were growing up; not fitting in, feeling left out. Obviously, from the way he reacted to seeing me again, they were not the happiest days of his life. I wished he could know that I wasn't the same person I'd been then. I wanted to be redeemed in his eyes. But I didn't want to win him over by forcing him to talk to me, either, as if I were competing against his stubborn memories of our past.

Putting Daniel out of my head, I turned on my PalmPilot to retrieve the number of one of my new clients. I saw a note that I'd made to myself on the schedule screen.

"Photo shoot," I wondered aloud. Then it hit me. I was supposed to have been at Blythe's apartment a half-hour earlier to help soothe her savage nerves when Josh took pictures of her art for the Web site.

"Why the hell didn't she call me?" I yelped at the waifs, who only stared in silence as I dashed around the apartment, changing into more presentable clothes, stuffing my notebook and PowerBook into a shoulder bag. I flipped open my cell phone to give her a quick call as I raced outside to catch a cab, then cursed a blue streak when I remembered that Blythe had no phone.

I couldn't believe I'd forgotten the photo shoot. In addition to fretting about Daniel Stephenson, I had a more pressing problem on my mind. Ray Patel had informed me that Prajna would be returning from Nagpur in ten days and would obviously want her apartment back. I hadn't expected to be displaced so abruptly, but I figured it was one of the drawbacks of my open-ended stay in the Big Apple. Ray had assured me that he would find another place for me to live, at his expense. But I wondered how long that offer would last once Prajna discovered the state of her plants, whose condition warned me that it might be time to find a botanical Dr. Kevorkian.

I glanced from my cab as it stopped at a light and said, "I changed my mind. I'm getting out here."

The driver gave me an annoyed look, since my fare was barely over the two-dollar minimum. I shoved a five at him and hurried from the cab into a Sprint Wireless storefront. Vowing that Blythe would never be unreachable again, I added another cell phone to my account to give to her. I also added more minutes to my plan, since I didn't know where I would be living next, and I wanted to be sure I had plenty of phone access for my clients.

A half hour later, Josh let me into Blythe's loft, which seemed eerily vacant. Even though it was minimally furnished, Blythe's personality usually filled the apartment like a grand piano, and her laugh reverberated through its space like a Beethoven symphony. But something seemed amiss; there was a different kind of energy inside. It was like the feeling you get just before you realize your house has been broken into.

"What's going on? Where's Blythe?" I asked Josh.

"She's stuck in the closet," Josh said, a hint of exasperation in his voice.

"That's funny; I always thought she was straight," I joked. "Seriously, I'm sorry I'm late."

"It doesn't matter," Josh said. "Sheila and I have been here for an hour, waiting on Blythe. She answered the door in a carnival tent, said something about hating all her clothes, then disappeared. That's the last I saw of her. Sheila's in there with her now."

I scanned the loft but saw nobody.

"In where?" I asked.

Josh pointed to the screens that surrounded Blythe's mattresses and said, "Back there. Tell them to hurry. Sheila and I are having dinner with her agent later."

I went to the screens and peered behind them, unsure what I'd find, as if the screens were a clown car containing Blythe and the cast of a Fellini movie. A few blankets messily covered her stack of mattresses. I noticed a door next to the bed that wasn't visible from the living-area side of the screens.

The door was ajar, so I opened it to find a small room with no windows. On one side there was a rolling rack with Blythe's clothes on hangers. Toward the back of the room were stacks of canvases leaning out from the wall, all individually covered in sheets. To the left of the room, Blythe sat despondently on the floor with several pairs of shoes and a pile of clothes scattered around her. Sheila stood over her with one hand on her hip and the other raking back her hair as if she were about to rip it out in chunks. When I entered, they both looked at me like I was an angel about to give them a message of guidance.

"Cinderella, have you tried on the glass slipper? Does it fit?" I asked Blythe. She threw a shoe at me and missed.

Sheila glared at me, and I knew that if she had a shoe, she wouldn't have missed.

"We've been trying to get Blythe ready for the photo shoot," Sheila said.

"I see we haven't had much luck," I said, and another shoe flew threw the air. "Stop that! Josh tells me he's been waiting for an hour; what's going on?"

"I can't find anything to wear. The paintings I selected don't look right. Suddenly I feel like they're not finished. I don't think this is a good idea, Adam. And where have you been? None of this would've happened if you'd been here. You got me into this," Blythe sulked.

I felt like throwing a few shoes, myself.

"Sheila, can I have a moment alone with Dan Marino?" I asked, pointing at Blythe. Sheila smirked and strode out of the storage room, shutting the door behind her.

"Do you think we'll have enough air in here?" I teased.

Blythe said nothing, sucking in her lower lip like a little girl. I had seen this face before, usually when she was deep in thought, so I let her be.

"I don't know if I can do this, Adam," she finally said.

"You're going to have to do better than that."

"What do you mean?" she asked, playing with the zipper on a boot.

"Blythe, nobody is forcing you to do anything you don't want to do. I offered to make a Web site for you because I thought it would be a good tool to showcase your talent. I wouldn't have made the offer if I didn't believe in you. But I did, and you accepted. You also accepted Josh's offer. He's a professional photographer donating his time—which I'm sure is valuable—to help you out."

"I know, Adam," Blythe said, rolling her eyes and tossing the boot aside. "I'm not a child."

"Then stop acting like one," I said. She stared at me, so I added, "I'm sorry, but you are. Sometimes it takes a friend to—"

"Okay. I get it," she interrupted and stood up. I saw what Josh meant when he described what she was wearing. It was a rainbow-striped ball gown, which made her look like a circus tent crossed with a barbershop pole. She saw my horrified look, laughed, and said, "I traded with a drag queen at the Pride Parade last year. He gave me the gown, and I body-painted everyone on his float this year. Can you please tell Josh and Sheila that I'll be out in ten minutes?"

I did, and she emerged a few minutes later in black jeans, a black T-shirt with Keith Haring's Radiant Baby on it, and bare feet. I helped her bring out twenty canvases, which she uncovered and hung on a bare wall, one at a time, for Josh to photograph. Josh, at first wary of Blythe's temperamental ways, warmed when he saw the artwork. He grew animated and intent on shooting the right angle or making sure the lighting was perfect. Blythe shyly told him about each painting—the story behind it, what she felt while the image emerged from her subconscious, or what frustrated her about it. Josh related similar experiences as a photographer. I'd never heard Blythe speak so frankly about her work, and I shot Josh an admiring glance. Evidently, fashion photography provided good training for putting people at ease.

Sheila gently tugged at my arm and motioned me to a window at the opposite end of the loft.

"Let's not bother the geniuses," she said and opened the window.

We put on our jackets and climbed onto the fire escape.

"Are you okay? It's not too cold, is it?" I asked Sheila.

"No, it's gorgeous today," Sheila said, her face radiant in the afternoon sun as she looked across at the old buildings around us. "And we seem to be out of the path of the autumn breeze."

"Autumn breeze? Is that the male counterpart to Autumn Dusk?" I asked.

Sheila rolled her eyes and said, "I'm never doing another douche ad as long as I live. It's been nothing but fodder for all my friends' lame jokes. Or their stage acts. Anyway, I'm on the verge of becoming the Zodiac Girl."

"What's that? A part in a Jack the Ripper movie?"

"No, silly. Lillith Parker's Zodiac is a new line of cosmetics. It's bright, flashy, very glam. Silver and glittery eyeshadows, blue lipstick, yadda yadda yadda," Sheila explained. She was obviously excited, which captivated my interest. Her face grew brighter as she continued. "The ads so far have been minimal. Just words on a blank page: *The Future: Zodiac.* Stuff like that. Now that the new year is approaching, they're looking to attach a face to the product." She framed her face with her hands and struck a Garbo pose, and I laughed. "It would be huge!" she exclaimed, quickly turning around and peering through the window to see if her outburst had disturbed Josh and Blythe. It hadn't. Josh was reloading film, and Blythe was chattering away while hanging another painting on the wall. "The whole Zodiac line has twelve divisions, mainly different colors and looks for each month. So it's a whole year's worth of constant work."

"Geez, what a brilliant marketing plan," I commented. "It sounds like fun. I hope you get it. When will you find out?"

"I don't know. Soon, I hope. Josh and I are having dinner with my agent tonight. I guess I'll find out if I'm seriously in the running."

"That would be great. And it would make a good Web site," I mused.

Sheila's eyes glazed over for a moment; she appeared to be deep in thought. Just as quickly, her head snapped toward me, sending blond hair flying over her shoulder.

"Have you decided whether or not you're going to take on more clients from the East Coast?" she asked.

"I have," I answered. "Taken on clients, I mean. I met several people at Wade Van Atterson's party who turned out to be perfect client material. I've already started work on three new Web businesses."

"That's fantastic," Sheila said and put her hand on my arm. "I'm so glad for you, Adam. Maybe we'll make a New Yorker out of you yet."

"I don't think so. But thanks for trying," I said, a sardonic undertone creeping into my voice. "I don't think New York is exactly the place for me."

"What do you mean?" Sheila asked. Her concern was evident in the furrows across her forehead.

"Forget it. I'm just being stupid," I said, trying to brush away the topic with a wave of my hand.

Sheila pulled her hair behind her ears and grabbed her knees, as if she would have to be physically dragged away from the subject, and asked, "What's bugging you?"

"I ran into someone from Eau Claire not too long ago. Daniel Stephenson," I began.

"I didn't know you had a car," Sheila quipped. I groaned and pretended I was going to hurl my body off the fire escape. "Sorry; old joke. Go on. How was that?"

"He wasn't glad to see me at all," I lamented. "Which is understandable, given our history."

"Yeah, I heard. I mean, I understand," she said and immediately cringed when I grinned. "Okay, you got me. I know more than I'm letting on. Daniel is a friend of mine, so I heard all about it. Try to see it from Daniel's point of view. He had a rough time in high school."

Though I was surprised to hear that she was a friend of Daniel's,

it was a relief to talk to someone who knew him. I explained everything that I'd been thinking about and how awful I felt as a result
of my actions when I was young and naive. I wondered aloud if
Daniel would ever understand the pressures I faced in order to fit
in.

"He understands," Sheila said. "Sometimes it's just as difficult to
fit in and be accepted as it is not to. Daniel learned that when he
moved here and became a performance artist. He and I talk about
it a lot, since we're in similar professions—constantly under
scrutiny, trying to fulfill someone else's vision. It's hard to deal
with, but he's really come a long way with who he is. I think he
might come around where you're concerned, too."

"Does he—" I began, but was unsure how to finish my thought.

"Know you're gay? Yes," she answered.

"How'd you know I was going to ask that?" I asked, amazed by
her perception.

"Because it was the one thing that gave Daniel pause for thought,"
she explained. "He changed the subject shortly afterward. That's
why I think he'll come around if we give him time. We have to
think of some common ground or a way to get you two in the same
room again."

"I don't want to put you in the middle of anything," I said, and
she laughed.

"I don't want to be in the middle, either. But I tend to get put in
that position a lot. If I were a gay man, I might not mind so much,"
she joked, and did a "know what I mean?" eyebrow wiggle.

We sat silently on the fire escape for a few moments. I shivered a
little and realized it was getting colder as the afternoon light
waned. Then Sheila gave a little yelp and grabbed my arm.

"Plants!" she shrieked.

"What grows out of the ground? I'll take 'Adam Is Clueless' for
five hundred, Alex."

"Blythe mentioned that you need someone to rescue the plants
in your apartment," Sheila explained, ignoring my sarcasm.
"Daniel loves gardening. He could grow a rosebush in the Sahara if
he put his mind to it."

"Not me. If I were in the Sahara, I'd forget to water the cactus
and kill it."

"Cacti don't need watering," Sheila said. "I'll be sure to include
that comment as evidence of your ignorance when I report you to

Daniel for herbicide. Seriously, he's like me, he can't stand not helping. It'll be the perfect opportunity to get you two together. Then it's up to you to show him that you've changed. I'll call you after I talk with him and let you know when he'll be by to save those poor plants from imminent doom."

"You're nuts," I said. "Helping me is the last thing you'll ever talk Daniel into doing."

"Never doubt my powers of persuasion," Sheila said with confidence.

"Aren't you two cold out here?" Blythe asked, sticking her head out the window. "Josh is finished, Sheila, and here you sit jawing with Adam while your agent waits for you."

Sheila laughed, and we went back inside. After they were gone, I looked at Blythe.

"I'm so sorry I was late," I apologized again.

"Not a problem," she said, airily waving her hand, all thoughts of her earlier tantrum dismissed. "Though it is unlike you not to be punctual."

I took the new cell phone from my bag and handed it to her. "What's this?"

"This is my peace of mind," I said. "Don't worry; it's a business expense for me, since you're a client. I'm tired of not being able to reach you."

For once, Blythe didn't argue with me, her eyes tearing up behind her cat glasses as she asked, "Why are you always so nice to me?"

"Because you're my best friend. Over dinner, I'll show you how to program it, help you set up your voice mail, and all that. In return, you can give me your wisdom. Sheila and I have a mutual acquaintance in the city. Unbelievably, he is not an admirer of mine. Sheila thinks she's contrived a way to get us together. Now I have to charm him."

"And you want *my* advice?"

"You can be charming when you want to be," I said.

Throughout the evening, and over the next few days, Blythe came up with increasingly more humorous ways for me to win Daniel over, most of them involving sexual favors of one type or another. I called her as soon as I got a message from Sheila telling me that Daniel had finally agreed to come to Prajna's apartment to look at the plants.

"Have *Bolero* showing when he gets there," Blythe advised. "Make sure honey is nearby."

"All I could think about was the mess on the sheets when I saw that," I argued.

"Okay, *Ghost.* You can make pots together for the revived plants."

"No mess there," I said.

"Adam, you are hopelessly practical. I'm done with you. Good luck!"

I laughed and hung up, returning my attention to Carl Nash's Web site. I was startled later by someone knocking. Though Prajna's apartment was in a small building without a doorman, visitors did have to announce themselves through an intercom system to get through the door at the top of the stoop. Of course, that didn't mean that an industrious person couldn't come in when someone with a key left or entered.

It was, in fact, Daniel who stood there when I opened my door. His expression wasn't hostile, the way it had been the last time I saw him. Instead it was neutral, almost indifferent. Then he spoke in a voice that was less than friendly.

"This wasn't on the top of my list of things I wanted to do today. I wouldn't be here at all if there'd been any other way to make Sheila stop talking about it. Plus, I spend half my time working in my garden, or volunteering for Parks and Recreation, trying to make things grow or keep them alive. Maybe I just have some morbid need to see again exactly how destructive you are to other living things."

"Hello to you, too," I said.

"Is that supposed to be an orchid?" he asked, looking past me.

"I have no idea."

He kept space between us as he walked to the plant in question, which to me looked like a couple of barely green sticks poking out of dirt.

"Vanda orchid," he pronounced. "Is there some reason why you'd keep a tropical plant so close to the air conditioner? In fact, why is it colder in here than it is outside? There are all kinds of tropicals in here."

"My computer equipment," I explained meekly.

"This one, and all of those," he indicated some other pots, "should have been kept in a warm place in a gravel-lined tray, with water in the tray to keep them humid. I can probably revive them at my place, but it's going to take a while. Your best bet is to replace them with thriving plants." He looked around and continued, "You have now disproved the statement that no one can kill a philodendron. It should be replaced, too. Are there more victims?"

"In the bedroom," I said, gesturing in that direction.

He started to walk away, then stopped dead still and yelped, "What the *hell* is *that?*"

I followed his horrified gaze to the saucer-eyed girl and dog who were staring back at us.

"That's part of Prajna's art collection."

"Good god," was all he said.

I let him explore the apartment without me, though I could hear him muttering from time to time.

"This is going to cost you," he said when he finally returned to the living room.

"Of course. I'll be glad to pay you," I agreed.

He frowned and said, "I don't want your money. I meant it's going to cost a lot to replace the dead and critically ill plants. There are some that just need pruning and fertilizing. I can trim the dead leaves off the ones that'll pull through and move them to the window in the bedroom. The light is better in there. And just so you know, there's plant food under the sink in the kitchen. You might try using it every now and then."

"Yes, Martha Stewart," I said, trying to lighten the mood.

"Plant food," Daniel said primly, "it's a good thing."

I laughed; he didn't.

"I can replace some of the plants from my own garden. The more exotic ones I can pick up from a greenhouse I frequent in Chelsea."

"That's the first time I've heard the words *pick up, frequent,* and *greenhouse* in the same sentence," I said, making another valiant attempt at humor.

"Obviously," Daniel stated, casting a look in the direction of several plants. "I got the idea from Sheila the situation is urgent because what's-her-name—"

"Prajna?"

"Right, Prajna is coming home. I'm busy tomorrow, so I'd like to take care of this today."

"You're going to have to let me pay you," I insisted.

"Some of these plants are expensive."

"Money's not an issue. You can take my credit card to the green-house and spend whatever you have to."

"Of course, you're paying for the new stuff. My point was, if you let me keep the unhealthy plants, that will repay me for my time. I really don't want your money," he said firmly. "And I'm not taking your credit card anywhere. I'm not lugging plants and soil all over Manhattan; you are."

Once again I could offer nothing but meek agreement. It was obvious Daniel was not going to warm up to me. I'd endure a day of his company to get the plant dilemma resolved, then we could go our separate ways.

"I guess there's no time like the present," I said.

He watched as I logged off my computer and got my keys and wallet; then he followed me from the apartment, where he took charge, hailing a cab and giving a Chelsea address. I'd thought we might walk, since it was a nice day; then I realized that Daniel, like me, was doing what he had to do as quickly as possible to limit the amount of time we spent together.

Once we were at the greenhouse, however, he forgot me. He was obviously in his element, and the employees apparently knew him well. I wandered around feeling useless while they quipped their way through botany chat. It did give me the opportunity to see Daniel's personality when he wasn't sullen or resentful.

"Hey Daniel," a guy called as he came through a door. "We've still got that fountain you want."

"And it's still too expensive," Daniel said.

"No job yet, huh?"

"I've done some more auditions."

"You should let that rich boyfriend of yours buy it," the guy said.

The other employees shot a questioning glance my way, as if wondering what my presence with Daniel indicated about his boyfriend status.

"Oh, sorry," Daniel said. "This is Adam Wilson. The stuff I'm get-ting today is for his place. Adam, this is Billy, Paul, Krista, and Brian."

Everyone nodded or gave me a wave. As they began talking about Daniel's order again, I managed to sidle over to Billy.

"Can you do me a favor?" I asked quietly after making sure Daniel was engrossed elsewhere.

"What's that?"

"The fountain Daniel wants. Can you add it to my purchases and have it delivered to his place without him knowing?"

Billy's eyes widened, and he said, "It *is* expensive."

I shrugged and said, "It will help me take care of a debt to him that money won't cover. He's not watching now. Take my credit card and run it through while he's busy."

In less than five minutes the transaction was finished, with no one the wiser. I glanced at the receipt to see the damage, which wasn't as bad as I'd thought. The cost of the fountain was nothing compared to a piece of my computer equipment, but I supposed everything was relative. To someone looking for a job, a luxury item like a fountain probably wasn't worth the cost.

Hopefully, by the time the fountain was delivered and Daniel figured out what I'd done, it would be too much of a hassle to return it. Or maybe the nice Daniel I was seeing now would allow me to atone for the way I'd mistreated him when we were kids.

The greenhouse had a van, and I paid the extra cost for delivery after seeing how many plants Daniel had picked out and what sizes they were. Daniel and I rode back to Prajna's in the van with Billy, both of them talking easily about the neighborhood or mutual acquaintances while I listened. At the apartment, I hauled the soil and heavier stuff up, while Daniel and Billy gently transported the more delicate plants. Finally, after giving Billy a nice tip, I found myself alone with Daniel again.

"This will take a few hours," Daniel reminded me as I looked at him.

"Is there anything I can do to help?" I asked.

"Tempting, but for the sake of living things, no. You don't even have to be here if you've got stuff to do."

"I do have stuff to do, but this is where I work," I said, pointing toward my array of computers.

"Okay, I'll try not to disturb you," Daniel said. He shot another glance at the print on the wall, gave a little shudder, and went into the kitchen.

I worked for a while, then found myself listening to Daniel as he went about his work. Though I couldn't hear what he was saying, he was apparently talking to the plants. If I disregarded his disdain for me, there was something comfortably domestic about the situation. I found myself wondering about his boyfriend, what kind of relationship they had, how they'd met. I glanced over my shoulder to make sure I was still alone, then typed the name Daniel Stephenson into a search engine, scanning the many results without finding anything that seemed related to him until suddenly, the name Club Chaos popped up.

I could hear him in the kitchen, so I went to the site to find an archived article about an auction the club had held the year before to raise money for AmFAR. I read on, fascinated. Apparently, Daniel had worked at Club Chaos for several years. The auction sold many of the outfits he'd worn onstage, most of which had been replicas of dresses worn by Princess Diana. Daniel had performed for several years as a Diana impersonator, Princess 2Di4.

Everything clicked for me as I recalled the picture I'd seen at the club, and Sheila's sad comment that she'd missed the chance to see the Princess Diana and Judy Garland impersonators perform there. Of course, I hadn't recognized Daniel in drag, but I wasn't surprised. He had been terrific in our high school plays; female impersonation was another form of acting. Also, he'd talked to the guys at the greenhouse about auditions, which meant he was still acting.

My heart seemed about to explode out of my chest as I remembered something else, the night I went to the Big Cup with Blythe and heard Andy ask Jeremy, "So how is Daniel? Do you see him often? Are you still carrying a *torch* for him?"

With another cautious glance toward the kitchen, I did a search on "Princess 2Di4 Manhattan" and came up with many results. As I did a quick perusal of the list of interviews, Pride Parade appearances, and news articles, Daniel stepped out of the kitchen, and I quickly minimized my screen.

"Looking at porn?" he asked.

"What?"

"You look guilty. You're not one of those people whose face hides things."

"Unlike you," I commented.

Now it was his turn to ask, "What?"

"You're an actor. Don't actors wear masks? Figuratively speaking."

"I suppose we do."

"You used to appear at Club Chaos, huh?"

He frowned and said, "I guess Sheila told you that. She said that you and she caught my friend Martin's act one night."

"Yeah. He was great. But actually, Sheila didn't tell me. I was just remembering a conversation I overheard at the Big Cup. I didn't realize it was you at the time, of course, but the subject of Daniel came up in a conversation between Club Chaos's owner, Andy, and a guy named Jeremy."

Daniel gave a little snort and said, "I'm sure it did. Jeremy is my ex-boyfriend."

"Really? Your ex-boyfriend?" I asked, trying to keep the excitement out of my voice and not put too much emphasis on the "ex" part.

Daniel gave me an odd look and said, "You did know I'm gay, right? That couldn't have been news. At least, not news like I got when Sheila told me that *you're* gay."

"I guess that was a shock," I agreed. "Considering our history."

"Yeah, it makes your obnoxious behavior in school even worse."

"Didn't you ever watch a John Hughes movie or some after-school special about confused teenagers who torment the person they're afraid of being?"

"The only thing special about after-school for me was getting the hell away from you and your buddies."

"Okay, you're not going to forgive me. I accept that. But could you do one thing for me?"

"I'm already saving your plant-killing ass. Isn't that enough?"

"No. Tell me Jeremy's last name."

Daniel gave me a bewildered look and said, "Caprellian. Why?"

I turned back to my computer, went to the original search page, and said, "Could you spell that?"

He spelled it, then stepped up behind me to see what I was doing.

"You're researching Jeremy?"

"Yep."

"Why?"

I ignored his question, feeling elated as several results appeared on my screen, including one that said, "Review: Anything Goes."

"He's an actor, too?" I asked.

"Right. But he's not in *Anything Goes* now. He's got a recurring role on that new sitcom *Man of the House.*"

"Oh geez," I muttered. "You mean if I ever watched television I could have found him?"

"If you like sitcoms that are doomed by going up against *Must*

See TV, yes," Daniel said. "All this interest stems from seeing Jeremy once at the Big Cup? He must have made quite an impression."

"He did. I even crashed a party because I knew he was going to be there."

I turned to look at Daniel as he started laughing.

"I don't believe this. My high school nemesis has a crush on my ex-boyfriend. I can't wait to tell Blaine this."

"Blaine? Dunhill? Why would he care?"

"Because Blaine is my current boyfriend."

"Blaine Dunhill is gay?" I yelped.

"He was the last time I had sex with him," Daniel answered calmly.

"That explains a lot," I said, thinking it over.

"Like what?"

"Like why Sheila and Josh were so weird when I asked about Blaine. Nobody back home knows he's gay. They think he and his wife broke up because of another woman. I even got the idea Sheila was the other woman."

"I'm the other woman," Daniel pronounced dramatically. "But he and Sydney were already broken up when I met him. You're right; his family has no idea he's gay. Since he's not on speaking terms with them these days, that's one bit of news they don't have."

"I won't say anything," I reassured him. "It's his business."

"I guess you know a little bit about the closet yourself," Daniel commented.

"Not really. I told my family when I was eighteen. I didn't make any secret of it at college or at any of my jobs."

"How wonderful for you," Daniel said in a somewhat bitter tone.

"I don't believe it. I find what would have to be the greatest source of information on Jeremy: an ex-boyfriend. And you can't stand me."

"Sucks to be you." He walked toward the bedroom, then turned around. "He's happily single. After he stopped seeing the man who broke us up, Robert, he dated some other guy for a while. Now he's sworn off of love and relationships to devote himself to his career and inner peace. He's going to need a lot of inner peace when his sitcom gets canceled. By the way, the phone isn't in his name. It's Orso. Robert Orso."

As he disappeared into the bedroom, I felt my grin spread from ear to ear. Daniel wasn't quite ready to give up his grudge, but he was intentionally making it easy for me to find Jeremy. Considering his feelings for me, maybe he intended to settle scores with his ex-boyfriend and his high school antagonist by inflicting us on each other.

I followed him into the bedroom and caught him in the midst of a Three Stooges impression, waving two fingers in front of the waif painting as if to poke a pair of myopic eyes.

"Isn't she awful?" I asked.

"She looks like Nancy Reagan," Daniel said. "I don't know how you sleep in here."

"I dream of Jeremy," I said, and Daniel rolled his eyes. "It's nice of you to tell me how to find him. Does that mean—"

"It doesn't mean anything. After I saw you in Central Park, I called Bill Hamilton to tell him about it. He made me see that no matter what a jerk you are, if I let you get to me, you're still in control. I can either stay that scared kid who used to hide from you, or I can get over it. I control my own life. You're the one who's still living at home with all your old buddies around you, all of you clinging to your teenage glory days. At least I moved on with my life."

"So did I. I grew up. And wised up."

"Whatever."

It was obvious I wasn't getting anywhere with him, so I really had nothing to lose by asking him about Jeremy.

"This Robert guy. He's just Jeremy's roommate now?"

"Yes. He's also an actor. He's still in *Anything Goes*. Good old Robert always takes care of himself."

"Who takes care of Jeremy?" I asked softly, wishing it could be me.

Daniel turned to give me a measuring look. I could tell my question had gotten to him. Jeremy might be his ex, but apparently he retained enough feeling for him to be affected by the sincerity in my voice.

"Lately, Blaine complains that we do. But Jeremy leads a charmed life. He's enjoying his moment as 'the single redeeming attraction in another dismal sitcom,'" Daniel said, obviously quoting a review. "While the rest of us are dealing with all kinds of crap, Jeremy floats somewhere above it all. In fact, that's the new bromide he keeps serving all of us: *Detach from outcome.* He's lucky Andy and Martin haven't detached his body parts."

"Are things not going well for Andy and Martin?" I asked.

Daniel's expression grew suspicious again, and I said, "Come on, Daniel, it's a friendly question. We'll never move beyond our unhappy past if you don't at least try to believe I'm not some evil homophobe in disguise."

His facial expression let me know he had a quick retort that he was deliberately suppressing. He finally answered, "It's the club. They're having a hard time holding on to their crowd since my friend Ken died. Ken was the creative force behind most of the entertainment at Club Chaos. In fact, it was Ken who gave me my start and helped me develop and perfect my act. I was the headliner. After I left, Ken filled that slot again for a while. When he got sick, Martin stepped in. Martin was Ken's boyfriend, so he had to leave to take care of Ken. Now he's back at work, and his act is good, but the momentum is gone. Competition between gay bars is fierce; everyone tends to flock to the latest bar du jour, and a lot of gay men don't like drag shows. And Club Chaos has started losing a lot of its straight and tourist clientele to a couple of other drag clubs. I don't know why the hell I'm telling you all this."

"Because I asked, and I'm really interested," I responded. "In fact, I know a little bit about Andy's competition. I've met Wade Van Atterson and been to Disorient XPress, though I've never seen a show there."

Daniel gave a short burst of laughter and said, "There's a name I hoped never to hear again. Wade Van Atterson."

"You know him?"

"I've never met Wade, but he has quite a past with Andy. Ken probably knew the whole story, but all I ever heard was Andy invoking the name. If anything bad happened at the club, Andy would say something like, 'Great, as if it's not enough that Wade Van Atterson is breathing down my neck, the toilet's backed up.' Or, 'I've got Wade Van Atterson trying to ruin me, and you want a raise? You're all going to bankrupt me!' We heard it so much that it became a mantra for us in any disaster. 'My boyfriend left me, and Wade Van Atterson's breathing down my neck!' 'The condom broke, and Wade Van Atterson's trying to destroy me!' Whenever my financial advisor, Gretchen, has to give me bad news about an investment, she starts the conversation with something like, 'So I let Wade Van Atterson look at your portfolio.' Then I know to brace myself." Daniel laughed again and said, "Only a couple of days before Ken died, the doctor came in with some bad news.

After he left, Ken turned to me and said, 'My T-cells are fucked, and Wade Van Atterson wants to destroy me!' We all laughed so hard. But no, I don't know Wade."

"Ken must have been quite a guy," I said, noticing how Daniel's eyes softened whenever he mentioned Ken's name.

"Nothing could keep him down. He was the perfect foil for Andy. Do you know Andy's last name?" When I shook my head, he said, "Vanedesen. Eerily similar to Van Atterson, huh? We used to tease Andy about that, though it would never last long, because any mention of Wade would cause him to go into a cavalcade of screaming. We'd say, 'Did you see the new ad your brother ran for Disorient XPress?' Or, 'Your wife called. She's running late closing the XPress tonight.' Andy would start shrieking about how their names are *nothing* alike, and 'Shouldn't you be *practicing* or *something*, instead of *reminding* me how that man is trying to *ruin* me?' He's a piece of work, that Andy."

"You do the most dead-on imitation of Andy," I said, laughing at him. "You must be a really good actor. I heard you tell the guys at the greenhouse that you'd been auditioning. Anything look promising?"

"Maybe. Although normally I'm not interested in TV, I tried out for a soap opera role. It's a small part to start, but seems to have promise of developing into something bigger. The soap is *Secret Splendor.* Have you heard of it?"

"Oh yes," I kidded. "That's the one that's on right before Donohue, but after 'As the Stomach Growls.' "

"Very funny. It's actually the oldest running soap on TV, but they're introducing some new characters to help their sagging ratings. Of course, it's only on against the news, which is how it's stayed around so long. People will watch anything other than the news. And Donohue isn't on anymore, you Neanderthal," Daniel finished with a laugh, which he cut short, the wary look returning to his eyes as if he'd suddenly remembered he was talking to an enemy.

"It's too bad about Club Chaos," I said quickly, wanting to keep the mood friendly now that he was actually talking to me. "I had a great time there with Sheila."

"It is too bad," Daniel agreed. "Regardless of Andy's flaws, he's worked his ass off to keep that club going through some tough times. Not only was it my home for a long time, but I still have a lot of friends there, including Martin. Gretchen, who is Andy's financial advisor as well as mine, has warned him that unless he manages to draw younger gay guys away from dance clubs and pick-up bars, his days are numbered. I feel like there will always be a place for impersonators and drag queens, but I could be wrong. You said you had a great time, but would you have gone to Club Chaos on your own?"

"Probably not," I said thoughtfully. "There aren't that many gay bars in Eau Claire. In fact, I usually go to straight bars unless I'm specifically looking for sex. I don't go to any of those things like Mr. Leather contests or drag shows. I like to dance, but the guys at dance clubs are so young."

"I never even knew Eau Claire had gay bars until my sisters told me," Daniel said. "It's weird to think of being an adult gay man there. Even weirder to consider that if I'd gone into a gay bar and seen you, I'd have run screaming into the night."

I thought his willingness to make jokes about our past was a promising sign.

"Maybe Andy and I are dinosaurs," Daniel finally said. "The era of taffeta and tiaras is over. Now it's all technology and—"

"That's it!" I interrupted. "Technology. Do you have any online chat experience?"

"I hate computers. I had to do Internet research in a job I had for a while, but I'm not exactly wired in."

"Because you have friends, a career, and a boyfriend," I said. "There are a lot of lonely young guys hanging out at copy places and coffee cyber-bars using computers, or sitting home alone in front of their PCs while they search for the man of their dreams online. Those are the people Andy needs to lure into Club Chaos. They shun bars, so he doesn't have to compete with the dance clubs and meat racks for them. He only has to help them overcome their shyness and fear about meeting people by giving them an environment they already feel comfortable in."

"I'm not sure I follow," Daniel said.

I thought about the layout of the club and said, "The walled-off area at Club Chaos that probably used to be a balcony. What does Andy use that space for now?"

"Storage, mostly, and the projection room is in there, so it has all the lighting stuff for the shows. Why?"

"If you go there with me, will Andy let me look at it? I have a great idea that I want to pitch to him."

Daniel hesitated for only the briefest of moments before he said, "I guess. I need to finish the plants, though."

"Can I help you?"

"Hell, no," Daniel said. "I've seen your work."

"All right, all right. How about if I do some research while you finish up? Then will you go with me?"

"Are you sure you know what you're getting into?" Daniel asked.

"Computers are my livelihood," I assured him. "And I'm used to working with neophytes."

"Nothing," Daniel assured me, "has prepared you to work with Andy Vanedesen."

SEVEN

Two weeks later, I was standing at a makeshift table in the balcony of Club Chaos with a set of plans in front of me. The electrical and construction foremen flanked me as I explained for what felt like the millionth time what we were trying to accomplish. I drew a breath, exasperated that I wasn't making myself clear, and told the less-than-dynamic duo that it was time for a break, at least for me. I watched them walk away while I thought of what had transpired to get me into this mess.

Although Daniel had not seemed particularly enthusiastic about what I saw as my exciting plan for the club, he'd brought me to meet Andy the same afternoon that he blew the breath of life into the plants at Prajna's. Andy's expression upon being introduced to me wavered from lust to confusion, then back to lust, only to be followed by more confusion as I explained my idea for the bar. Once in a while Andy would produce a dramatic outburst, coming up with reasons why my idea wouldn't work.

"What on *earth* do you think I'm going to do with all these *boxes?*" Andy whined, looking from Daniel to me. He gestured dramatically, using his arms in a sweeping motion, then dropped them at his sides. Daniel shrugged and looked at me.

"Andy," I began, "it's not all that many boxes. Put them in storage. If you really need them, you'll know right where they are."

"And the extra *cost!* Do you know how much all of this is going to *cost?* Not only for the construction, but all the rest of it?" Andy implored.

"The way I see it," I said, "it's going to be nothing compared to how much it'll cost you if you don't do it. I know times are tough, but you have to stay current. You have to do something new and fresh. Think of it like this; you have to be the Madonna of the club world, constantly reinventing yourself, evolving, to reach the broadest audience possible."

"We've been holding their interest at Club Chaos for *years,*" he spoke with more than a hint of disdain. "I don't see how a bunch of computers sitting on tables is going to pique the curiosity of *any-one* but our local librarians."

"That's just it. It's a *venue* that piques curiosity." I paused, concerned that I was starting to emphasize words the way Andy did. I didn't want him to think that I was mocking him. "What you have here is wonderful. Now you need to reach beyond the audience that comes for your shows."

"That's what the double bar in the lobby is for," Andy pointed out.

"Right. But let's consider that. When a guy goes to a bar, he sees someone he's attracted to, then he tries to get to know him. Initially, it's all based on looks; there's no real substance behind the meeting. If he's really lucky, that good-looking guy shares some of his interests and is able to carry on a conversation. But most of the time, for whatever reason, things don't work out that way. When you meet a guy online, there has to be a connection to something other than looks from the get-go. Trust me when I say that more than half the guys who come in here on any given night have hooked up with someone this way. In fact, one of the things we can do is enable people to send messages in-house that are queued up to a large screen. Someone could send a message to a guy who's not even logged on to the network. It could be displayed for every-one to see, which might serve to bring others who aren't as computer savvy into the loop, so that it's not just a clique of computer geeks up here. It'll work, Andy. I know how to do it, and I know it'll be a success."

Andy looked at me, and I could tell he was seriously weighing my proposal. I was asking him to take a risk on something about which he knew nothing. But if Daniel was right, Club Chaos wasn't drawing the crowds it once had. It was time for a change, and Andy had to realize that.

"Oh, all right," Andy said, doing his best to sound taxed and burdened. "I'll think about it. I'm not making any promises. There's a lot more to consider than just my ability to evolve. This will be an *enormous* undertaking—expensive and time-consuming, not to mention *very* dusty. I have to speak with some people about the cost. Lord only knows *where* I'm going to get the money for all this."

"Andy, remember that I'm not taking away from what you're already doing. Your customers are still going to be loyal to you. But adding this will bring you a whole new group of patrons. It'll help your business grow."

"All right, all right," Andy muttered. He waved his hands as if to dismiss me and said, "I've heard enough of this for one day. Daniel, I really *have* to get back to rehearsal, and you really have to get *this* one"—he gestured with his head in my general direction—"out of here. Things haven't *evolved* that much. Our rehearsals are still closed. I'll be in touch with you, Adam."

A couple of days after our first meeting, Andy called to ask if I'd join him and his financial advisor, Gretchen Schmidt, for lunch. I covered my apprehension when he named the Sequoia Restaurant in the South Street Seaport. Remembering my lunch with Ethan in Central Park, I knew it was likely that a restaurant in Manhattan on the water could mean only one thing: seafood.

I arrived early to get the lay of the land, which was probably the wrong term, as the Sequoia overlooked the fishing boats coming to the Fulton Fish Market on the East River. The restaurant was beautiful, with a nautical theme. But a look at the menu confirmed my suspicion that the entrees were a wet dream—if you were a person who dreamed of food that was once wet. I decided I would let Andy and Gretchen order first, so I could see what price range they stayed in before I decided between a steak and the turkey club sandwich.

I liked Gretchen immediately upon being introduced to her by Andy. My Gemini nature was tantalized by the contrast between her no-nonsense suit and the subtle white streaks in her tousled chestnut hair. She projected an image that was both businesslike and fun.

What really struck me, however, was the change in Andy. It was as if the whining, hand-wringing, belabored shrew had been replaced by a skilled negotiator. Once the niceties were dispensed with, he cut right to the bottom line.

"Gretchen agrees that your plan has merit and assures me it would be in my best interest to consider your idea," Andy said. "However, there's one expense you left out of your sales pitch."

"What expense?" I asked with a frown, certain that I had covered everything with Andy in our initial meeting.

"Your fee," Gretchen said, pinning me with her hazel eyes. "I assume you don't work for free."

"Right," Andy said, then slipped into his old persona with his next words. "While it's very *touching* that you would enjoy the challenge of giving Club Chaos a makeover, I'm sure you're a business-man, not a *philanthropist.*"

As we began hammering out details, I decided to order the steak. It might be the last free meal I got out of Andy. By the time lunch was over, I was grateful that my other clients didn't inflict me with a sharp businesswoman like Gretchen.

However, I'd come to wish that Gretchen had been *my* advisor when I hired my subcontractors. The crew I'd used for Patel, Inc. had been unavailable, and I felt like Bob Newhart stuck with Larry, Darryl, and Darryl on this job.

It was my plan to have the upstairs balcony of Club Chaos wired and outfitted with basic PCs and various colors of the just-released iMacs along the walls. I also wanted tables in the center of the room, where computer monitors could be positioned to angle up-ward beneath Plexiglas surfaces surrounded by comfortable chairs. This would protect the equipment from drinks and ashes, and the users wouldn't have to be shackled to the counters along the room's perimeters. The upstairs area would be called Cybeeria and was sure to be the talk of Manhattan if I could just get "Larry" and his cohorts to cooperate.

I heard footsteps coming up the stairs to the balcony and was surprised to see Daniel.

"Wow," was all he said, looking around. "It hardly seems like the same place."

"It always gets worse before it gets better," I offered. "What's up?"

"Not too much. I thought I'd come by to see how things are pro-gressing."

"Really?" I asked. "I got the impression you didn't care."

"I've spent a lot of time here over the last decade. Of course I care, especially since I introduced you to Andy. I don't entirely understand this scheme of yours, but it does intrigue me. I considered sneaking in at night to check things out, but I'd have felt like Gladys Kravitz coming over to borrow a cup of sugar."

I detailed some of my ideas for him, leaving out the technical aspects and focusing on how it would all look and work when it was done. He listened, then surprised me with a couple of questions about the cost.

"Why do I get the idea this is more than idle curiosity?" I finally asked. "You don't think I'd take advantage of Andy, do you?"

"I'm not sure he'd let that happen, but in this case, it's not only Andy's money that's at risk."

"What do you mean?"

"One of the reasons Gretchen got involved, other than as an advisor to Andy, is that some of this expansion is being funded by a trust she administers as part of Ken's estate. There's a lot riding on the success of this venture."

"I won't let any of you down," I assured him.

"Good. I have enough on my mind without baby-sitting you and Andy."

"Anything you want to talk about?"

"I had this weird conversation the other day with my ex, Jeremy," he said, his eyes fixed on me as if trying to gauge my reaction to Jeremy's name.

My heart skipped a beat, and I gave him my full attention. But the sound of footsteps coming up the stairs behind him made Daniel stop and turn. I groaned inwardly as Andy appeared, wondering why it wasn't possible to ban him from his own club.

"I heard you were here," Andy said to Daniel, pulling up a chair to share in the festivities. "Want your old job back? Or are you just here to keep Adam from *working?*"

"I wanted to talk to Adam about an acquaintance of his," Daniel said, a malicious gleam in his eyes as he continued, "Wade Van Atterson."

"Good god!" Andy exclaimed, jumping from his chair with such zeal that I thought he must have been shocked by an electrical cord. "Isn't it enough that I have the whole upstairs of my club torn apart? Now you're saying this is all part of some *horrid* scheme of Wade Van Atterson's?"

He stared at me as if I were Tokyo Rose, transported directly from Disorient XPress to infiltrate and destroy his business.

"I've only met Wade once," I defended myself. "At a party. There were lots of other people there."

"Damn," Daniel said. "I was hoping you knew him."

"Would you like for me to arrange a cab to take you over to Kabuki Country right now?" Andy asked. "The two of you can just cozy *right up* to Wade Van Atterson and destroy me."

"This has nothing to do with you, Andy," Daniel said. "If you'll sit quietly while I talk to Adam, I'll be happy to explain."

Andy clamped his jaw shut and glared at the two of us.

"As I was saying," Daniel continued, "I got a call from Jeremy, who's sworn off men in an effort to *find* himself." Daniel rolled his eyes and Andy clicked his tongue in disapproval. "Although I'm not sure when or where Jeremy disappeared, evidently the search is supposed to begin at a weekend retreat that Wade Van Atterson has organized at Columbia University. The main speaker is a friend of Jeremy's, a man named Ethan Whitecrow, who does these New Age talks all over the country."

"Puh-*leeze*," Andy interjected.

Daniel clenched his jaw, shot a look at Andy, then said, "Jeremy is hopping on this tent revival bandwagon and plans to attend the retreat. In spite of knowing that I don't put a whole lot of stock in New Age stuff, Jeremy invited me to go because apparently, one of Ethan Whitecrow's more devoted disciples is Bonnie Seaforth-Wilkes."

"She was at Wade's party, too," I commented.

"Oh, so it wasn't just *a* party, it was *Wade's* party," Andy snapped.

"Her family owns Seaforth Chemicals," Daniel went on, talking over Andy. "Makers of Fiberforth, because *'Sometimes nature needs a little helper.'*"

"They really say that?" I asked.

"Yes," Daniel assured me. "Fiberforth sponsors *Secret Splendor.*"

"You *know* Wade Van Atterson and Bonnie Seaforth-Wilkes are friends," Andy spat. "*He* saved that stupid soap opera from the extinction it deserves with his dreadful *Secret Splendor* Saturdays. It's the only show his club *has* with *any* kind of audience. Heaven only knows what other tricks he's got up his sleeve over at that Farcical Far East to hurl me into *bankruptcy.*"

Daniel chose to ignore Andy, saying, "Jeremy is sure Bonnie will be at the retreat. He thinks this might be an opportunity for me to cement some kind of relationship with her. It couldn't hurt. The part I auditioned for is small, but I really want it. I'm actually thinking of going. It's not like I have to rub stones or gaze into crystal balls or anything like that. According to Jeremy, I can just kind of hang out. I feel like if I can meet Ms. Seaforth-Wilkes, she'll know I'm right for the part."

"Because sometimes fate needs a little helper," I suggested.

"That's the spirit!" Daniel agreed.

"All I have to say is, I'm *sure* it won't be long now," Andy warned. "The clock is ticking, you mark my words, Daniel Stephenson." He wagged his finger in Daniel's direction to emphasize his point. "You take a role on that soap, and it's only a matter of time before Beastly Bonnie and the Wicked Witch Wade use *you* to bury me once and for all."

"Andy, first of all, Bonnie Seaforth-Wilkes is not out to destroy you. I don't expect to have anything to do with Wade Van Atterson at this retreat. Just because he helped organize it doesn't mean he'll be there. This is about me getting a job. Nothing else. Not Club Chaos, not Wade Van Atterson, and certainly not you."

Watching Andy and Daniel trade quips was like watching a Ping-Pong match. They were completely oblivious to the fact that several members of the construction crew had joined us, a few working on something electrical while others carried lumber up the stairs.

"Don't you think you're being melodramatic?" I finally asked Andy.

"I don't think I'm being melodramatic enough," Andy disagreed, twirling to head down the stairs, throwing his sweater over his shoulders like a cape and leaving his arms free to hold the railing on his way down. One of the workers swung a two-by-four plank across the top of the opening to the stairs, narrowly missing Andy's head. Seeing the catastrophe coming and knowing there was nothing to be done, I felt Daniel hold his breath just as I did, until the board successfully cleared Andy. We exhaled together.

I waited until I felt sure that Andy was well out of earshot, then said to Daniel, "You know, I've met the guy you're talking about."

"Wade?"

"Ethan Whitecrow."

"Oh?" Daniel raised an eyebrow and sat down. "Do tell."

"Remember I told you that I crashed a party to meet Jeremy? That was Wade's party. I saw Bonnie and Ethan there. When I realized he was Jeremy's date, I contrived to meet Ethan a few days after the party."

"I'm beginning to think you contrived to meet Sheila and Josh for lunch, not to mention run into me at Bethesda Fountain, as a way to get to Jeremy."

"I didn't know either of you knew Jeremy," I said, then realized by his smile he was kidding. "But if I had known, I probably would have," I admitted. "Anyway, Ethan's not a bad guy. He's also easy on the eyes. His talk could be interesting; you might get something out of it. Other than meeting Bonnie, I mean."

"You think so? Then why don't you go with me?" Daniel asked with a devilish grin.

"Me?" I yelped. "I don't go for that New Age crap."

"Blaine isn't remotely interested in going, and he's working like a dog right now, anyway. It might help your career, too—your dating career, that is. Jeremy will be there."

"I don't know," I hedged. I wasn't exactly eager to watch Ethan and Jeremy make eyes at each other for an entire weekend.

"C'mon," Daniel taunted, *"Ethan's not a bad guy."*

"Might have known that would come back to bite me," I said. I drew a deep breath. "Okay, I'll do it. I'll go. Our last venture together turned out pretty well. Look around you!"

Daniel turned his head from one side to the other, observing the carnage of what would be Cybeeria.

"Hmmm. It always gets worse before it gets better, huh?" he asked, once again evoking my words to haunt me.

I frowned as I turned to face the electrical and construction contractors who were thumping up the stairs. I excused myself from Daniel to discuss my plans with Larry, his brother Darryl, and his other brother Darryl, for the million-and-first time.

Daniel waited until I finished my discussion, then said, "I'm supposed to meet Blaine at his gym. It's about twenty blocks from here, between Seventh and Eighth. Are you ready to leave? Do you feel like a walk? I need to clear Andy drama out of my system."

"I'm not accomplishing much here," I said. "A walk might help. Anyway, that's close to my new apartment."

"How's that working out?" Daniel asked.

"It's one of those sterile corporate things. Very clean, which I don't mind, but none of those personal touches to make a man feel at home."

"Uh, like dead plants and scary bug-eyed children hanging on the walls?"

"I did get used to Nancy, Anorexia, and their friends," I admitted.

"It's a good thing you got out when you did. What if you'd started looking like them?"

"Sounds like a good science fiction story," I said.

He waited while I got my stuff together; then we stepped outside.

"It's definitely getting colder," Daniel commented. "Winter's on the way. Before you know it, you'll feel like you're right at home."

Daniel seemed lost in thought as we walked north on Seventh Avenue. I found it somewhat touching that, as inattentive as he appeared, he still guided me through the throngs of people hurrying along the sidewalks. I decided that navigating the city on foot was probably a trait that, once acquired, became automatic. Like a tourist, I still wanted to look everywhere, especially up, but Daniel's purposeful stride propelled us forward. I wondered if I would ever blend, as Daniel and Blythe did, into this urban landscape.

We were waiting for a light to change, when Daniel suddenly pulled me away from the crowd and said, "I need to ask you something."

"Sure. What's up?"

"I got the fountain. I'm not sure I understand why you did that."

"You helped me get the job working for Andy. It's a token of my gratitude."

"But you did it while we were at the greenhouse, right? I was being an asshole to you then. And the Club Chaos thing hadn't come up yet."

"You did me another favor, too. I felt really guilty about Prajna's plants. I honestly did try to take care of them, because I wanted to respect her space the way I'd expect someone to respect my home. Looking back, I realize I should have immediately found some kind of plant-sitter before the damage was done. When Ray called me to tell me Prajna was coming home earlier than expected, I was in a panic, with no idea how to make things right. You fixed it. You didn't have to. In fact, I never dreamed Sheila could talk you into it. Since you refused to let me pay you, and the fountain seemed to be something you wanted, I thought I'd try to make things even between us."

"You sure you weren't trying to buy my love?" Daniel asked with a faint smile.

"Is it for sale?"

"No. Neither is my forgiveness," he said, his face serious again.

"It was meant as an apology," I admitted. "I'm sorry about our unhappy past."

"Honestly, I've been thinking about our dear old school days," Daniel said. "You weren't the worst of the guys who tormented me. I just lumped you in with them as another jock asshole. I'm over it."

"Damn," I said. "Should I return the fountain?"

"It's already installed and running," Daniel said with a smile. "You can't take it back now."

I grinned and reached over to grip the back of his neck, giving him a little shake, happy to see that he didn't flinch or jerk away.

"Thank you for the fountain," Daniel said. "You know what you said about respecting your home? I realize an apartment doesn't always have the same . . . warmth as a home of your own, but my garden is my sacred space. The fountain is a nice addition."

"Good," I said. "Whenever you see it, you can think of me."

"Noisy and wet?"

"Soothing and generous," I argued.

We began walking again, and this time my stride was more confident because I had the promise of a real friend by my side. Though I was grateful for all that Blythe offered, I felt the first stirring of hope that Daniel and I could actually develop the kind of friendship I'd long wanted with another gay man. It was better than a boyfriend. Well, almost . . .

We stopped in front of glass doors marked *bodyWorks*.

"This is it," Daniel said.

My cell phone chose that moment to ring, and I pulled it out to see Blythe's name on the display.

"Wait just a second?" I asked Daniel, and he nodded while I answered the phone. "Hi, Blythe."

"How did you know it was me?" she asked.

"Your number is stored on my list. Can I call you right back? I'm just saying goodbye to someone."

"That's okay," Daniel said. "I'll wait."

"Never mind," I spoke to Blythe. "What's up?"

"I just finished talking to my parents. They're thrilled that I have a phone. They're going to Italy next month! I'm so excited for them. They've always wanted to go to Florence and Rome to see all the art. Since they won't be here on Thanksgiving, they want me to come home for a visit now. They're wiring me the money."

"That's great. When are you leaving?"

"Tomorrow. I'm taking a train. I wanted to tell you where I'd be."

"How long will you be gone?"

"I've left that open. Four or five days, I guess. I'll call you and let you know."

"Okay. I'll miss you. I hope you have a good time."

"It will be nice to get away," she said. "As long as I know I'm coming back. I have to do laundry before I leave, so I'd better let you go. Love you!"

"I love you, too," I said, grinning. It was the first time she'd ever said that to me, and I liked the way it made me feel inside. I hung up and said to Daniel, "My friend Blythe. She's adorable. You'll have to meet her sometime. She's my one friend in Manhattan."

"Now you have two," Daniel said. As my grin widened, he said, "I meant Sheila!"

I laughed and said, "No you didn't. So this is where Blaine works out? I still haven't found a permanent gym in the city."

"Why don't you check this one out?" Daniel suggested. "Then you can meet Blaine, too."

I didn't know if it was the gift of the fountain, if I'd passed some kind of test at Club Chaos, or if my agreement to go with Daniel to the retreat had done the trick, but I recognized that introducing me to Blaine was a clear invitation into his personal life. I wasn't about to refuse. I was eager to meet the man who'd snatched my high school acclaim from me. I also wanted to see how Daniel and Blaine interacted as a couple.

Daniel led me through the glass doors to confront a sensory feast. The unforgiving white light that I was accustomed to in gyms was nonexistent. Colors streamed and pulsated through the room as if it were a disco. Indeed, across the floor of gleaming state-of-the-art gym equipment, I could see a DJ booth, which explained the high-energy dance music. Over the usual smell of clean sweat and disinfectants, I detected scents that made me think of Blythe's essential-oil blends. Daniel laughed when he realized that I'd stopped to stand still and inhale.

"Men working out, men getting massaged, men taking show-ers—and the personal trainers are all gods. Blaine swears he only comes here because it's halfway between home and the office, but"—he glanced toward the room, which was, as he'd said, full of shining, pumping, preening men—"I'm pretty sure it's for the juice bar."

I laughed and followed him into what actually did look like a neighborhood bar. The lights were more subtle here, but it was still easy to see how new and clean everything was. My scan of the men sitting at tables and at the bar was not quite as fast as Daniel's. He was obviously looking for Blaine; I was just looking.

We walked to the counter, where he ordered a chocolate-banana smoothie. I opted for a bottle of water and a kiwi-lime shake. The only available table was in a far corner, but Daniel said he was cer-tain Blaine would find us.

"Tell me more about Jeremy swearing off men," I said after we sat down. "Do you think that means he and Ethan have only a pla-tonic, spiritual interest in each other?"

"You've got it bad," Daniel said.

As he laughed at me, I saw Blaine approaching us. I recognized him from the large pictures that were in the lobby of Dunhill Electrical. Though he'd been a few years younger and dressed in a football uniform in those photos, he hadn't changed much. His frame had filled out more. His muscles were pronounced, since he'd just finished a workout, but weren't overly developed. Like everyone, his face was more interesting now that he had a few more years of life behind him. His dark hair was still wet from a shower, his eyes were the greenest I'd ever seen, and he was looking at me as if I were a rodent about to get caught in a trap he'd set. His ex-pression was a mixture of interest, distaste, and faith that whatever I got I had coming to me after having invaded his territory.

I understood and liked him immediately. There would be no Andy-like catty comments or subtle jabs from this one. He spoke my language, and at that moment, as clearly as if he'd said it aloud, I could hear, *You have thirty seconds to explain what the fuck you are doing with my boyfriend before I decide if you live or die.*

"Adam Wilson," I said, standing and holding out my hand. I saw my height and build register in his eyes, but his hand remained at his side. "Jake's friend from Eau Claire."

He hesitated a moment, still sizing me up, then clasped my hand. His grip was firmer than it needed to be. I no longer had to fear execution, but I was still on probation.

"Adam, this is my bodyguard, Blaine Dunhill," Daniel said with a perceptive smile. "Testosterone chaser, anyone?"

The expression on Blaine's face when he tore his gaze from me to look at Daniel would have made me forgive anything I hadn't already understood. He was a man completely smitten. The look that passed between them made me remember all the reasons why I wished I had a boyfriend.

"How you doing?" Blaine asked.

"I'm okay," Daniel said. "I didn't hear from the soap yet."

"You will," Blaine assured him. He dropped his gym bag on the floor and glanced at me. "Need anything?"

I shook my head and watched as he went to the bar to order.

"I might take one of him," I said softly.

"You *are* one of him," Daniel answered with another grin.

When Blaine returned with his smoothie, he sat between us, looking at me.

"Where do you work out?"

"I'm a member of a fitness center in Eau Claire. I've been to a few gyms here. A guy I'm doing some work for has his corporate offices in Weehawken. I use the gym in their building whenever I go over there. I'm not really sure how long I'll be in New York, so I don't know about getting a membership."

"I'm more consistent if I have one place to go," Blaine said. "The memberships here are pretty steep, but as my guest you can get three free visits. I don't know what kind of schedule you're on, but if you want to work out with me and see how you like this place, I get here around five o'clock at least three nights a week."

"My schedule's flexible," I said, adding my thanks as he handed me a business card with his work, home, and cell phones listed.

Daniel listened, absently rotating a stirrer through his smoothie, as Blaine and I discussed Jake and other mutual acquaintances in Eau Claire, then sports, and finally our work in Manhattan. Blaine was in advertising at what I comprehended was a highly successful firm, where he handled a single account, Lillith Allure Cosmetics.

"Is that anything like Lillith Parker?" I asked.

"She's one of the partners. You're familiar with her?" Blaine asked with a surprised expression.

"Only that Sheila told me she was trying to get an assignment as Lillith Parker's Zodiac Girl."

"She is?" Blaine asked, looking at Daniel.

"She didn't want you to know," Daniel explained. "She wants to get it on her own."

"She had to realize I'd be seeing all the models' test layouts," Blaine said. "Naturally, Lillith Parker and Frank Allen will make the final decision, but they'll take my opinion into consideration."

"I'm sorry if I said something I shouldn't have," I said.

"I'm glad you did," Daniel said with a relieved expression. "I was having a terrible time not telling Blaine."

"Yeah, don't worry about it," Blaine said. "Sheila doesn't even have to know. I'm sure she's got a great shot at the job, with or without my help. I don't know why I didn't think of her myself."

The chill from Blaine had thawed considerably, and I was pretty sure Daniel was pleased that Blaine had decided not only to let me live but to make me one of the jock brotherhood. I knew that if I hadn't invoked the name of Jake Meyers that might not have happened so quickly.

When Daniel excused himself to go to the rest room, Blaine watched him leave, his expression thoughtful, then he turned to me.

"I heard about you from Sheila and Daniel, but I had the idea you still lived in Eau Claire and were working here temporarily."

"It is temporary, but I'll be here another couple of months, probably until Christmas." I glanced up to make sure Daniel wasn't on his way back before I took a deep breath and plunged. "Look, I realize you don't know me, and you have no reason to trust me, but I'm only interested in being friends with Daniel. I treated him like crap in high school, and I want to make that up to him."

"Is that what the fountain was all about?" Blaine asked.

"Yes."

"It was a nice gesture. Of *friendship.*"

"That's exactly what it was. I respect your relationship," I assured him.

Blaine's eyes crinkled into a semismile as he looked at me and said, "Even if you didn't, I trust Daniel completely. But thanks for saying that. He's been through a lot over the past few months. I think he could use a friend who isn't connected to all that."

"I heard about his best friend's death."

"Losing Ken hit him hard. I have to travel so much, and I worry about him. I wasn't surprised when Sheila was able to talk him into helping you with the plants. It's in Daniel's nature to be generous that way. Sometimes people take advantage of that."

He trailed off, as if not wanting to say more.

"You two look awfully serious," Daniel said as he sat down.

"You know how seriously I take my carb intake," Blaine said. "Speaking of which, it's my night to cook at your place. Adam, you should join us."

"I don't want to impose," I said.

"Oh, you're coming with us," Daniel ordered. "I've been very patient while you and Blaine bonded over jock straps"—he broke off, considering how that sounded, and shook his head—"Anyway, we can start talking about our strategy for the retreat."

"You decided to go?" Blaine asked Daniel.

"Uh-huh. Adam's going with me. He knows some of the people who are organizing it."

When we got into the cab, Daniel further explained the plan he'd concocted to meet Bonnie Seaforth-Wilkes and, hopefully, get an edge on landing the soap role. Blaine said the whole thing sounded improbable to him, but if the two of us wanted to spend a weekend contemplating our navels, he was grateful he didn't have to be part of it. He said he had enough of that "mystical bullshit" from Lillith Parker, who ran her life and business in constant consultation with various astrologers and psychics. He'd recently undergone an aura-fluffing to humor her.

Once we were in the apartment, Daniel gave me a tour of his garden, including the newly installed stone and bronze fountain. Then we sat at the bar so our conversation could include Blaine. From time to time, as he sautéed vegetables or prepared a marinade for the chicken breasts, Blaine would get Daniel to taste-test something. I felt a blend of longing and envy as I watched the easy intimacy between them.

"You know," I finally said, "I have an ulterior motive for going on this retreat." Before Daniel could say anything, I went on, "My friend Blythe seems to have some kind of connection to Ethan and Wade that she doesn't want me to know about." I gave them what background I knew on both men, then told them Blythe had pretended not to know Wade. I explained how she had evaded my questions after the party, where it had been obvious to me that Wade knew her, and finally, how she'd warned me away from both Wade and Ethan. "She's entitled to her privacy, of course. But I had lunch with Ethan one day and he seemed curious about her. I guess I feel protective of her."

Blaine pulled the chicken from the oven, gave it an intense look, then said in a joking tone, "Wade and Ethan are a couple. They're willing to pay large sums of money to Blythe if she'll have their turkey-baster baby."

"I'm pretty sure Wade and Ethan are not a couple. Their relationship seems to be one of economics and maybe friendship."

Blaine frowned; then his eyes brightened as he came up with another improbable scenario.

"Wade's art that you described: all forgeries. Blythe copies masterpieces for him, and he sells them to investors."

"Thank you, Perry Mason," Daniel said.

"He was gay, you know," Blaine commented.

"I didn't know that," I said.

Daniel gave a deep sigh and said, "Perry Mason—not gay. Raymond Burr—gay. Ever since I dragged Blaine kicking and screaming from the closet, he's been obsessed with who's gay."

Blaine laughed and said, "I've never screamed in my life. Anyway, your friends say I'm still in the closet."

"Actually, the partners at Blaine's firm asked him to evaluate their performance on diversity issues," Daniel said proudly. "And they're changing their benefits package to include domestic partners."

"That would never have happened in the first companies I worked for," I commented. "It's good to see things moving forward."

"Okay, that takes care of the mandatory politically correct stuff," Daniel said. "Back to your secret, Adam. You haven't told Blaine your real ulterior motive for going on this retreat."

"Uh—"

"Adam has a crush on *Jeremy!*" Daniel announced.

"Geez," Blaine said distastefully. "Why does everybody always know everyone else in this city?"

"If there are seven million people in New York, and ten percent of the general population is gay and lesbian, that means there are about seven-hundred-thousand of us," Daniel said in a singsong voice. "If fifty percent of the population is female, then we can assume that means there are only three-hundred-fifty-thousand gay men in Manhattan. Let's say ten percent of them are too young or too old to go out, ten percent of them are agoraphobic, ten percent of them are self-loathing social misfits, ten percent of them are—"

"I should never have taught him about demographic research," Blaine interrupted. "We get the picture. Six degrees of separation."

"No, ten percent of six-tight-jeans-of-separation," Daniel said. "Or five percent if you take out the lesbians."

"I'd never take out a lesbian," I said. "I don't support violence."

"They're rarely in season anyway," Daniel said.

"And that takes care of the politically *incorrect* portion of tonight," Blaine said. "Dinner's ready."

I got the idea that Blaine would rather not talk about Jeremy. But Daniel was not to be deterred.

"Jeremy has been so obnoxious with this new spiritual pursuit of his. I can't wait to see how his determination to keep his body pure holds up when Adam begins his seduction," Daniel said in a gleeful tone.

As he followed that thought down some road inside his head, I complimented Blaine on the food. That led us into a conversation about the best dietary needs for certain workout programs.

"I was serious," Blaine said, "about you being my guest at bodyWorks. It's been years since I had a workout partner."

"I've tried it a few times. My friends say I'm too competitive so they don't like to work out with me. When I lived in Madison, I had a really good workout partner, but I think that was because it was the only relationship we had."

"My worst problem is when I do free weights," Blaine said. "I'm never sure when I ask someone to spot me if he thinks I'm trying to pick him up."

"Oh, please," Daniel said. "I went to the gym with him once. The trainers were falling all over him. That's why I stick to running."

"You don't like working out with trainers?" I asked.

"Only because they don't fall all over *me*," Daniel said.

Later, as I helped them clear the table and clean up, I realized I hadn't felt that kind of camaraderie since sharing a place with roommates in college. It made me reluctant to return to my empty, boring apartment, but I finally gathered my stuff and shrugged into my jacket.

"I enjoyed this," I said. "Thanks for inviting me."

"I knew you and Blaine would get along," Daniel said. "As will you and Jeremy. You can see I have great taste in boyfriends. At least when they're not threatening your life."

"I protect what's mine," Blaine said without a trace of remorse.

We laughed and said our good-nights.

EIGHT

I had never been one for primping and preening. The way I saw it, if a guy wasn't interested in my natural first impression, he wasn't boyfriend material. Then again, I had never actively pursued anyone for more than a little fling or a one-night stand.

It was the first truly cold morning of November. I put the flannel shirts aside and pulled out a new black sweater. I ran my hand through my hair and looked in the full-length mirror in the bedroom. I actually missed getting ready under the watchful, super-sized eyes of Nancy the Waif. Once again I bemoaned the sterility of my corporate apartment. Even the scraggly plants in The Waifs Land had provided a certain comfort.

At least Prajna had been thrilled by the replacement plants. Daniel had warned me that some of her plants might hold sentimental value for her. He'd promised to return any of them that she missed if she was willing to wait until he had them flourishing again. But when I'd met her in Ray's office in Weehawken, she'd been understanding and said she was happy they were all in a good home.

I picked up my backpack and laptop and headed out the door. I got a cab almost immediately and directed the driver to Daniel's apartment so we could go to the retreat at Columbia University together. The introductory pamphlet said the retreat's title was "Spirit Matters: A Journey Through the Infinite Plain," and the keynote speaker was Ethan Whitecrow.

Daniel was sitting outside on the steps with a cup of coffee in one hand and the pamphlet in the other, dark glasses covering his eyes. The driver honked the horn, and Daniel got up and walked to the car, lugging a large leather duffel bag at his side. I reached across the backseat and let him in.

"Good morning," I said cheerfully.

"Isn't it, though?" he replied. "This should be an interesting weekend."

"Are you going to any of the workshops, or is this weekend fully dedicated to charming the turban off of Madame Fiberforth?"

"I thought of doing a past-life regression, but decided I don't need a shaman to tell me I was once a princess," Daniel said. "Who knows? Some of this stuff might actually work."

"I'll keep an open mind, but I'm not sure how much I believe in all this."

"I'm not sure if I believe in DKNY, but I still buy it. Anyway, if it's helpful to some, then more power to 'em," Daniel said.

As the cab made its way up the West Side, Daniel gave me more details about Jeremy's newfound spirituality and how his conversation recently had been filled with "Ethan says," "Ethan thinks," "Ethan believes." My heart sank for a second, but rebounded quickly. I was not one to be deterred by a little competition.

The car pulled up in front of our building just as I imagined myself tackling Ethan to the ground before he could score the final touchdown of the homecoming game.

The building stood proudly at the edge of a great expanse of rolling green lawn. A large banner hung down between two columns: deep-red writing on an ochre background announcing the retreat. A few college students walked across the grass; a small group sat in a circle in the middle of the lawn with cups of coffee in their hands and books on their laps.

Outside the building, attendees were gathering with ochre-colored folders in their hands. A group of women, each dressed in either a purple or green batik dress, stood beside one of the columns. As Daniel and I made our way up the steps, I heard one of them say, "Ethan is a dream. Not only is he handsome, but he has helped me make sense of all the questions that have plagued me all of my lives."

Her voice trailed off as we entered the building, and Daniel and I exchanged an amused glance.

"Apparently, Ethan couldn't help her work through her fashion issues," Daniel said. "Is that a laptop computer?"

"Yes," I said.

"Did you read the entire pamphlet? 'No watches, no cell phones, no pagers unless you're a healthcare provider,' " Daniel recited. "No laptop computers."

"I left my watch at home, my cell phone ringer is off, and if you don't tell them about the laptop, I won't."

"Mutinous Mac User Impedes World Peace," Daniel intoned in his best newscaster voice.

After registration, Daniel and I parted ways to drop off our belongings in our rooms. Daniel was staying in the East Campus Hotel, while I was at the Union Theological Seminary. I was led to my room, which overlooked a garden and was a far cry from the kind of freshman dorm space I'd expected. As I stared from the window, I heard the door open behind me and turned to see a tall, thin man whom I immediately dubbed Ichabod Crane.

"Hello, I'm Harold Smith. You must be Adam."

"Adam Wilson," I agreed, shaking his outstretched hand.

"Yes, Wade told me we'd be rooming together for the weekend." When I merely gave him a blank look, wondering how Wade had known that I would be at the retreat, he continued, "Wade Van Atterson. I clerk for his attorney. One of our secretaries helped Ethan and Wade coordinate the weekend's activities."

"Right," I said for lack of any other intelligent comment.

"I just want you to know, Adam, that I'm not gay."

I wondered if the man thought I had designs on him, but I merely repeated, "Right."

"It's not a problem for me that you are, of course. I embrace your—er—gayness."

With his bad toupee, I knew he wasn't embracing anything of mine.

"That's not a laptop in that case, I hope," Harold said, glancing at my bed, where I'd dropped my bags.

"A laptop? Computer?" I asked. I wondered if I had lost all ability to form a meaningful sentence.

"You know, we're not supposed to have any electronic connection to the outside world. That's why it's called a *retreat*," he said with a grin that looked more like a grimace. "I'm sure they'll be happy to keep your computer safely locked up for you."

"I, uh—"

"We really should be going if we're going to make the opening reception." He plucked my laptop from the bed. "We can turn this in on our way."

"No! I mean, don't trouble yourself. I can turn it in later."

With a smug shake of his head, he said, "Nuh-uh-uh, Adam, rules are rules. Believe me, once you get involved in the retreat, you'll be glad it's in a safe place and you don't have to worry about it." Harold obviously considered this his mission, so I gave in, deciding I could sneak back later and retrieve the laptop from whomever he checked it with. As if reading my mind, he said, "In fact, if we hurry, they'll still be checking in the late arrivals. The retreat organizers can put your laptop with all the cell phones and pagers that have been turned in."

I couldn't wait to find Daniel and berate him for getting me involved in this ordeal. The thought of being without computer access for a weekend was even less appealing than my roommate.

I sighed and surrendered myself to the gods of the "infinite plain," or whatever the hell brand of spirituality Ethan and Wade were selling. If they'd been kinder gods, I might have drawn Jeremy as a roommate instead of this escapee from Sleepy Hollow.

After relinquishing my laptop to the wardens of Feasley Hall, I ditched Harold to look for Daniel. The banquet room bustled with men and women doused in patchouli, a smell that reminded me of dirty sweat socks. Some appeared to be wealthy homemakers who were trying to fill a void. Others, like me, seemed to be neophytes who had come out of curiosity or perhaps felt they needed a sense of spirituality in a high-tech world. I began to feel more at ease and hopeful that being at the retreat wasn't such a bad idea.

Lunch was casual. Tables stretched up and down each side of the hall, leaving the center clear for attendees to wander and mingle. Those who were holding workshops wore special name badges to differentiate them. I noticed a tall man who looked more like a college professor than a New Age guru. People seemed to be descending on him from all directions. A voice spoke from behind me.

"That man is one of the top hypnotists in the country. I hear he works wonders."

I cringed, realizing whose voice it was.

"Hello, Wade. What a"—I paused to conjure up a little tact—"pleasant surprise."

"Don't be surprised. I'm funding this spiritual gala."

"Will you be attending any of the workshops?"

"Oh, yes. I have gained such a respect for Ethan's work." Someone seemed to catch his attention. "That one over there has, as well. He follows Ethan around like a lost puppy."

I followed Wade's gaze to see Jeremy talking to Ethan and Bonnie Seaforth-Wilkes. She was, as I'd warned Daniel, wearing a turban. Not far from them I saw Daniel looking expectantly around the room. I figured he was trying to find a way to corner Bonnie, but I needed an excuse to get away from Wade.

"If you'll excuse me, Wade, my friend is waiting for me."

"Of course."

It sounded as if he said something else, but I lost it as I wedged myself into the crowd and wove and ducked until I reached Daniel. I also kept one eye on Ethan and his entourage, looking to see if Jeremy had pulled away.

"Daniel," I moaned when I finally reached him.

"Problem?"

"You better have a really shitty roommate or I'm going to do terrible things to you," I vowed.

He gave me a bright smile and said, "I got lucky. My guy canceled at the last minute, so I have a room to myself."

"Not anymore, you don't. The first chance we have to make a break for it, we're getting my stuff and moving me to your room."

"Don't tell me you ended up with Wade Van Atterson?" Daniel asked.

"That better not be happiness I see in your eyes," I warned. "Actually, my roomie wants to embrace my inner gayness to prove how tolerant he is. And he's a dead ringer for Ichabod Crane!"

"Your roommate looks like Johnny Depp?"

"Johnny Depp?"

"Yeah, isn't that who's doing the remake of *The Legend of*—"

"No, he looks like Tiny Tim."

"That's Dickens."

"Not that Tiny Tim, you ass, the one who tiptoed through the tulips."

"As long as he only wants to embrace your *inner* gayness," Daniel laughed. When I stared at him he said, "Okay. Operation Move Adam will take place whenever we have our first break. Have you figured out your schedule?"

"Yes, and you?"

"I have. It would seem that Bonnie and I are both in need of some cleansing."

"I hope that doesn't mean taking a bath together."

"I don't think so. The description said something about crystals. I chose it because I happened to catch a glimpse of Bonnie's schedule and noticed it was the only workshop that would give me a chance to interact with her."

"I haven't gotten close enough to Jeremy to find out anything like that."

"I think I can arrange for you two to meet. But handle him carefully. He's at that stage of celebrity where he pretends to be bored by admiration."

Before I could argue with Daniel, the strike of a gong caught everyone's attention and killed all conversation. In one motion, the entire congregation whipped their heads around to the front of the hall. The New Age guru, whose name I noticed in the program was Ernest Berman, was calling us to attention. He stood behind a podium and tapped the microphone, which caused a screech to fill the entire hall. He cleared his throat, then began speaking in a calming, hypnotic voice.

"Welcome," he began, "to the tenth annual Festival of Inner Light. This year's theme, Spirit Matters . . ."

He continued to speak as my gaze fell on Ethan, who was leading Jeremy behind a curtain. I clenched my jaw and felt the blood rush to my face. No one else seemed to notice, or if they did, they didn't care. Ten minutes after Ethan absconded with Jeremy in tow, the crowd was released with a half-hour more to mingle or figure out how to get to the rooms or lounges where the various workshops were taking place. Daniel and I both stepped outside before embarking on our separate spiritual journeys. As I stood between two columns looking over the lawn, I noticed two girls being chased by a group of whooping guys. As they neared, I had a realization. Daniel did, too, and burst into a fit of laughter.

"Who knew? Jocks do drag!"

The two "girls" were actually two beefy guys dressed as cheerleaders. They were both wearing blond wigs done up into pigtails, their faces were blushed and freckled, and their bosoms were stuffed with jockstraps. I figured that out only because the lead "girl" lost one of her straps as the group ran around the corner of

Feasley Hall. They stopped in front of the steps and began doing a very clumsy routine. Their pursuers all stood around and clapped. After they landed in faux splits, got up, and readjusted themselves, they were off and running again.

"They could use some makeup tips," Daniel commented.

"A lot of my friends had to undergo similar rituals to get into their chosen fraternities," I said. "I'm glad I chose a different kind of Greek experience."

"You go, Caligula," Daniel said.

"He was Roman. I think you mean Spartacus."

The gong alerted us that it was time to move on. Daniel and I quickly agreed to meet at my room later, when everyone else converged for the communal dinner, to carry out Operation Move Adam. He was sure we'd make it to dinner in time for me to get a proper introduction to Jeremy.

I'd chosen a workshop with the promising title "Retrieve Your Power Animal." I walked into a small, candlelit room with blankets and pillows scattered on the floor. I felt an immediate affinity for our facilitator, Mae, because her tiny body swathed in diaphanous layers of fabric made me think of Blythe's Stevie Nicks getup. She introduced herself as a shamanic practitioner and explained a bit about the concept of drumming, journeying, and soul retrieval.

Gradually, I found that all thoughts of Jeremy, Daniel, and the retreat itself faded as I focused on Mae's discussion of power animals. I had to smile when she said that most parents unconsciously provide their children with animal protectors from infancy, with stuffed toys like teddy bears, lambs, and rabbits. I thought about my own teddy bear, Oscar, who still sat on the mantel in my parents' house in all his worn and tattered glory.

By the time we went through all the meditation exercises, I could easily have curled up on the floor and slept. Instead, I lay next to a woman named Linda, our sides touching, while Mae beat a steady, mesmerizing rhythm on a shamanic drum. I had no problem with the visualization technique Mae had taught us. Whenever I closed my eyes, I was immediately transported to a place on my property in Wisconsin. I could see the pond that sat in a copse of trees behind my house. I imagined myself sitting on one of the large flat rocks that overlooked the pond.

Mae had explained that the first animal that presented itself to me four times was Linda's power animal. Among the array of hawks, deer, and beavers that came into my head, only the hawk appeared four times. When the meditation ended and I told Linda what I'd seen, she seemed delighted by the hawk. Mae explained that the hawk teaches us to be observant and not overlook things such as a talent we don't use or a blessing we have not been thankful for.

I was a little nervous as we began the next meditation, during which Linda would retrieve my power animal. I was surprised to find myself taking it all so seriously. I had genuinely put aside my skepticism so I could learn something—I just wasn't sure what that might be or whether I'd like it.

When Mae began drumming, I didn't try to journey again. Instead I let myself think about Jeremy. It baffled me that someone I'd seen only a couple of times, with whom I'd never shared a real conversation or seemed to have much in common, and who apparently had sworn off dating, had invaded my waking and sleeping hours as Jeremy had. Even though I'd felt that rush of jealousy when I saw him leave with Ethan, I couldn't chalk up this preoccupation to my competitive nature. I'd been interested in Jeremy at first sight, after all.

I realized the drumming had stopped and everyone was sitting up. Others in our group heard the identities and meanings of their power animals. Linda just smiled at me, waiting our turn.

"This time I didn't see my meadow," Linda finally said. "I was at the edge of a huge, grassy plain. I wasn't sure where I was. I saw a buffalo, so I thought it was the Midwest." I nodded, thinking that made sense; then she went on. "But then I saw an elephant and a tiger, so I thought I might be in India. Then I heard this rumbling noise, and I thought the buffalo was running back, but I saw a lot of zebras. After that, I saw all kinds of animals, but one zebra came back to look at me three more times. Adam's power animal is a zebra."

Mae nodded, and I sat still, awaiting her explanation.

"Zebra," she said, "is about dualities. For example, the zebra is safe from predators, who can't distinguish one zebra from another. But other zebras recognize all the members of the herd as unique. Zebra as a power animal helps you maintain your individuality while being a supportive member of your community. Also, the contrast of the black-and-white stripes teaches you something about integrating the opposite sides of your nature to see a deeper truth. Remember that your power animal is not only a protector but a guide, strong in qualities you may be lacking."

Mae held my gaze for a few seconds longer. I felt as if she were trying to convey a message to me, as if she'd seen something I didn't know I was revealing. Usually, that would be unnerving, but once again she reminded me of Blythe, who often made me feel like her little black glasses were a microscope.

My first instinct was to run to my laptop and look up everything I could about power animals and zebras; then I remembered that was no longer possible. As the others went on talking, I recalled the words of my buddy the limo driver: *"Look around at what your life has brought you . . . Life's bigger than the Internet . . ."*

Later I walked back to the Union Theological Seminary in a daze. Daniel was waiting outside, so I tried to compose myself. But he, too, seemed a bit subdued.

"Did you get to talk to Bonnie?" I asked.

"You know, I fully intended to," Daniel said. "But the weirdest thing happened. I really got into this discussion of crystals and energy. I know some of these people are really out there, but some of them seem so . . ."

"Enlightened?" I suggested.

"Or at least sincere. I found myself wanting to protect them from my cynical inner voice."

"I know exactly what you mean," I said. "But I'm still not sleeping with Ichabod."

"Oh, hell no," Daniel agreed. "He was in my group, I think. Harold something?"

"That's him."

"Let's get your stuff."

There was no one else around, so we proceeded without detection from my room to Daniel's. After I dropped my bag on the bed, we figured we had time to catch the end of dinner. Several people frowned at our late arrival, but we got our food and found a place to sit together. As I ate, I scanned the room but didn't see Jeremy, Ethan, or Wade.

"Did you talk to Bonnie at all?" I finally asked.

"You don't really talk to Bonnie. You listen. She's been all over the world seeking spiritual guidance. She doesn't seem very comfortable with the whole Seaforth Chemicals thing."

"Would *you* want to be known as the heiress to Fiberforth?" I asked.

"Somebody made a cleansing joke to her," Daniel said. "She wasn't amused."

"Like Sheila and Autumn Dusk," I suggested.

Daniel almost spit out his baked chicken, and we both cracked up.

"Having a good time?" Ethan asked, stopping by our table with Jeremy.

We composed ourselves as Daniel introduced me to Jeremy, and I introduced Daniel to Ethan.

"I've already heard all about you," Ethan said, putting his hands on my shoulders. "The contraband laptop, and now your roommate is worried because you've vanished without a trace."

"I haven't vanished," I argued. "I'm right here."

"I suppose you'll do whatever you want, but I would like to remind you this weekend is meant to be *spiritually* enriching," Ethan said a little reprovingly, stepping around me so I could see his face.

His gaze was measuring, and I had a sudden thought. If Ethan had noticed my name on the list of retreat participants, maybe he'd assumed that I was attending as a ruse to see him again. Since I'd made no effort to connect with him during the day, he must have been rethinking my motives, and Daniel probably seemed like the answer. That was fine with me, since I had no intention of letting him know that Jeremy was my real quarry.

"I think I told you in our last meeting that I was looking for a way to step back from the frantic pace of the city," I reminded him. "Daniel presented me with the perfect opportunity."

"I hope you find what you're looking for," Ethan said.

"I intend to."

Jeremy's face was puzzled, as if he sensed a current of animosity between Ethan and me, then he looked at Daniel.

"Could I talk to you for a minute, Daniel? Alone?"

Daniel glanced at me then said, "Sure."

They walked away from the table, and I returned my attention to Ethan.

"I'm looking forward to your talk tomorrow," I said. "What little I learned about shamanism today was interesting and—"

"Daniel's friend Jeremy is a very honest person," Ethan cut me off. "He told me Daniel's main reason for attending was to meet Bonnie. But Jeremy also says Daniel has been through some painful experiences recently. Jeremy hopes the weekend will give him a few coping skills. As I said, this conference was designed for spiritual enrichment, not as a romantic getaway."

"Does that go for the organizers as well as the inmates?" I asked, suddenly annoyed by his tone and his assumptions about Daniel and me.

"Of course."

"Good. I'll be sure and tell Wade if he makes anymore suggestive comments to me. And Harold can rest without fear that I might lose control and ravish him."

Ethan laughed in spite of himself and said, "Harold can be a bit of a jerk, I know. Believe me, the sleeping arrangements were made entirely at random. But we do try to keep friends and couples separate."

"I won't be ravishing Daniel, either," I reassured him with as much graciousness as I could manage.

As Jeremy and Daniel made their way back to our table, Ethan quickly said, "We kept missing each other's calls after the day we met in Central Park. Then I got so busy—"

"I've been busy, too," I said.

"I'm sorry if I sounded harsh earlier. I enjoyed our lunch that day, even if it was cut short. Maybe after my speech tomorrow night, we could meet for a while. Just the two of us."

I couldn't resist taunting him a little and asked, "In an *un*romantic way?"

"Just to talk."

"Sure."

"Good," Ethan said. "Jeremy, are you ready?"

Jeremy nodded, barely glancing at me before the two of them continued on their way.

"So much for making a good impression," I commented.

"On Jeremy? Ethan gave him the idea there was something going on between you and me, but I took care of that. I told him you were one of my high school tormentors."

"You *what?*"

"I'm kidding," Daniel said, grinning at me. "He did ask about Blaine, and I told him things were fine at home. I think he got a bit of a scolding from Ethan about the Bonnie mission. That's what he really wanted to talk to me about, to make sure I hadn't ambushed her. He doesn't want me to make him look bad. I don't know what kind of hold that guy has over him. I've never seen Jeremy so submissive. I think we may have to call in one of those deprogrammers before he shaves his head. Saffron is *not* his color."

"I wonder what it would take to get his attention," I mused.

"What is it about Jeremy that intrigues you so much?" Daniel asked. "You haven't even gotten to see the best of him."

"I've been trying to figure that out," I said. "It's not like me. Generally, I see what I want and take it by the most direct route possible. If it resists, I move on."

"Maybe it's time you had a challenge," Daniel said.

"Maybe. That gong is starting to make me feel like I'm being herded," I complained as it sounded again.

Daniel sat as quietly as I did through that night's talk, titled "Compassion in Action." He may have been paying attention, but my thoughts were all over the place. I wanted to know exactly what the relationship was between Jeremy and Ethan. I wondered whether, if I had time alone with Jeremy, I could make him look at me as he had the night of Wade's party, or whether he would continue to look through me. I'd certainly had no trouble getting Wade's attention, but I suspected that might have something to do with Blythe. For the hundredth time I suppressed my curiosity about why she'd concealed knowing Wade. Instead, I thought about her Web site; then my mind drifted to other clients and the work I'd planned to do on my laptop over the weekend, which was no longer possible. I'd counted on having time to further develop my Club Chaos project before a Tuesday meeting with Andy.

My reverie was interrupted by a gentle snore, and I nudged Daniel, whose eyes flew open.

"Did I just snore?" Daniel asked.

"Yes," I whispered.

"At least I wasn't drooling."

"Yet," I said.

We were both relieved when the talk ended. Since we couldn't seem to spot either Bonnie or Jeremy among the crowd, we decided to walk back to our room. Daniel flopped down on his bed while I went in the bathroom and brushed my teeth and washed my face. When I came out, he seemed to have fallen asleep again, so I kicked off my shoes and pulled my sweater over my head. When I unbuttoned my jeans and slid them down, I heard Daniel laugh. I turned to look at him.

"What?"

"What does this sound like? Two high school enemies go away to some remote spot and find themselves rooming together. One is half asleep; the other begins to undress."

"Perfect beginning of a porn flick," I said.

"It's like one of my high school fantasies. Rooming with a jock. As I'm falling asleep, he's overcome by lust and starts to ravage me. I wonder how many times I visualized that happening with Bill Hamilton when we were stuck in that teenage wasteland you call home. Unfortunately, it never happened. Bill's as straight as he can be."

"With me it was Lars Ziegler," I said. "Only mine came true."

"No shit?" Daniel sat up on his bed and stared at me as I crawled under the covers on my bed. "Do tell."

"As long as this conversation falls under the code of silence," I said.

"Who the hell would I tell? Okay, maybe Blaine. But I don't talk to anyone else from Eau Claire. Except Sheila, and I won't tell her."

He listened with wide eyes as I told him the whole story of Rachel Monroe's graduation party.

"I always knew Rachel was a bitch," he said when I finished.

"It's funny, though; she never told anyone what happened. Or if she did, I never heard about it."

"Did you and Lars ever talk about it afterward?"

"Not for a long time. He spent that summer working for his uncle in St. Paul. By the time he came back, I'd left for college. Once I came out to all our friends, he avoided me. It's only been over the past couple of years, since I moved back to Eau Claire, that we started talking again." I broke off, then decided to trust Daniel. "He makes me sad. He's so unhappy in his closet. He's really let himself go. He'd have been much better off if he'd done what you did."

"I can't picture Lars in drag," Daniel said.

I laughed and tossed one of my pillows at him, saying, "Not that, you nut. Moving away so he could get comfortable with himself and have a more fulfilling life."

"At least he didn't get married and make some woman as miserable as he is," Daniel said. "Besides, a lot of those guys who fled to the cities are dead now. I don't know how I dodged that bullet."

"I know how I dodged it," I said. "I think Lars and I were each other's first. Then I got lucky with the first man I dated in college. He was a professor—not one of mine—and he'd moved to Wisconsin from San Francisco, so he was politically and socially aware. As little as I liked his lectures about being safe, he had too many stories of lost friends for me to shrug off his warnings. And once my parents got involved with PFLAG, I got the same lectures from home."

"Ken filled that role for me," Daniel said. "He went with me to get my first test. He was so happy when it came back negative. It was the first time I really felt like what I did mattered to someone. Staying well became a way I could repay him for all the ways he took care of me."

"Were you and Ken ever lovers?" I asked.

"No. I wasn't attracted to him at first. Later I went through a phase when I felt like I was falling in love with him. But Ken never had those feelings for me. He'd had a great love, a guy named Samuel, who had a heart attack and died not long before I met Ken. In a lot of ways, Ken never got over that loss. He wasn't looking for a lover."

"But you said he and Martin were together."

"Yeah, that started less than a year before Ken died. I never realized it, but I think Ken had his eye on Martin for a long time. He was always protective of him. I think he worried about the difference in their ages, or about infecting Martin, or about dying and leaving him behind. I don't know how they got past all that, but they made the most of those final months. Ken was happier than I'd ever seen him, and nobody could have been more devoted than Martin was. Martin can be quite a flake, but he kept Ken laughing until the end. I'll always love him for that."

Daniel broke off, his eyes faraway, as if he were watching scenes from his past. I suddenly sensed how fragile he was. I remembered Blaine expressing his concern for what Daniel was going through. His loss was so recent . . .

I left my bed and went to sit next to him, pulling him into a hug. He didn't resist, instead seeming to melt into my embrace. I'd never held a crying man before, but my instincts told me to stay quiet.

"Well," Daniel finally said, "this is probably what Jeremy and Blaine wanted me to do. I don't think anyone would have guessed you'd be the lucky witness."

"Is this the first time you've cried?" I asked softly, reaching for the box of tissues next to the bed.

He blew his nose and mopped up.

"Since Ken died? No. Just the first time with anyone else around."

"Why is that, do you think?"

"Why not with anyone else, or why with you?"

"Either. Both."

"I don't know. Maybe because I didn't want to set anyone else off. Maybe because you didn't know Ken. It's funny; the last time I cried like this was when Jeremy and I made peace after our breakup. Now I'm wondering if anyone's been taking care of Jeremy."

"Maybe Ethan?" I suggested.

"I don't think so. Jeremy's eyes are like looking into a mirror and seeing my sadness. He probably got shut out of a lot, because he and Martin barely tolerate each other. It's possible Robert has been supportive. Although Jeremy has spent a lot of time with his family lately. There's a huge clan of Caprellians in Brooklyn. They're so good to him. But I feel like Jeremy, Martin, and I are all locked into our separate ways of mourning right now. Ken would have disapproved. He counted on us to take care of each other."

"It hasn't been that long since he died," I said. "It could be that you all need some space for a while. I think it will work out. This may sound crazy, but in spite of what you've lost, I'm jealous."

"Jealous?"

"I've got a great family, like Jeremy's. But after I left college, I never took the time to make a family of friends. My mother tells me I'm missing out. She practically forced me to come to New York for that very reason."

"She was right. Other than Blythe and Sheila, you've met Blaine and me. And it's just a matter of time until you connect with Jeremy."

"Don't forget Andy, Wade, and Ethan," I said, scrunching up my face in distaste.

"Every family has its—oh, my god, I have the most brilliant

idea!" His face was transformed, and I waited, wondering what scheme he was devising. "Do you know about the town house?"

"What town house?"

"Ken owned a town house on Jane Street in the Village. Martin moved in with Ken prior to Ken's death."

"I would hope Martin didn't move in with Ken *after* his death," I joked, then cringed because the comment might have seemed in poor taste.

But Daniel started laughing and said, "Ken would've adored you. Your sense of humor is a lot like his. Anyway, Ken left Martin a trust fund, but he left the town house to me. I'm sure he had no idea how much trouble that would cause. Blaine's all for Martin moving into my apartment, and Blaine and me moving into the town house. I think that's heartless; to me it would be like forcing Martin to lose Ken all over again. But no matter how often I tell Martin it's his home, he's sure I plan to kick him out. In anticipation of that, he treats me like the cruel landlord. Which pisses me off, because I've had to take crap from Blaine about it. I feel like I'm caught in the middle no matter what I do."

"So what's your brilliant idea?"

"You hate the apartment you're in now. If you moved in with Martin, he'd finally believe I wasn't going to displace him. The town house has three stories. The main floor was Ken's apartment. The other two are rented. One to a couple who just got married last spring, and the other to a woman who might have settled here when the city was still called New Amsterdam. Ken didn't have the heart to make her move when he bought the place. He felt he had more than enough room for himself on the main floor. So he told her she could stay and reduced her rent to fifty dollars a month. If I promise Blaine that when one of the other floors becomes available he and I can move in, he'll probably stop hounding me about it. What do you think?"

"Are you sure Martin wants a roommate?" I asked.

"Did the retreat ogres confiscate your cell phone, too?" Daniel asked.

"No. It's in my bag."

"Martin should be home from the club by now. Let's call him and see what he thinks."

I got the phone for Daniel. I had no shame about eavesdropping, and Daniel and I stared at each other while he talked.

"Hi, Martin. How are you? Uh-huh . . . Uh-huh . . . You do not have crow's feet. . . . Nuh-uh . . . Nuh-uh . . . You do not. Listen, an old friend of mine needs a place to stay, and I was thinking maybe"—Daniel broke off and rolled his eyes, holding the phone away and frowning at it as if a Sprint representative was on the other end trying to get him to switch his long-distance. "Martin, I'm not bringing him there tonight. I'm away for the weekend. Monday . . . Uh-huh . . . Uh-huh . . . A feng shui expert? Why . . . ? It is not. The feng shui is not all wrong for two people there. Two people lived there once before, Martin. You and Ken lived there and nothing bad happened," Daniel said, an obvious strain in his voice. "Ken died of AIDS. He did not die from bad feng shui. . . . I know you weren't suggesting that. . . . No, you're not a moron. . . . Fine. I'll see you soon."

He disconnected the phone and handed it to me.

"Not crazy about the idea?" I asked.

"Sometimes I feel like I have a teenage daughter," Daniel said. "Once he meets you, he'll be fine. Just remember not to believe anything he says about Jeremy. Those two are like Zsa Zsa Gabor and a cop."

"Which one is the cop?" I asked with a leer.

Daniel laughed and said, "This is the only inside information I'm going to give you. Jeremy will *not* disappoint you in bed."

"Bed? I can't even make him look at me!"

"Please," Daniel said. "Trust me. He's checked you out. I don't know Ethan, but I suspect that Jeremy will quickly tire of being one in a flock of many. Jeremy is high-maintenance in the attention department. And unless he's done a one-eighty, he's not cut out for celibacy. Jeremy can be one of the most self-assured people I know, but his weakness is his career. I'd be willing to bet this whole spiritual quest he's on has something to do with his fear of his sitcom being canceled. These New Age zealots have probably convinced him that success is all a matter of visualization, tarot cards, and astrology, when in fact he's a brilliant actor. He'd do better with Scientologists."

"Oh, I love Tom Cruise. What sign is he?" I asked.

"Tom Cruise?"

"Jeremy."

"Do you believe in that stuff?"

"I do have all the qualities of a Gemini," I admitted.

"I'm a typical Virgo, too. Jeremy's a Leo."

"I dated a Leo once. They're exciting, charming, and funny, but a little self-absorbed. They have a tough time laughing at themselves, and they hate being laughed at."

"That's Jeremy."

"You know what the best sign for a Leo is?" I asked.

"Beware of cat?"

I laughed and said, "Gemini. Speaking of astrology, our seven AM return to the spirit world will be brutal if we don't get some sleep."

I crawled back into my bed while Daniel went to the bathroom. He came out and turned off the lights before he settled into his own bed.

"Adam?"

"Mmmm," I said, already half asleep.

"Thank you."

"You're welcome," I mumbled and the next thing I knew Daniel was shaking me awake.

"It is not morning," I protested, pulling the covers over my head.

I felt comforted by the sounds of someone else getting ready— the shower, the hair dryer, the little coffeemaker gurgling in the corner. I might never know what it was like to live with a boyfriend, but it could be nice to have a roommate. I was actually looking forward to winning Martin over.

It was a dreary Saturday, cold with the promise of rain, but I felt like the sun was shining down on me when I discovered Jeremy in my chakra-balancing workshop. He smiled when he saw me come in and gestured for me to sit next to him.

"How'd you sleep?" he asked.

"Like a quartz crystal," I said.

"Vibrating?"

"No, we didn't have any quarters," I said. "What about you?"

"I've got plenty of quarters."

"Maybe I should sleep in your bed tonight."

His eyes widened for a second; then he burst out laughing. Several people, apparently in the throes of morning meditation, turned to frown at him.

"Wouldn't you think the means to enlightenment would be to lighten up?" I whispered.

"I personally think the means to enlightenment is watching a *Simpsons* marathon on TV."

It was my turn to be frowned at as I released a most unseemly guffaw. We settled down like two chastened schoolboys as our facilitator turned an eye on us.

I wasn't sure what Jeremy got out of the ensuing discussion of energy centers in the body, but I definitely felt a shift in the charge between us, especially when Jeremy lay down and I positioned crystals on him as directed by our facilitator, Phil. When I placed a rose quartz on Jeremy's heart, his eyes fluttered open. I wondered why I'd never realized how rich and deep brown eyes could be. Our gazes locked for a moment.

"Adam," he said softly.

"Jeremy?"

"Stop."

"Stop what?"

"You know what."

I put a turquoise on his throat and said, "That's for communication. Stop what?"

"Stop looking at me like you're going to devour me."

I gently placed a piece of lapis on his forehead and said, "That one is for awareness."

"I'm not having a problem with awareness," he said.

"Good."

"Are you two focusing on your chakra colors?" Phil asked, appearing next to me and moving the lapis between Jeremy's eyebrows.

"I'm very focused," I said, still looking into Jeremy's eyes. An actual blush crept over his cheeks as he stared back at me.

When Phil moved away, Jeremy closed his eyes. I could feel him shutting himself off, but I wasn't worried. He had definitely felt the electricity between us, and he would remember it long after he forgot what color corresponded to his root chakra.

I was even more convinced of that when he practically fled from the room as soon as our session ended.

I didn't care if he was running back to Ethan. I was sure he'd never look through me again.

After lunch, Daniel and I dozed together through a dream interpretation workshop. Then he went to a tarot reader while I explored the wonderful world of numerology. Finally, it was time for dinner, where Jeremy sat at a table with Ethan, Wade, and Bonnie, his back resolutely turned to me. As everyone walked to the auditorium later, however, Jeremy caught up with Daniel and me.

"After Ethan's talk," he spoke hurriedly to Daniel, avoiding my eyes, "I've gotten Bonnie to agree to do a meditation with me in my room. Drop by, as if it was unplanned, and I'll ask you to meditate with us. Then you can walk her to her room and talk about the soap role."

"Thanks, Jeremy," Daniel said. As Jeremy rushed away, Daniel turned to me. "You could go with me. When I leave with Bonnie, you'd be alone with Jeremy."

"Damn it," I said. "I told Ethan we could get together after his talk."

"Maybe he forgot," Daniel suggested hopefully.

"No, my numerology facilitator gave me an envelope with the key to Ethan's guest suite at the International House," I said. "I'm supposed to wait for him there."

"Does it occur to you that Ethan might think there's something going on between you and him?" Daniel asked.

"The thought has crossed my mind."

We found two seats together just before a woman took the stage to introduce Ethan. As frustrated as I felt about missing the chance to be alone with Jeremy, once Ethan began talking, he had my full attention. Daniel's rapt expression indicated that he, too, felt the power of Ethan's personality.

"When I was eighteen years old, the day after I graduated from high school, I found myself cast into an indifferent world. A boy without money, without prospects, without family support. I had been told by my parents that if I was honest and worked hard, I would never be disadvantaged by my status as a Native American, a descendant of the Wyandot tribe. In fact, I was taught to see my heritage as a gift. At eighteen, my gift became my curse. Adhering to my code of honesty, I told my parents I was gay. As their only son, they heard my news as if it were a bell tolling the end of their dreams. I would not marry and have children and continue our proud heritage. I would live outside the American dream of clean living, hard work, and great accomplishment. In their disappointment, they were the first to cast me out." Ethan paused, as if looking back at his past, then smiled. "It is wise to remember that our curse often becomes our blessing."

"It takes guts to tell an auditorium full of strangers that you're gay," Daniel whispered.

"Yeah," I agreed, wishing I didn't admire the man who was my competition for Jeremy's affections.

Ethan went on to detail what he called his "wander years," when he worked on communal farms, lived on the streets, and traveled through the United States as well as India and Egypt, expanding his consciousness by many means, including teachers, shamans, gurus, nature, drugs, wealthy and poor men, yoga masters, sisters, priests, and animals. Even when a benefactor gave him the opportunity to go to school and earn degrees in Native American studies and adolescent psychology, he felt that he still carried with him that wound inflicted at age eighteen.

"Spirit matters," Ethan said after another pause. "It's a clever title on many levels. Spirit is important. Or it is good to examine matters of the spirit. But the meaning I most like is that spirit and matter are one thing. Spirit is not some ephemeral concept divorced from the body or from the mind. Spirit, like the body which houses us, or the physiological systems that give us thought, is also matter. And it is only by bringing all this different matter into harmonic alignment that we can be healed of our wounds, whether they be psychological, emotional, physical, or spiritual."

He continued talking about the various workshops available over the weekend and what we might take from them. Then he said, "From my own perspective, in light of my past, I believe I'm on a healing journey. Healing my Self. Healing those with whom I share the planet. Healing even the planet itself. Shamanism was a natural progression from my psychology background and interest in Native American tradition and history. I enhanced it with many different philosophies and practices I learned during my 'wander years.' Shamanism integrates the whole—physical, spiritual, emotional, mental—into healing. When I say I'm a shamanic healer, what I mean is that I assist people, and my Self, on a healing journey."

"But what does this mean to me?" Daniel suddenly whispered.

"It's always about you," I teased as quietly.

"You may be asking yourself, what does the story of my life and journey mean to you?" Ethan asked.

Daniel turned wide eyes to me, then we both stared straight ahead at Ethan, wondering if he had supersensitive hearing.

"So often," Ethan continued, "I encounter people who are lost. They are in grief. They are in denial. They are in recovery or addiction or in places of abuse. They search and they suffer. They meet quacks and charlatans and often cannot discern them from true healers and nurturers. They isolate themselves on mountaintops, bury themselves in work, desperately seek relationships to fulfill an aching inner need. Spirit matters. What does not matter is your method. The challenge of your journey is to acknowledge spirit in all that you touch or that touches you, in everything you see and hear, in every act and every choice not to act. When you accept this challenge, you begin to feel oneness with all. Everything becomes a lesson and a gift. And healing happens. Because of us, sometimes in spite of us, healing is ongoing. Infinite."

Ethan paused as if to consider his next words, and the entire audience seemed to hold its collective breath.

"Breathe," he suddenly said with a brilliant smile. "There are hundreds of words for peace. I leave you with these: *Shanti. Shalom. Ashti. Sidi. Mina.* Peace on your journey."

As Ethan stepped away from the podium, the room exploded into applause. Daniel turned to me.

"He's so strong," he said.

"I'll pass that on when I'm stuck with him while you meditate with Jeremy," I said without any real hostility. I was impressed with Ethan in spite of myself.

I walked alone to the International House. Ethan's suite had a sitting area separate from his bedroom. All the makings for herbal tea were set out, which I took as my cue to brew it. I looked toward the door as I heard a key turn in the lock.

"Wade!" I said, stunned.

"Adam F-for-Fortunate Wilson," Wade said, his confused expression quickly replaced by gloating. "I had no idea you'd be here."

"I'm supposed to meet Ethan," I said quickly, turning back to the tea.

He slipped his arms around me from behind and murmured, "Come here often?" I patted his arm, then removed it from around my waist. "What's the matter, Adam? Don't you think I'm attractive?"

"It's not that, Wade—"

"I know I'm no youngster anymore, especially by gay standards, but I don't think I'm too bad for an old guy. You could do lots worse."

Blythe's voice came to me: *"He collects everything."*

I felt my jaw tighten with determination.

"You're very handsome, Wade. It's just—"

"Come on, then. Give us a kiss." He reached for me. I evaded him and slipped around the opposite side of the tea cart. We squared off and each worked our way clockwise around the cart, keeping equidistant from each other in our rendition of the Tea Tray Tango.

"Wade, stop," I said, trying to discourage him. "My head is full of Ethan's talk. I've got a lot to think about."

"Oh, please, Adam. You're not going to hop on his bandwagon, too, are you? And start following Ethan around like that pathetic Jeremy?"

I was really starting to dislike Wade Van Atterson. As he lunged for me, my old football training came in handy. I faked to the right, then dodged to the left. Wade's momentum carried him to the right, causing him to trip over an ottoman. His arms were nowhere close to breaking his fall, and his head crashed against a chair. When I knelt down to see if he was hurt, I was assaulted by the unmistakable smell of gin.

I knew then he was okay. Drunks always were. I easily dragged him into Ethan's bedroom and deposited him on the bed. To be on the safe side, I left the suite and went outside to wait for Ethan. I didn't care how cold I got. I had no intention of fending off more of Wade's advances if he regained consciousness.

I was relieved when Ethan finally walked up.

"What are you doing out here?" he asked. "It's freezing! You got the key, didn't you?"

"Yes. I also got a dance with Wade."

When I told him what had happened, Ethan sighed.

"Could you tell if he'd been drinking?"

"Most definitely," I said.

"I guess I'd better check on him," Ethan said, sounding resigned. I got the feeling he'd been down this road before.

I went with him to his suite, dropping to a sofa while he went into the bedroom. He came out immediately.

"He's not there. Let me go check his room." I nodded and waited. When Ethan returned, I could tell by his frustrated look that he hadn't found Wade. "Damn, damn, damn. I guess I'll have to go look for him."

"Remember, your curse is your blessing," I said.

"You can be a real asshole sometimes, can't you?" Ethan asked.

"I think your friend Wade is the asshole. But I'll help you look for him. After all, between the two of us, we can probably cover all of Manhattan in, say, a month."

"Riverside Park or Morningside Park," Ethan said, closing his eyes as if trying to do a remote viewing on Wade.

"What makes you so sure?"

"I know him. Both parks are closed at this hour, but Riverside Park is bigger. Let's start with Morningside. Maybe we'll get lucky."

We didn't talk as we made the short walk to the park, managing our furtive break-in without being spotted. Ethan stood still a moment, as if trying to sense Wade's presence. I glanced down and saw what appeared to be an expensive leather glove. I knelt to pick it up.

"Is this familiar?" I asked.

"You are good tracker, white man," Ethan deadpanned.

"Can we cut the comedy and find Wade so I can get some sleep? It's been a long day, and I'm not interested in acting out *Nancy Drew and the Mystery of the Drunk Moron*," I snapped. Ethan stared at me in stony silence, and I felt embarrassed. "I'm sorry for being belligerent, but like I said, it's very late and I'm tired."

"I understand," Ethan said.

"I also don't want to be wandering around aimlessly in a dark park in the middle of New York City."

"Darkness was at first by darkness hidden," Ethan said. When I only stared at him blankly, he added, "It's a Hindu creation hymn."

"If I get home before daylight, I just might get some sleep tonight. The Grateful Dead," I countered.

"Touché," Ethan said, his dark eyes dancing in the lamplight.

He began walking, and I kept pace with him.

"Do you always have to take care of him this way?" I asked.

"He's my friend," Ethan said.

"You two don't seem to have anything in common."

"Wade is the person I mentioned in my talk tonight," Ethan said. "My benefactor. He took care of me when I was lost and alone. Now we're friends, and if sometimes he needs someone to take care of him, it's an honor to do that. Yes, he can be a tiresome man, especially when he's drinking. But I think you judge him too harshly. Everyone carries pain, Adam. Sometimes pain makes us behave in unattractive ways."

"What is Wade's pain?" I asked.

"It's not *my* place to tell you that," Ethan said.

Something about his emphasis on the word *my* seemed to hold a message for me, but I had no idea what it was. Before I could ask more questions, Ethan caught my arm.

"There he is," he whispered.

I followed the direction of his gaze. Three trees stood in a makeshift triangle around a little clearing. Wade was in the middle of the canopy of branches. He was kneeling on the ground, one hand raised to the sky, the other sweeping dirt off the ground and sprinkling it at his feet. He was chanting, but I couldn't understand what he was saying.

"What's he doing?" I whispered to Ethan.

"He's chanting," Ethan whispered back.

"I realize that, but what's he saying?"

"Once, there was no Moon, for it had been stolen," Ethan translated quietly. "The tribe asked, 'Which one of us will be the Moon?' Yellow Fox tried to be the Moon, but he was so bright it made the Earth hot at night. The tribe asked Coyote to be the Moon instead, and he agreed. Coyote was a good Moon. Not too bright and not too dim. From his vantage point in the sky, Coyote could see what everyone in the tribe was doing. Whenever he saw someone doing something dishonest, he would howl, 'Hey! That person is stealing meat from the drying racks!' Or, 'Hey! That person is cheating at the moccasin game!' Finally, the tribe, who wished to do things in secret once again, got together and said, 'Coyote is too noisy. Let's remove him from the sky.' So someone else from the tribe became the Moon. Coyote can no longer see what everyone else is doing, but he still tries to snoop into everyone's business."

As Ethan talked, I could see Wade acting out the story in movements combined with his chanting. He was graceful and powerful at the same time, not at all the clumsy, tipsy man I had seen earlier.

"Is Wade part Native American?" I asked.

"Seminole," Ethan answered.

"Maybe I was wrong to judge him so quickly," I admitted, moved by the power of Wade's dance.

"I can take care of him now," Ethan said. "I'm sorry that once again Wade has kept us from talking. Maybe another time."

"Maybe," I said. "Are you sure you don't need help getting him back?"

"I'm sure."

I gave him the key to his suite and trudged back to my room at the East Campus Hotel. Daniel wasn't there yet. I hoped his meeting with Bonnie had been more rewarding than mine with Wade and Ethan.

I had no real answers to my questions about Wade, Ethan, and Blythe, and I'd made no inroads with Jeremy except for that brief moment of contact in the chakra class.

But, I reminded myself as I crawled beneath the covers, I now had a power animal, a deeper friendship with Daniel, and a potential new roommate and apartment.

NINE

Daniel took me to the town house, which was nestled in the middle of a block on Jane Street. The location was quiet and charming, with rows of houses and trees lining the street. If there had been cobblestones, I'd have felt like I was on a tiny street in London at the turn of the century. When we stepped out of the cab onto the sidewalk, I looked at the steps leading up to the front door. I imagined myself sitting on them in the sun with my laptop, a cup of coffee by my side, periodically looking up from my work to wave at my neighbors as they passed by while walking their dogs or bustling off to work.

Daniel rang the doorbell and said to me as we waited, "Think of this visit like a trip to ancient Greece. I don't know what mood Martin may be in. He could be Aphrodite, full of goodness and love. Or he could be Cerberus guarding the gates of hell."

The front door suddenly swung open to reveal Martin, with a face full of makeup, his head wrapped in a towel, and wearing a terry-cloth bathrobe, which was open enough to display a nipple ring.

"Hell. Definitely hell," Daniel said in a *Rain Man* voice.

"Daniel! What a surprise. And you brought company; how nice. Come in. My god, I'm a fright, but I was just getting ready to go to the club. It's much easier to do my makeup here and go. I hope I don't scare off your friend. Where are my manners?"

"In the gutter with your mind?" Daniel suggested.

"Don't forget my morals, bitch," Martin said and air-kissed Daniel. He shook my hand and said, "My name is Martin Blount. Hello."

"I'm Adam Wilson," I responded.

"You look so familiar. If I've met you, I can't believe I don't remember. Names do escape me, but I never forget a chest."

"I saw your act at Club Chaos a while ago. I was there with Sheila Meyers."

"The laptop pornographer!" Martin exclaimed. "Yes, now I remember. I hope I didn't embarrass you too much."

"No, it was fun. You were great. I've never seen anything like it," I said.

"That's just about the best compliment I could get. No matter how you liked it. Why haven't I met you before now? Daniel, where did you find him?"

"I grew him in my garden," Daniel muttered and walked into the apartment.

Martin took my arm, and we followed Daniel into a large front room with Early American furnishings and various antiques scattered in eye-catching places. A large brass lantern hung from a post by a doorway. A brass teapot sat high on a bookshelf. Nothing was ostentatious, but the room looked regal in its simplicity.

"Are you coming to see me perform again, Adam?" Martin asked as he led me into the room. "I'd love it if you did, but I have to warn you. Seeing me a second time could develop into a nasty habit. You'll keep coming and coming."

"What great lines, Martin," Daniel commented. "You'll have to write those into your show. Oh, wait; you already did. That was from your opening night, wasn't it?"

"Lighten up," Martin said, dropping my arm and turning to look at Daniel. "Who used your mascara and gave you pinkeye? I'm just having fun. I'm performing. See, Adam, I'm the performer. Daniel's the responsible *actor* now, who has no time for the little people he left behind."

Daniel chose to ignore that and said, "Adam, let's look at the apartment while Martin gets ready for work."

"You're the one who's going to move in?" Martin asked me with glee.

"I'm thinking about it," I said.

"That's great!" he exclaimed.

"I thought you said this place is too cramped and the feng shui is all wrong for two people," Daniel accused Martin.

"I did not," Martin said, laughing nervously. "I said I'd have to rearrange some of the things I've moved around to divert the energy flow to accommodate two people. There's a difference. As for being cramped, this place is huge. So is Adam. It's perfect."

"I could have sworn you said it's too cramped," Daniel said.

"Maybe you were thinking about your cramps," Martin suggested. "You're certainly acting like it's that time of the month."

"Adam, I'm sorry about this. Maybe this isn't such a good time to look at the apartment. We could come back later when the evil spirit that haunts it goes to work."

"Bitch!" Martin yelled. "You say you don't mind me living here, and then you say spiteful things like that. *Haunts it,* indeed. I guess it's just the guilt talking."

"Guilt? What do I have to feel guilty about?" Daniel asked, but Martin stood quietly and glared at him.

"Um, guys," I tentatively spoke. They turned and looked at me as if I were a statue in the corner that had suddenly come to life. "If you two are done yelling at each other, I was just wondering when I might be able to move in?"

"You want to live here?" Martin and Daniel asked simultaneously, but in very different tones.

"Temporarily, yes," I answered.

"With him?" Daniel queried, pointing at Martin.

"Yeah," I said. "Besides, after attending that retreat I feel fairly attuned to the spirit world. Maybe we can get our friend Ethan down here to help us work on expelling that evil spirit."

Martin grinned, ran his tongue over his upper teeth, and said, "You can move in tomorrow. What's your friend's name? Ethan? More importantly, is he built like you?"

"He was being sarcastic, Martin. Surely, one so gifted in the art of sarcasm would recognize it from the mouths of others," Daniel said.

"Of course I knew he was being sarcastic," Martin clarified. "I was using humor to lighten the mood in here. You remember humor, don't you?"

"Daniel and I just got back from a spiritual retreat," I explained to Martin. "It was called 'Spirit Matters: A Journey Through the Infinite Plain.' "

"How interesting," Martin said with a beatific smile, returning to his role as the perfect host. "What did you boys learn?"

"There were workshops on crystal healing, power animals, spirit guides, past-life regression, and harmonic balance through guided meditations," I said.

"I see this one learned a lot," Martin said and gestured at Daniel. "He's about as balanced as Keri Strug and Hulk Hogan on a see-saw."

Daniel's mouth opened, and I quickly said, "We weren't really there to balance our chakras. Our reasons for attending the retreat were purely material."

"Silk?" Martin said, not comprehending, or maybe he wasn't listening, which caused Daniel to snort loudly.

"Oh, my god," Daniel said vehemently. "Adam, you're wasting your breath. Martin's most enlightened moment was when he looked into a mirror for the first time."

"This coming from a man whose aura is the color of Burberry plaid," Martin said.

I felt uncomfortable, to say the least. At the retreat Daniel had implied that things were strained between him and Martin, but I hadn't expected outright animosity. Their banter reminded me of a new sitcom that had caught my attention because two of its main characters were gay men. Though I seldom had time for television other than *Nick at Night,* I tried to watch *Will and Grace* because it made me laugh. I'd thought its sarcastic, over-the-top dialogue was somewhat unrealistic, but Daniel and Martin disproved that theory as I watched them squawk at each other like two buzzards fighting over a dead buffalo. I saw a remote control laying on top of a table and wished I could point it at them and flip to a lighter topic. I decided the best I could do was continue my Pollyanna routine and pretend like nothing was amiss.

"What made you seek a course in miracles, Daniel?" Martin asked. "Madonna's enlightened, so now you are, too?"

"No. Like Adam said, we're still material girls," Daniel said. "I went to get in the good graces of a woman who might hold the key to getting a role on *Secret Splendor.* And Adam went along—well, I probably shouldn't say."

"Oh?" Martin asked, his eyes lighting up. "Out with it. Confession is good for my soul."

I laughed, remembering his act as Sister Mary Amanda Prophet, and said, "I went to help Daniel. But mainly because a guy I have a crush on was there."

"A pornographer *and* a stalker!" Martin exclaimed. "A man after my own heart. But I wasn't there, so whose heart were you after?"

Daniel smirked as I answered, "Jeremy Caprel—"

"Stop!" Martin shrieked, holding up his hand, like a traffic cop. "What is it with you boys and that soulless cardboard cutout masquerading as a human being? Why do you fall all over him like dying swans at the Met?"

"He's hot," Daniel and I chorused together.

Martin rolled his eyes and fell to the sofa. He pulled the towel off of his head and wrung it in his hands as he spoke. This was my first look at his closely cropped brown hair tipped with blond highlights. He was one of those adorable guys I always wanted to put in my pocket and take home with me but wouldn't because he didn't come with an "off" switch.

"I'd think Daniel, of all people, could tell you what a two-timer that one is," Martin huffed. "The dick is always bigger on the other side of the fence to Jeremy. He's had more boyfriends than a virgin in a communal shower in prison."

Daniel noticed my disgruntled expression and said, "Martin, don't let us stop you from getting ready for work. I'll give Adam your number so he can call you to work out the details of his move. He's got a lot of computer equipment that he'll need to set up."

As he spoke, he resolutely led me to the door, careful to keep himself between Martin and me. Martin could get no more than a hurried goodbye out before Daniel shoved me through the door and prodded me away from the town house.

"All right," I said, once we had turned the corner and stood on the avenue. "We escaped. Are you sure you want me to share the town house with Martin?"

"I just can't deal with him right now," Daniel exploded. Then he got quiet, standing in the middle of the sidewalk as if he'd lost his sense of direction. "He brings out the worst in me, and apparently the worst is a bratty child."

"Maybe I should take you for an ice-cream cone or something," I said, hoping to lighten the mood.

"I don't feel like doing anything but taking a walk."

"Perfect," I said. "You can walk me home. It's not that far."

"Okay," he agreed, "but only if you let me use your cell phone to check my machine for messages."

I handed it over, and he entered his number while we walked, periodically pressing numbers to save or delete messages from his machine. His face lit up just as I pulled him out of the way of an oncoming cab when he stepped into a crosswalk against the light.

"I got it!" he yelled after I hauled him back to the curb.

"You almost got hit," I said. "What the hell are you talking about?"

"I got the part! That was my agent," he said, pointing at the cell phone. "I got the part on *Secret Splendor!*"

A woman in the throng of people waiting on the corner with us said, "Oh, I just love that show! You're on it? Who you gonna be, child?"

"I probably shouldn't say," Daniel said to her. "Should I say? I can say. No, I shouldn't. Oh, why not. I'm going to be Angus Remington."

"Get out of here!" the woman shrieked. The people around us seemed to obey her order; then I realized the light had changed and they were crossing the street. "That's not possible. You died three years ago when your sister Brianna found out you were the one who ruined her chances of taking over the family company. She fixed the brakes in your car. You went over a cliff! How can you come back?"

"Angus wasn't in that car," Daniel explained and seemed oblivious to the woman's mounting hysteria. Her wide eyes glazed over with horror, which was how I imagined the actress who played Brianna on *Secret Splendor* would look when Angus returned.

"Uh, Daniel," I said, deliberately emphasizing his name so his psycho fan would realize we were on the street rather than the television in her living room at home, "we really need to get going."

"But you don't even look like Angus!" the fanatic shrieked as I grabbed Daniel's arm and started walking as quickly as I could up the avenue. "You were ten years older and had brown hair!"

"Plastic surgery has come a long way," Daniel called back to her.

"You'll never get away with it!" the woman screamed after us. "I'm gonna write Brianna and tell her you're coming back, Angus Remington!"

Four blocks after the altercation, Daniel was still laughing about his encounter with the zealous *Secret Splendor* fan.

"She was scary," I said. "If Angus is as evil as she seemed to think, you're going to run into a lot of crazies, I guess. You'd better be careful."

"I thought it was fun," Daniel said. "I used to deal with Diana fanatics all the time when I did Princess 2Di4. Besides, after Martin, she was a piece of cake."

"At least Martin has a grip on reality," I stated.

"Don't be so sure," Daniel said with a laugh. "I'm kidding. I'm sorry for the way we acted. Believe it or not, I really care about Martin. I told you that ever since Ken died, he's treated me like the cruel landlord."

"And I told you it's probably one of those things time will take care of," I said as we stopped outside my apartment. "I can't predict the future, but I'm sure everything will be okay. When I move in with Martin, I'll do whatever I can to help."

"I'd think after what you saw between us today, you'd want to stay out of it," Daniel said in a wry tone.

"Friends help each other," I stated. "Besides, I'm bigger than Martin. If he gives me grief, I'll kick his ass."

Daniel laughed and said, "I'm not going to worry about Martin when I'm the new Angus Remington!"

"That reminds me. Plastic surgery aside, how can Angus come back from the dead after going over a cliff in a car?"

"Like I said, Angus was never in that car," Daniel said airily, as if that sort of thing happened all the time. "Angus knew about the brakes and sent this guy named Philip Trask on an errand in his place. It killed two birds with one stone, so to speak, because not only did Brianna and everyone think he died in the crash, but Philip was the only other person who knew that Angus was the father of Gayle Harmon's baby."

"Good grief, how do you know all this?"

"Research," Daniel said and shifted in place. I stood silently in the doorway of my building until he confessed, "Okay, I've watched *Secret Splendor* for years. My mother used to watch it, and I've been hooked ever since."

I laughed and said, "Go home and get handsome for Blaine. You've got some partying to do."

We hugged goodbye, and I went upstairs, thinking how lucky Daniel was to have someone to celebrate milestones with.

Before going to Martin's with Daniel, I'd spent most of my

morning and early afternoon sending e-mails to Tracy in Eau Claire about various business matters that needed my attention. Then I'd gone to bodyWorks and signed up for a membership. With all my errands out of the way, I decided it was time to devote my full attention to the Club Chaos plans before my meeting with Andy the next day. I went into the bedroom and retrieved my laptop, which I hadn't set up after returning from the retreat the day before. After reconnecting it to my network, I reached into the bag for my case of Zip disks and came up empty-handed. I panicked as I searched through the various compartments of the bag, sure that I'd packed the case before I left for the retreat. But there was nothing in the bag but some floppy disks and a couple of legal pads.

I looked around the desk and floor, trying to retrace my steps from the Friday before, but I didn't see the case anywhere. Finally, I went to the bedroom and went through my other bag, which held nothing but dirty laundry from the weekend.

"Think," I commanded myself aloud, reconstructing every move I'd made since Friday. I knew I'd packed the Zip disk case, though, because I'd intended to prepare for the meeting with Andy, until that idiot Harold Smith had made me turn in my bag—

"Holy shit," I said, thinking of the woman at the retreat who'd taped my name on the bag before putting it with the others to be stored during the weekend.

But I couldn't have been robbed. It was ridiculous to think that a thief would take a few Zip disks and leave the expensive computer and PalmPilot that were in the bag. The disks had to be somewhere.

I went through both bags again, then shook out all the clothes I'd taken with me, including the dirty laundry, to see if the case had somehow been lost among them. Then I went over every square inch of the apartment, including each drawer and cabinet. But I knew my search was futile, because I was sure I'd packed the disks.

I took a deep breath and found the retreat pamphlet, looking for someone to call. If the Zip disk case had slipped out of the bag, would it be somewhere in Feasley Hall?

I called the number listed in the brochure and explained my problem to a receptionist. After being transferred to several other people, I repeated my story to the sympathetic voice on the other end of the phone.

"No, I have some items from the conference, but nothing like that," she said. "I wish I could be of more help. I do have a number for the organizers, if you want it."

I wrote down the number, staring at it after I hung up the phone. Harold Smith had told me that a secretary for Wade Van Atterson's lawyers had helped organize the retreat. I didn't even try to convince myself not to trust my instincts. Wade had financed the retreat; he'd been responsible for helping organize it; and he'd no doubt had access to every room and office they'd used at Columbia. He'd even had a key to Ethan's room. Ethan had known I'd turned in my laptop, so Wade probably knew, too.

Taking the Zip disks had nothing to do with their monetary value; that was why my equipment was still in the bag. It was a malicious act directed at me personally, probably out of vindictiveness after I rebuffed Wade's advances. He'd no doubt awakened with a hangover after his little moonlight dance and decided to get even in some slimy, indirect way.

The idea that Wade Van Atterson had plundered my bag for those Zip disks made me furious. I didn't care what pain Ethan inferred that Wade was carrying; it would be nothing compared to the pain he'd feel when I got hold of him. I looked up the street address for Disorient XPress, fully intending to go directly to the club and confront Wade.

Then I realized how pointless that was. A man who was underhanded enough to go to the detestable lengths Wade had was not likely to confess his misdeeds or hand over my property. He would deny all wrongdoing with a smile on his face and usher me right out of his office, perhaps with the assistance of the oversized Brenda Li. I needed to get inside his head and figure out why he'd stolen the disks. Was it just vindictiveness? Was he curious about me, my clients, or the work I did? If I reacted too strongly, it would only enlighten him as to the importance of what he'd stumbled on.

My heart sank as I searched my desk again, hoping against hope that the Club Chaos plans, so recently developed, had not been on one of the Zip disks in the case. But I knew they were. If Wade figured out a way to access the disks, he would not only have confidential financial information about a competitor; he'd also have the inside track on Andy's plans for his club's expansion. I had never betrayed a client's trust, and I felt sick thinking of all the people who might be affected: Andy, Daniel, Martin, even Gretchen, who had so trustingly e-mailed sensitive information about Club Chaos to me. I couldn't bear the idea of telling any of them how careless I'd been.

As I had so many times in my life, I picked up the phone and called home. When my mother answered, I felt like crying with relief. I quickly explained the situation, then waited while she thought about it.

"What you need is someone with an inside track on Wade," she said. "You need to find out where he's likely to have the disks. Does he have a home office like you do? Does he do most of his work out of his nightclub? Is he likely to hand over the disks to someone he knows, someone you can trust? What about Jeremy? If he's Daniel's friend, he'd surely be willing to help you."

"I don't think Jeremy and Wade know each other very well," I said. "The things Wade said about Jeremy weren't exactly flattering. And I'm not too sure how Jeremy feels about me. He'd think I was a lunatic if I descended on him with a bunch of accusations and demands. He'd probably go straight to Daniel."

"And the fewer people who know about this, the better," my mother said. "What about Ethan? It sounds like he's gotten Wade out of scrapes before."

"Yes, and that would be his main interest. Protecting or helping Wade. I don't know if I can trust him."

"Do you know anyone else who knows Wade?" she asked.

"Maybe Blythe. But I told you before: for whatever reason, she doesn't want to talk about him."

"But Blythe is *your* friend," my mother said. "Isn't it possible she could give you some helpful information?"

"I guess it's worth a try," I said. "She's the best connection I have right now. This makes me feel sick. If I'd left the stuff at home like I should have, or kept that idiot at the retreat from turning it in—"

"There's no point beating yourself up. After all, you had no reason to know anything like this would happen. Hold on to two thoughts. The first is that Wade may have no idea what valuable information is on those disks. The second is that he may be unable to get past your password protections. You may get the disks back before he has a chance to do anything with them. He may have even destroyed them if he was just being spiteful. Do you have the information saved anywhere else?"

"Most of it is on my PC," I said. "And a lot of it is on Tracy's computer, too. I can probably recreate what I don't have. But all my time and work would be lost. Not to mention the hit my reputation will take if I have to notify all my clients. What an asshole."

"Talk to Blythe," she urged. "Now."

I didn't even try to call Blythe after my mother hung up. I went directly to her apartment, hoping she was back from Vermont.

She opened the door in her paint-spattered overalls, frowning at the sight of me.

"It's not that I'm unhappy to see you," she said without preamble. "I missed you. But I'm working, Adam."

"I'm sorry. But I have to talk to you. About Wade Van Atterson."

She rolled her eyes and said, "Didn't we have an unspoken agreement not to talk about him?"

"You don't have to tell me how you know him or why you don't like him," I said. "But I have a problem, and I don't know where else to turn."

"If you've gotten into some kind of predicament because of Wade, please remember that I warned you to stay away from him."

"It wasn't my intention to go anywhere near him. It was an unfortunate consequence of something else."

I gave her a brief rundown on Daniel, Club Chaos, Jeremy, Ethan, and the retreat, finishing with my discovery of the missing disks and my conviction that Wade had stolen them.

"Why Wade?" she asked. "Anyone who was part of the retreat could have done it."

"If it was just some thief, they'd have stolen the laptop, the Zip disk drive, and my PalmPilot. Those have much more material value than the disks. They were stolen deliberately by someone who wanted me to know it was directed at me. My gut instinct tells me that was Wade. Maybe he did it Saturday night when he was drunk. Maybe he's sorry for it now and doesn't know how to correct it. Hell, maybe he doesn't even remember doing it. I don't care. I want my disks back."

"How do you want me to help you?" Blythe asked.

"Tell me anything you know about Wade. Is he computer literate? Is his office at home or at the club? Do you know what kind of security he has? Do you know anyone who might be able to reason with him or get the story out of him?"

Blythe thought a moment; then she said, "He has an office at home and an e-mail account. There's a manager at Disorient XPress who runs everything. I know he cuts checks using the computer printer, and he told a group of people at a party that Wade once accidentally erased his hard drive, so he won't let Wade near the computer there. Does that help?"

"Do you know the manager well?"

"No. I don't know any of them well. Oh, Wade has a very elaborate security system at his apartment because of the artwork. There's a motion-sensitive alarm in his gallery. I don't know about the rest of the apartment."

"Is there anything else you can tell me? Other than 'I told you so'?"

"Believe it or not," she said, "I'm probably as upset about this as you are."

For the first time, I noticed that the eyes behind her glasses looked angry, and her lips, when she stopped talking, were pressed tightly together. I watched as she went to her backpack and took out her cell phone, pushing in a number without looking it up.

"Wade Van Atterson, please. It's Blythe Mayfield." She waited, listening, then said, "When he gets back, please have him call me at this number." After she gave the number of her cell phone and disconnected the call, she turned back to me. "Wade left for Zurich a couple of hours ago. He won't be back until some time next week. Now what?"

"I have no idea," I said. "Thank you. I know you don't want to have anything to do with him."

"You better believe that when he gets back, I'm going to have plenty to say to him," she answered. "He has no right to mess with you this way. I don't care what you did or said to him, or whether or not he was drunk when he stole your disks. There's no excuse for what he's done, and it's exactly the kind of underhanded, vicious, stupid thing I'd expect from him. I'm sorry you had to see for yourself why I want nothing to do with him. He's petty and destructive and—"

"If I'd listened to you in the first place—"

"No, this is not your fault. I mean, you'd think you could go away for a fucking weekend to the same place as that conniving, miserable excuse for a human being and not be victimized by him."

"I didn't mean to get you so worked up."

"You didn't. He did. Oh, I can't wait until he gets back."

"Don't do anything without talking to me. It's possible that I can figure something out before he gets back."

"What are you going to do, Spider-Man, scale the walls of his building and break into his apartment?"

"I don't know. But the more reaction he gets, the more suspicious he'll be about what's on those disks. Especially if he finds out I'm doing some work for Andy." I looked at my watch. "I have to go; I'm supposed to meet Blaine Dunhill at the gym to work out. Promise you won't do anything? When I figure out a plan, I'll tell you."

"I promise."

I felt terrible about leaving her when she was upset, and gave her a hug, saying, "Call me when you want to get together. We'll talk about anything but Wade. You can tell me about Vermont, and I'll tell you all the good stuff that's going on in my life, okay?"

She nodded and walked me to the door. I had just enough time to take a cab to my apartment to get my gym bag before meeting Blaine.

He'd arrived before me and was waiting at the desk to sign me in. He grinned when I showed him my membership card, then we worked out. I pushed all thoughts of Wade and the Zip disks out of my head. After we showered, we decided to get a smoothie before going our separate ways.

"All right," Blaine said, "out with it."

"What?"

"It's obvious something is bothering you. I know a rage workout when I see one. Daniel told me pretty much everything about the retreat. Are you upset about Jeremy?"

"No. I think I made some progress there. I mean, he's not exactly putting my number on speed-dial, but I got his attention. I'm relatively sure a lusty thought or two may be creeping into his inner Jeremy."

"Is it work? Daniel says your subcontractors at Club Chaos are a real headache."

"I do have a lot on my mind," I said.

"I know how that is. If you want to talk about it . . ."

"I'd be putting you in an uncomfortable position with Daniel."

"If this is about moving in with Martin—"

"I'm looking forward to that," I assured him.

"I know Daniel's friends can be a little frustrating, especially the more colorful ones like Andy and Martin. Like I said, if you want to talk about it, I'll be glad to listen. Of course, if this is something about Daniel, you don't have to tell me."

"Oh, hell, why not?" I asked.

Blaine listened intently as I told him the whole story. When I finished, he thought for a few minutes, then said, "Wade could have been motivated by either of the things you mentioned. Striking out at you or getting information about a rival business. But if he's as computer illiterate as Blythe thinks, I doubt he'd take your disks with him on a business trip. He either left them at home, or he may have given them to his office manager at Disorient XPress with instructions to find out what's on them. I'm betting he didn't have time to do that before he took off on his trip. What you need to do is find out exactly when he'll be back. Then you can confront him immediately, before he has time to do anything with the disks."

"Unless he's already destroyed them."

"No matter what, there's not much you can do until he gets back. But if I were you, I wouldn't tell my clients yet. There's no point getting everyone upset about a breach of confidence you don't even know has taken place. You've got a few days to think it over. Can you reconstruct most of what's on the disks?"

"I think so. It will be time-consuming and annoying as hell, but I guess I have no choice at this point."

"Right. And there's no reason for Daniel or Andy to know."

"Ultimately, I'll probably end up telling Daniel. Especially if I have to tell Andy and Gretchen."

"That will be your call," Blaine assured me.

"Thanks. But if you decide to tell him, I'll understand."

Over the next few days, I suppressed my anxiety about the disks and got everything ready for my move to Jane Street. Ray Patel, relieved of the burden of paying for an expensive apartment, offered to take care of any wiring needs for my computer systems. When Daniel found out that I would need some electrical work done, he asked me, at his expense, to have the electrician check out all three floors and make sure everyone's needs were being met and everything was up to code. In this way, I got to meet my new neighbors.

As for my future roommate, Martin's ideas for how we would rearrange things surprised me. He wanted to give up the master suite because it opened into a small sitting room lined with built-in bookcases that he thought would be ideal for my office. Though I agreed that the space was perfect, I expressed my concern that he was giving up the room he'd shared with Ken.

"Do you mind sleeping in there?" Martin asked.

"No, but—"

"Here's my reason," Martin said. "I was talking with Josh and Sheila about you. Josh said you were thinking of finding more clients here and getting your own place to work from whenever you're in Manhattan. Maybe you intended to live with me just a little while. But if it works out, if we get along, then why not make it permanent? There's a security system, so when you're away, you can leave your stuff here without worrying about it. I can't even turn on a computer, so no one will bother it. And it would be dumb to put you in the second bedroom and try to convert another room into an office when we have an office I don't use. Of course, we can pack some of Ken's books—"

He broke off with a little frown.

"I wish you wouldn't," I said. "I don't need all the shelf space, and the books make the room seem so comfortable. Besides, I can already see several I want to read. But it's your *bedroom.*"

"Honey, at some point I'm going to want to share my bed with a man. Frankly, I'd rather it not be that bed. Can you understand?"

I nodded, still feeling like I was kicking him out of his room, which must have shown on my face.

"I need this," Martin finally said. "I'm excited about redoing the other room and the bathroom and making them mine. Think of the trips to Pottery Barn and Pier One! So many retailers, so little space . . . Anyway, I like this more than the idea Blaine came up with."

"What idea was that?" I asked.

A stricken look flitted across Martin's face, as if he'd said too much, but when I continued to stare at him, he admitted, "Blaine wanted Daniel to trade apartments with me. He wanted them to move in here together. When Daniel told me that, I thought it was his subtle way of asking me to move out. Now I think maybe Daniel didn't want to move anymore than I did. Do you think they're having problems? Do you think Blaine will be upset about all this?"

I couldn't tell if Martin's tone was concerned or hopeful, but I said, "I don't think they're having any problems. I think if Daniel's happy, Blaine's happy. If Daniel doesn't want to give up his apartment, it's probably more about his garden than whether or not to live with Blaine."

"No kidding," Martin said. "You can take the boy out of Minnesota, but you can't—"

"Wisconsin," I said. "Daniel is from Wisconsin. Like me."

Martin laughed and said, "Inside joke. So we're agreed? I can empty the master bedroom by this weekend. I'd already packed Ken's stuff—you should have been here for that. At least thirty people, most of them drag queens, ecstatic over everything they touched, like it was the Shroud of Turin."

His light tone was belied by a sad look in his eyes.

"Can I be totally honest?" I asked.

"It may be a new experience for me, but please do," Martin said.

"I got the idea you weren't too thrilled about a roommate in the first place. I feel like I'm inconveniencing you."

Martin thought that over before he said, "One thing Daniel and I agreed on after Ken died was that the nicest people get predatory when it comes to real estate. At Ken's memorial service, people gave Daniel their cards with hints that they were ready to negotiate whenever he was ready to sell."

"What assholes," I said.

"I *know!* But even some of our closest friends started hinting about how much space I had, or how they wanted Daniel's apartment if he moved out. It had gotten to the point where I was afraid to pick up the phone. I didn't know if it would be some apartment-hunting vulture posing as a friend, or Daniel calling to evict me. I felt like Greta Garbo." He went to the window, drew the curtains closed, and threw himself on the bed. "I vant to be alone."

"Then why did you answer the phone when we called from the retreat?" I asked.

"I had just ordered kung pao chicken. I thought it was the delivery boy calling. He always gets lost. When I found out it was Daniel on the phone, I had no idea what he was going to ask me to do about the apartment. Of course I leaped to conclusions, but once I met you, I could see you were okay. My biggest fear was that Daniel was going to make me live with Jeremy, because I know Robert is ready for Jeremy to move out."

"Uh-huh," I said in a way that made it clear I wanted to hear more.

"I don't know how much you already know about this, but

Jeremy left Daniel for Robert," Martin explained. "It didn't last long. From what I understand, it never does last long with Jeremy." Martin paused for a laugh, but when I didn't, he kept talking. "Jeremy wanted Daniel back, but Daniel was done with him. And good riddance, I say. So now Robert is stuck with a roommate he doesn't want. Even though I like Robert, it serves him right for getting involved with Jeremy in the first place. And I can't believe Daniel is friends with Jeremy now. He should have kicked him to the curb with the rest of the trash."

"Boy, you really don't like Jeremy. Did you like him before he and Daniel broke up?"

"Jeremy is a narcissistic, shallow slut," Martin pronounced. "If that Whitebird guy is dating him, he'll see through Jeremy fast enough."

"Whitecrow," I corrected him. "I admit I don't know Jeremy that well yet, but I obviously don't see him in the same light you do."

"I understand," Martin said, looking in a mirror and pulling the skin tight around his eyes. "You see him through a Vaseline-coated lens with soft lighting. This, too, won't last. So we're agreed? You'll start moving in this weekend, and these two rooms will be enough space for you?"

"Of course. And we'll be splitting the bills, right? For one thing, your expenses will be affected by my equipment." Martin's eyes danced, and I could see him running through a variety of comebacks to that, so I quickly said, "You should keep paying about what you have been, and let me pay the rest of it, because you'll notice a huge surge—"

"Oh I hope so—"

"But your phone line will be unaffected," I went on, doggedly talking over him. "You don't want to hear all the details, I'm sure, but my equip—uh—stuff and your stuff will be separate and—"

"Yes, it can get so messy when everyone's stuff—"

"Stop!" I said, putting my hands over my ears and laughing at him. "It's not safe for me to say anything!"

"Double entendres are my life," he noted.

So it was settled. My first night on Jane Street was wonderful. I slept so hard that I never heard Martin come in after his two performances at Club Chaos. The next morning, my systems booted up with only minor problems that were easy fixes. I checked in with my employees in Eau Claire; everything was running smoothly, as were things at Patel, Inc. We'd made a nearly seamless transition, which seemed nothing short of miraculous.

So far, there had been no consequences that I knew of from the stolen Zip disks. I recovered the work I'd done for Carl Nash's jewelry Web site and made an appointment to meet him later in the week. The work I'd lost for my new clients had to be started over from scratch. Thankfully, my clients were all computer illiterate and didn't question me when I said my computer crashed and I lost everything. They simply resubmitted the figures, photos, and information I'd need to get the job done. I told them I'd knock five percent off their total bill for the inconvenience, which wasn't a lot but made them happy.

Their Web sites ended up looking better than they had before the Zip disk debacle. It should've made me feel better, but it was hard not to think of information about their companies, not to mention my own, floating around somewhere out of my control.

All that was weighing on my mind one afternoon when I took a break from recreating my design for the Club Chaos Web site and went to make a sandwich. The kitchen was at the back of the apartment and had windows that overlooked an alley. The alley created a wide enough space between the buildings to allow a generous amount of light to filter through the kitchen windows during the day.

While the rest of the town house appeared to be the home of a colonialist or a sea captain in the early part of the past century, the kitchen looked as if it were owned by Arnold from *Happy Days* due to its retro fifties decor. Chrome Sunbeam appliances and a flip-front breadbox rested on white Formica countertops with a blue-and-red boomerang print. The refrigerator was solid robin's-egg blue, and a neon Route 66 clock hung above the matching blue General Electric stove.

Feeling like a kid in my grandmother's kitchen, I slid in my sock-clad feet across the black-and-white-checked linoleum to the refrigerator. As I brought out the makings for a roast-chicken sandwich, Martin swooped into the room like June Cleaver about to fix the Beav's lunch to take to school. Although I'd never known June to wear daisy dukes and a *Flashdance* sweater.

"Good morning, starshine," Martin sang out and brought down a tin of coffee from a cupboard.

"It's two in the afternoon," I said.

Martin paused, gave me a blank look, then resumed fixing his coffee.

"Good morning," he brightly chirped again.

I laughed and said, "You may be the only person I know who still uses a percolator to make his coffee."

"Oh, yeah," Martin said in a blasé tone and stopped assembling the percolator to give it a good, hard look. "It's Ken's, of course. It's weird how the whole house looks like Little House on the fucking Prairie and the kitchen looks like an *I Love Lucy* rerun. But that's Ken. I think he wanted to create the kind of kitchen he always dreamed of growing up in when he was a little boy. From what I gather, he never had the perfect home life. I don't know, but he had that kind of duality thing going on in his life. Not only as a gay man, but from working as a female impersonator, and I guess it spilled over into his decorating. You should know all about that since you're a Gemini."

He plugged in the percolator, and I finished making my sandwich. Then something dawned on me.

"How did you know I'm a Gemini?" I asked as I sat down at the vinyl-covered kitchen table.

Martin squirmed uncomfortably and said, "You may have left your wallet in the living room the other night. And I may have looked at your driver's license."

"I see," I said with a smirk. "You *may* have?"

"If it's any consolation, your picture looks so much better than mine does," Martin offered. "Anyway, why are you in here moping around?"

"I'm not moping," I protested. "I'm avoiding work. There's a big difference."

"Good, you can go to Bed Bath and Big Queen with me."

"Got to get back to work!" I said.

Martin frowned and asked, "What proof do I have that you're gay?"

"I'm attracted to Jeremy?"

"That just proves you're easily swayed by pretty boys with deep brown eyes, chiseled good looks, and—oh hell, you're gay."

"Damn it."

"What? Now you don't want to be gay?"

"I just realized I'm missing something I worked a long time on," I said, thinking aloud.

"I only looked in your wallet," Martin said. "I didn't steal anything. And you might want to throw out that vintage nineteen eighty-two condom."

"That's my lucky condom," I said.

"Apparently not."

"Long story," I said. "I do have to get to work now."

I walked back to my office and sat down with a thud, depressed as I stared at my computer. Martin's use of the term "chiseled good looks" had reminded me of an illustration of a beautiful man I'd intended to put on the Club Chaos home page. The file had been so large that I'd put it on a Zip disk and deleted it from my Power-Book, planning to put it on my laptop later. Now it was lost in the black abyss that should have been occupied by Wade Van Atterson's ethics.

"I guess you're tired of hearing snide remarks about Jeremy," Martin spoke from next to me, and I jumped, startled that he'd been standing so close by.

"That doesn't bother me," I said. When he looked unconvinced, I said, "I lost some work I did for the Club Chaos Web site."

"Oh, that," Martin said with an expression of distaste. "Too bad you didn't lose the whole concept."

"I'm surprised to hear you say that. Cybeeria could help get Andy's operations back in the black."

"Whatever," Martin said, looking injured.

I stared at him, concerned, and asked, "You don't want Club Chaos to succeed?"

"I didn't realize live talent wasn't enough. Not only are computers replacing people in offices, I guess they're replacing performers as well."

"Oh, my god, is that what you think?" I asked. "Your show is great, Martin. In fact, now that I've spent some nights working at the club, I'm impressed by everyone's shows. What you all do is amazing. Cybeeria is meant to draw a new crowd that will undoubtedly become an appreciative part of your audience."

"Or take away what audience we have."

"I promise you, Martin, Cybeeria will generate a buzz and make the atmosphere there even more exciting. That buzz won't be just local, either. You'll be national." That got his attention, and he shot me a quizzical look. I decided to appeal to his Joan Rivers-like zeal for the inside scoop. "Some of these ideas I haven't even discussed with Andy. It would be wrong to tell you first."

"If telling me is wrong, you don't want to be right," Martin sang.

"You *are* a big part of my plan, so maybe I should tell you. I was thinking about those *Secret Splendor* Saturdays at Disorient XPress, and some of the things Daniel has told me about the large number of gay men who watch soaps. I thought it would be perfect if Club Chaos had a sort of virtual soap opera. I would imagine a lot goes on behind the scenes there."

"If those walls could squawk," Martin agreed.

"So my idea is that we do a Web bio on anyone at the club who's interested in participating. We can either keep you in character, which would mean a bio on Sister Mary Amanda Prophet, or if you guys prefer, we can use your real first names, or even a fictitious name. The site can be set up to have a chat room, where you can talk online to people all over the country. You can talk about the club, backstage antics, each other, the local scene, anything that will generate interest. As you can see, there are a lot of details to work out, but it's the performers themselves—and Andy—who will set the parameters for how it's done. I can make it happen, but the rest of you will be what makes it exciting. As word of mouth grows and people start logging on, your audience will probably play a large part in how things develop."

"How does this help the club? More tourists will know about us?"

"Sure, but not just that. Here, look at this."

Martin looked at my screen, and I went to several Web sites and showed him banner ads, pop-up ads, and product promotions.

"This is advertising," I said. "So, for example, when someone enters the club's Web address, at the bottom of the site you'll see ads for, say, *Advocate* magazine, or Calvin Klein underwear. Those companies pay for that. The more hits the site gets, the higher the ad rates. Make sense?"

"Yes," Martin said. "It's another way for that greedy queen Andy to make money."

"Right. But say he donates even part of that money to gay organizations, the club builds goodwill."

"Like the auction last year. Or Dunk-a-Diva."

"Uh-huh. The site ends up paying for itself many times over. The club gets publicity, you become the next RuPaul, community organizations have another source of funds, and advertisers reach the audience they want. Everyone wins."

"The next RuPaul?"

"You never know where it all may lead."

"You're a bee charmer, Idgie Threadgoode," Martin said in his best Mary-Louise Parker accent.

"Is it working?"

"Maybe. So what's the problem?"

"The problem?"

"You said you lost some work you did."

"Oh, that," I said in a flat tone. I'd almost forgotten until Martin reminded me. "Another long story. Something I hope to get fixed in a couple of days."

"Anything to do with those missing disks?"

I was sure the blood drained from my face as I stared at him.

"Missing disks?" I repeated in a daze.

"When I was dusting your desk, I may have seen an e-mail from your mother on your computer screen and—"

"You *may* have read it? You're wasted at Club Chaos. You should be a corporate spy or something."

"I'm not used to having a roommate," Martin said with a cherubic look. "I have to relearn about boundaries and such. And I'm a very curious boy. At least I'm honest. I keep telling you, confession cleanses the soul."

"Then your soul must be as clean as my desk. Yes, I mislaid some disks."

"I read the *whole* e-mail," Martin said. "Your mother is a riot, by the way. So you're giving up? You're going to let Wade Van Atterson get away with this?"

I frowned at him, realizing he read me as easily as he read the contents of my wallet and computer monitor. I wasn't just worried about my clients' confidentiality or annoyed about redoing my work. I resented feeling like Wade had scored a victory over me.

"There's nothing I can do until Wade gets back into town," I said.

"And you think you're going to bully him into giving those disks back? You've got a lot to learn about bitter old queens, girl."

"What would you do?" I asked. "I mean, not that you're a bitter old queen."

"Nice try. In any case, I've worked with enough of them. He sneaked through your stuff to get what he wanted. Now it's your turn."

"That's not my style," I said.

"You're not stealing anything of his. You're taking back your own property. Think about how he'll squirm when he finds out, because there won't be a thing he can do to you without admitting he started it."

"I can't break into his apartment," I argued.

"Break in? Why would you have to?"

"How else can I get into his office?"

"Your mother told you to talk to Ethan Whitehawk—"

"Crow."

"I will as soon as you successfully complete your mission," Martin said. "I'll bet Ethan can get you in the apartment."

"Ethan White*crow*," I said, emphasizing the last name, "is not going to let me in Wade's apartment to snoop through his office. First, he'll defend Wade. If I'm adamant about my suspicions, he'll tell me to speak to Wade directly. He's a nice guy; he may even agree to go with me to talk to Wade. And I have no doubt Wade would lie to both of us."

"You don't have to tell Ethan that you want in the apartment. Did you not tell me a while ago that Ethan may think you're after him? Ask him out on a date."

"How will that get me in Wade's apartment?"

Martin mulled it over for a moment, seeming to go through a mental Rolodex of harebrained schemes.

"Fire? No, not after the last time. Flood? No, he's too high up for that. You could tell him Andy broke in and—"

"Are you nuts?"

"That's perfect. Tell him Andy's nuts and he broke in with a torch."

"I'm not going to do any such thing, and I want a lock on my bedroom door."

"I'm joking. Just ask him if Wade was affected by the recent break-ins in his building. If Ethan knows Wade's out of town, if he has a key, he might be anxious to check on things for him."

"That's a lot to leave to chance. And what am I supposed to do if it works? Go wandering around the apartment and hope Ethan doesn't notice?"

Martin sighed and said, "If you're going to make this difficult, I'll have to go to plan B."

"Which is?"

"The less you know, the better."

"A lock *and* an alarm on my bedroom door."

"Does Ethan have a cell phone?"

"Yes."

"Does he keep it with him? Keep it on?"

"He did the only time I was out with him."

"Do you have the number?"

"Yes."

"You ask him out. Give me the number and leave the rest to me."

"Not unless you tell me what you're going to do."

"I'm going to ask an old friend of Ken's for a favor. She'll give Ethan an urgent reason to interrupt your date and go to Wade's apartment. And you'll convince Ethan you don't mind going along. In fact, maybe it will be a computer problem, so Ethan will be glad to have you with him."

"Is there some connection between this friend and Wade?"

"She works for Wade. In fact, she'd still have a key if it weren't for that whole fire thing."

"Fire?"

"Never mind that. Have you ever tried to get the smell of smoke out of twenty kimonos?"

"Not recently," I said, laughing at Martin in spite of myself.

"And Wade made Brenda pay for it, that cheap bastard."

"Brenda Li?"

"You know Brenda?"

"Not really."

"Believe me, she'll be happy to help, since her closet smells like she bought out Boy George's fire sale. And the best part is that you'll be using Wade's own people against him. That one-ups the score, doesn't it?"

"I've been living with you less than a week, and you already know how to push my buttons."

"Which should tell you that an alarm on your bedroom door would be useless."

"Remind me not to make you mad at me."

"I don't get mad," Martin said sweetly. "I get even."

TEN

I stepped out of my bedroom feeling fresh and clean and ready for some action worthy of James Bond. I assumed Martin had left for Club Chaos, since the Spice Girls were no longer singing about what they really, really wanted. I only wanted my disks back and all spy games out of the way so I could concentrate on getting the guy. I took my jacket from the coatrack and noticed a pair of black leather gloves on the table by the door, with a note attached to them that read: *Don't leave any fingerprints! Yours in espionage, M.*

I chuckled, wondering if Martin realized how appropriate it was that he used only his first initial. I was beginning to think he was smarter than he sometimes let on.

I'd arranged to meet Ethan at the bar of a restaurant called Savoir Fare. It was a popular place among the newly rich and always-trendy dot-com-ers. I was surprised that Ethan had chosen it, but as I did a quick scan of the menu in the window, I was relieved to see only a small selection of seafood.

"I hope you weren't waiting long," I said, stepping back as Ethan stood up from the bar.

"Not at all. Our table will be ready in a few minutes. I do have to warn you about something." Ethan paused. I wasn't sure what he would say. I hoped it wouldn't be a speech about how he liked me as a friend, but that I really needed some spiritual guidance. He continued with a semisheepish look on his face. "Wade is out of town, but that doesn't mean I won't be summoned away."

"Don't tell me you may have to jump up and take a cab to JFK."

"No, nothing like that," he assured me, "but Wade did leave my number at Disorient XPress in case of any emergencies."

"At least I know what to expect if anyone at Wade's club has an urgent need to have their rune stones read."

"Touché. Sometimes Wade keeps things related to the club in his apartment. I'm the only one with a key. So far, there haven't been any problems, so we should be safe."

The maître d' approached us with menus in hand and said, "This way, gentlemen."

He led us to a corner table, nicely separated from the rest of the diners by the dangling tendrils of what even I could recognize were the fullest spider plants I'd ever seen. I realized that Ethan's eyes were resting on me as if he were trying to read my mind. I hoped he couldn't detect that I had an ulterior motive for asking him out. I dropped my eyes and immediately picked up my menu, hoping that Brenda's call would come soon.

"As you'll see, this menu has very few seafood choices."

"I'm glad you remembered that I don't like fish."

Ethan smiled as he set his menu aside without even looking at it. Because he was such an attractive man, I had a hard time resisting his gaze. I wouldn't have been surprised to find out that some of his followers were interested in him for more than his spiritual guidance; I wished I knew if Jeremy was among them.

I set down my menu, deciding on the coq au vin. Our server appeared and took our drink orders. When she left, Ethan let his eyes rest on me again.

"May I be blunt and ask you a question?"

"Yes," I drawled, wondering what I was in for.

"Jeremy's friend at the retreat. Daniel. Are you and he dating?"

"No," I said, flooded with relief. "We know each other from Eau Claire. Daniel is in a relationship. He and I are just friends."

As Ethan smiled at me, my relief was replaced by anxiety. I didn't want to lead him on about the reason for our meeting. Then again, he'd left me an opening I couldn't resist.

"What about you and Jeremy?" I asked. "Are you two a couple?"

"Jeremy is a wonderful man," Ethan said. "But right now, at least, our relationship isn't really in that place. We're more like healer-client."

I kept my face blank so he wouldn't misinterpret my pleasure over his answer as interest in him. But I was thrilled to hear that, at least in Ethan's mind, there was nothing romantic happening between Jeremy and him.

Our server returned and set our drinks in front of us. Just as she left, ducking around the dangling plants, Ethan's phone rang. His first few words made it clear that the call was from Brenda, and I forced myself not to listen or look at him, still worried that he could read my mind. I remembered the night at the retreat when Ethan seemed to "hear" Daniel's thoughts from across a crowded room. Whether or not he could read minds, he had an uncanny ability to see into people.

I looked up only after he had flipped his phone shut. He wore an apologetic look.

"It seems we're meant never to finish a meal together."

"You have to go?"

"The new karaoke machine at Disorient XPress is having problems, and tonight is karaoke night. Brenda, who works at the club, thinks that Wade may have left the manual at his apartment so yes, I have to go."

"Why don't I go along to keep you company? We could always grab a quick bite after running the manual down to the club."

"Are you sure you don't mind?"

"Not at all. Besides, I have a few questions about some things I learned at the retreat," I lied, hoping that my interest in spiritual matters would make him as unguarded as possible.

We talked about power animals on the short cab ride from Savoir Fare to Wade's apartment, where the doorman greeted Ethan and waved us to the elevator. I followed closely behind as we stopped outside Wade's door. Ethan fumbled with the keys, then unlocked all three locks. I slipped into spy mode, watching inconspicuously over his shoulder as he punched in the code to deactivate the alarm system: 3-1-2-7-7.

The lights came on automatically as the door opened. A pile of mail was stacked just inside on a small antique table. I followed Ethan through the apartment, gaping at its immense space. It seemed almost triple the size it was on the night of the party, probably because it had been filled with people then. Fortunately for me, however, Wade believed in minimalism. The disks would have practically blared their presence from any of the nearly bare tables and shelves. I was certain if they were anywhere, they'd be in his office.

An empty vodka bottle sat on top of the grand piano. Ethan grabbed it and tossed it into the recycling bin in the pantry, just off of the kitchen. He gave me a long-suffering look as I followed him from the room.

"I'll check in the library first," he said, ducking into the small, shelf-lined room. A few law books were spread across an oak table, which had a built-in light coming up from the center. Other than that, the library was as immaculate as the other rooms, without a Zip disk in sight.

"Do you mind if I pop into the bathroom?" I asked.

"Not at all; this should only take a minute."

"So should this," I said with a laugh, hoping he wouldn't detect my nervousness.

I remembered from my tour that Wade's office was right next to the bathroom. It was just down the hall from the library, so I knew I had to make it quick. Hopefully, there weren't any special tricks to get in.

The door to the office was closed. I was about to put my hand on the knob when I remembered the note from Martin. As silly as it seemed, there was no reason to be careless. When I slipped on the black gloves, I noticed a small square beside the office door. I looked over my shoulder as I pressed the square, determined to err on the side of caution. I could hear the rustling of papers coming from the library as Ethan continued his search for the manual.

My instincts had been right. The square flipped up to reveal a keypad exactly like the one outside the apartment door. The LCD display read *ARMED*. Sweat formed at my temples. I had my doubts that the code would be the same as the one Ethan had used at the other door. I also wondered if I should just wait for him, since Ethan would probably want to look in the office. Then I did it; I punched in the code. It beeped and the LCD display changed to *DISARMED*. I sighed and pushed open the door, flipping on the light to reveal a sparsely furnished office. Against the far wall was an oversized marble-topped desk. A lone PC sat humming away. I hurried to it and immediately saw that there was no Zip drive on the computer. I opened the three drawers of the desk, unsurprised to find them empty except for a pad of paper and an array of

Disorient XPress pens. I shrugged my shoulders and turned, remembering that I had to be quick. I turned off the light and closed the door behind me as I walked out.

Ethan stepped into the hall right after I flipped the alarm box closed. I had forgotten to set the code and felt another bead of sweat forming at my temple. I put my hands in my pockets and wiggled out of the gloves.

"It wasn't in the library," Ethan said.

"Could it have been in the den with the candlestick?" Ethan gave me a confused look as he turned to the wall and flipped up the square panel. "I guess you've never played Clue."

"I don't play games," he said. "Ugh. Wade didn't set the alarm to the office."

"That's odd," I said nervously. I was not cut out for these cat-and-mouse games and felt like my guilt was written all over my face.

"Not really," Ethan sighed. "Wade has been forgetting a lot of things lately. The drinking binges don't help, especially since he's at the club so much now that he converted the back room into his office."

"That's too bad," I said, firmly convinced that my disks were at Disorient XPress. Unfortunately, I had no idea how I would get into that office short of breaking in after hours, although Brenda Li had proved cooperative so far. Maybe Martin could talk her into looking for the Zip disks.

"It really is too bad," Ethan was saying. "Wade's a smart guy with a lot of potential to be really great." He paused with a disturbed look on his face. "To be completely honest, though, it's been tough playing baby-sitter, no matter how much I owe him." He quickly moved away, which I perceived as his way of avoiding elaboration. He made a quick search of the office, then stood in the center of the room with a pensive look, wrinkling his brow and biting his bottom lip. "Why don't you wait on the sofa while I search the rest of the apartment? I'm really sorry about this. I had hoped we would get a chance to talk more."

"Don't sweat it. Like I said, there's no reason why we can't still have dinner, whether or not we take the manual to the club. It's not that late."

I went to the living room and sat down on a sofa, facing a breathtaking view of the city. I suddenly had a different impression of Ethan. He seemed more vulnerable, at least when it came to Wade. Maybe I was imagining it, but he appeared to have a side that was just as lost as the people he tried to help with spiritual guidance.

I noticed a shock of bright pink in the middle of a picture frame on a small table in the corner. I walked over and picked it up. It was a photo of a smiling Wade and an uncomfortable-looking Blythe with a group of people I had never seen. I recognized the location as Tompkins Square Park. I laughed to myself, thinking about how thrilled Blythe must have been to pose beside Wade. Just as I replaced the picture, Ethan reappeared, flipping his long, dark hair over one shoulder.

"It's not here. Knowing Wade, my guess is that if it isn't somewhere at the club where no one thought to look, it's probably in a landfill in New Jersey. Let me call Brenda and let her know."

I followed Ethan from Wade's apartment as he put his cell phone between his shoulder and ear after hitting a button to speed-dial the club. As he locked the door and reset the alarm, he explained to the person on the other end that he'd had no luck finding the manual. He then turned to me and rolled his eyes and groaned. His face gave way to a smile that looked half frustrated and half amused. He disconnected the phone.

"Brenda says she found the manual on top of a case of Absolut in the basement. Nice of her to call and let me know. How Disorient XPress survives with that staff I'll never understand."

The night was crisp and clear, winter descending upon us with sharp wisps of cold air. Amazingly, I could see the stars. I was finding that there were certain parts of Manhattan with less light pollution, including the Upper East Side. Out of the corner of my eye, I saw Ethan also look at the sky. As I spotted the North Star, I was reminded, when a wonderful aroma hit my nose, that I hadn't eaten. I took my eyes from the sky to find its source. A lone hot-dog vendor looked like he was getting ready to close up his mobile shop for the night.

"Come on," I said, tugging at Ethan's sleeve. "Have you ever had a New York vendor hot dog?"

"I try not to eat food that's too processed. It interferes with the proper flow of energy."

"Do you ever lighten up?"

He compressed his lips and looked away, then pulled me in the direction of the vendor.

"What harm will one intestine filled with by-products, parts, and chemicals do," he mused, relenting with a smile.

"I must have eaten a million of these as a kid," I said. "I turned out okay, didn't I?"

"Better than okay," Ethan agreed.

I ordered one hot dog with the works, a bag of roasted peanuts, and a Diet Coke. I let Ethan decide how he wanted his wiener to be adorned. After we had our dinner in hand, we found a bench beside the stone wall on the periphery of Central Park that afforded a good view of the sky.

"That little patch of sky reminds me of nights I've spent on the roof of my farmhouse in Eau Claire, thinking about a story my grandmother told me when I was a kid," I said between bites. "She used to say that each star in the sky is a ball of energy; when one's life on earth ends, it continues up there, the essence of the person jumping from one star to another. If you're lucky enough to see a shooting star, you're witnessing a soul returning to earth to be reborn. She only started telling these stories in her old age, so most of my family thought she was losing it. I, on the other hand, thought she made a lot of sense."

As I talked, I realized this was one of the first moments since I'd come to Manhattan that I felt absolutely relaxed. There was something about Ethan's presence that was soothing, especially his voice when he began speaking.

"You can see an entire constellation right there," he said, pointing to an area of the sky just below the North Star. "Of course, if we were in a place where more stars were visible, you could see the whole story evolve. A Canadian tribe passed down a tale that follows the movement of that constellation, the Bear, called 'The Great Hunt.' I never heard it until after I came to New York. Wade knows it. He'll only tell it at this time of year or in early summer, which is when it was traditionally told."

"What's the story about you and Wade?" I asked boldly.

Ethan sat in silence. At first I perceived this reaction as one of uncomfortable restraint. When I studied his face, however, I realized it was more likely that Ethan felt conflicting emotions when it came to Wade and had never really opened up about them to anyone.

He took in a great gulp of air, the last bite of his hot dog, and a swig of water, then began to speak in a hushed voice.

"Remember in my speech at the retreat how I said I'd traveled around trying to find spiritual enlightenment through various means?"

"Yes."

"That's the way I present it for the benefit of those who trust and believe my words, my advice—those who need me to appear strong. The reality is that I was just lost. I'd gotten mixed up in a lot of things I don't care to go into detail about. My experience with drugs went well beyond using them for spiritual enlightenment. I had more than a few scrapes with the law and hit rock bottom with a suicide attempt. It was right after that when I met Wade. I'd made friends with a group of artists living in the Southwest, taking an interest in the Native American artists who were part of the group. I dabbled in art as part of my therapy. Wade saw some of my work and was impressed. It began with a few innocent conversations. As we became closer, just as friends—never anything more—he made an offer to send me to art school. I wasn't sure if that was really what I wanted. Finally, I agreed to go to a liberal arts school. As I've said before, I eventually chose a double major in psychology and Native American studies and later fully immersed myself in the spiritual side of what I learned. Wade was always encouraging. He helped me find a publisher for my books. Then, when I came to New York, he helped me get established here, too. Do you understand why I feel so indebted to him?"

"Yes, but don't you believe there are limits to indebtedness?"

"I'll have to give that some thought." He paused to take a drink. "It happened again. I blathered on about myself. We never seem to get around to talking about you, do we?"

"I've pretty much told you my story," I said.

"About your technical and business background, yes," Ethan agreed. "But not much about your artistic side. I think I remember you telling me that you minored in graphic arts in college. You mentioned a project you were working on with Blythe Mayfield. She's a painter, right?"

"Right," I said, suddenly suspicious that I wasn't the only one with an ulterior motive for this meeting.

"And the two of you are collaborating on . . ." he said in a leading tone.

I glanced at my watch and said, "Oh, my gosh, look at the time."

Ethan didn't miss a beat, saying, "The Buddha advised, 'Do not

dream of the future, concentrate the mind on the present moment.' "

"And the Doors said, 'The day destroys the night; the night di-
vides the day.' I've got an early meeting in New Jersey tomorrow. I
should call it a night," I explained.

"Adam, I'm disappointed in you. If you're going to quote the
Doors, you should've used the line about the clock saying it's time to
close now." He stood up from the bench, stepping toward the street to
hail a cab. "Anyway, I've got an early morning tomorrow, too. Thanks
for being understanding, once again, about a change in plans."

"I'm a Gemini. You know how flexible we can be about that kind
of thing."

"You're going south, right?" he asked when a cab stopped in response to his wave.

"Right."

"Then you take this cab. I need to catch one going north."

"All right," I agreed.

He gave me a quick, platonic hug just before I climbed into the
cab. As we pulled away, I glanced back to see him crossing the
street toward Wade's apartment. Though I never got the idea that
Ethan lived with Wade—and he was certainly eager to inform me
that the two of them were not romantically involved—I still sensed
there was more to their story than he wanted me to know. I was
sure it had something to do with Blythe.

I felt frustrated. Not only had our meeting not resulted in the retrieval of my Zip disk case, but I was left with more questions than
answers about the connection between Ethan, Wade, and Blythe.
Or maybe I was just imagining all of that to assuage my guilt about
using Ethan. And I did feel guilty, because I was certain that Ethan
was a good man. I remembered Daniel's assessment of him at the
retreat: "*He's so strong.*" I had to agree. Ethan exuded strength and
decency, and he'd obviously traveled a long distance from his troubled youth. No matter what plots or schemes Wade had ensnared
him in, and whether or not they involved Blythe, I believed that
Ethan's motives were good ones.

I was determined that any future schemes of my own, involving
either Wade or Jeremy, would exclude Ethan. I'd been wrong to
use him, and I wouldn't do it again. In fact, it was time to be true to
my nature, doing as Blaine had advised, and simply wait for Wade's
return from Zurich to confront him face to face about the disks.

With that decided, I spent the rest of the cab ride marshalling any possible arguments for Martin. It was time for James Bond and M to turn in their secret decoder rings. When the cab rolled up in front of the town house, I paid the driver and wearily made my way up the stoop. Jane Street was beginning to feel like home. All I wanted to do was tuck myself in bed for a solid night's sleep.

As I let myself in, a whistling Martin, obviously just home from Club Chaos, breezed through the living room from the kitchen, carrying four large shopping bags. I gave him a quizzical look as he headed toward his bedroom.

"Shopping?" I asked, following him.

"Not exactly," he said shoving the bags into his walk-in closet. "Borrowing."

"What's it all for?" I asked suspiciously.

"Plan B, of course. Or do I mean plan C?"

"How do you know I didn't get the disks back?" I asked.

"I don't, but not too long before becoming a whirling, twirling diva, I was a Boy Scout." He stopped arranging the bags and whipped around like a cyclone, a horrified look on his face. "Don't you dare tell a soul!"

"Don't worry, Martin, I won't tell anyone. I'll just use it as leverage."

Martin beamed as he closed the door and threw his arms in the air.

"I'm so proud! You're learning!" He collected himself, then continued, "Be prepared; that's my motto. I have all the tools for this mission, but I still have to find two more secret Asians."

"Seeing as how this is my problem, do you mind sharing plan B? Or C?"

"Oh hell, let's make it plan D, for 'don't worry about a thing.' It will all come together tomorrow evening. I arranged to have my shows at Club Chaos covered by someone else. Operation Disco Disk has become a wonderful distraction."

"Fine," I muttered, trudging off to bed with the slightest flicker of hope that leaving this to Martin wasn't a mistake. As long as Ethan wasn't involved, I was willing to listen to Martin's plan when he decided to share it.

I woke early Friday morning and went straight to Weehawken to work with Ray. He seemed so solid and sensible as he efficiently ran his business that it was a relief to be around him. I decided that I would nix whatever new plan Martin had formulated. I was a businessman, not an undercover agent.

The town house was quiet when I got home, and I went into the kitchen to forage for food. Though Martin kept the apartment in good condition, he wasn't exactly Julia Child when it came to stocking the place with groceries. While I was standing in front of the refrigerator trying to make something appealing appear for lunch, Martin waltzed in humming.

"I hate to spoil your mood," I said, "but I've made a decision. No more covert activities involving the disks. I'm already up to speed on all my work. When Wade gets back from Zurich, I'll talk to him directly. I'm not involving anyone else in this nonsense."

"That might be a problem," Martin said. "Daniel came by Club Chaos last night."

"So?"

"Apparently, you told Blaine about Wade and the disks. Blaine told Daniel."

"That's fine. I told Blaine he could tell Daniel if he felt it was necessary."

"Daniel is really pissed."

"Oh," I said, my heart sinking. "He's mad at me?"

"At you? How well do you and Daniel know each other?"

"I had hoped well enough that he'd understand how terrible I feel about all this," I said.

"Of course he understands!" Martin said. "Blaine told him how upset you were. Daniel came here to talk to you about it. Since you weren't here, he came to the club. He seemed worried that you might do Wade bodily harm."

I gave a half laugh, wondering if Daniel thought I'd traded in the spit wads and taunts of youth for more sinister weapons as an adult.

"One of Daniel's more appealing qualities is his loyalty," Martin was saying. "Of course to Andy and the club, but his real concern was you. He wasn't angry at you. He was angry on your behalf. And amused when I told him about your mission last night."

"He doesn't blame me for the precarious position Club Chaos is in?"

"Not at all. Anyway, after talking to him, I decided if you didn't find the disks in Wade Van Atterson's apartment, we'd have a go at the club."

"I thought about that, too. Brenda Li was very helpful last night. Do you think she'll look for the disks in Wade's office and give them to me if she finds them?"

"*Hel-lo,*" Martin said in a Valley Girl voice. "She was the first one to think of that. She went through the office, at great risk to herself, I might add. When this is all over, you'll have to meet Vic, Wade's pit bull of an office manager. Brenda says he barely lets Wade into that office. There's a stack of plastic and leather cases with unlabeled disks, and they all looked alike to her. Vic apparently thinks knowledge is power, and he's not giving any away."

"Oh," I said, feeling defeated. "I don't have my disks marked either, since I'm the only one who uses them."

"Maybe Ethan Whitefish's next retreat can include a session on intuiting disk contents."

Just then our buzzer rang. Martin put his hands together as if praying, slipping momentarily into his Sister Mary Amanda persona, and did a quick curtsy while looking at the ceiling with a thankful expression on his face. He grabbed me by the wrist and nearly dragged me to the door. I didn't expect this slight man to be so strong and allowed myself to be led.

When Martin saw our visitors, his face seemed to slide off and fall to the floor with a squish. He quickly composed himself.

"Daniel! What exquisite timing. Too bad about your choice in accessories," Martin snarled, curling his lip toward Jeremy, who stood beside Daniel, looking as if he'd rather be anywhere else.

"Martin, can we call a five-minute truce?" Daniel asked.

"Oh, okay," Martin said, letting Daniel in but closing the door on Jeremy.

"Martin," Daniel warned.

Martin sighed and opened the door to let Jeremy in, while Daniel turned to me.

"I wanted to stop by and see how you've settled in. Did you get your disks back last night?"

I wasn't sure how much Jeremy knew, so I merely said, "No. They weren't where I hoped they'd be."

"That's too bad," Daniel said.

The atmosphere seemed to be filled with uncertainty about who knew what and what should or shouldn't be said. I found myself wishing the damn disks had never existed. I had the object of my desire in my home, but instead of being able to enjoy his company,

I was caught up in a drama I'd never wanted. I searched my mind for some way to get rid of Martin and Daniel.

Martin slunk into the room and plopped himself down on a brown leather chair. He had a mischievous gleam in his eye and a rather proud grin running across his face. Jeremy, on the other hand, looked like a cat who had just been doused with water. He sat next to Daniel and seemed to avoid looking at Martin.

"Does anyone want a drink?" I asked, adopting the Manhattan tradition of cocktails anytime, day or night.

"Yes," the three of them chorused.

"I'll help you," Daniel and Jeremy said at the same time.

Daniel ignored my meaningful glance and said, "Relax, Jeremy. I'll do the honors. Why don't you put on some music?"

"I'll do that," Martin snapped, obviously feeling proprietary about the apartment.

As Daniel and I prepared the two gin-and-tonics and two sparkling waters that were ordered, I softly asked, "Does Jeremy know about the disks? Or about my pseudodate with Ethan last night?"

"No," Daniel said. "He and I met for a late lunch to celebrate my *Secret Splendor* role. I suggested stopping by here afterward."

"He looks thrilled," I said.

"It's not you. It's Martin. I told you they don't get along."

"I know. But it's not exactly helping my cause." I turned, alarmed, as I heard what Martin was saying.

". . . all Andy's wonderful plans going down the toilet because of your friends Ethan Whitewing and Wade Van Atterson."

"Martin," I barked, "why don't you just write a story about it for *HX?*"

"Wade stole property from you at the retreat?" Jeremy asked, his tone stunned. "Adam, believe me, I had no idea. I barely know Wade!"

"No one's blaming you," I said, turning to glare at Martin just in time to see him shoot a little glance of victory Daniel's way. I looked quickly at Daniel, who was giving Martin a slight nod.

"That's so sleazy," Jeremy said. "He must have found out that you're doing work for Club Chaos. I can't believe he's using you in his longstanding rivalry with Andy."

I shut up, content to let Jeremy see me as the wronged party. It was obvious Daniel and Martin had something up their sleeves; I figured I might as well let it play out.

"What's the story with Andy and Wade?" Daniel asked. "Does anyone know?"

"I know how it began," Jeremy said. "Ken told me a long time ago."

"Why would he tell you?" Martin asked.

"Martin," Daniel spoke patiently, "Jeremy and Ken were friends."

"It involved something theatrical. Since I work in the theater—"

"Your sitcom was canceled? You're working the ticket booth?" Martin asked.

Jeremy ignored him, saying, "Twenty years or so ago—who can tell with Andy's birth date jumping from one calendar year to the next?—Wade and Andy were as tight as Martin's daisy dukes. They formed a small band of radical performers known as the Lavender Players. For about two years everything went well. They became successful and took their show on the road. Andy had written, directed, and produced a one-act comedy called *Tell It to Me Blondly*. The media loved it; the audiences loved it, so they entered it in the Coriander Festival at NYU one summer. Andy was hospitalized for some medical problems, so Wade handled all the arrangements. When the program for the festival was printed, all of the credits for the play were given to Wade. Wade claimed that it was the printer's error, but the play caused such a frenzy that he never bothered to fix the mistake and ended up taking home the grand prize and all of the profits for the off-Broadway run of the play."

"Why didn't Andy sue?" I asked.

"According to Ken, Andy was way too trusting at that time and had no substantial proof that he'd written the play. Ken thought that was one of the reasons Andy's been so difficult and bitter all these years. As much because of his own error as because of Wade."

"I guess it's no surprise that Wade stole Adam's disks," Daniel said. "He obviously has no scruples."

"And to think you made it possible!" Martin said to Daniel.

"What's that supposed to mean?" Daniel growled.

"You're the one who dragged poor Adam to the retreat, in your lust for getting that role on *Splendid Squalor*. And you," Martin pointed at Jeremy, "are probably the reason Wade even knew Adam was doing work for Club Chaos."

"Me?" Jeremy demanded. "What are you talking about?"

"I bet you told Ethan Whitetail, and he told Wade."

"Jesus!" Jeremy flew off the sofa, sending his drink crashing into a signed photograph of Sarah Ferguson that sat on the end table. "I didn't even know Adam, much less that he was connected to Club Chaos. And Daniel had no way of knowing Wade would steal from Adam. Besides, what proof do you have that Wade stole anything?"

"Thank you, Ms. Lansbury. Since you require evidence, I've come up with a foolproof plan to get it for you."

"Who knew that a fool could come up with a foolproof plan?" Daniel chided.

"I will ignore that ridiculous remark. This plan will involve everyone's full cooperation. It will also require everyone to be in drag."

"I don't think so," I said, casting a look of horror Martin's way.

"We are going to infiltrate Wade's office at Disorient XPress," Martin went on, ignoring me.

"I am not breaking into Wade's nightclub," I said adamantly.

"We won't be breaking in. I'm not a criminal, after all. We'll go to the club, and we *will* get into that office, but it won't be with a crowbar. Just high heels and mascara. Adam, have you ever done drag?"

"Oh, no, Martin. I don't think that's going to be a good idea," I pleaded.

"Everyone has to do it at least once. It's a gay man's rite of passage. Don't you think this would make a fantastic debut for you?" Martin asked.

"I won't be part of this," Daniel said, giving me a supportive look. "I gave up drag last year, and I have no intention of doing it again. Besides, the last time I got involved in one of your little plots, Martin, I ended up in the emergency room getting cactus needles plucked from my ass for three hours." Daniel turned quickly to me and said, "Don't ask."

"Oh, again, you're just worried that you might jeopardize your soap role. Traitor! After all the years Andy gave you! Not to mention your childhood friendship with Adam!"

While Daniel and Martin continued to exchange verbal barbs, Jeremy stepped up beside me.

"As stupid as it sounds," he said softly, "maybe you should go along with this. It's the first time these two have acted normal with each other since Ken died."

"This is normal?" I asked, suspecting that Daniel and Martin were only seconds away from physical violence.

Jeremy nodded, watching them as they bickered.

"Daniel and I will cause a distraction," Martin was saying.

"Adam, since he knows what he's looking for, will get into Wade's office. We're also lucky enough to have Brenda Li helping us, only she required a small payoff." Martin blushed when he revealed this last part.

I had no clue as to what Martin could have traded to get Brenda to agree to help us a second time. Silence descended upon the room, all of us needing to take in what he'd said.

"Come on, Daniel," Jeremy finally prodded. "You can do it. Look at it like any other role. You're an actor, after all."

"And you," Martin said, pointing at Jeremy, "will be responsible for getting and driving the getaway car. You, too, will need to be in drag."

I could see a small vein pulsing in Jeremy's forehead.

"Oh no, I'm not getting mixed up in this . . . this debacle. It goes against all of my beliefs," Jeremy said.

"Debacle?" Martin mimicked. "Has your live-in tutor Robert still not gotten you past the *D* words after all this time? You should have bought one of those abridged dictionaries."

"This is not my battle," Jeremy said firmly. "I'm sorry about what's happened to you, Adam, but—"

"Come on Jeremy," Daniel mocked, *"look at it like any other role. You're an actor, after all."*

"Besides," Martin added, "you can put your retreat lessons to work and do something for the greater good. Think of the karmic repercussions if you deny the universe this chance to return things to their natural balance."

Jeremy's mouth opened as if to offer a retort, but before he spoke, I said, "Jeremy is right. This is my battle, not his."

"It's your *property*," Daniel said. "The battle is actually between Wade and Andy. Maybe none of us should be involved in it."

"But it isn't just between Andy and Wade," I disagreed. "Club Chaos is in trouble, and Wade Van Atterson is swooping in like a vulture to finish it off. When he does, all the people who have time and money invested—"

"I'll do it," Daniel said.

"So will I," Jeremy said.

Martin looked at them, seeming baffled by their change of heart, but I understood. It might be Andy's club, but it was Ken's money that was at risk here, money he'd left to take care of Martin. No matter what old rivalries and clashes existed among the three men in front of me, Ken was their common bond. And whether Martin knew it or not, on Ken's and his behalf, they would work together.

I was sure that most of the bickering between Daniel and Martin had been an act to cover up a plot they'd devised the night before to throw Jeremy and me together. I suspected Martin had thrown Daniel a curve with his idea for infiltrating Disorient XPress. Beyond that, I wasn't sure who was manipulating whom. I hadn't meant to conjure up Ken's ghost, and I'd been sincere about being willing to drop the Disorient XPress idea and confront Wade directly. But if this whole thing was going to help them work together as a group, not to mention allow me to spend time with Jeremy . . .

Martin clapped his hands and said, "Fabulous. We're all on the same page. Daniel, I'm running a little late for the club. Come into my bedroom so I can quickly explain what it is you and I are going to do. Jeremy, you have to make arrangements for a car."

Daniel and Martin walked out as I collected the empty glasses from the coasters and picked up Jeremy's overturned glass, wiping up the spilled water with a dish towel. Jeremy went to an antique cabinet and opened a door, smiling as he found what he was looking for—the Yellow Pages.

"It's been a long time since I was here, but I guess Martin hasn't moved things around," he said.

"Thanks for helping us do this. I know you don't want to," I said.

He shrugged and said, "What Wade did to you was wrong." He paused, then added, "That's not entirely why I agreed to go along."

"You want to keep those two from killing each other?" I asked, inclining my head toward Martin's room.

"I want to feel like a part of things again. I've missed them."

He concentrated on calling car rental agencies, so I continued cleaning up. As I moved about the room, I noticed something odd. Martin's pair of Catherine Bach–autographed daisy dukes no longer hung on the wall beside the coatrack. I felt a real soft spot growing for him, realizing that they must now be in Brenda Li's possession.

My mother had been right. Coming to New York was exactly what I'd needed to teach me the meaning of a family of friends. I could understand why Jeremy didn't want to lose them.

ELEVEN

I approached Operation Disco Disk with dread. I was tired of the entire ordeal and wished no one else had ever found out about it. I did call Blythe early on Saturday to tell her what little I knew about the plan. She broke into a fit of giggles when I told her that Martin intended to dress me in drag.

"Adam, just enjoy the sheer silly adventure of it. Can you take pictures?" she begged.

"Gosh, if only they'd done that at Watergate," I said.

"Way before my time," Blythe commented. "Monica should have taken a little spy-cam into the Oval Office."

"She did the next best thing, blabbing her secrets to anyone who would listen. Much like me."

"Could you repeat the details of your plan a little louder and more clearly?" Blythe asked. "Not that I'm making a tape."

I did feel better after talking with her, deciding she was right. Even without the disks, even without the sense that the trip to Disorient XPress would revive or forge new bonds between Daniel, Martin, Jeremy, and me, I was having an adventure.

Martin had taken great delight in finding something for me to wear. He had also chosen an outfit for Jeremy, who wouldn't arrive at the town house until after he picked up the rental car. When I last saw Martin, before I went to my bedroom to get changed, he was sitting in front of the television watching *Judge Judy* without the slightest care in the world. I, on the other hand, worried about how

long it was going to take to get ready, what I'd look like in my costume, and what would happen if Martin's plan went wrong. Not to
mention what Jeremy would think about the whole scheme now
that it was really happening.

I showered and, per Martin's instructions, shaved closely. Then I
went to the closet and took the kimono and wide sash from a satin-
padded hanger and laid it across the bed. I didn't know if I should
dress first, then put on my makeup, or do the reverse order.

"To hell with it," I muttered and went into the bathroom to
apply my makeup, something I would have bet Lars a thousand dollars I'd never end up doing.

Earlier, Martin had approached my makeup as if he were Mike
Ditka leading the Chicago Bears to the Super Bowl in 1986.

"First you're going to do your base, which will be white. The base
sets the whole face for the rest of your makeup, which is your eye-
liner, eyeshadow, and eyebrows," he listed, drawing a diagram on
paper like a football play on a chalkboard. "A dust of blush on each
cheekbone. Then the lips. Then you set your face with dusting
powder."

"I thought the base sets your face," I said with confusion.

"No! The powder sets the makeup in place so your eyebrows
aren't sliding down into your lip liner."

"You didn't say anything about lip liner," I grumbled.

After calling me a yeti, Martin calmed down and took a different
approach. He told me to think of applying makeup as painting a
picture. My face was the canvas and my medium was Lillith Allure
cosmetics. He then trashed his original list and drew me a paint-by-
numbers diagram of how my face was supposed to look and the
order it would take to achieve perfection.

He had said that he or Daniel would be available to help, and as
I wiped the first bit of white makeup across my forehead with the
sponge, I heard the doorbell ring. The barking voice of Judge Judy
was cut off, and I heard Martin open the front door for Daniel.
They exchanged a few words before Daniel came down the hall
and paused outside the bathroom door.

"Knock, knock," he said.

"Who's there?"

"Daniel."

"Daniel who?"

"If you're expecting me to come up with some kind of punch

line, forget it," he said and swept into the bathroom where I stood in front of the mirror.

He looked at the makeup I'd applied already and said, "You look like a cross between a Kewpie doll and—I don't know what, but it can't be good."

"I don't know about this, Daniel. I don't see how it can work. Look at me. This is ridiculous."

"It's nothing Hop Sing can't fix," Daniel said, pushing up his sleeves.

"Hop Sing? The cook on *Bonanza?*" I asked in bewilderment.

"See? You're already becoming an authority on Asian lore."

I laughed. I could hear Martin bustling about in his room, humming "Sukiyaki Song" as he got ready. Once in a while I saw a flash of blue as he breezed by the open door of his room with something over his shoulder.

The sound of the doorbell a half hour later signaled Jeremy's arrival at the town house. Martin let him in and pointed him in the direction of my room. Although there had been plenty of moments when I thought it would be nice to have him in my bedroom, applying lipstick and putting on dresses was not quite what I'd had in mind.

"And don't come out of there until you're good and made up!" Martin shouted to Jeremy. I couldn't tell if he was kidding or not.

"I can't believe I'm doing this," Jeremy said, echoing my thoughts when he passed by the open door to the bathroom.

"But'cha ahhhh, Blanche. Ya ahhhh," Daniel said without missing a beat while reapplying my makeup.

"Ha-ha," was all Jeremy said. He paused to look at me. Though I was facing Daniel, I could see his image in the mirror.

"Hi," I said to his reflection, feeling vulnerable.

"Hi," he responded, then set a case that looked like a fishing tackle box on the counter and opened it. After rummaging through its contents, he blurted out, "Dang, that's what I was afraid of." He looked over the small pile of makeup that Martin had provided for me, then called out, "Martin?"

"Yeth?" Martin replied from his bedroom with an exaggerated lisp.

"Do you have any powder?"

Martin came into the bathroom to see how my face was progressing.

"Sure," he replied to Jeremy, and his brow furrowed when he gave my makeup a once-over. He closed his eyes and shook the sight of my face from his head as if it were an Etch A Sketch, then said to Jeremy, "Walk this way."

I took a blush brush from the counter and said, in my best Groucho Marx impersonation, "If he could walk that way, he wouldn't need the powder," while tapping the blush brush "cigar."

Martin and Daniel groaned in unison, but I felt redeemed when I saw a smile dance across Jeremy's lips before he followed Martin out of the bathroom.

"I guess I'm done," Daniel pronounced. "I'm sorry, Adam. I hate to say this, but your face is too masculine to be pretty. This is the best I can do."

I was reminded of the scene in *Batman* when the Joker laughed maniacally at his image before breaking his mirror. I stared in horror at my reflection before saying, "You're kidding, right?"

"No," Daniel said gravely, as if he were a general informing a war widow of a terrible loss. "I'm not."

"Daniel, I've seen pictures of you on the walls of Club Chaos. How can *you* look so beautiful and I end up looking like this?"

"Honey, good drag doesn't mean the person necessarily looks pretty. You have to work with what you've got. You're a marvel of a man, Adam, but you're not cut out to be a woman."

The contrast of the white makeup and the thin black eyebrows Daniel had painted on me made me think I was beginning to resemble my power animal more and more. The only things that kept me from looking like a Sumo-wrestling zebra were my rosebud lips and the garish red paint around my eyes.

"Get dressed while I put on my face," Daniel said, pushing me toward the bedroom. He brought out his own makeup case, setting out jars and brushes with the efficiency of someone who knew what he was doing. "We really should have dressed you first. Be careful not to smudge your face when you change clothes."

"I will *not*," I heard Jeremy say a short time later as he stormed across the hall.

"You're going to have to wear it. It's the only thing I have that'll fit you."

"Absolutely not. Daniel? We have a problem."

"Oh, what now?" Daniel asked.

"Martin has picked out a special outfit just for me," Jeremy announced, coming into the bedroom partially made up and holding what appeared to be a large dismantled bird, sewn back together with patches of different colors of lamé, slung over his shoulder. Feathers flowed in every direction behind him.

"He doesn't have to look like us." Martin presented his case to Daniel. "He's just going to be in the car, right? Oh, my god, you did bring the car, didn't you?"

Jeremy's expression changed from anger about the outfit to looking somewhat sheepish.

"Yeah."

"What? What's wrong?"

"I got the last one they had. We're lucky, actually. It was only because I called that I was able to rent it."

"Spill," Martin commanded, hands on the hips of his terry-cloth robe, a towel twisted around his head.

Jeremy looked pleadingly at us but only received anticipatory stares from Daniel and me. Martin shot a frosty glare back at Jeremy.

"It's like this," Jeremy began. "I guess there was something going on at the car rental place, because when I called, the guy I spoke with sounded really busy. I asked for a large car, just like you said."

"And when you got there?" Martin prompted, trying to get Jeremy to cut to the chase.

"He said everything was fine on the phone, but when I got there—"

"Oh, god," Martin interrupted and tore the towel off his head, perhaps to strangle Jeremy with it.

". . . when I got there, they said they didn't have any four-door rentals."

"And you let them feed you that crap?" Martin demanded. "That's the oldest line in the book. This is just your way of getting back at me."

"For what?" Jeremy demanded.

"I don't know, but you better believe I'll think of it before we leave. Now what kind of car did you get?"

"It's new," Jeremy stated, as though the car's model year would somehow balance out the bad news yet to come.

"Go on," Daniel prompted in his most patient tone. I could tell it had been practiced over some period of time.

"It's a Volkswagen Beetle."

"*Oh—*" Martin started.

"It's really quite roomy," Jeremy said.

"—*my*—" Martin took a step toward Jeremy.

"It was all they had!" Jeremy yelped and stepped backward.

"—*god!*" Martin twisted the towel in his hands as if wringing out an image of how we'd all look jammed into the tiny car in full drag.

I looked with pity at Jeremy, who, I believed, had done the best he could with the assignment he'd been given. I knew from all the traveling I'd done what it was like to be shafted by the rental car companies.

"A Beetle? Were they out of rickshaws?" Martin fumed. "How in the hell are we supposed to fit into a Volkswagen?"

"That's enough," Daniel said and placed a calming hand on Martin's shoulder. "The clock is ticking. We can stand here and debate this, or we can work with what we've got. I suggest we continue to get ready or we'll miss the *Secret Splendor* crowd. Don't forget, we need to go while it's still busy, so Adam can carry out his part of the plan. I've heard the crowd thins out after the showing. Jeremy, Martin, I want you in separate corners getting dressed. Adam, put on your outfit, and I'll help you with your wig in a minute."

Daniel went back into my bathroom to finish getting ready. Martin scowled one last time at Jeremy before returning to his room, and Jeremy laid his dress on my bed. I picked up the kimono and shrugged it on over my shoulders. It was surprisingly comfortable, and the cool silk felt good against my skin. I wondered with a frown what it meant that I kind of liked the way it felt on me.

I glanced up to see that Jeremy had taken off his shirt and was watching me. He looked incredible. Though his frame was smaller and less developed than mine, he'd obviously put some work into his well-defined muscles. The sight of just his abs would have made Martin forget whatever mishap had occurred with the car. My eyes roamed over his exposed torso.

"What's wrong?" Jeremy asked.

"Huh?" I tore my eyes from his chest and looked intently into his eyes. "Nothing. I mean, this thing feels good."

"It's a silk robe. It ought to feel good. And don't worry," he said, as if reading my mind, "you're not going to have an overwhelming urge to dress like Doris Day anytime soon." He flashed a grin at me, getting the birdlike thing that he'd laid over the bed, and added, "Not that there's anything wrong with that."

I sat down on the bed and said, "I'm being narrow-minded, I guess. This is all new to me. I like Halloween as much as the next guy, but I always stick to more realistic costumes, like firemen, sailors, or cowboys."

"Then I'm definitely sorry I missed seeing your costume last month," Jeremy teased, and the lights on my mental scoreboard started flashing.

"Actually, you didn't miss much," I said. "All I did was watch the parade in the Village dressed as a displaced hick from the Midwest."

· "That sounds better than the network party I went to for the TV show," Jeremy said with a scowl and sat on the corner of the bed. "We didn't dress up either. It was just the cast, crew, and a bunch of producers in suits. It took two hours of yoga and a bag of Snickers miniatures to bring me down after pretending to be interested in the producers' wives, who were only there so they could fill pages in their autograph books. I'm sorry; you must think I'm awfully cynical."

"No. Not at all," I said, relieved that he had diverted himself from the topic of yoga. I wanted to hear more about him instead of his karmic path or anything else relating to Ethan Whitecrow. "I'm interested in hearing what's it like to be a big television star."

"I'd hardly call myself a 'star,' " Jeremy protested. "Our show is new and has barely made a crack in the ratings. Also, I'm just a supporting character."

"That's not the impression I got from Daniel," I said, then cringed, realizing I had just admitted that I'd never watched the show.

If Jeremy caught my faux pas, he didn't let on. Instead, he shrugged his shoulders and said, "Despite all the crappy theatrical roles I've done, and even though I was a crappy boyfriend, Daniel's always been my biggest fan. He'd say I was brilliant even if I was cast as a tree in an elementary school play."

I laughed at the idea and asked, "What about drag? Have you ever done this before?"

"Yeah," he answered and looked briefly at the ceiling as if it were a window into his past. "A couple of times. Ken, Daniel, and I went to this thing called the Unnatural Blonde Party once. I went as Loni Anderson. If you think you look ridiculous, you should have seen me."

"I'm sure you were stunning," I said, making it a point to look into his brown eyes. Just like at the retreat, Jeremy ducked his head and smiled.

"Daniel's career as a female impersonator was huge when we were together," he went on. "It was inevitable that I'd make an appearance or two in drag, I suppose."

"Onstage with him?"

"No," he said with a laugh. "It never came up. Some people thought that was strange, but we never even talked about it. There was a lot Daniel and I didn't talk about."

"Do you think that's why you broke up? Because of poor communication?" Jeremy didn't answer, and I suddenly realized I was prying. "Geez, listen to me. I sound like I'm interviewing you for some entertainment magazine. You don't have to answer. It's none of my business. Besides, Daniel is right in the next room."

"It's okay," Jeremy assured me. "Daniel and I have talked about all this. It's not like I'm revealing anything he doesn't already know, so I'm not breaking any barriers of confidence. I've done a lot of soul-searching lately, as you may have guessed, thinking about mistakes I've made. Simply put, where my past relationships are concerned, when the going gets tough, I've sometimes been selfish. Daniel and I were having problems, and instead of communicating, we both turned to other outlets to deal with our fears. Daniel's outlet was Princess 2Di4. Mine was the less honorable, unfortunately."

"Robert," I surmised. When Jeremy looked at me in surprise I said, "I'm learning that Martin isn't exactly the poster child for a kept secret."

"That's true. It doesn't matter, because it's not really a secret. Anyway, that's why I'm not rushing into another relationship. I want to work on myself first and figure out where I'm going. I want to have more to offer the next person I get involved with."

I didn't know what to say. I sat on my bed with what I hoped looked like an endearing smile, but given my costume, I'm sure I looked like the cat who swallowed the tuna roll instead of the proverbial canary. Jeremy had just confirmed for me that my instincts had been right all along. He was exactly the levelheaded, beautiful yet flawed man I had been looking for.

Jeremy broke eye contact with me and picked up his dress from the bed when he heard the sound of the bathroom door opening.

"I can't believe I'm going along with this," he said. "But I know if Daniel and Martin are involved, it's going to be interesting."

On his way to the bathroom, Jeremy passed a fully transformed Daniel, who joined me in the bedroom. He wore a dark wig and looked like someone I'd seen before. His slinky black dress with its high, broad shoulder pads was cut in such a way that it showed his cleavage.

Cleavage? Obviously this wasn't his first time at the rodeo.

I racked my brain trying to think of who he looked like. He walked across the room, turning for me like a runway model.

"Well? What do you think? Not bad, huh?"

"Amazing," was all I could say. "Are you sure I can't look a little better? Don't take this the wrong way, but I'd like to look . . ."

"Pretty? Let it go, Adam."

I sighed and turned again toward the door when Martin flounced into the bedroom, ready to be seen. He wore a royal blue dress with shoulder pads as large as Daniel's. The two of them looked like linebackers for the Packers. Like Daniel's, Martin's dress was cut low and showed an ample bosom. On his head was a sandy-blond wig, parted down the middle, with long feathers of hair that swept back from the front. He, too, looked vaguely famil-iar, but I couldn't put my finger on whom he resembled.

Daniel and Martin looked at each other and, as though planned, extended their arms.

"Krystle, darling!" Daniel proclaimed.

"Alexis, dear!" Martin countered.

They met each other in the middle of the room, air-kissing each cheek, and turned to face me. I was dumbstruck. A vague recollec-tion of the characters from the eighties nighttime drama *Dynasty* became clearer as I watched them.

"Wow," was all I could manage to say.

"Amazing, aren't they?" Jeremy said from behind them. He'd managed to put himself together quickly, probably because of his theatrical background. I wondered if being a gay man in New York required some sort of performing history.

Daniel and Martin parted to make room for Jeremy, who looked ridiculous. His outfit was a mishmash of crisscrossed feathers up and down the entire length of the long, tight dress. Interspersed among the feathers were triangular and rectangular patches of gold, silver, and copper lamé. A silver lamé turban covered his head, making him look somewhat like an ostrich after a brawl with a baked potato.

"I don't understand why I have to be dressed like this. I'm only driving the car. I don't even know how I can sit behind the wheel in this thing."

"You can sit, dear," Martin explained. "Just don't try to cross your legs. Not that you've ever tried that strategy before."

"Martin, please," Daniel began.

"Besides," Martin continued, "it's all about mood. You know how long it's been since Daniel's done anything like this. He needs all the help and support he can get. Think of it as part of your quest for spiritual enlightenment. You have to give off positive drag energy for the highest good of the mission."

Daniel carefully pinned a large black wig on my head, which made me feel even more like an alien than before. It was pulled up into a bun the size of a basketball, with a pair of chopsticks stuck into the back of it.

"Always thinking of others, Martin," Daniel chimed in. He glanced at a jeweled watch, then placed a black pillbox hat with a white band around it on his head and tilted it ever so slightly. With a hint of Joan Collins's English accent he said, "Let's go, shall we?"

When we made it to the sidewalk, we gazed at the bright-red Volkswagen Beetle, for the most part ignoring the stares of pedestrians. A few people allowed smiles to turn their lips upward as they watched us stand beside the car in silence.

"Subtle," was all Martin had to say.

"Okay, let's do this," Daniel added with a certain finality as Jeremy fumbled with the keys. The car blipped a couple of times, and the door locks sprang up after he pushed a button. "Come on, Krystle, into the back with you."

"Why? So you can ride shotgun? I think not," Martin said as he gingerly descended into the passenger side of the car.

"No, Adam is riding up front with Jeremy. You and I are in the backseat. We have experience with this stuff, and Adam is going to need the extra headroom."

I stood in my long, green robe and sandals and shrugged. I suspected I was being put in the front seat so that I could sit with Jeremy, a thought that somehow made the whole experience more palatable.

"I still don't understand why I have to be here." Jeremy tried one last-ditch effort to get out of this charade. "Why couldn't you just call a cab?"

"I've told you," Martin began, "we have to have a car waiting. You know as well as anyone that you can't count on a cab to wait for you."

Daniel and Martin squeezed into the backseat and coached Jeremy and me into the front seats of the car. I had to duck way down to get my head in and couldn't really sit upright once I was inside. Luckily, I was able to extend my legs a bit more than I thought I'd be able to.

Martin, who was sitting behind me, squelched that when he said, "Adam, dear, would you be a lamb and move your seat up a bit? I can hardly breathe back here. Yes, that's it. Just a bit more. Okay, good. No, wait. Can you move a bit more? Oh, thank you. That's perfect."

I couldn't turn my head, but I adjusted the side mirror to see Martin's reflection. Although I knew that "objects in mirror are closer than they appear," Martin now had enough room to stretch his legs comfortably under my seat while I ate my kneecaps.

Jeremy, on the other hand, was still trying to get into the car. His dress was so tight that every time he bent to try to sit in the driver's seat, the dress constricted around his hips, pulling down in the front and riding up in the back, exposing his chest and calves.

"This isn't going to work," he proclaimed.

"Jeremy," Daniel began, once more using his patient tone, "pull the dress up a bit from your thighs before you sit, and it won't pull down in the front. It'll give your hips more room to move."

Jeremy did as he was instructed, and was able to assume a seated position when he moved behind the wheel in a stationary pose, simultaneously ducking down so that the turban would clear the door frame.

"Before we go," Jeremy began, "I should tell you that I'm not very good at driving a stick."

"Unless you've learned a new trick since we broke up, you've never driven a stick shift before," Daniel said.

"Yes, I have."

"When?" Daniel asked.

"I drove this one from the rental place," Jeremy said.

Martin clicked his tongue and rolled his eyes as Jeremy started the car. He pulled away from the curb like Cruella De Vil, jolting and lurching us into traffic as the horns of drivers sounded their displeasure with Jeremy's daring maneuvers.

As we got closer to Disorient XPress, Martin said, "Wait. Pull over here."

"Why?" Jeremy asked.

His knuckles were white on the steering wheel, and his eyes were wide. His was the face of someone clearly not accustomed to driving. He looked like Karen Black in the movie *Airport,* and I half expected him to say, "I can't fly this plane!"

"We can't all go in at once," Martin explained. "We'd be too obvious. Pull over and let me out. I can walk from here and arrive after you. Daniel, you and Adam need to stagger your entrances a bit. The two of you certainly don't look like you're together. But Daniel and I can't be seen together until we create the distraction."

The Beetle took one last forward lurch to the curb. The engine died when Jeremy remembered the clutch a little too late. I ducked low and got out of the car, allowing Martin to emerge from his luxurious quarters in the backseat.

He pecked me on the cheek, saying, "Don't forget to look for Brenda Li to give you the 'all clear' sign. Good luck."

I felt like Mr. Phelps in *Mission Impossible.* I got back into the car, and Jeremy swerved recklessly into traffic, setting off another series of honking horns. We pulled into a space that, miraculously, was open at the corner of the block Disorient XPress was on.

Daniel said, "Adam, you go first. I'll come in just a minute after you. I know we don't look like we're together, but I don't want to take any chances. Martin ought to be along anytime."

"Don't abandon me," I begged Jeremy as I once again uncurled myself from my seat.

"I won't. I hope you find your disks."

I went into the club. I was glad I'd been there with Blythe, because it meant I was already familiar with the layout. I glanced around the main room, looking for the office door. Brenda Li casually approached me. Out of the corner of my eye, I saw Daniel stride past us on his way to the bar.

"Hey, hot stuff," Brenda's gravelly voice greeted me.

"Hi," was all I could say in my nervous state.

"Don't worry, sweet thing. It'll be a big crowd today. A lot happened on the show this week, and this place'll be packed with queens who've waited for this moment to squeal with each other over the taped highlights. Just keep an eye out for my signal; you're on your own from there."

"Okay." I drew a deep breath and let it out.

"By the way," Brenda paused to say before leaving me, "what have ya got on under that thing? And does the sash have a combination?"

She winked at me, then made her way through the assembling crowd. As the door opened, a flood of light came in from outside, and Martin glided in. Heads turned his way, and I saw a few patrons gesture toward Daniel in his Alexis garb at the bar. They chuckled as they put the pieces of the two characters together and anticipated a showdown.

I spotted a nearly invisible door across the room. The only things that set it apart from the wall were its brass doorknob and the sign that read, *Office*. I meandered toward the door as *Secret Splendor's* introduction music swelled to fill the bar. Monitors strategically placed about the room went from solid blue to a series of pictures that I didn't stop to watch. The announcer's voice, rich and deep from years of voice-over work, boomed, "*Secret Splendor,* brought to you by Fiberforth. *Because sometimes nature needs a little helper.*"

Some patrons burst into applause, while others cackled with delight. I heard bits and pieces of one-liners being shared at different tables, and the energy level in the room picked up considerably.

I glanced at Martin, who was gradually making his way to the Fiberforth display set up near the corner of the bar, close to where Daniel sat. Martin picked up a pamphlet, glanced through it, and rolled his eyes as he set it down. He looked around and casually dropped a few free samples into the bag he carried. I was hoping he'd seen me, since I was wandering closer to the office door, until someone stopped me by taking my arm.

"Hey, honey," he began, and I turned to look at a man sitting at a table. My eyes widened in horror at the thought of somebody bringing attention to me and foiling our carefully planned mission. The man gawked at me and said, "I was gonna ask you to bring me a drink, but I think you need to spend the time working on that face of yours. You look like Michael Jackson on a bender." I looked at him, speechless. "But as long as you're here, bring us two Bloody Marys and two greyhounds, would you?"

"Sure. I'll be right back with that," I replied, and felt proud of my ad lib.

From the other side of the room, I heard Daniel's and Martin's voices rising above the din of the speakers.

"You!" Alexis screeched and pointed a finger at Krystle. "I might have known I'd find you here!"

Daniel and Martin had finally met at the bar, obviously seeing how near I was to the door of the office. Brenda Li swooped into my view from out of nowhere and flashed me "the sign" by taking her right index finger and pulling down on her right cheek. I reached for the doorknob and found, as promised, that the door had been left unlocked.

"Yes, Alexis. I thought I'd stop by and do a little early Christmas shopping. Here, these are for you." Martin reached into the bowl of free Fiberforth samples and tossed some at Daniel.

The crowd, as planned, turned their attention from the television above the office door to the drama unfolding between Krystle and Alexis.

"Say what you like, Krystle, darling. But by the time I gain control of Denver Carrington, *you're* the one who'll be dependent on free samples," Daniel retorted in his clipped English accent.

I slipped through the open door and shut it noiselessly behind me. Luckily, a small desk lamp was lit, and I could scan the room quickly without having to fumble for a light switch. My eyes darted to a desk strewn with papers, a high-tech phone, and a small computer table. The monitor of the computer displayed a screen saver: the letters of Disorient XPress twisting and changing color. The keyboard tray was pushed in, and I frantically looked through several piles of disks for my case.

An unexpectedly loud cheer rose from outside, and I knew I was taking too long. As I fought a sense of panic, my eyes were drawn to the server sitting on the table, where my Zip disk case was placed in plain sight.

I snatched up the disks and spun around to bump chests with Ethan Whitecrow. His lip curled, and the thought flashed through my mind that he looked awfully enraged for one so spiritually enlightened.

"What are you doing in here?" he challenged.

I thought for a moment and realized I couldn't lie. He'd obviously caught me red-handed, but what he probably didn't know was that I wasn't taking something that belonged to someone else. I was taking what was rightfully mine.

But maybe he didn't know it was me. I didn't normally look like the offspring of Connie Chung and—

"I asked you a question, Adam."

So much for not recognizing me.

"How did you know it was me?" I asked in an effort to divert his attention from the situation at hand.

"There aren't many geishas with your build," he answered. "What are you doing in here?"

"I came to get what's mine," I said matter-of-factly.

I quickly sized Ethan up, knowing I could take him if I had to. He was well built, but I had height on my side. I also had faith in my ability to move and knew I could outmaneuver him if I had to. The crowd gave another roar of approval outside, but I could no longer hear the television monitors. The presentation of *Secret Splendor* had been replaced by Krystle and Alexis as the main attraction. I didn't know what else to do except get out of Disorient XPress the only way I knew how.

In a blaze of leftover high school glory, I threw a block that knocked Ethan against the open door of the office and rushed past him with the disks tucked like a football into the crook of my arm. Ethan came racing after me. Heads turned from the live replay of *Dynasty* to watch our version of *Monday Night Football* as Ethan's legs powered his body toward me. I ducked and swerved around tables, with Ethan scrambling after me, until a deep voice yelled, "Stop!" As if a penalty flag had been thrown, for a moment everyone did.

Daniel and Martin stood frozen in place at the bar, gawking at Ethan and me. We were on opposite sides of a table that had cleared after we came crashing noisily out of the office. A figure moved behind Ethan; I recognized the large frame of Brenda Li. She took his arm, practically lifting him from the floor, nodded her head to me, and said, "Let's go."

I saw another opportunity to look like I worked for Disorient XPress and took Ethan's other arm to assist Brenda. In the confusion, Daniel and Martin made their exit just moments before us. Brenda and I ushered Ethan through the door and onto the street. As the door swung shut behind us, the bar burst into thunderous applause.

Daniel and Martin dove into the back of the car, flinging the passenger door open into traffic. Brenda and I shoved a bewildered Ethan, who was starting to fight back, into the backseat with them. I jumped into the passenger seat and pulled the door shut in one motion.

Brenda stood next to the car shouting, "Drive! Drive like the wind!"

Jeremy, with some not-so-delicate manipulation of the clutch, hurled us into traffic and sped away.

"What the hell is going on here? Get your hands off me!" Ethan cried from the back seat.

I whipped my head around, chopsticks clacking against the window, and said, "Be still and keep your mouth shut, and you won't get hurt."

"I feel like Lily Tomlin in *Nine to Five*," Martin commented to Daniel.

"You won't get away with this. I'll press charges. Let me out of this car!"

"Oh, transcend," Martin said. "And let go of my shoulder pad."

A silence fell over the rest of us as we contemplated the potential ramifications of our actions. Without any further instructions, Jeremy parked the car after turning onto a side street. We all got out, seeming dazed by the night's events. I was sure this was a story that would be retold.

Ethan, still agitated, angrily turned his gaze on Jeremy and said, "How can you be involved in this? I thought I knew you better. I believed you were on the path to enlightenment, but now I question your level of commitment."

"I question his choice in shoes," Martin chimed in. "Who on earth would wear those things with that outfit? Your fashion chakra must be blocked, Jeremy." Martin rummaged through his bag and found the pilfered Fiberforth samples, tossing them at Jeremy while saying, "Here! Cleanse! Cleanse!"

Jeremy looked apologetically at Ethan, letting the samples fall to the pavement. I decided that unless you were Martin, there were no words to say at this point.

"And you," Ethan said, turning his angry eyes to me. "You used me."

"Used you? How the hell was I supposed to know you'd be at the club?"

"I'm talking about Thursday night. It's obvious Brenda was in on this. Do you think I don't remember her calling me and interrupting our date?"

"Thursday night?" Jeremy asked. "Date?"

"Fine," I said. "I used you. I had to get into the apartment to look for these disks. But they're *my* disks. They were stolen at *your* retreat. Jeremy was willing to help me get them back. He's apparently more upstanding than some of the people who work with you. As far as I'm concerned, finding them in Wade's office doesn't speak very well of him, either. Blythe told me not to get involved with the two of you. I should have listened to her."

"Blythe?" Jeremy interrupted in the same bewildered tone he'd used before. "What does Wade's daughter have to do with this?"

Everyone's heads turned in unison to Ethan, as if watching a line drive hit by Jeremy. Ethan's face turned scarlet. My mouth opened in surprise. I suddenly wondered who had been using whom.

"Wade's *daughter?*" I asked.

"Jeremy," Ethan said, closing his eyes as if seeking divine guidance, "I told you that in confidence."

Martin made an odd strangling noise and said, "Blythe, I am your father. Darth Wader."

Daniel and Martin broke into nervous laughter and clutched each other.

Ethan took a deep breath, exhaled, and admitted, "Yes, Adam, Blythe is Wade's daughter. But it was her choice not to tell you. She doesn't want to have anything to do with him."

"And you kept pumping me for information about her, didn't you?" I demanded.

"He just wants a chance to know her. He's missed a lot of her life and wants to make up for that. Blythe's mother and stepfather have agreed not to interfere if Blythe wants a relationship with him."

"Forget *Secret Splendor,*" Martin stage-whispered to Daniel. "We've got Dysfunction Junction right here."

Ethan continued, "Wade's not all bad, Adam. I don't know why he would have taken your disks."

"Because Adam's doing work for Andy Vanedesen at Club Chaos," Jeremy said. "They've been rivals for a long time."

"And they've both made mistakes," Ethan said. "But just as Andy has redeeming qualities—"

"I could count them on one finger," Martin said.

"Will you shut the fuck up?" Ethan yelled, finally losing patience with Martin.

"Wow, your aura just changed colors," Martin said.

"Martin," I warned.

"It's for the best," Martin said. "You shouldn't wear a white aura after Labor Day."

"Are you ready to go?" Ethan asked Jeremy.

"Yeah, I'm ready."

Jeremy got into the Beetle, pointedly locked the doors, and jerked away from the curb alone. Ethan turned without a word and walked down the street, disappearing around the corner.

Martin, Daniel, and I began walking in the opposite direction, not speaking. I wondered if I'd see Jeremy again and what it would be like if I did. We trudged up the street: Krystle, Alexis, and Adam Butterfly.

TWELVE

I was lying in bed the next morning, thinking about the ramifications of Operation Disco Disk, when the phone rang. I decided to ignore it. It was Sunday. I was tired of work. My best friend was the daughter of a thieving lecher. I'd offended the sensibilities of Ethan, a good man who had done nothing to me. And as things looked right now, I'd lost my shot at making Jeremy my boyfriend.

Besides, the call was on the apartment phone. My clients all used my cell phone. And of course, the call could have been for Martin.

"It's for you," Martin said from the doorway to my bedroom. "It's Blythe."

"Ask her if I can call her back in an hour," I said. "And for god's sake, don't tell her what we found out last night."

"Can he call you in an hour?" Martin said into the phone. "Hold on. Did you get your disks back?" he asked me.

"Yes," I said.

"Yes," he said into the phone. "I'll let him tell you about it later. Bye."

"Thank you," I said.

"Would you like coffee?"

"Solitude."

He faded from the doorway, and I turned over to face the windows. I wasn't in a bad mood; I wanted to think. And if I had to call Blythe in an hour, I decided to start by thinking about her, the news I'd learned last night, and how I planned to handle it with her.

I had to laugh when I recalled Martin's Darth Wader joke. The moment had been fraught with more melodrama than a *Secret Splendor* script, and Martin's humor had undercut the tension. But I also had to remember that behind the melodrama were real people with real feelings. Blythe had gone to great lengths to keep me in the dark, and I hadn't made it easy. I'd insisted on going to Wade's party and bugged her with questions afterward. It was obvious that she'd warned him not to explain their relationship to me. She'd also advised me to stay away from Wade and Ethan, though I felt that was as much to protect me as herself. I believed that her confusion about the two of them, their morals, and whether they could be trusted, was real.

Had she known I was going to the retreat beforehand, no doubt she would have endured some uncomfortable moments. It had never been my intention to cause her any distress. And no matter what, she was entitled to her privacy. I decided it was best to let sleeping dogs lie. She could tell me about Wade when and if she wanted to. It wasn't her secret that bothered me. It was the reason for her secret.

I thought about her behavior at Disorient XPress on the day I'd wrangled that party invitation out of Brenda Li. I'd been surprised that Blythe, an artist, had flicked ashes and stubbed out her cigarette on the Noguchi table. Apparently, that had been her small way of showing disrespect for Wade. I could also remember what she'd said about success: *"If it means having my art: my thoughts, my emotions, hell, my soul—hanging on the walls of someone like Wade Van Atterson's gilded showcase of an apartment, then no, thank you."*

I sighed, wondering how much I'd contributed to her bad opinion of her father. I'd told her about his making a pass at me. I'd called him slimy and probably half a dozen other insulting things. While everything I said might be true, that didn't mean that he'd be a bad father or that the two of them didn't deserve a shot at a relationship. There were other sides to Wade, too, as I'd seen the night of his moonlight dance and heard from Ethan. He'd had a profound and positive impact on Ethan's life, after all.

Then again, he also behaved as if that entitled him to Ethan's time, care, and attention. Blythe would never tolerate being bought that way; she was too independent. In fact, now that I thought about it, when she'd told me what she knew about Wade's office setup, she'd mentioned his manager printing checks from their computer. Either she'd taken money from Wade and regretted it, or Wade had tried to give her money and she'd turned him down. I certainly wouldn't put it past Wade to try to use his money to buy her a place in the art world, or at least a better living space. That didn't make him a bad person, though, just a man trying to be a parent to a young woman he didn't understand. But they never would understand each other if they didn't talk.

If Blythe's mother and stepfather were open to her having a relationship with Wade, then he couldn't be all bad. Although I had no intention of bringing up the subject, and certainly would not push her into Wade's fatherly embrace, I could at least stop belittling and insulting him in front of her. I could trust that Ethan knew what he was talking about when he assured me that Wade was not a bad guy.

Ethan . . . The thought of him made me groan. My decision to leave him out of my scheming had come a little too late. Last night's caper would have been no more than something I could gleefully recount for my mother on the phone, except for Ethan. I didn't mind so much that he'd caught us at Disorient XPress. We'd done nothing more than reclaim my property and offer the crowd a good show. I could snicker over Martin and Daniel's *Dynasty* act, and it wasn't every day that you got to see a hundred-ninety-pound running back demonstrate his football prowess while dressed like one of the three little maids from *The Mikado*.

Somehow, though, I felt like the humor had completely bypassed Ethan. He'd been disappointed in Jeremy and felt used by me, all with good reason. We'd roped Jeremy in against his will. And I *had* used Ethan, not only to get into Wade's apartment but to get information on Jeremy, though that was probably still my little secret—at least from Ethan and Jeremy, if not from Martin and Daniel.

The worst part of the whole night was watching Jeremy drive away alone in that stupid red Beetle. When we'd talked in my bedroom, I'd started to feel a connection develop between us. Our conversation flowed freely, and I liked that Jeremy was so honest with me when talking about himself.

Moreover, Jeremy had proved to me that he wasn't interested in a person's exterior, which pleased me when I forced myself out of bed and looked at my exterior in the mirror. Even after washing my face three times, there were residual traces of black in the corners of my eyes, and my lips still looked a shade darker than normal.

Although my character the previous evening had hardly been womanly, I felt different, somehow. I was conscious of how my bare feet felt and moved on the floor as I walked to the closet. They moved freely and with perfect balance, unlike when I'd worn my sandals the night before. The flannel shirt I put on felt smooth against my skin, but not airy and soft like the silk of the kimono.

The Adam in the mirror in his flannel shirt and boxers looked the same as ever, so I wondered why I felt so different. Somehow, getting my Zip disks back was not the triumph I had expected.

I followed the sound of "Open Your Heart" by Madonna, which grew louder as I reached the living room and found Martin dancing across the floor. The furniture had been pushed back to the perimeter of the room, save for a single chair, and Madonna's video was turned up on the television. Martin obviously knew the choreography for the video, since he matched Madonna's every kick, shimmy, and turn around the chair. I was impressed and surprised to find my melancholy fading. Martin was having fun, and it was rubbing off.

Even though there were hurtful repercussions to Operation Disco Disk, I felt grateful for my glimpse into Daniel and Martin's world, and the chance to walk a mile in their fashionable shoes for an evening. I felt like I understood why Daniel had moved to New York City to become an actor. Putting on a new face and clothes I normally would never dream of wearing, and becoming someone else for an evening, was an altering experience for me. Despite feeling bad for using Ethan and possibly ruining any chance at a relationship with Jeremy, I'd had fun.

I remembered how I'd felt before I left Eau Claire for the WebTek convention. My mother had been right when she said I was stuck in a rut, doing little more than work, work out, and sleep. Even my occasional pool game at the bar didn't count, because I'd always felt guilty for not using the time more constructively.

I decided to do something Adam of Eau Claire would never do. As Madonna and Martin both left the peepshow, I bolted in front of the television to join Martin for a raucous dance, just like Madonna and the little boy in the video.

Martin grinned, danced around me, and said, "You missed the part where I kiss you awake. Let's rewind."

"But we haven't skipped down the street yet," I protested. "That looks like fun."

"Okay," Martin agreed.

We both skipped in step across the room and fell onto the sofa, laughing the whole time.

"It *was* fun," I said.

"When you were in your room, Mr. Grumbleface, I thought this was going to be a PMS kind of day for you," Martin said. "I'm glad I was wrong."

"I wanted some time alone to think about our adventure last night. It was fun, but I'm not thrilled about—"

"How you looked compared to the rest of us?" Martin interrupted. His arms shot out to turn my face in his hands as if he were inspecting a melon at a farmers' market. "Actually, you look worse this morning. Didn't I explain about cold cream? No? Obviously not."

As Martin babbled about the myriad uses for cold cream, I realized it would probably be useless to explain my feelings to him. Maybe Daniel was right. If the subject wasn't about Martin, Martin wasn't interested. Unless, of course, the subject was gossip.

"Don't forget to call Blythe back," he reminded me and stood, stretching his arms in the air. "I still can't believe she's Wade's daughter."

"Why can't you believe it? You don't even know her."

Martin threw his foot over the back of the sofa, began stretching, and said, "No, I don't. I just think it's odd that she didn't tell you. I mean, you're such good friends and all. Do you think she'll talk with you about it? Do you want to?"

"I'm going to leave that up to her," I replied. "I've been thinking about it all morning. She's not good at being vulnerable. And she's obviously been avoiding the topic and doing anything possible so I wouldn't find out about it. She can't stand Wade, and I'm afraid my dislike of him influenced her. I don't know, Martin. It might be best to let her tell me when she's ready. I'm sure she'll find out fairly soon that I know."

"I think that's a smart decision on your part," Martin airily replied and brought his foot off the sofa and up to his forehead. "I may not know Blythe, but I understand about that vulnerability thing. I've always marched to the beat of a different drum machine. When Ken died, I wasn't keen on talking about how I felt to everyone who forced their way in here. I'm not saying it's the same situation, but it sounds like Blythe and I might have a little in common."

"I'm not sure about that," I pondered aloud. "I don't think she's as adventurous as you are. Though she is outspoken, just like you."

"Why hide what you're feeling?" Martin asked and switched legs, stretching the other one on the back of the sofa. "I think that's what gets me in hot water with Daniel, though. We didn't always bicker the way we have been lately. He used to like having fun with me."

"He seemed to enjoy himself at Disorient XPress last night," I pointed out.

"Thanks to you, yes," Martin admitted and held his leg at a ninety-degree angle from his body. "When he worked at Club Chaos, we collaborated on projects together and did it very well. I guess we needed another project to help bring us back together. You and your slipped disks came along at the right time."

"Zip disks," I corrected him.

"Whatever. Anyway, as much as I'd like to take the credit, I didn't cook up that little scheme on my own. Daniel helped me. And it was great performing with him again. I really miss it. But people come and go. It's a fact of life." Martin paused, held on to the back of the sofa, and began methodically rising up and down on his toes. He snapped out of his reverie and said, "Anyway, what was I saying? Oh, yeah, I was talking about Daniel and me. I'm just glad you helped steer us back to our friendship. When Ken died, things changed."

"Daniel said the same thing to me," I said.

Martin seemed about to make a snide remark, then changed his mind. Instead, he smiled and said, "I'm glad you and he became friends. You're a lot alike."

"You think?" I scoffed at the idea. "He's talented, in a stable relationship, and—I don't know—glamorous. And he can touch a plant without killing it. I don't think we're anything alike."

"You're both handsome men," Martin observed, standing still for once. "And you're both funny."

"I don't think I'm that funny," I protested. "I've only recently learned how to have fun. I may have only learned this weekend, in fact."

"I'm an excellent teacher of Fun One-oh-one," Martin said, perhaps a bit wryly. "Daniel likes to have fun. But I feel like he can't see me as anything but everybody's fun boy. As if I never see the bigger picture, or I don't listen to anything but the sound of my own voice. I guess there *are* times when I take it too far. Sometimes I think that's what drew Ken to me, though. I used to believe he only wanted to date me so he'd be sure his last moments would be fun."

"That's a bit maudlin."

"Maybe," Martin admitted and did a quickstep, followed by a grand bow. "But I'm everyone's court jester."

"Daniel also told me that Ken loved you deeply," I stated.

"I loved him, too," Martin said, standing upright and becoming serious. "I loved someone more than myself for once in my life, which I'm sure would shock everyone. My point, Adam, is that it's easy to pigeonhole people into certain roles. It's difficult to accept them when they act differently. Or when they turn out to be something you didn't, couldn't, or wouldn't let yourself see all along. I'm sure your family and friends back home in Big Bear—"

"Eau Claire."

"Whatever, would balk if they knew you were dancing to Madonna videos in your bare feet. Or if you told them you broke into an office dressed like Mister Eddie's father's housekeeper."

"You're right," I agreed. "Although when I tell my mother, she'll want to see pictures."

"You're lucky. My mother no longer has a son. She does, however, have seven cats. From what I understand, they live in my old bedroom. Which now probably smells like cat pee."

"Martin, that's terrible," I said softly.

"I know! It takes years to get rid of the smell of cat pee," Martin agreed, pretending to misunderstand me. He moved the coffee table back in front of the sofa. "I just couldn't believe they didn't know I'm gay. I was studying ballet, for god's sake. As soon as they found out, they stopped funding my schooling and told me not to come home."

"What did you do?"

"I fell back on my law degree," Martin quipped. "I danced at the Bullpen in a thong at night and auditioned for other ballet companies and theaters during the day. It didn't work out, though. I couldn't get anything. But I heard about Club Chaos and caught a few shows to check it out. Ken knocked my socks off when I saw his Judy tribute. And Daniel as Princess 2Di4 was beyond belief. He had this way of spoofing the royal family that was funny, yet very touching. He was more Diana than Diana, so people ended up loving Diana *and* 2Di4. Anyway, I didn't want to be a stripper, and my professional dancing career seemed to be on hold, so I thought Club Chaos was the place to be. I was a class clown of sorts, but didn't really have theatrical training, so I was a little worried about that aspect."

"Apparently, it didn't matter," I said. "Look where you are now."

"Yeah, I'm Club Chaos's reigning drag queen. Or headlining female impersonator. Whatever you want to call it. People get so touchy these days. Half the reason I created Sister Mary Amanda Prophet was because nuns seem kind of asexual to me. All that fabric they wear hides everything and makes you wonder what's really underneath. I went to a Catholic school when I was young. I used to sit in class wondering, do nuns have knees? What about elbows? Do they have hair, or are they bald as a bowling ball under that wimple?"

I laughed at the idea and began to wonder, too. Billy Zane, Homer Simpson, George Foreman, and Michael Jordan all flashed through my mind dressed in nuns' habits. I shook their images out of my head and continued to listen to Martin ramble.

"Accepting the headlining act at Club Chaos as Sister Mary was a mixed blessing. It was great to take on the challenge and gain notoriety, but it only happened because the people I love left me. And it cut down on the hours it used to take doing makeup. That way I could spend as much time with Ken as possible, race to the club to do my show, and get home. Or race to the club and back to the hospital. Or race to the club and back here to cry my eyes out after Ken died. Revisiting female impersonation last night as Krystle was fun, but I'm not anxious to do it anymore. I think I'm getting to a point where I want to move on, too. Just like Daniel and Ken did. Although not quite the way Ken did."

I laughed nervously and put my hand over my mouth in surprise, embarrassed at my reaction.

Martin smiled and said, "Oh, please, don't worry about it. I love making people laugh. I learned a lot from Ken, but the main thing I picked up is that it's okay to keep laughing, because there's a funny side to everything. On that note, get dressed. You're coming with me on a mission."

At the word *mission,* the scoreboard in my mind started flashing, *Foul!*

"Oh, no," I protested. "Not another mission. I think I've had enough adventure for this lifetime."

"This will be nothing like what we did in Disorient XPress. Nobody will get hurt. I'm serious."

"Right. And I'm Dr. Ruth Westheimer."

"I swear," Martin said solemnly and held one hand over his groin.

"All right," I warily agreed. "As long as you're sure nobody will get hurt. And no costumes or disguises."

"We'll be out in broad daylight, but you will have to wear old clothes, which shouldn't be a problem for you. Wear something you won't mind getting dirty, because we'll be digging," Martin added and quickly vanished into the kitchen before I could protest. My body went rigid, and I stood in place until Martin came back into the main room, carrying something in a black plastic bag.

"How are we getting dirty, and why? What are we doing?" I demanded.

"I have plans to meet Daniel in a half hour in Sheridan Square to help him plant something," Martin said. "I'd like you to come with us. We should get moving or we'll be late."

"How do I know you two haven't cooked up some scheme again?"

Martin rolled his eyes and said with exasperation, "You are so suspicious, Adam. Trust me. I understand that's probably difficult after last night. But Daniel volunteers for the Sheridan Square Viewing Garden, where the three of us will be tossing some dirt around and kicking up a little dust. Doesn't that sound harmless? You make it sound like I'm asking you to toss tubs of Cool Whip off the top of the Empire State Building or something."

"You had me up until the Cool Whip part."

"Sheridan Square is in the Village, and the Empire State Building is way up in Midtown. We'll be nowhere near there. Now get dressed. Go!" As I went to my room to change, I heard Martin mutter, "Besides, the restraining order is still in effect. I can't go near the Empire State Building."

Despite my fear of marring my public record by going anywhere with Martin, I walked with him to Sheridan Square to meet Daniel. It was a clear day, the sun was shining, and there was a cold wind fighting to pierce its way through our coats. Daniel was waiting for us outside the gate to the large, triangular-shaped garden bounded by Washington Place, Barrow, and West Fourth Streets. At his feet was an old metal bucket containing a bag of dirt and hand tools. He held a small bush with its roots wrapped in brown paper.

"Where the hell have you been? It's freezing, and I've been standing here trying to think of excuses in case anyone from the garden association comes by," Daniel said in a hissing whisper.

"I thought you were a volunteer," I said, confused. "Why would you need an excuse?"

"You didn't tell him?" Daniel asked Martin. "What's he doing here, anyway? Never mind. My volunteer time is up in an hour, and someone else is sure to be by soon. We don't have much time to bury Ken."

"Bury Ken?" I shouted in shock. Daniel and Martin cringed and made loud shushing noises while looking around to see if anyone had heard my outburst.

"We're burying Ken's ashes under that thing," Martin explained, pointing at the plant in Daniel's hands.

"It's a juniper bush," Daniel said. "It's a rare type called—"

"Who gives a rat's ass?" Martin interrupted. "I thought we were short on time."

As Daniel unlocked the garden gate and we went inside, Martin explained how Ken had grown up in New York City and always felt that the Sheridan Square area was his home.

"He lived nearly his entire life around here," Martin said wistfully as Daniel began digging in the center of the garden. "He had something to do with every bar on Christopher Street."

"You make him sound like an alcoholic," Daniel muttered.

"Or a hustler," I added.

"You know what I mean," Martin declared. "He kept going to Stonewall even after the raids."

"And he wasn't even old enough to drink," Daniel mused.

"He was also in Act Up and Queer Nation," Martin added.

"Then I agree that it seems perfectly natural to put his ashes here," I said. "But is this private or city property? Is what we're doing illegal?"

"I don't know, and who cares?" Martin implored, obviously getting upset by what we were doing. "If it were up to me, I'd throw great big handfuls of Ken up and down the streets. Not only so he could be part of the city he loved, but hopefully, right into the face of some ratbastard politician who kept blocking AIDS funding and denying its existence for so long. Let him fill a lung with one of the people he helped kill."

"Martin, calm down," Daniel gently said, putting an arm around him. I stood by, not knowing what to say or do. "I have no idea if this is illegal, either, but we're doing it. I'm angry and upset, too, but Ken wouldn't want us getting hysterical. And as political as he could be, I'm sure he wouldn't want us getting arrested. Or dragging Adam down with us."

"You're right," Martin sighed and wiped a tear off of his cheek. "I didn't mean to get worked up."

"It's okay," I said. "And perfectly understandable."

"Are you sure about this?" Daniel asked. "I could just plant the juniper and we can do this another way, if you want."

"No," Martin said, exhaling with an air of finality. "Let's do it."

"Okay. Where are the ashes?"

Martin opened the black plastic bag and brought out a cookie jar shaped in an exact likeness of Lucille Ball's head.

"Oh, for god's sake!" Daniel exclaimed. "What the hell is that?"

"The ashes!" Martin shrieked.

"We can't bury *that* under the juniper bush! It's too big! Someone's liable to dig it up sooner or later."

"We're not burying it, you simpleton!" Martin shouted. "I was just using it to hold the ashes. I'll pour some of them in the ground under the bush, and the rest we'll scatter over the garden. Besides, this jar is autographed by Lucy herself. There's no way in hell I'd bury it."

I couldn't hold back any longer and began laughing out loud with my hands over my mouth. Daniel and Martin looked at me as if I were laughing in the middle of a funeral, which in a way I was. But it was like a funeral being led by the Odd Couple. After a minute, they looked at each other, then at the Lucy-head cookie jar, and began laughing, too.

"So much for not attracting attention," Daniel said.

"I can't help it," Martin explained. "It's what I do best. Can we get on with this?"

Martin opened the jar and poured some of Ken's ashes into the hole Daniel had dug. I held the juniper bush in place while they swept the dirt back then patted it down.

"Just like he did with so many people in his life, Ken will help this juniper grow," Daniel said philosophically.

"Too bad it's not something flashier, like a big, pink rosebush," Martin said.

"I had to keep with the plan of the garden, and it was the best thing to plant in this cold weather," Daniel said. "Besides, it'll grow all year. Forever."

"It's perfect," Martin said and wrapped his arms around Daniel from behind, the Lucy jar held firmly against Daniel's chest. They stood like that for several minutes, staring at the juniper bush.

I didn't feel awkward at all watching their moment. I was glad Martin had asked me to share it with them. I was somewhat in awe of their friendship. Though they weren't lovers, they obviously had a similar bond. I wondered if that kind of friendship took years to develop, or if it was like true love and spontaneously sparked when the right people met. Not that I knew anything about true love.

"We should get moving," Daniel finally said.

"I have to scatter the rest of the ashes first," Martin said.

"Are you sure that's such a wise idea?" I asked.

Martin opened the Lucy jar again, scooped out some of Ken's ashes, and said, "I don't give a shit."

Daniel and I shared a look of agreement and stepped forward, each of us taking a handful of ashes from Lucille Ball's head. We scattered them around us, watching as the cold wind swept them over the grass at our feet, around the plants, and through the fence encompassing the perimeter of the triangular garden. Martin grinned, throwing another handful of ashes high into the air and watching as they were carried into the streets like he'd originally wanted.

The clanging sound of the gate being opened made our heads snap around in unison, and we stared in horror as an older woman carefully shut it behind her.

"It's one of the garden association members," an aghast Daniel informed us.

"Why, hello, Daniel," she jovially said. "Is it cold enough for you? I didn't know you were tending our lovely garden today. What a delight. I see you added another juniper to our mix. They always look lovely in the winter. Did you boys come to help him?"

Before Daniel could open his mouth to reply, Martin answered, "Actually, we're scattering the ashes of my dead lover. Care to join us?"

The woman's mouth opened and shut a few times like a goldfish's before she composed herself and said, "No, thank you. But do shut the gate behind you when you leave, dear." She nodded politely to each of us before she left.

"What a dear, sweet woman," Martin observed. He peered into Lucy's head and said, "Just as I suspected. Empty. There's a little left, but I think I'd like to hang on to them. I have a small marble box back at the apartment that I can keep them in. Maybe I'll put it on top of Ken's piano. Don't worry; I'll wash out Lucy if I ever put cookies in her again."

We filed silently out of the garden, and Daniel locked the gate behind him. We hugged each other goodbye, Daniel taking his tools and soil home, and Martin taking Lucy back to the town house. I decided to walk across town to drop in on Blythe, so Martin could have some time alone with his emotions and memories.

Even though I had forgotten to return Blythe's call before we left the town house, I still didn't call her to let her know I was coming or to see if she was home. I finally felt like someone who could enjoy taking chances, having learned that life was far more interesting when you allowed yourself a little risk. Unfortunately, I couldn't figure out a way to apply that lesson to winning Jeremy over. Or to make up for the mistakes I had made with my previous efforts.

One of Blythe's neighbors was leaving her building, so I let myself into the stairwell and climbed to her floor. When I knocked on her door, I heard her yell, "Hang on! I'll be right there!"

"It's me," I answered loudly. "Take your time."

After a few minutes, she opened the door looking like she'd wrestled with a wet painting and the painting had won. She wore her overalls, as usual, but I could see she had no T-shirt on underneath, was barefoot and was frantically buttoning a denim shirt to cover herself.

"Am I interrupting something kinky? I could come back," I said.

"No, silly. I'm working, but I'm more than happy to take a break," she said, and I followed her inside. "I'd give you a hug, but I'd ruin your clothes. Watch your step, too."

She held up her hands, which looked like she was wearing gloves made of oil paint. Several large canvases lay on the floor of the loft with tubes of paint, bottles of linseed oil, and brushes scattered around them. There seemed to be just as much paint on the floor as there was on the canvases. Footprints in different hues led from the canvases to the kitchen and other areas of her studio.

A set of purple tracks went from the door to where she was standing in front of me. She smirked and lifted a foot; the bottom matched the prints on the floor.

"I see you've been throwing yourself into your work," I observed. "So to speak."

"Yeah, it's fantastic. I've been painting nonstop all weekend. Come take a look."

She led me to the canvases on the floor but plucked a small painting off the wall before I could look at anything else.

"I was doing this one and hated how it was turning out. The colors weren't blending right, and it looked more abstract than I wanted it to. Like a Rothko without any purpose. Anyway, I put it aside and started working on something else when the cell phone rang. Of course I stepped on the canvas when I went to answer the phone, but I didn't care. The next day, I tried to paint over it, but the footprint had dried into the painting. I could've thinned it out and scraped the paint off, I guess, but I really took to the idea of that footprint. Like you said, I liked that I put myself into the painting. So to speak."

"Yes, so to speak."

"The colors finally blended the right way, and everything looked right. So I kept it up and did these," she said, pointing to the canvases on the floor.

The paintings could best be described as layered. At first glance there were no discernible figures or objects in them. Just layers of muted colors creating the appearance of a sunset as it might appear in a photographic negative. But when my eyes relaxed, I could see the outline of an arm, a hand, and various parts of her body. In the largest, I could see where she had laid her whole body over the canvas. One painting was a self-portrait done in muted greens staring out of a wash of hard brush strokes; the outline of her profile was faintly visible beneath the surface.

"It's interesting," I said, still staring at her self-portrait. Beneath the paint I saw a handprint I hadn't noticed before.

"Ew," Blythe said, cringing. "You sound like my parents."

"No, really," I said apologetically. "Give me a few minutes. I'm still taking it all in."

Blythe smiled, and I knew she was just teasing me. Though she valued my opinions, she didn't need to hear them about her art. As long as her work reflected what was in her heart, that was all she needed. We had talked enough about art for her to know just by looking at my face whether or not I liked what I saw.

"I love them," I said. "I don't know what else to say. The colors are really dark. Even though the body imagery underneath the paint is playful, the colors make them seem serious."

Blythe nodded and said, "That's pretty much what I've been going for. It's one thing to create a great painting and have it outlive you. But it's a different feeling when you've put something physical into it, too. It's kind of like combining painting with sculpture. I'm not sure I'm expressing it correctly. Anyway, remember the last time I saw you?"

"When you practically kicked me down the stairs?" I replied. "Yes, it's hazy, but I think I remember."

"It wasn't that long ago, drama queen," Blythe said. "That was a few hours before I stepped on the painting, when I was getting all frustrated. I knew I wanted to do something different. I'm sure someone else has done something like this. I just mean it was time to change my painting style a little. I've been feeling stagnant."

"There seems to be a lot of that going around," I said. "Martin was saying the same thing this morning."

"Hold that thought," Blythe said. "I want to catch up, but I have to shower this paint off before I absorb any more of it."

While she showered, I looked at all her canvases again, amazed as always by her originality. Then I made a pot of coffee and had a steaming cup waiting for her when she joined me again, her wet hair spiking in all directions.

"Martin," she reminded me, sitting next to me on the sofa and sipping her coffee, then lighting a cigarette.

I told her about my conversation with Martin and our morning with Daniel at Sheridan Square. Blythe kept quiet until I was finished with my story.

"You know what's really strange? Lucky strange, I mean," she said. "I don't know anybody who's died of AIDS. I hope I never do."

"I've known a few who have," I said. "I hope you never do, either."

"Maybe when I have children, AIDS will be wiped out," Blythe mused. We sat in silence for a minute, hoping. "Or maybe by then Republicans will be wiped out."

"I'd settle for that," I said.

"Ever since I learned about sex, I've also known about AIDS. Know what I mean?" Blythe asked. "It's always been around for me."

"Think about my generation," I said. "We grew up in the seventies, hearing all sorts of rowdy stories from our friends about sex. Then we reached puberty, and it was a brand-new decade. Finally, it was our turn to have sex. We were so ready. It was going to be fun and everything we'd heard sex could be. And then—*bam!*—no, we couldn't. AIDS meant we'd die if we had sex. But we were teenagers, extremely selfish, saying, 'No way, man; it's not fair!' I was too scared to have sex for years."

"Did you ever have sex?" Blythe asked. "With a woman, I mean?"

"Actually, no. I didn't. By the time I learned how to do it safely, I didn't see the point. What about you?"

"It sounds like you had quite a morning," Blythe commented, pointedly changing the subject. "Why do you think Martin asked you to go with them? It seems a little strange to me, since you never met Ken."

"I was wondering the same thing. Maybe he wanted a neutral party along in case things got volatile between him and Daniel again. Or maybe after last night, they feel our friendship is stronger and wanted to include me for moral support."

Once again my mental scoreboard began flashing the foul sign, and I tried not to visibly cringe at my gaffe. Of course, Blythe responded to it naturally.

"Why? What happened last night? Oh, that's right. The disks! Martin said you got them back."

I thought about lying but decided Blythe's friendship was too important. Besides, I reasoned, I didn't have to tell her what I'd learned about her family tree.

"Martin and Daniel tried to bring those stolen Zip disks, Jeremy, and me together as one happy family. Unfortunately it didn't work out the way they planned," I explained.

I filled her in on the whole story, minus the part where Jeremy spilled the beans about Wade's being her father. If she was worried about any incriminating evidence I might have discovered in Wade's apartment or office, she never let on. She sneered when I told her about my night alone with Ethan, looked hopeful when I told her about how Jeremy and I connected in my room before we left for Disorient XPress, and laughed her fat laugh when I described our outfits and the events that led to our getaway in the little red Beetle.

"It sounds like you owe Brenda Li big-time. Aren't you ashamed that you stood her up at Wade's party?" Blythe gibed.

"I never promised her a rose garden."

"I think that was Lynn Anderson, not Brenda Lee."

"How do you know this stuff?"

"All my parents ever listened to was country music," Blythe explained. "I'm glad you got your disks back, Adam, but I'm sorry things didn't work out between you and Jeremy."

"Me, too," I sighed.

"I guess we were right about Wade," she said and got up from the sofa to shift some paintings around. "He really is a thieving, corporate shrew instead of the benefactor he pretends to be. I wonder what he hoped to gain by taking your disks? Would it really have damaged Club Chaos in the long run? I guess I don't understand all that cutthroat business stuff. Then again, if Wade is any indication, I don't think I want to."

She propped one of the larger canvases against the wall and stared at it while I stewed about what she'd said. It appeared my conflict with Wade had fueled her desire not to let him into her life, just as I'd feared.

"I'm a businessman, and I'm nothing like Wade," I offered.

"You're just now learning how to let go, Adam," Blythe said. "And you're too creative. Wade feeds off of and uses other people's creativity. There's a huge difference between the two of you. I don't think you could hurt anybody even if you tried."

"I don't think you should write people off like that," I said. "Even Wade."

"You know, don't you?" she asked, not looking at me.

"Know what?"

"Don't make me say it, Adam."

"Yes, I know Wade is your father," I said tentatively. "Ethan must have told Jeremy some time ago, because they let it slip last night when we were all arguing after we got the disks. Apparently, Ethan was trying to get closer to me to learn more about you on Wade's behalf."

"Is there anybody in this city without an angle?" Blythe asked, her voice full of sarcasm.

"So far, only Josh and Blaine," I offered.

"From now on, I only want to hang out with them."

"What about me?" I asked, wondering if she would drop me like a bad habit now that everything was out in the open.

"I suppose you want to hear the whole story," she said with a sigh.

"Only if you want to tell me. You don't have to."

"I know I don't. But I will," she said, finally turning to face me. "My grandparents moved to Florida when they retired. When my grandfather died, my mother went to be with my grandmother. She ended up staying there for a few years. From what I understand, Miami was just beginning to develop in the seventies. My mother loved it. There was a thriving bohemian underground, but quiet and solitude were never far away. She never got tired of the ocean scenes and colors that found their way into her paintings."

She broke off to stare at her own paintings again, then went on.

"Wade's family had a winter home in Boca Raton and spent their time within the 'appropriate' social circles. Wade, on the other hand, with the ink still fresh on his Ivy League diploma, preferred the artists and squatters of South Beach. Wade and my mother met, had a fling, and I was made."

"Apparently, your mother didn't have her gaydar turned on."

"My mother says sexual boundaries were more blurred back then. Bisexuality and androgyny were all the rage. Anyway, Wade was in the closet." Blythe shifted and lit a cigarette before continuing. "I think he was afraid too much honesty might cost him his inheritance. By the time my mother realized she was pregnant, Wade was back in New York working in a brokerage firm. She came to Manhattan to give him the news about me."

She paused, and I said, "Please tell me he didn't turn her away."

"No, nothing like that. In fact, her arrival was timely. As he explained it to her, at the age of twenty-five, he would inherit the bulk of his parents' estate as long as he was married. If his twenty-fifth birthday passed and he wasn't married, he would get his trust fund, but the estate would be dispersed among other relatives and various charities."

"How old were Wade's parents? Two hundred?" I asked.

"I know," Blythe agreed. "It sounds like a Henry James novel."

"Or Jacqueline Susann."

"That's more like it," Blythe said after letting out a hearty laugh. "Where was I? Oh, yes. An already rich Wade wanted to get richer, so he asked her to marry him. To be fair, he did tell her the truth. About the money and being gay. She went into it with her eyes open. She wanted security for me. He also provided care for my grandmother until she died."

"How long were they married?"

"Until I was four. I don't remember him at all, but my mother says that's because we weren't around him much. He liked living the fast life in Manhattan. She preferred a country house he bought in Vermont, where she could paint surrounded by nature. That's where she met my stepfather. They fell in love. Wade, happy with his inheritance, gave her a divorce and the Vermont house, and that was the end of it."

"He just dropped out of your life?"

"He paid child support. Believe me, I never missed out on a thing. I love my stepfather. I was loved and adored by my parents. I had a good childhood."

She lay down on the sofa, putting her head in my lap.

"How did you end up here?" I queried, smoothing her hair. It was surprisingly soft for having been colored so much.

"Manhattan is where all artists go," Blythe said innocently, looking up at me from my lap. I blinked pointedly at her, and she laughed. "Okay, so I was more curious about Wade than I let on to anyone. I *did* move here to be a starving artist, though."

"Except for me, you'd be successful."

"I found out about Disorient XPress and started hanging out there. Just to see if I'd run into Wade. Unfortunately, when you become a regular at a gay bar in Manhattan, it's not easy to remain inconspicuous."

"I find that hard to believe," I said, adding wryly, "especially for someone as subtle as you."

"I really did try. After a few hours, the cocktail waiters know your drink. After a few visits, they know your name. After a few weeks, they know your blood type. It's ridiculous. Even more so if you sit at the bar. Bartenders remember everything. It didn't take long before everyone who worked there knew me."

"Did everyone yell, 'Blythe!' when you walked in?"

"Pretty much," she said. "The night I went there with you, I was scared someone would blow the whistle on me. Luckily, Brenda Li knows when to keep her mouth shut. Anyway, one night Wade was there and overheard the bartender introducing me as Blythe Mayfield, the brilliant artist, though of course the bartender had never seen even one of my paintings. Wade stepped in, introduced himself, and we had an awkward conversation. My parents never said, 'By the way, your father is a gay tycoon,' so you can imagine my shock."

"Wade, in any form, is a shock," I agreed. "Does it matter that he's gay?"

"No," Blythe protested; then her face twisted with thought. "Maybe. It's hard to say. I don't think of him as my father yet. But when I do, it does make me kind of uncomfortable. Does that make me homophobic?"

"On some level, I guess it does."

"What if your father told you he's gay, Adam?"

"Okay! I see your point. I guess on the same level, I'm homophobic, too," I said quickly, wanting to change the subject and get the thought out of my head. "But does it make you want him not to be a part of your life?"

"The fact that he's gay? No, of course not. He is who he is. But on the other side of the coin, he is who he is, which is not the most endearing person. That's what makes me wonder if I really want him to be in my life."

"Maybe you could change that," I said. "We'll call you Little Orphan Blythe."

"I have parents," Blythe said and gave me a light rap on my forehead with her knuckles. "I'm done. Let's change the subject. What are we going to do about getting you and Jeremy together?"

"I don't know," I said, the hopelessness returning like a baseball to my stomach. "Next subject."

"Okay, how is Cybeeria? When does Club Chaos reopen?"

"It's not closed; the construction is all upstairs and out of the way of business. It's going well and right on schedule. I can't wait to show it to you."

"What, I don't get a sneak peek? Let's go," Blythe said, sitting up.

"Right now?" I asked, momentarily forgetting everything I had learned about being spontaneous.

"Yes!" Blythe exclaimed. "I haven't been out of my apartment in days. And you said Martin taught you some new moves this morning. You can show me how Cybeeria is coming along; then we'll have some fun."

"Maybe we could stop by Disorient XPress afterward, and your daddy could comp us a few drinks," I joked.

"Sure. And you could finally hook up with the bewitching Brenda Li," Blythe said, disappearing behind the screens that blocked off her bedroom. Then she stuck her head out and said, "Don't push it, Adam."

"Yes ma'am," I said meekly, and added in a defiant whisper, "Wade's still out of town anyway."

THIRTEEN

I'd begun to understand why the zebra was my ideal power animal; I couldn't change my stripes, either. Once I felt that things were resolved between Blythe and me, and that Martin and Daniel seemed to be on the right track with each other, I threw myself into my work. I decided to take the fact that I'd retrieved my apparently intact disks as a win. As for the fiasco with Ethan and Jeremy, if I kept myself busy, I didn't think about it.

My deadline for wrapping up my various New York projects and returning to Wisconsin was mid-December. When I'd thought I might get something started with Jeremy, time seemed to be racing toward my departure date. But now that I just wanted to go to Eau Claire and be surrounded by familiarity and sanity, the days were crawling along.

To make my schedule even busier, I held interviews until I found the ideal person to take over my duties for Ray Patel. Lester Jenkins was a computer information systems major at City Tech in Brooklyn. Since Lester had been struggling to put himself through school, he was not only thrilled about having a good income, but he knew that if he met my expectations with his work on Patel, Inc., he'd eventually be my liaison to all my New York clients and work his way up to a partnership. Ray, bored by my futile pursuit of Jeremy, was thrilled when Lester professed himself to be something of a ladies' man. Their ribald conversations amused me. Not only did I know that Ray was a devoted husband and father, but between work and school, Lester was too busy to have made all the conquests he claimed. I figured such talk was just part of the heterosexual male-bonding ritual.

My other New York Web sites were launched and would require nothing beyond maintenance and occasional updates. I'd received Josh's photos of Blythe's paintings, so I worked on her site at night when Martin was at Club Chaos, where I spent my days. It was my intention to have Cybeeria up and running on the Sunday before Thanksgiving and to be finished with Blythe's site shortly thereafter. I could then spend my remaining two or three weeks in New York pursuing new business leads and shopping for Christmas presents before going home for the holidays.

It didn't make me sad to think of leaving Daniel, Blythe, and Martin behind, because I knew I'd be coming back. I was just moderately disgusted at myself for all the energy I'd spent dreaming about or pursuing Jeremy. I felt like I'd fumbled the ball just short of the goal line. Rather than stay on the field and humiliate myself further, I was running back to a game where I was undefeated—my career.

Martin had told me about a place where he, Daniel, and Ken had once shared Sunday brunches, the Screening Room, where they could watch movies while they ate. I checked it out and discovered that the restaurant had a smaller room, the i-Room, with a large screen for private parties. Since I wanted to set up the training and demo for Cybeeria's site away from interruptions at Club Chaos, I reserved the room for several hours on Friday and let the club staff come in shifts for training on the chat room, instant messaging, and message board features. My final session included Andy, Martin, and Gretchen, who planned to remain afterward so Daniel and Blaine could join us for dinner.

Surprisingly, Martin had managed to withhold the story of Wade Van Atterson's corporate espionage from Andy. Something in Gretchen's attitude made me think she knew all about it, but if she did, she kept it to herself. While Andy and Martin tapped out instant messages to each other, Gretchen asked smart questions about the way Cybeeria's features would function.

"I'm thinking you're no stranger to online chatting," I said.

"I enjoyed it when it was a novelty," Gretchen said, "then I got bored with it."

"Got burned by a woman or two, did you?" I asked knowingly.

"I attract enough weirdos in my daily life," she said. "I didn't need to add any online psychos into the mix."

"The virtual world can be scary," I agreed.

"Did you ever hook up with anyone online?" she asked.

"Once," I said, remembering Sam69wu. "He was adorable, but not for me."

"At least you got adorable," she said. "I got someone who was calling me her wife and we hadn't even met in person. I was only able to get rid of her by dumping her for another online fling. It was very dramatic. The second woman, I did meet in person. She stole my ATM card and a picture of my childhood dog. How weird was that?"

"This is not exactly *reassuring,*" Andy called out, frowning at Gretchen.

"You can't judge online stuff by my experiences," Gretchen promised him.

"Right," I said. "I've heard much worse."

Martin was still cackling at Andy's distressed expression when Daniel strolled in, Blaine and Jeremy trailing behind him. I felt my heart turn over. The cold wind had left Jeremy with ruddy cheeks and bright eyes. I wanted to sweep him into my arms and kiss him, but my exhilaration faded as fast as it flared when he didn't meet my eyes as we all exchanged greetings. He dropped to a chair next to Andy, while Daniel and Blaine looked over Martin's shoulders so that Martin and Andy could demonstrate everything they'd learned about Cybeeria's messaging systems.

The Screening Room staff began bringing in food while I put things away. I left the equipment connected so the six of them could talk via a chat room that Martin had created. Jeremy was the least computer literate of any of them and the most enchanted by the whole setup. I suspected it wouldn't be long before he had his own PC and Internet provider and was breaking hearts all over the place.

I frowned. I'd have to be in love with him to be nursing a broken heart. I couldn't possibly be in love with someone I'd shared only a half-dozen conversations with. Someone I barely knew. Someone who—

At that precise moment, Jeremy met my eyes from across the room and smiled at me. I almost pantomimed, *Who, me?* in response, but decided simply to return the smile. I waited for him to turn back to the computer, but he didn't. He kept his eyes locked on mine until, for the first time ever, I looked away before he did, unsure what was going through his head.

When the others started filling their plates from the buffet, I continued to pack my equipment. Finally, Daniel demanded that I stop what I was doing to sit down and eat. We all made small talk for a while about Cybeeria and its likelihood of success; then Martin and Andy began pestering Daniel for details about his first week on *Secret Splendor.*

"I haven't taped any of my big scenes yet," Daniel said. "Right now, we're taping flashback scenes, where different characters are remembering all the vile things Angus did before he supposedly went over the cliff in his car. They aren't showing my face. Just the back of my head, or my eyes, or my body from a blurry distance. So by the time they do show me, the viewers will accept me as Angus, after some plastic surgery, in place of what's-his-name."

Daniel clapped his hand over Martin's mouth before Martin could supply the previous actor's name.

"Daniel's been watching the show for years," Blaine explained. "He wants to forget the other actors who've played Angus so he can develop the character his own way."

"That's a good idea," Jeremy said. *"Secret Splendor* rarely gets rid of characters, so you can bet there's a reason why they killed Angus. On most shows, the official word is that it's for the story line, but a lot of times they just don't like the actor. Naturally, you wouldn't want to repeat any of his mistakes."

"I haven't seen much evidence of politics so far," Daniel said. "Most of the cast has been there forever. Like you said, they don't write people off very often. They're all comfortable with each other. Kind of like a boring family. I think that's why they're bring-ing in new characters and resurrecting Angus. To infuse life into the show. It's going to be a lot of fun to play him. He's one of those evil characters you love to hate. But they're planning on throwing in a couple of surprises to show motivation for his evil."

"Like what?" Martin asked.

"I don't know," Daniel said. "They don't give us much advance information. We tape a couple of weeks ahead. My first real scene, the one where I show up in Splendor Falls and start wreaking havoc, airs some time after Thanksgiving."

"Whereupon those vile *Secret Splendor* Saturdays at Disorient XPress will be helped along by *you,* " Andy accused Daniel.

"But Cybeeria is your trump card," Gretchen reminded him. "Adam, I definitely think you've given Andy a winner."

"*Given* me?" Andy complained. "For what it cost—"

"I hate to eat and run," Gretchen said, "but I have a date with some financial statements."

"We need to get to the club," Martin said to Andy.

After kisses and hugs all around, the three of them left me alone with Daniel, Blaine, and Jeremy. Once again, I had the feeling Jeremy and I were being stage-managed. But I no longer felt very hopeful about the outcome.

As Blaine and I piled more food onto our plates, I heard Daniel say, "I have to thank you again, Jer, for telling me to audition for the *Secret Splendor* job. Not to mention putting me on the path to Bonnie. She has a lot more input into the show than we realized. She and the producers are old friends."

"I know you didn't intend to do TV," Jeremy said, "but you never know where this could lead."

"I'm not thinking of it that way," Daniel said. "I want to work. The money is great. Whether I end up an old geezer on the show or it springboards me into other things, I'll be acting. That's all I want."

"Oh, I know," Jeremy teased him. "Adulation, awards—who cares? It's all for love of the craft."

"My real goal is to become a male Susan Lucci," Daniel confided. "Every year, a new chance to look stoic in the face of defeat at the daytime Emmys. You can't buy that kind of publicity!"

"Sure you can, with enough dollars for advertising, an agent, a publicist, and stamps to answer all your fan mail," Jeremy argued. "You've landed in a nice spot, no matter how long you choose to stay there. The contented mood of the cast and crew of *Secret Splendor* is legendary. That's why no one ever leaves. They get great perks, including time off if they want to have babies or facelifts or do theater or prime time. Not to mention closed sets, minimal public appearances to promote the show, and no one to tell you how to live your personal life."

By now Blaine and I were sitting across from Daniel and Jeremy. At Jeremy's last comment, we exchanged glances while Jeremy stared moodily at his barely touched plate.

"I take it things are not going well on *Man of the House?*" Daniel asked.

"It doesn't matter," Jeremy said. "I quit."

This was followed by tense silence until Daniel asked, "You what?"

"I quit today. You don't have to give me any speeches about what a mistake that was. My agent couldn't believe it. Everyone knows the show's going to be canceled. All I had to do was hang in there and collect my oversized paycheck until they pull the plug. Instead they're threatening to sue me for breach of contract and vowing I'll never work on their network again. Blah, blah, blah. Who cares?"

Jeremy shrugged and dropped his eyes again. I had an urgent desire to console him and wished Blaine and Daniel would vanish. But it was apparent from Daniel's expression that Jeremy had his full attention. Any signals I sent would go unnoticed.

"It's unlike you to walk out on a job," Daniel said. When Jeremy gave him an annoyed look, Daniel hastily added, "You must have had your reasons. What happened?"

"Our production is nothing like *Secret Splendor.* We've got infighting, ass-kissing, and manipulating that makes a VH-1 diva concert look like kindergarten. I spend more time doing meet-and-greets than rehearsing or taping. Executive spouses, advertisers, advertisers' spouses, advertisers' kids, advertisers' fucking maids. Then there's the press. As if the perfume of publicity could cover up the smell of this dead dog of a show. We're supposed to smile all day and be little troopers. Then I go home to hear Robert talk about how great everything is on *Anything Goes,* and what shows everyone is going to audition for next, and I can't say a word because he'll just remind me that he told me not to do TV."

"But like you said, it's bound to be canceled, and you'll be free. Why quit? Just keep collecting the money and the glowing reviews *you've* been getting."

"I can't," Jeremy said. "I can't be this unhappy every day for something so irrelevant."

"It's your career," Daniel argued. "The show may be irrelevant, but your career isn't."

Jeremy's laugh sounded surprised, and he said, "Are you listening to yourself? Does any of this sound familiar?"

"What do you mean?"

"Last year, when Princess Diana died and you quit performing as 2Di4, everybody was telling you to do a new act. But you didn't do that. You were ready to make changes in your life. Big changes.

Now it's my turn. It seems like you'd be the one person who could understand how I feel."

"I didn't want to do female impersonation anymore," Daniel said. "But I didn't give up acting."

"Bullshit," Jeremy said. "You gave up acting years ago. After you retired 2Di4, you decided to work in an office. You only auditioned for parts because you had to quit working for Blaine when he became your boyfriend. However, amazing as it may be, we're not talking about you. We're talking about me. I've never had to pretend to be anything I'm not. I came out when I came out of the womb. Now I'm being told to flirt with the wives of assholes, to squire their daughters or some flavor-of-the-month actresses to network functions and public events. Downplay the whole 'gay thing.' I'm not putting on a front for anybody or any job. I can't do it."

"You shouldn't," Daniel agreed. "After the sitcom is canceled, go back to the theater. Audition for TV or film roles working with people who won't expect that from you. But don't let this show get you a reputation as a troublemaker. *Man of the House* is the problem, not you. If you stick it out, it'll be better for you."

Jeremy didn't answer, retreating into sullen silence, so Daniel kept at him while Blaine looked on, seeming less than pleased by how much attention Jeremy was getting from Daniel. I understood how he felt. The two of them were obviously arguing in a pattern that formed when they were a couple. I wasn't enjoying the moment either, and Jeremy wasn't even my boyfriend.

"You said," I interrupted Daniel midsentence, "that right now acting seems irrelevant to you. Do you have any idea what you'd rather be doing?"

Jeremy gave me a grateful look and said, "I do, in fact. I wouldn't have quit the show without a plan."

"Please enlighten us," Daniel said.

"It's something Ethan and I have been talking about for a while," Jeremy said. I ignored the exasperated glance Daniel cast my way, and kept my mouth shut. "Ethan understands how unhappy I've been. How I want to do something more meaningful with my life. He's offered to make a place for me in his plans."

"In his plans? What plans?" Daniel asked.

"Give me a chance to tell you," Jeremy muttered. "Ethan has spent several years helping at-risk Native American kids. I don't know if you remember him saying that he has a degree in adolescent psychology. Recently, he got financial backing to develop pilot programs in Oklahoma and Wyoming. These programs will connect with children—teenagers—through the arts, helping them express themselves creatively, and hopefully keep them out of trouble. Ethan's people will work with Native American community leaders and local colleges on all of this. Artists, dramatists, musicians, voice teachers—all kinds of people in the arts will be trained, and I want to be part of it. Ethan wants me to start by teaching acting to teenagers, but later I'll probably help train local people to teach them."

"So wait. You're going to move away? From Manhattan? To Oklahoma? Leave your family in Brooklyn? You're going to give up acting to teach acting? Without any teaching experience?" Daniel asked. "And this was your idea? Or Ethan's?"

"It was my idea," Jeremy said. "I told you that I feel like what I'm doing is irrelevant. Daniel, it's not just the sitcom. I don't want to do what Robert's doing, either. I don't want to have some successes and make money and get a few glowing reviews that nobody but other actors read so they know who to resent. I want to feel like what I'm doing matters."

"Then what I'm doing doesn't matter either, does it?" Daniel asked.

"I told you this is not about you," Jeremy snapped, then continued in a more patient tone. "You gave away your time and talent for years as Princess 2Di4. You raised consciousness and money while all I did was scrounge around for parts and wait for a break. I got a break. I'm on a prime-time show. If I played the game right, like you said, when it's canceled someone would take care of me. There would be another show. But I don't want to play. I want to feel good about myself for a change. Ethan's offering me that chance. A chance I intend to take. I'm sorry if you don't understand."

"I think you should do it," I said before Daniel could respond. "I can honestly say that I think artists, just by doing what they do, make the world a better place. They enlighten or entertain or enrich us. That's why I like working with them. But it's important that *you* feel like what you do matters. If this is what you think is best for you, then go for it. I'm sure you and Ethan and the others can have a positive impact on those kids' lives."

"Thank you," Jeremy said, once again staring into my eyes. "I wasn't sure you'd feel that way."

"Why not? I'm a teacher, after all."

"I know there are problems between you and Ethan."

"I've never said Ethan is a bad person," I answered. "Sounds like the two of you will be quite a team."

"I think so," Jeremy agreed.

"That's great," I said and glanced at the computers, wishing I could book an immediate flight to Eau Claire. "Speaking of work, I need to finish packing this stuff and get out of here."

"We should be heading out, too," Blaine said. "Can we help you do anything, Adam?"

"No. I could do this in my sleep. You'll be at Cybeeria's opening on Sunday night, right?" I asked.

"Blaine and I will be," Daniel said. "Jeremy?"

"Sure. I want to try out this whole computer thing for real. It seems like it could be a lot of fun," Jeremy said, smiling at me.

"You're welcome to bring Ethan," I said as graciously as I could.

"I doubt that Ethan, as Wade's business associate, would go," Jeremy said, then broke into a little smile. "Besides, he wasn't too happy after his last meeting with all of us."

"Yeah, I picked up on that, too," I said, smiling back even though it was the last thing I felt like doing.

Once the three of them were gone, I sat down, staring disconsolately at my computer equipment. I knew I'd done the right thing by encouraging Jeremy, and I honestly did support his need to try something different. I viewed his potential influence over teenagers in the same way I viewed mine. We were both honest, well-adjusted guys from decent families and could have a positive impact on impressionable kids. Jeremy would be taking what he loved and using it in a good way, just like I did with the computer class I taught at Stout. In fact, his plan gave us something in common, something that could have been part of our interaction with each other.

Instead, it would be Ethan who shared it with him. Jeremy and Ethan had obviously made up after the Disorient XPress caper. It even seemed like they might be a couple, since Jeremy felt it was his place to accept or decline an invitation on Ethan's behalf. It made sense. Ethan, like Jeremy, was a decent guy. They would, as I'd said to Jeremy, make a great team. I might as well be as agreeable about it as possible and leave the field with some shred of pride intact.

With that in mind, I called Ethan the next day and left a message on his voice mail, taking a chance that he would hear it before that afternoon.

"Ethan, it's Adam Wilson. It's Saturday morning about ten o'clock. I have a meeting near Central Park in the early afternoon. I was wondering if we could meet at Bethesda Fountain around three. I swear I won't make you eat a hot dog, but I'd like to maybe share a cup of coffee or something with you. And apologize. In person. For what happened last week at Wade's club. Anyway, if you don't show up, at least know that I'm sorry for making you feel used. And for any embarrassment I caused you at the bar. So maybe I'll see you later."

The sun didn't even begin to take the chill off the afternoon as I went to Central Park that afternoon. I tucked my gloved hands under my arms as I walked around the fountain, thinking of other times I'd been there. The day Ethan and I had walked to the Boathouse for our aborted lunch. The day I'd first spotted Daniel and thought I recognized him. I'd intended to use Ethan, a potential friend, to get to Jeremy. Instead it had been Daniel, who considered himself an old enemy, who had brought Jeremy into my life. And in the end it hadn't mattered; I ended up with nothing.

Only that wasn't exactly true. I thought further back, to that lonely day in Café Pick Me Up, when I'd started writing a make-believe life on my laptop, and Blythe had appeared in a flash of cigarette smoke with humor, friendship, and a zest for adventure. She had made all of Manhattan seem like a friend to me. I'd never written another word on that story because I'd been too busy living life to write about it. Maybe when I went back to Eau Claire, during those long, snowy nights in my cozy farmhouse, I could pick up the story again, writing my own tales of the city.

My disappointment over Jeremy notwithstanding, I'd had a great three months. I'd met people who had become real friends, like Blythe, Daniel, Blaine, Martin, Sheila, and Josh. I'd met millionaires, like Bonnie and Wade. I'd met high-society elite, like Betsy Pelham. I'd worked with interesting and diverse clients, like Ray Patel, Andy Vanedesen, and Carl Nash. The work I'd done had been fun, appreciated, and lucrative. I had a gym, an apartment, favorite places to hang out, and a group of people to enjoy it all with. Manhattan had become a second home with a second family, just as my mother had promised it could if I was open to it.

So what if I hadn't gotten the guy? I'd seen some of the greatest art in the world. I'd been in the tallest buildings, eaten at fantastic restaurants, danced the night away in crazy nightclubs, retrieved my power animal, and dressed in drag. Maybe I hadn't been pretty as Adam Butterfly, but I cleaned up okay, and now I had a little polish I hadn't had before. There would be other men to woo and win.

It was cold, and I was done waiting for Ethan. I'd given him his apology; it was time for me to move on. I turned abruptly to leave the park and, just like at Wade's party and in Wade's office, bumped into Ethan. Only this time he was holding two large cups of steaming coffee, and we barely avoided being scalded.

"Sorry," I said.

"You're always apologizing to me," Ethan answered. "Fortunately, only a little spilled, and since we're both wearing coats and gloves . . ."

"Any harm can be fixed by the dry cleaner," I finished, gratefully taking the cup of coffee he held out.

"You might have chosen a warmer spot to meet," Ethan said.

"But this one has meaning. I hoped we could start over. From the beginning."

"Then we'd have to go to Wade's apartment. That's where we first met," Ethan reminded me. "Should I ask Wade to throw another party?"

"Uh, no. Unless we can be there without him. I know the alarm code, after all."

"I wondered if you were watching as I punched that in," Ethan said. "It made me nervous that you were going to figure out the secret."

"The secret?"

"About Blythe."

"I don't get it," I said.

"Wade's alarm code. It's Blythe's birthday."

"Oh, geez, I never picked up on that," I admitted. "Some undercover agent I turned out to be."

"It's not in your nature," Ethan said. "Which is why you really don't have to apologize to me. I know you were driven to desperate measures by Wade. Okay, yes, I was humiliated at Disorient XPress that night, and angry, but the more I think about it, the more I enjoy the memory. What a sight you were in that wig and kimono, using your football moves on me."

We both laughed a little awkwardly. I was sure he wouldn't be so forgiving if he knew the whole story, that I'd been using him from the very beginning—not for the disks, but to get information on Jeremy. But I figured that was news I could keep to myself.

"I was just as uncomfortable about what I was doing," Ethan continued. "I really wanted to get to know you better, but our meetings were tainted by Wade pressuring me to ask you questions about Blythe. Now that everything is out in the open, we can start over. No Wade, no disks, no seafood, no hot dogs, no Blythe. Does that sound okay to you?"

"As friends?" I asked, a little confused. Surely Ethan didn't intend to date both Jeremy and me. That would be a little too weird.

"Yes, as friends," he said. "You're a handsome man, Adam, and I've enjoyed some of our conversations, but I don't feel attracted to you. Except in a friendly way. I don't think you feel attracted to me, either."

"Not really," I agreed. "Though I have to say it surprises me, because I think *you're* a handsome man. I guess sometimes the chemistry isn't there."

"I'm glad we both feel that way. Sometimes in our previous meetings, I felt like I was giving you the wrong idea."

"Same here," I said.

We both laughed again.

"So now that we agree to be friends," Ethan began, "I was wondering . . ."

He trailed off, so I asked, "Wondering what?"

"I know you moved, and you have a new roommate and a new phone number. All I have is your cell phone number."

"You want my home number?" I asked, now feeling really confused. "It's always easier to reach me through my cell phone—"

"Not to reach you," Ethan said, and I was sure he blushed, though it could have been the freezing wind coloring his face.

"Huh?" I asked, feeling exactly like the dumb jock I always swore I wasn't.

"I'm kind of . . . interested . . . in calling . . . Krystle."

"Krystle?" I asked blankly. "You mean Martin? You want to call *Martin?*"

"I do," Ethan said.

"Why?"

"For obvious reasons?"

"They aren't obvious to me," I said.

"He made me laugh. Okay, not at the time, but later. He's a funny man."

"He was awful to you!" I said. "All those rude comments about auras and fashion chakras and Darth Vader—"

"Darth *Wader*," Ethan said and snickered. "He was so irreverent."

"You should see his nun act," I said, dumbfounded. Ethan and Martin? How was that possible? "You don't even know what he looks like under that blond wig and makeup."

"How shallow of you, Adam," Ethan said reproachfully. "I'm glad I don't know. It's his personality, not his looks, that I find appealing. Do you know how seldom anyone talks to me like I'm a regular person? I'm so tired of having to be unworldly and above it all. I'm a man, not a mystic or a swami. I'm a normal, healthy gay man with the same desires everyone else has. Physical and emotional."

"What about Jeremy?"

"I'm sure he has the same desires," Ethan answered, looking as bewildered as I was feeling. "You'd have to ask him. It's not something he and I talk about."

"Huh?"

"What?"

We stared at each other until I decided to try again.

"So you and Jeremy are dating other people?"

"Other people? I don't know what Jeremy is doing, but—"

"Wait," I interrupted. "Are you and Jeremy dating each other?"

"No!" Ethan said. "I could never date Jeremy. He's exactly the kind of person I'm talking about. I'm sure as far as Jeremy's concerned, I don't have a dick. I'm like some kind of spiritual mentor to him. Besides, he's not really my type. I mean, not that I have a type. But what we were saying earlier about chemistry—there's nothing like that between Jeremy and me. I got more of a charge being crammed in the back seat of that Volkswagen next to Martin than I ever did in all my meetings with Jeremy."

"Oh, my god," I said, grabbing Ethan to hug him, causing both of our cups to collapse and coffee to stream down our chests.

"Adam, sometimes you're like an obnoxious puppy," Ethan moaned, trying to brush the liquid off his coat. "Am I to assume from all this exuberance that you are interested in Jeremy?"

"Yes," I said. "But I thought you and he were together, so I planned to bow out gracefully."

"'Graceful' is not the word I'd use," Ethan said, taking my crushed cup from my hand and dropping it into a trash can with his. "As far as I know, Jeremy is as free as a bird. And now you do owe me an apology."

"I'm sorry about spilling coffee all over you," I said.

"No, because I just figured out that you've been using me from our first meeting. Not to get your stupid disks from Wade, but to find out more about Jeremy after seeing him with me at Wade's party. Am I right?"

"Yes," I admitted. "I never intended to lead you on—"

"And I was worried that I was leading you on," Ethan said with a rueful smile. "Are we both just a bit conceited?"

"Possibly."

"So last night, when you lent your support to Jeremy, you did that in spite of thinking he and I were an item?" Ethan asked.

"You heard about that?"

"It meant a lot to Jeremy," Ethan said. "He has so much respect for Daniel. Daniel's reaction hurt his feelings, but he felt like you understood him. And you must have, since by supporting his decision you thought you were pushing him into my arms."

"I'm not usually a generous loser," I said, "but whether or not it involves you, I think Jeremy should feel fulfilled by what he does. Nobody should be miserable in their work. It takes up too much of our lives."

"Remember what I said? That it's not in your nature to be secretive or sneaky? How come you never just asked Jeremy out?"

"Rumor had it that Jeremy wasn't interested in dating anyone," I said. "By the time I maneuvered myself into a position where I could ask him out, I thought something was going on between the two of you. I don't mind a little competition, but I'm not the kind of guy who'd break up a relationship."

"Very admirable. Now you know there's no relationship. But Jeremy does have some baggage. Including Daniel and Robert. Think you can handle it?"

"I'm willing to give it the old college try," I said. "So you and I are good?"

"No!" Ethan said.

"We're not? What else can I do to make things right?"

"Didn't I ask you for Martin's phone number?"

I grinned and took out a business card, writing the number on the back for him. We hugged goodbye, and as I walked away, the sun felt a lot warmer than it had earlier. Jeremy and Ethan were not a couple. They never had been. I was back in the game.

I decided against telling Martin any details about my meeting with Ethan, leaving it at the simple explanation that we had cleared the air between us. I figured Ethan deserved his shot at romancing Martin in his own time, his own way, and I didn't want to do anything to mess it up. I had a feeling Ethan would do the same thing regarding Jeremy and me.

Lester joined me at Club Chaos on Sunday afternoon so that we could launch and test the new site before Cybeeria's opening. Everything proceeded without serious problems, and the last time I saw him, he was on the dance floor with Blythe and Sheila. Blythe had snatched a cowboy hat from someone, and Sheila was teaching them a line dance. I loved the new openness of the club now that the wall had been removed from the balcony. Anyone at the computers could look over the dance floor or catch the shows onstage, just as I'd planned. Thus, they could talk to people online about things going on at the club.

Ray and his wife came by early in the evening to congratulate me before going downstairs to catch the first show. I had warned Ray it might be a little risqué, but he had merely rubbed his hands together with a happy, evil look, much like Mr. Burns, Homer Simpson's boss. At that thought I had to smile. *The Simpsons* was the one current TV show I'd seen a lot of, and I remembered Jeremy's quip at the retreat that watching it was the path to enlightenment.

At a prearranged time, I met my mom and dad online in the Club Chaos chat room called "Back Stage" so I could tell them how everything was going. Unfortunately, MixALot, one of the club's bartenders, was regaling the chat room with stories about the bar, and my parents were much more into him than me.

I couldn't have asked for a more successful opening. As Cybeeria filled with guys eager to try out the online messaging features, Andy sent in bottle after bottle of champagne as his treat. It was his cheapest champagne, of course, but it was still a nice gesture. At different times Gretchen, Daniel and Blaine, and Josh came in to check things out and wish me the best. Sheila took a break from dancing to let me know that Blythe was being well taken care of and I could concentrate on my work. The computer screen near the dance floor drew onlookers into Cybeeria, and the two crowds mingled throughout the night. I could think of only one thing that was missing from my evening: Jeremy.

I hadn't caught even a glimpse of him. Since Daniel hadn't mentioned him, I decided Jeremy must have changed his mind about coming. My disappointment was acute. It wasn't just a matter of wanting to see him. It wasn't even wanting him to see my success. It was more a need to share the moment with him, to somehow feel like we were part of it together. I knew it was presumptuous and hopelessly romantic of me, but I wanted one of those movie kind of moments where everything got wrapped up in a tidy ending, with music swelling and a slow fade to black.

As one of the computer stations against the wall cleared, I sat down and signed on with my Club Chaos screen name, GeminiGuy. I checked out the chat room again, then blinked when an instant message appeared on my screen.

ActingOut: Are you the hot one wearing the red flannel shirt over the white Henley, blue jeans, and could those be cowboy boots?

I glanced up to quickly scan the bar and saw Jeremy watching me from another computer station across the room. As our eyes met, he smiled at me and gave a little nod. I typed a response to him.

GeminiGuy: They are cowboy boots. I'm glad you made it.

ActingOut: I told you I'd be here. My typing is a little slow. Will you be patient with me?

GeminiGuy: I can be very patient.

I didn't dare look up at him after typing that, not wanting him to see that my patience had nothing to do with his typing.

ActingOut: I'm glad. I've been told I take a LOT of patience.

I suppressed my grin. Jeremy was definitely flirting with me. It was one of the quirks of talking online. Sometimes you typed things you wouldn't say face to face. Even though Jeremy was in the same room with me, having computers between us might make him feel a little bolder than usual.

GeminiGuy: Don't believe everything you hear. Did Ethan tell you he saw me yesterday?

ActingOut: Yes. He said you apologized for the DX mission. And he apologized about Blythe. Is that how you spell her name? Is she here tonight?

GeminiGuy: Yes. And yes. Last time I saw her, she was on the dance floor.

ActingOut: I hope I get to meet her. After hearing so much about her.

GeminiGuy: I'll make sure you meet her. Try not to be overwhelmed. She packs a lot of energy into her small self. She reminds me of Martin.

ActingOut: Now I'm scared!

I smiled. Before I could type a response, he went on.

ActingOut: Ethan didn't say much about your meeting. But he said you gave him Martin's number. Can you believe that? That he wants to go out with MARTIN?

GeminiGuy: I wonder what he'll think of Martin out of Krystle drag?

ActingOut: It will be a good surprise. Even I can admit Martin is cute. If you like obnox—I'm not sure how to spell that. Rude little shitheads.

I started laughing and glanced up to see Jeremy scowling at me.

ActingOut: Stop laughing at me. I know my spelling is atro—awful. This is all new to me.

GeminiGuy: You're doing fine. Have you given Ethan your opinion of Martin?

ActingOut: No. Let him learn for himself. He might even be a good influence on Martin.

Though I thought it was more likely that Martin would be a good influence on Ethan, I decided not to say so.

GeminiGuy: I figure their relationship can last only until Martin runs out of variations on the name Whitecrow. Like, 'Hi, this is my date, Ethan Whitebird—no, wait, I used that one—White—er—I'm sorry, Ethan, it's over!' BTW (which means 'by the way'), the appropriate response to every clever thing I say is LOL or ROFL.

ActingOut: What does that mean?

GeminiGuy: Laughing out loud or rolling on floor laughing.

ActingOut: ROFL.

GeminiGuy: Liar. I can see you and you are NOT rolling on the floor.

ActingOut: I am in my head. I'll bet when Ethan finds out Martin used to study ballet, he'll be all into that. Before you know it, he'll have Martin dancing for the Dalai Lama.

GeminiGuy: Jeremy?

ActingOut: Adam?

GeminiGuy: Did you just poke fun at yourself and Ethan and your spiritual endeavors?

ActingOut: Why yes I did. I DO have a sense of humor. Please don't believe everything Daniel says about me.

GeminiGuy: Daniel says only good things about you, I promise.

ActingOut: You, too. Well, except for all the ways you tormented him when you were kids.

GeminiGuy: He said he didn't tell you that!

ActingOut: He told me in only the nicest way. Really. I promise.

GeminiGuy: Sure he did. Is that why you're sometimes a little aloof with me? Because I used to pick on Daniel?

ActingOut: You want the truth?

GeminiGuy: Of course.

ActingOut: I thought you were kind of a slut.

GeminiGuy: What???

ActingOut: I heard you were interested in Ethan. But at the retreat, I thought you had something going with Daniel, only you were flirting with me, too.

GeminiGuy: I was never interested in Ethan or Daniel.

I glanced up to see Jeremy smiling at me again. When he looked back at his monitor, so did I.

ActingOut: I'm very impressed with Cybeeria. I've got an idea.

GeminiGuy: What?

ActingOut: Will you help me pick out a good laptop to buy and teach me how to get online? So that when I start traveling with Ethan, I can keep in touch with people that way?

GeminiGuy: I'll be happy to. After I get Blythe's Web site up this coming week, I'll be at a loss for something to do until I leave. We can go shopping!

ActingOut: Until you leave? Leave where?

GeminiGuy: Leave to go home to Eau Claire.

ActingOut: For Christmas?

GeminiGuy: Well, that, but it's where I live.

There was a long pause and I looked up to find Jeremy staring at me.

GeminiGuy: You still there?

ActingOut: I guess I didn't realize you were going back. Did I know that?

GeminiGuy: I don't know. I'm keeping my place here with Martin. I plan to travel back and forth. But I'll be in Eau Claire for a while.

Again there was a long pause, and I finally began typing again.

GeminiGuy: I guess you don't understand why I'd want to be anywhere but New York. Eau Claire probably seems about a million miles away from anywhere you'd ever want to be.

ActingOut: Actually, for a couple of years of my life, I wanted to go there more than anything in the world. But Daniel never invited me. He wasn't spending much time with his family then.

GeminiGuy: Sorry, I didn't mean to bring up any unpleasant memories.

ActingOut: No problem. Daniel never said anything good about Eau Claire. Do you really like it there?

GeminiGuy: I love it. I've lived in bigger cities, but Eau Claire is home. It's got a small-town appeal for me. My family and friends are there.

ActingOut: Tell me about your family.

GeminiGuy: It's my mother, father, brother, and me. My dad is retired, but he and my mom are always up to something. Mike is older than I am. He's married to Julie and has two sons, Kit and Cody. What about you?

ActingOut: My mother's a homemaker. My father owns an architectural salvage company. I have four older sisters. Reva and Roni are twins, then Anita, Adele, and me. I have lots of nieces and nephews. And about a million cousins. My parents are still in Brooklyn, but their kids are scattered over all the boroughs. None of us really moves too far from home. I understand what you mean about Eau Claire.

GeminiGuy: I renovated an old farmhouse on my own land. I miss my house. In fact, I can show you how to see it on the Web sometime. I've got a Webcam in my front yard.

ActingOut: A Webcam?

GeminiGuy: It's a live camera hooked up to a computer. It's always pointed at my house and broadcasts the picture over the Internet. I can go to a Web site and see my house day or night.

ActingOut: You're joking! So if you stand outside your house, people can see you on their computers?

GeminiGuy: Yes. It's why I never have sex on the lawn.

ActingOut: LOL.

GeminiGuy: See? You're learning. Will it be hard for you to leave the city and go to Oklahoma? Or wherever you end up? Not just leaving your family and friends, but all the great things about Manhattan?

ActingOut: You don't know much about me. After I graduated from Juilliard, my grandmother told me to take a year off, on her, and do anything I wanted. So I traveled all over the country. I did a lot of camping and hiking. After Daniel and I got together, we took a trip to the Northwest. I love New York. But I never get tired of exploring other parts of the country.

GeminiGuy: Wow. I had no idea.

ActingOut: I'm not just a city slicker! Anyway, I'm not really moving away. I'll spend time working with Ethan wherever, then come back here. Sort of like commuting. But different.

GeminiGuy: Just like me.

ActingOut: Yes. That's true.

GeminiGuy: Jeremy?

ActingOut: Adam?

GeminiGuy: Did Martin's act just end?

I saw Jeremy look over the half wall toward the stage.

ActingOut: Yes.

GeminiGuy: Is the dance floor filling up?

ActingOut: Yes.

GeminiGuy: Jeremy?

ActingOut: Adam?

GeminiGuy: Would you like to dance?

ActingOut: Yes. I would.

I signed off, hoping he was doing the same, and stood up. Jeremy walked across the room toward me, his blond hair a little messy from where he'd been running his hands through it. I resisted the urge to fix it. I didn't know if I should be that forward, and besides, he looked adorable.

"That was fun," Jeremy said. "I can't wait to get a computer of my own. And then, no matter where we are, we can still talk. I just wish I could type faster."

"You will," I promised, "the more you do it."

We walked downstairs, where the gods of nightclubs showered approval on me by allowing the DJ to start Duncan Sheik's rendition of "Embraceable You" just as we reached the dance floor. Jeremy smiled and moved easily into my arms. We fit. I wondered if he felt that way, too; then he pressed his body more closely against mine. I grinned. Jeremy was definitely happy to see me.

I looked past him to see Sheila and Blythe at a table next to the dance floor. They each had their chin propped on their hands as they watched me dance with Jeremy. They both looked a little misty, and I knew I had it—my movie moment.

Jeremy raised his face and said, "Are you going with everybody else to Gretchen's place upstate for Thanksgiving?"

"No. They invited me, but Blythe is dog-sitting for a friend of hers and can't leave town. I don't want her to be alone on Thanksgiving, so she and I are going to spend the day together."

"That's funny, I'm cat-sitting for Blaine," Jeremy said. "If you'd like, you and Blythe could come to Brooklyn on Thursday. The Caprellians put on a great Thanksgiving. Before you say no, let me tell you that my family is—"

"Yes," I said.

"Yes?"

"I'd love to."

"What about Blythe? Don't you need to ask her—"

"She'd love to, also," I said, thinking that she'd damn well better. I was not going to miss this opportunity to spend time with Jeremy. Especially with no Daniel, no Ethan, and no Martin around.

"I was just wondering," Jeremy said.

"Yes?"

"Do you think you could wear that pretty little kimono? You looked so stunning in it."

"Only if you wear your ostrich costume."

I could feel him laughing as he rested his head against my shoulder.

FOURTEEN

"**C**ome in!" Blythe hollered.

As I went in, I dropped the bag with my laptop by the door. Karma, the mutt that Blythe was dog-sitting—obviously named by people who thought it would be funny to spend twelve to fifteen years saying, "Good Karma!" or "No, no, bad Karma!"—was stretched on the floor and lifted a lazy head to check me out, then gave a contented sigh and went back to sleep. He wasn't even interested when I began unloading groceries into the refrigerator. I decided he was a refreshing change from my parents' hyper weimaraners, the Glutton Sisters.

"So?" Blythe came bounding out of the bedroom. Her energy swept through the room like a tidal wave.

"It's a surprise," I said, suppressing a laugh at Blythe's timing. "C'mon. Tell me."

"I have something to show you," I said, taking her hand in mine and leading her to the sofa. I opened the laptop and powered it on. We sat in silence waiting for the computer to boot up. I moved the cursor around the desktop, clicking and double-clicking, until finally I got to the window I wanted.

"Ready?" I asked.

"I suppose so." Blythe shrugged. "What am I agreeing to be ready for?"

"Sit tight for a second, and you'll see."

With one final click of the mouse, the screen went black.

"Impressive, Adam."

"Shhhh. Here it comes."

Seemingly random letters came from all sides and corners of the black screen to dance across the monitor. After about twenty seconds, the letters settled to form the multicolored name *Blythe Mayfield* under a banner announcing, *Welcome to the World of . . .*

Her mouth dropped open just a bit. She looked from the computer screen to me, then back to the computer.

"Oh," was all she said.

We continued to watch the screen as a button appeared at the bottom of the page, inviting us to ENTER. I got a nervous pang in my stomach at Blythe's reaction, but clicked on the button anyway, forging ahead. I figured that before I asked if she liked it or not, maybe she ought to see the whole site.

The next page popped up in a flash. Blythe remained silent as I clicked on each picture, showing her how they enlarged in a new window. Even I was amazed at how well Josh had managed to capture the colors and feelings of her paintings, as well as how effectively those emotions carried over to the Web site. The final page showed a small, nonclickable picture of Blythe in her apartment, sitting in front of a half-completed canvas, and included a small biography.

I moved the cursor and brought us back to the home page before saying, "It's pretty basic, but in time, of course, there'll be more on the Web site. Exhibits, galleries that sell your work, your reviews. The site will grow with your career." Neither Blythe's facial expression nor her body language held any clues about her reaction, so I said, "If there are any links you want to add, to your favorite museums or to pages of artists who influenced you . . ."

I trailed off, hoping for a response, and Blythe announced, "I need a minute so I can take this in."

She got up from the sofa and walked to the kitchen, leaning with both hands on the counter in front of the sink. I was worried because she'd told me from the start that she was apprehensive about doing a Web site of her work, even fighting with me on the day Josh came to take the pictures. I wondered if I should have left well enough alone.

I approached her to let her know that it was okay and we didn't have to launch the site if she wasn't comfortable with it. She turned to face me, her cheeks flushed, and put her arms around me.

"Adam," she said, "it's amazing. I didn't know what to expect, but that certainly wasn't it."

"You're not disappointed?"

"Disappointed?" She pulled back from me. "Are you kidding? I think it's terrific. I can't believe I made such a fuss about it. I love it."

"What a relief."

"You know," Blythe continued, busying herself between cupboards and the refrigerator, "I'm not in the habit of taking things for free." She pulled out a new jar of jam that I'd brought and looked at it before shrugging her shoulders and putting it back in the refrigerator door. "I insist on paying you."

"I don't need money."

"Who said anything about money?" She walked back out to her studio and found the painting that I'd admired when I first met her. "I want you to have this."

"Oh, man," I said. "This is great. Thank you."

"All right, all right, enough of this. What's for dinner?" she asked.

"I brought stuff to make stroganoff, but now I'm thinking maybe we'll go out."

"Why? I love it when you cook for me."

"I thought since we're eating in tomorrow, you might want to go out tonight."

"We're eating in tomorrow?" Blythe's eyes searched my face as if she were Miss Marple studying a suspect. "Stop being so cryptic, Adam, and tell me what you've done."

"We're going to Jeremy's family's for dinner."

"I see," she said, giving me a knowing look. "Aren't you Adam F-for-Fancy-Footwork Wilson?"

"Footwork?"

"When you and Jeremy were dancing, Sheila said you fit together like pieces of a puzzle," Blythe said. "I was simply impressed that you managed to get him to the dance floor."

"I wish we could have had that moment in a less public place," I said. "If something is finally starting to develop between Jeremy and me, we don't need the added pressure of all the history between him and his friends."

"Sheila introduced me to Daniel and Blaine. They seem like really nice people," Blythe said with a shrug. "Of course, I understand about not wanting everyone watching. But even with his ex and friends there, you got more than a dance. You're having dinner with the family. You don't need me there. I'm a big girl and can take care of myself."

"Of course you are," I said. "Daniel says that I have to move slowly. If I show up without you, he may think I'm assuming too much."

I looked at her with the biggest puppy-dog eyes I could manage.

"Ugh." Blythe rolled her eyes. "All right, all right. Just stop doing that thing with your face. I'm taking care of one dog already. Besides, you look like one of those paintings from Prajna's apartment." We both laughed, and Blythe added, "You'd better make extra stroganoff, too. I'm hungry. That's your penance."

I bustled around the kitchen, putting dinner together. Blythe watched in silence for a while until she bluntly asked, "Did you kiss him?"

I looked at her, feigned shock, and replied, "No."

"Did you try?"

"If I'd tried, the first answer would have been different," I said with a leer.

"But his friends were there," Blythe surmised, as she began to open a bottle of wine. "And Daniel was there."

"And you were there, too, Scarecrow," I joked and dumped the onions into the pan to brown with the meat. "I want to do it right this time. I've been with a lot of guys. But Jeremy's not like the others. At least I don't want him to be. I've never put this much energy into getting to know someone before getting physical. Do you think it's crazy that I feel like he's the one? Even though I barely know him?"

Blythe wrested the cork from the bottle of wine with an opener and said, "I think you just answered your own question."

We speculated on what Thanksgiving would be like as we ate our dinner. Blythe was full of questions.

"What do you know about his family?"

"Not too much. He was going to tell me something about them when we were dancing, but I think I cut him off before he could get it out."

"We know you didn't stop him by kissing him."

I rolled my eyes and countered, "I was busy accepting our invitation to Thanksgiving."

"So what you're telling me is that we're flying into this blind?"

"Not exactly. We know Jeremy."

"I don't. What does his father do? Are his parents still together? How many people will be there?"

"Architectural salvage. I think so. I'm not sure," I answered. "What is this, the Spanish Inquisition?"

Blythe sighed and mumbled, "Apparently not. You've told me nothing. I guess I do have to go if I want to find out anything."

"I don't want to force you. If you'd really rather not go—"

Blythe interrupted in a long-suffering tone, "No, no. I'll go. So Jeremy won't know how relentlessly you're stalking him. What are friends for except to shield your worst traits from prospective boyfriends?"

"You're the one who's only going to dinner to get information. Maybe *you're* stalking him."

"If I were stalking him, I'd have gotten a kiss already," Blythe said. "And I wouldn't need help to get into his apartment, the way you used poor Ethan to get into Wade's."

"Hey!" I objected, and she laughed at me.

Our laughter was silenced by the sound of someone knocking on Blythe's door.

"Expecting company?" I asked. Blythe shrugged and got up to answer the door.

"Oh, crap," she said, and I turned to see Wade.

"Wade!" I exclaimed in shock. As if on cue, Karma got up and padded into the bedroom.

"Adam, what a pleasure," he said as he stepped into the room.

"Oh, crap," Blythe repeated and closed the door, lightly banging her forehead against it. "You're early, Wade. Very early."

"I'm sorry, Blythe," Wade said. He unbuttoned his coat, looked around for something to put it on, and of course found nothing. His nose wrinkled as he took in his surroundings, and I realized he had never seen Blythe's shabby-chic loft before. "My dinner meeting ended sooner than I expected, so I came right over. I didn't realize you had company. But if I'd known I'd be seeing Adam this evening, I'd have rushed over sooner."

"For god's sake, give it a rest, Wade," Blythe groaned. "You can throw your coat on the sofa. Adam made stroganoff, if you're still hungry."

"No, thank you. Though I'm sure it's delicious. I think I'll keep my coat on. It's quite cold in here. Don't you have heat?"

"Only in the bedroom, because Adam gave me a space heater," Blythe answered and resumed eating.

"Would you like some wine, Wade?" I offered, thinking at least one of us could pretend to be a gracious host.

"Yes, thank you," Wade said. He looked around him with a disgruntled expression, as if he wanted to sit down but was afraid to touch anything. I poured him a glass of wine and offered him my chair, which he accepted. Since Blythe had only two chairs, I pulled up two milk crates and balanced myself on top of them.

"Adam, stop being so nice to him," Blythe said. "He owes you an apology."

"An apology?" Wade looked surprised. "Is that why you asked me here? I think we've been set up, Adam."

"I wouldn't doubt it. Nothing Blythe does surprises me. She's an amazing woman," I said. Blythe glanced at me and smiled, then finished off her wine. "Since we're all here, Wade, how about it?"

"I suppose this is in reference to those computer disks?" Wade asked.

"Yes," Blythe answered. "The ones you stole from Adam. Endangering his career, I might add."

"Yes, now I remember," Wade said, leaning back in his chair, which I half hoped would collapse. "The same disks he broke into my apartment for, I imagine? Not to mention the office at my club? Wreaking havoc with his little friends every step of the way and ruining the club's Saturday night. Not to mention kidnapping poor Ethan! I think you owe *me* an apology, Adam."

"Adam, don't say a word," Blythe warned. She looked Wade in the eyes and continued, "None of that would've happened if you hadn't taken his disks at the retreat in the first place. I don't know what kind of crazy games you're playing, but you will not hurt my friends."

"Blythe, take it easy," I said. "I got my disks back and my jobs are all done. If he's not going to apologize, it's no big deal."

"Maybe not to you," Blythe said. "But it is to me. I feel like it's my fault."

"He took them," I said, pointing at Wade. "Not you."

"Yes, I did," Wade finally admitted. "I found out, from Ethan, that you were working on a project with Blythe. When I heard that your laptop was turned in at the retreat, I took the disks. I figured whatever it was you were working on had to be on those disks, and maybe I'd find out something about my daughter in the process. Instead, I discovered that you're working with Andy Vanedesen to restore his dinosaur of a club. How's that going, by the way?"

"Peachy," I said. "He's busier than ever."

"How lovely. Anyway, what can I say? I was drunk. I wasn't thinking ahead when I took the disks. I never intended for it to hurt you, Blythe."

"That's great, but I'm not the one you should apologize to," Blythe said.

"Not that that was an apology," I added.

"There is a bright side to this," Wade said. "I got to see the marvelous work you do for your clients. I'm sure I could create a position for you in my company, Adam."

"Working under you in any position is the last thing I want," I said, and he shrugged. I collected my laptop and coat. "Blythe, would you walk me to the door?"

When we stepped into the hallway, I said, "It was a nice try on your part, but I don't need an apology from him. Nothing he did was your fault, though."

"I know," Blythe said. "At this point, I'm just sorry I'm related to him."

"It doesn't seem possible. Are you sure?"

"My mother seems quite certain. Are we still on for tomorrow?"

"Of course," I said, kissing Blythe on her cheek. "I know Thanksgiving is traditionally a family day, but feel free to leave Wade at home."

"As long as he's not in my home," she said. "Speaking of which, let me send him on his way. See you in the morning."

The next morning, as we rode the F train, Blythe told me about the conversation she'd had with Wade after I left. She'd agreed to see him occasionally, as long as he stayed out of her business. She thought this would probably be impossible for him. But at least he'd promised not to bother her friends again, though we were sure Wade didn't include Andy in that group.

As we emerged up the steps from the Seventh Avenue station into Brooklyn, I was struck by the quiet of the neighborhood. There were only a few cars on the street, and the people on the sidewalks were in no hurry as they drifted along, smiling at their neighbors or stopping to chat. The congested feeling of Manhattan was absent as I gazed up at the wide-open sky. Gone were the towering skyscrapers I'd grown accustomed to, and in their place were brownstones and tenement buildings no higher than four to six stories.

"I wonder if it's so quiet because it's a holiday. Have you ever been here before?" I asked Blythe. "Do you know where we're going?"

"I don't leave Manhattan unless I absolutely have to," Blythe said. "Where the hell are we?"

I brought out Jeremy's scribbled instructions and said, "According to this, we're in Park Slope."

"That means nothing to me. Which way do we go, Magellan?"

We walked on, following the instructions, passing cigar stores, barbershops, and other small businesses tucked among the better-known chain stores. Almost everything was closed because of the holiday. When we passed an open bakery, I ducked inside, thinking it might be nice to bring some rolls or something for dessert.

"We're out of rolls," the man behind the counter said. "And pies. It's been busy. Who are you going to see for dinner?"

"The Caprellians," I answered tentatively, wondering why he asked.

"Oh, marvelous!" he exclaimed, clapping his hands together. He put two large loaves of Italian bread into a bag and handed it to me over the counter. "Take these and give Mama Caprellian my blessings. She'll be grateful, I'm sure. I don't know how she manages to feed that family every Thanksgiving. The woman's a saint. Stop next door and get some vino, too. She'll need it afterward."

We did as instructed, and I bought two bottles of red wine; then we walked around the corner to the address Jeremy had given me. I drew a deep breath as we marched up the steps to the Caprellians' brownstone. Blythe smiled and patted my shoulder as I rang the bell.

"I got it!" I heard a child yell as the sound of footsteps pounded toward the door.

"I better not be sitting at the children's table," Blythe warned me in a soft voice.

"Depends on whether you behave yourself," I countered.

The front door swung open and a voice from the area of my knees asked, "Who is it?"

"You've got the right steps, but in the wrong order," a beautiful woman said as she approached the open front door and nudged the child aside. "Hi, you must be Blythe and Adam. I'm Reva."

"Yes, I'm Adam. Nice to meet you. This is my friend, Blythe Mayfield."

"Jer's told us all about you," Reva said with a hint of a smile.

"Yeah, and we all decided to stay anyway!" a voice from the room behind Reva announced, then let out a raspy laugh that evolved into a cough.

Reva stepped back from the door and invited us in, saying over her shoulder, "Uncle Mario, stop that. Be nice to our guests."

Uncle Mario got up from the sofa, placing both hands on his knees and emitting a loud grunt to assist him.

"Hey, buddy. Mario Caprellian." I shifted the bag of wine so he could pump my hand a few times before he turned to leer at Blythe. "Hello, little lady," he said, with a different kind of smile than the one he'd used on me.

"Hello," Blythe answered, using the loaves of bread as a shield. She was obviously onto Mario's game.

"Nice to meet you, Mario," I added.

Jeremy came bounding down the stairs with movements obviously perfected by years of practice. He grasped the banister at the base of the staircase and swung around it while saying, "Uncle Mario, leave them alone. They just got here." He approached us and said, "You must be Blythe. We didn't get to meet the other night. I'm Jeremy." After he kissed her on the cheek, he turned to look into my eyes. "Hi."

I smiled and returned, "Hi."

I stood still, not knowing the protocol. The desire to kiss him returned. Not necessarily in a sexual way, but because it seemed like the natural thing to do. However, I didn't know the rules around his family and thought it best to follow Jeremy's lead.

He smiled and hugged me. In spite of the bag I held, I managed to hug him back. For just a moment he rested his head on my shoulder, much like he had when we'd danced. I could have held him like that all night.

"All right, you two," Reva's lookalike mock-scolded as she came from around the corner, "break it up, or I'll have Uncle Mario turn a hose on you."

"You met Reva. This is her twin, Roni," Jeremy said.

An older version of Roni/Reva came through a swinging door and said, "No one's turning the hose on anybody. Girls, would you please get in the kitchen and help your father with the chopping before he hurts himself using that knife? Year after year, he picks the one day that I don't want his help and tries to destroy my kitchen. He knows that once I see how much damage he can do, I'll run him out for at least another year. Jeremy where are your manners? Who are these people? I'm Jeremy's mother, Stella. I'm so glad you could join us, whoever you are."

"These are my friends, Mom," Jeremy explained, blushing, "Adam and Blythe."

"Nice to meet you," Stella said with a nod.

"The baker sent this," Blythe said, tentatively holding out the bread. "To Mama Caprellian, because he doesn't know how she feeds everyone every year."

Jeremy's mother snorted, then she said, "Ha! That woman hasn't touched a stove on Thanksgiving in thirty years."

"Mom, you know she made the meatballs," Jeremy argued.

"She mixed them up and brought them raw. I cooked them. That old woman fools you all. I bet the baker called her a saint, didn't he?"

"He did," I said. "And he told me to bring her some wine."

Stella took our offerings and said, "I'll open the wine so it can breathe."

"Yeah, its last breath before you swallow it," Jeremy teased.

She gave him a stern-mother look and said, "Listen, kids, we don't stand on a lot of formality here. If you're invited, you're family. Help yourself to whatever you want. I have to get back in the kitchen before Joe chops through the water main."

The doorbell rang, and again a voice shrieked, "I got it!"

Neither of Jeremy's sisters had moved after their mother's request, and Roni rolled her eyes and walked across the foyer. Two small children came bounding down the stairs, their expressions changing from elation to dismay as Roni opened the door.

"You can get it next time," she consoled them, and the kids turned and headed back up the stairs.

"Happy Thanksgiving," came the greeting from the door as another couple came in.

"Hello, Aunt Donna. Hi, Uncle Jack. Happy Thanksgiving," Roni said.

Before Roni had the chance to shut the door, more guests arrived. Children ran up and down the staircase, and cousins, aunts, and uncles flooded into the house, filling it with noise and commotion.

"I guess we beat the rush," I said to Blythe.

"How many people are you expecting?" Blythe asked, her eyes huge as she watched the flow of people around us.

"We never know," Jeremy said. "We just fix food and eat in shifts. It's been this way since I was a kid."

"I'll never remember everybody's names," I said.

"You'd better start studying; there's a quiz later," Jeremy said.

"Are you a real blonde?" Blythe asked Jeremy. "With these raven-haired beauties as sisters?"

"My father was blond before he went gray," Jeremy explained. "Come on. I want you to meet him."

Blythe and I followed him into the kitchen.

"I did not. Now leave me alone. I know what I'm doing," a tall man at a counter was saying in a disgruntled voice.

Another dark-haired woman, closer to Jeremy's age, stood at the counter and chastised him saying, "Pop, if you don't cut these smaller from the start, it just makes more work for me. Why don't you make sure everyone has wine?"

"Oh, sure. 'Why don't you go someplace and make yourself useful' is what you mean, huh?" The man at the counter turned around, wiping his hands on his shirt.

"Joe! I just laundered that shirt. Do you think I've got nothing to do but wash and iron all day?"

"Relax, Stella. It's water. It'll dry."

Jeremy's mother sighed before she turned back to a large pot on the stove.

"Pop, I want you to meet my friends," Jeremy said. "Adam Wilson and Blythe Mayfield."

Jeremy's father was quite handsome. I felt like I was looking at Jeremy some thirty years into the future.

"Nice to meet you, Mr. Caprellian. Thanks for having us today," I said.

He shook my hand and looked me up and down, saying, "He doesn't look anything like the last guy, Jer."

"Pop!" Jeremy said, while the black-haired girl and Jeremy's mother exchanged an amused glance.

"Nice to meet you, too, son. This one must be Blythe." He turned his gaze to tiny, pink-haired Blythe, bowed, and said, "Welcome to our home." He looked toward Jeremy, asking, "How was that? Better?"

Jeremy gave a sigh while Blythe laughed. I could tell she liked Jeremy's father's dry humor.

"Mr. Caprellian," she said grandly, "I'm pleased to make your acquaintance."

He allowed his mouth to betray him by smiling a bit before turning back to the counter.

The black-haired girl said, "I'm Anita, Jeremy's sister. I'd shake your hand, but you'd get gnocchi all over you."

"It's okay; I understand," I responded as she turned her attention back to the counter.

"You're Italian?" Joe asked.

"No. I mean, er, I meant that I know what it's like to have stuff . . ."

Blythe stifled a laugh as my voice trailed off, and Joe went back to his task of making a mess in the kitchen.

"All right, come on," Jeremy said, leading us from the kitchen into a room full of people.

Blythe stared around her in amazement. Some of the people in the room looked at her with amazement, too. But she walked away from us and into the crowd. She stuck out her hand at the first random stranger and was greeted warmly.

My secret hope had been that Jeremy and I might have a moment alone together, but I knew that wasn't going to happen as I saw people's eyes rest on us from time to time. I felt like I was under as much scrutiny as when I'd been on the ball field with a stadium of noisy fans around me.

Jeremy took my hand and said, "You have to meet Nana."

He led me across the room through people who smiled as if they knew some sort of surprise was waiting for us.

"Nana," Jeremy began, "this is my friend Adam. Adam, this is my grandmother, Lucia Caprellian."

"It's so nice to meet you, Mrs. Caprellian."

"Call me Nana," she said, casting her deep-brown eyes my way. Her eyes were just like Jeremy's, and her hair had the pure white color that made me guess it had once been blond, like Jeremy's and his father's.

"Okay, Nana."

"Tell me, Adam, what is it you do?"

"I own my own company," I replied, knowing enough not to go into detail. "I work with computers."

"Oh? Is there good money in that?"

"Nana! Don't ask that!" Jeremy exclaimed.

"I'm seventy-five years old. Don't you tell me what not to ask."

"Seventy-five? It's been years since—"

"Enough out of you." She swatted at him with a lacy handkerchief, cutting off his comment.

I laughed and said, "It's okay, Jeremy. Yes, Nana, I do okay for myself. I'm actually in Manhattan on business."

"Ah." She nodded. "I knew you weren't from New York. Where are you from?"

"Eau Claire, Wisconsin," I said.

She looked at Jeremy and raised an eyebrow.

"It's purely coincidental, Nana. Adam and Daniel went to high school together."

"Small world," she said.

"Daniel and I didn't know each other well when we were young, but we've become friends during my trip here," I explained.

"Daniel's a good boy. But this one," she said, then swatted at Jeremy again, calling him a name I didn't recognize.

"She just called me a little jackass," Jeremy said. "In Sicilian. Even though her family is originally from Tuscany, and she's never been out of Brooklyn. She gets this stuff from television."

In spite of Jeremy's light tone, I suspected that Daniel had left large shoes to fill as far as the Caprellians were concerned.

When we excused ourselves from paying homage to Nana, she took Jeremy's hand and said in a soft voice that I could barely hear, "He seems like a nice young man."

I was cheered by her vote of confidence.

As we made the rounds of the room, Jeremy introduced me to people whose names I'd never remember. I overheard Blythe say to a trio of cousins on a large sofa, "My biological father is gay, too. There's no escape for me. At least they're nice to look at."

The group of girls laughed and casually glanced at Jeremy and me to see if we'd heard. Although we both had, we pretended we hadn't.

"I assume that means you and she have talked about Wade," Jeremy said quietly.

"Yes. I wasn't going to mention it to her, but she could tell I knew."

"She seems pretty relaxed about it. I always got the idea from Ethan that she doesn't like Wade much."

"She doesn't. But she's under the influence," I said.

"Too much wine?"

"Too much family. I'm suddenly wishing I had eight hundred cousins, too. It's contagious."

Jeremy laughed and said, "It has its advantages. Including that," he said, nodding toward the dining room.

Food had been set out on long tables that lined the perimeter of the large room. One table had traditional Thanksgiving dishes on it, including a turkey that probably outweighed many of the children in the house, while on the opposite side of the room was more Italian food than some restaurants offered on their menus.

"Let's catch the cousins later," Jeremy suggested. "There's a break in the food line, and that doesn't happen often. We ought to get something to eat."

He couldn't have said anything sweeter to me at that moment. I was starving. I walked to the middle of the dining room and looked back and forth between the two tables. At my parents' house, we always had a traditional dinner. My memory told me that today was a day for turkey and dressing, but my heart told me to go for the Italian food. I tugged at Jeremy's sleeve as he took a plate and handed it to me.

"Which table should I head for?" I asked.

"There's nothing in the world like my mom's lasagna. But I'm sure if you want turkey—which, by the way, you can have any old time—no one would even notice or be offended, least of all Nana, who spent all morning mixing and rolling those meatballs."

I glanced from the corner of my eye to Nana, who sat where we'd left her, and couldn't help but notice that she held me under her watchful gaze. That made my decision for me.

I started piling meatballs onto my plate. Each time I set down a serving fork or spatula, some cousin, aunt, or other family member would lean over my shoulder to urge a portion of something else on me, saying, "You have to try that. Stella makes the best."

Jeremy smiled and glanced at me from time to time. When I was sure I couldn't fit any more on the plate, or that it might break from the weight of the food, we took a place at one of the oval tables set up in a large room off the dining room. Eventually, we were joined by most of Jeremy's immediate family. It was the first time I'd seen his mother sit down, although she had no plate in front of her, and his father sat across from her. Reva—or it could have been Roni—sat across from us next to Anita. I could see the other twin talking with Nana; there was no sign of Adele.

It occurred to me that I hadn't met any of the sisters' husbands, who were reportedly in the den watching television. I realized that I was probably missing a terrific football game. I was sure that when I called home later, Mike and my father would be amazed to find out I hadn't watched it. My mother, on the other hand, would want every detail about the kind of man who was more enticing than a football game on Thanksgiving.

"What?" Jeremy asked, noticing my smile.

"I was just thinking that our mothers would get along great," I said. "I mean, not that—"

"Would you relax?" Jeremy asked. "I wasn't going to accuse you of planning our wedding or anything."

I was saved from responding to that when Blythe slid into an empty chair at our table, her plate filled mostly by salad and a small helping of lasagna. She didn't fool me with her dainty portions. I knew that before the day was over, she'd refill her plate several times and probably manage to sneak something out in her purse, as well. I'd noticed that the one she was carrying was larger than usual and was probably stuffed with little plastic sandwich bags. I'd seen her work buffets before.

Within a matter of moments, Uncle Mario swooped in and took the last seat, directly across from Blythe.

"Mrs. Caprellian, aren't you eating?" I asked.

"Mom never eats when everyone else does," Anita answered for her mother.

"It's hard to eat when you've been around food all day. And it's *Stella*. Do you cook?" she asked.

"Adam's a great cook," Blythe said. "World-class stroganoff." She speared a piece of lettuce from her plate. As she raised her fork to her mouth, she suddenly stopped, glancing at Uncle Mario before eating the salad.

"Really? That's one thing I've never been very good at. You'll have to show me sometime how you make it."

"Mom," Jeremy said, "there's nothing you can't do in the kitchen. Give me a break."

"This is the guy you've been telling us about, huh?" Anita spoke out of the blue and pointed at me with her fork.

Jeremy almost dropped his knife, and his face flushed.

"Yes, this is Adam, who I said was joining us for dinner, Anita," Jeremy enunciated carefully.

"You were right. He sure *is* handsome."

"Jeremy, you look so nice today. We don't see enough of you," his mother commented. She turned to face me. "Don't you think he looks good?"

I pretended to size him up, taking in the details of his tousled blond hair and the fit of his deep-green broadcloth shirt and black jeans.

"Yes, I think he does," I agreed, and Jeremy ducked his head in that endearing way he had.

"There's that fake modesty," the twin said. "Remember when he got 'Best-looking' in high school? Pop had to widen the door frames so Jer could get his head through. He was impossible to live with."

"Reva, you know that's not true," Jeremy defended himself.

"Oh, it is so true!" Anita joined forces with her sister.

"You leave my boy alone, you two," Stella said, running a hand through her son's hair.

"Yeah!" Jeremy said, leaning over to rest his head on his mother's shoulder and winking at me.

"Good luck, Adam," Anita said. "You've hooked a real mama's boy."

"Couldn't be as much of a mama's boy as that guy you had the good sense to dump, Anita," Roni said as she passed by the table on her way to the kitchen.

"I'll never live that down," Anita said. "One error in judgment, and they won't let up on you."

Joe refilled everyone's wine glasses, including his own, then left the table, plate in hand.

"You're just jealous, Anita, because Jer always gets the hotties," Reva teased.

Blythe surprised me by saying, "You have a beautiful home, Stella. You've chosen great colors."

"Thank you, dear. I just had the whole thing redone. Joe finally said to go ahead and do it, so you'd better believe I wasted no time before he could change his mind. Speaking of color, I like your hair. What do they call that?"

"Magenta Madness," Blythe said.

"That's not magenta," Anita said. "Magenta has more of a burgundy to it."

"No, it's magenta," Reva argued.

"I think it's more like fuchsia," Roni said as she came back from the kitchen.

"It's pink," Uncle Mario said, which seemed to settle it.

"More power to you," Stella said. "I couldn't get away with it at my age, but I love it on you."

"What is it you do, little lady?" Uncle Mario asked.

"When I'm not busy fending off a game of footsie," Blythe said candidly, "I'm an artist."

"Mario!" Stella shot him a reproachful look.

"So I stretched my legs once or twice. Sue me!" He turned his attention back to Blythe. "An artist, huh? Do you have any etchings you'd like to show me?"

Joe sat down with another plate of food. His eyes were affectionate when he looked at Mario, but as soon as he realized I was watching him, he assumed his impassive expression again. It struck me that he was one of those people who took in everything and said little, but was generally amused by the people around him. I turned to look at Jeremy, wondering if he was sometimes so hard to read because he did the same thing.

"Can't say that I do," Blythe was saying with a small smile, not at all frazzled by the lecherous Mario. "But Adam just finished the most wonderful Web site that he designed to show off my work," she added, forcing me back into the spotlight.

"Oh? Is that what you do, Adam?" Stella asked, and Joe looked up.

"Yes, I have my own company. Building Web sites, setting up networks, stuff like that."

"Good money in that," Joe commented.

"It sounds nice," Stella said. "Do you live here in New York?"

"My home is in Wisconsin, but I have several clients in New York, so I'll be spending a lot of time here. What is it you do, Mr. Caprellian?"

"My brothers and I run an architectural salvage company."

"Pop sells the stuff they save from old buildings," Jeremy said.

"I bet there's no shortage of stuff to salvage in New York," I said.

"What do you think about Jeremy quitting his job, Adam?" Joe asked.

I was surprised but answered honestly, "I've already changed careers myself a couple of times. I don't think people should stay where they're unhappy or feel they're not in the right place. And I teach a college class, so I admire him for using his talent to help young people."

Joe nodded, and Stella smiled at me. Apparently, I'd given the answer they were hoping for. It made me glad for Jeremy that his parents thought he'd done the right thing, too.

"I've always said all I want is for my kids to be happy and feel productive," Stella said.

"And to wear clean underwear," Anita reminded her.

"Are you wearing clean underwear?" Blythe asked Jeremy in a stern voice.

"Always," he said.

"Mama's boy," his sisters chorused.

"Adam, you're almost done. What else can I get you to eat?" Stella asked.

"Nothing. I mean, not right this second, thank you. I couldn't eat another bite. Everything is so good, though. Can I help myself to dessert later?"

"Of course you can." She smiled approvingly. "Take a break. You should see the rest of the house. Jeremy? Why don't you show Adam around? We can entertain Blythe while you're gone."

"We certainly can," Uncle Mario said.

"I'd love to see it. May I be excused?" I asked.

"Go, go," Stella said with a wave of her hand, while the rest of the family watched us get up and make our way through a door to the hallway.

"I think next Thanksgiving I'll ride naked on a float in the Macy's parade. It'll be far less humiliating," Jeremy said. "This is the den, and my brothers-in-law Paul, Richard, and Freddy."

"Yeah!" the three of them yelled and jumped to their feet at the same time.

My head snapped to the television to see that the game was about to go into overtime with a tied score between the Lions and the Steelers. I was dying to stay and watch.

"You want to see the rest of this?" Jeremy asked, noticing that I was transfixed by the game.

"Huh? Sure. I mean, no. I mean, uh, do you want to see the rest of it?" I asked, and Jeremy smiled, watching me as I waffled on my answer. "No, you know what? I've missed it so far and lived to tell about it. Come on. Let's see the rest of the house."

"Okay, but don't say I didn't offer," Jeremy said.

He walked toward the door, but I stood rooted to the area rug, unable to tear myself from the game. Jeremy leaned on the door frame while I watched. As the game was wrapped up after a controversial call followed by a field goal, Jeremy's in-laws jumped up with ecstatic shouts. Being a die-hard Packers fan, I wasn't as thrilled, but I shook their hands as we introduced ourselves. They seemed like good guys.

On the way upstairs, Jeremy said, "You got your testosterone fix for the day, huh?"

"Almost," I said, deciding to test the waters, and Jeremy smiled.

We went up another staircase to the third floor of the brownstone. I couldn't get over the size of the house. I surmised that there was good money in architectural salvage. Even if they'd bought the house when prices were low, it would cost a small fortune to heat it.

"Is this the house you grew up in?" I asked.

"Yeah, but it's changed a lot. None of us are here anymore, except Anita after her divorce." I assumed he was referring to *that guy*. "Mom's taken liberties with some of the rooms, converting one to a sewing room and a couple to guest rooms instead of making them shrines to her kids."

"Not yours, though, I'll bet."

"I'm sure yours is still packed with football trophies and stuff," Jeremy taunted.

"Something like that," I admitted.

He opened a door on the third floor and said, "I thought we'd start here and work our way down. This was my room."

I'd been right. His room had bulletin boards and shelves filled with memorabilia. I saw his diplomas from high school and Juilliard, textbooks, *Playbills,* and stacks of clear plastic boxes containing what looked like lots of letters, photos, and newspaper clippings. There were also glossy magazine pages featuring pictures of handsome models, rock stars, and actors pinned to the walls. I thought of Sam69wu's room, but this was different. It was as if Jeremy had kept visible reminders in front of him of what he wanted to achieve.

The room probably hadn't been touched except to be cleaned since he moved out. The furniture was antique cherry and had obviously been taken care of. The bed was covered with fluffy old quilts.

"I wonder what that would say if it could talk," I said, pointing to the bed.

He laughed and said, "It would say, 'Jeremy slept here.' "

I wanted to tell him that I wished my bed would say that, too, but I wasn't quite able to read him yet, in spite of his sisters' hints that he was interested. At some point I was going to have to corner Daniel and find out if Jeremy, like his father, was always inscrutable.

"Is that Daniel?" I asked, spotting a framed picture on Jeremy's dresser.

"Yes," Jeremy said. "When we first started going out, I was still living here."

I crossed the room and saw more pictures of Daniel and Jeremy tucked around the mirror.

"You both look so young and happy," I said.

"We were happy. Once."

I lost myself in the pictures, realizing how little I knew about their relationship other than its unhappy ending.

"Hey." He touched my arm, and I jumped.

"Huh?"

"You okay? Or did you just go to the Bahamas for a minute?" He laughed but didn't take his hand off my arm.

I looked him squarely in the eye and said, "Something like the Bahamas, I guess."

We stood for a minute staring at each other; then it seemed like we were moving in slow motion. He moved his hand from my forearm to my biceps, while he turned slightly to face me. I put my arms around his waist, locking my fingers behind his back, holding him loosely. We stood a bit apart and continued to watch each other.

"I've been thinking," I started.

"Yeah?" he asked. "About what?"

"About the other night. When we danced."

"Yeah," he said softly. He blushed and looked away briefly before looking back.

"When you hugged me—when I first got here—it felt just like that. I loved dancing with you."

"Me, too," he agreed.

"I want to get to know you better, Jeremy."

"I want to get to know you better, too, Adam."

My breath seemed loud, and my heart was racing.

"So," I began as my arms settled around him, "can I ask you a question?"

"Sure."

"Can we go out some time? Like on a date?"

"I thought you'd never ask," he said.

"Is that a yes?"

"Yes."

I let out a huge breath that I hadn't even realized I'd been holding, and grinned.

"Can I ask you another question?"

"Sure."

"Would it be okay if I kissed you before our first date?"

He looked at me with a serious expression and nodded. I pulled him closer to me, and felt his hands tighten on my arms. I tilted my head slightly to the right, and he did the same, as if we'd practiced it a hundred times before. My closed lips met his, softly, then our lips parted at the same time. I instinctively tightened my hold on him, pressing my mouth harder onto his as our tongues met. I felt as though my heart would pound out of my chest and realized that I could feel his heart beating equally strong and fast. He wrapped his arms around my shoulders, kissing me harder and pulling me even closer. When we finally broke the kiss, I leaned back, keeping my arms around him.

"I can feel your heart beating."

"I can feel yours, too," he said.

"I want you to know something."

"Yes?" Jeremy asked.

I leaned my forehead on his and said, "I think you're someone special, and I don't want this to happen too fast, because I'm pretty new at this."

"You could have fooled me."

"No, I mean getting to know someone first. It's something I've wanted, to have someone special in my life, but I haven't had it before," I explained.

"Why don't we go on that first date and see how things work out?"

"You know, we *could* go on our first date and see how things work out."

"Good idea," Jeremy said with a smile. "Wish I'd thought of it."

We continued to stand like that for a while, holding each other, with his head on my shoulder again. I closed my eyes and immersed myself in the feeling, knowing that I wanted to put it in my memory so that no matter what, I'd always have it. I allowed my fingertips to trace up and down his back, and he did the same to me.

"You know what?" he asked.

"What?"

"If we don't go back downstairs, people will talk."

"I thought that's why they sent us upstairs, so they could talk."

He laughed and said, "You're probably right. Of course, in this family, there's no need to send people from the room to talk about them, in case you haven't noticed." I laughed, thinking again about Anita and *that guy*. "I'm so glad you came today."

"Me, too. Maybe I'll end up having even more to be thankful for."

He smiled at me and said, "You never know."

Jeremy showed me the rest of the house. By the time we got downstairs, several of the cousins and kids had left. Blythe was still chatting with Uncle Mario and Jeremy's father at the table. I could hear voices coming from the kitchen, and the clanging of pots being cleaned and dishes being washed.

"We should probably be going," I said. "Blythe has to take care of a friend's dog. And I need to call my folks."

"It's good that you're close to your family," Mario said, and Jeremy nodded.

Everyone seemed to stand at once as we thanked them for their hospitality and shrugged into our coats. Stella fluttered around, making sure both Blythe and I had brown paper bags filled with

Tupperware containers. I spotted lasagna, meat sauce, meatballs, turkey, dressing, and pasta salad. It was enough to feed an army, but I was sure Blythe and I would put it to good use. At least she hadn't had to use her sandwich bags.

After we thanked the Caprellians, Jeremy walked us outside.

"Thanks so much, Jeremy. I had a great time," Blythe said.

"I'm glad you enjoyed yourself. Sorry about Uncle Mario."

"Sorry? Don't be. We've agreed to have lunch some time next week." My mouth dropped open. She shrugged and said, "He's a nice guy. I had a good time talking with him."

As she bounced down the steps to the sidewalk, I said quietly to Jeremy, "I'll call you tomorrow, and we'll talk about specifics, okay?"

"Okay."

"I'm really looking forward to it."

"Me, too."

We hugged and kissed quickly and softly on the lips, then I joined Blythe to walk toward our subway stop.

"Not a word," I said, wanting to savor my memories of the day.

"Not from me," she said, tucking her free hand under my arm. "I'll pretend I didn't even notice that first kiss."

"It wasn't the first," I said.

"I knew I'd find out," Blythe said smugly.

FIFTEEN

I was glued to the front windows of the town house, watching snow fall and feeling nostalgic for snow days, ice-skating, and sledding, like when I was a little kid. However, most kids didn't have to live with Martin, who was glued to the television as he tried to learn the dance steps to a video by a girl named Britney Spears. After the fourth time he rewound and played the video, I was ready to hit them both.

"What the hell are you doing?" Martin asked, finally pausing the VCR to look at me.

"I'm watching the snow fall," I said. "It's beautiful."

"It won't be so beautiful when it's dirty, gray, and piled up in the gutters," Martin muttered. "I doubt it'll stick, but it does look good when it's falling." I didn't think it was possible for Martin to sit still for five minutes, other than when *Judge Judy* was on television, but he joined me on the sofa to stare out the window. "Maybe if we're lucky, we'll see someone slip on the sidewalk."

"Should we throw down some salt?" I asked.

"Nah, that's the landlord's job," Martin said. "Which reminds me, Daniel called earlier. He said something about getting together later for dinner. Are we available tonight?"

"I don't have any plans. Are you doing a show tonight?"

"No, it's my night off."

"Then I guess we're on," I said. "What's the occasion?"

"Sheila's rallying everyone together," Martin explained. "I have no idea why."

"That's fine. I feel like I haven't seen her in ages. Who else is going?"

Martin tore himself from the window to look at me and wrinkle his nose in disgust.

"I don't know. I'm not Julie the Cruise Director," he said disdainfully. "That's Sheila's job."

"Can you at least tell me what time we're leaving to meet them?" I asked. "Or is that not in the job description of a diva bitch from hell?"

Martin's mouth dropped open; then he took my face in his hands and said, "You've learned so much in so little time. I've taught you all I can. My work is done here." As I laughed, he got up from the sofa and pretended to wipe away a tear, saying, "I'm so proud. My little boy's growing up. We're meeting them in four hours."

I put on my coat, boots, and hat, then went to the corner deli to buy some overpriced rock salt for the steps and sidewalk. I didn't want Daniel to worry about his tenants' safety while he was busy taping his scenes for *Secret Splendor.*

In all honesty, I was bored. Lester had taken over managing my New York clients and was sending me daily e-mails to let me know how things were going. They were short e-mails, because he hadn't run into any serious problems. Major catastrophes would warrant a call from him on my cell phone. But other than an occasional call from Blythe, my cell phone had been quiet. It seemed the only thing I had to do was enjoy myself until I went back to Wisconsin for the holidays.

Though I had the promise of a date with Jeremy to look forward to, we'd already postponed a couple of times. He was out of town meeting people who would be helping Ethan and him with AFNAT, the acronym for Art for Native American Teens. He'd said he would call me when he got back in town.

I brushed snow from the top step of our stoop and sat down. Enjoying myself with nothing to do was easier said than done. I wasn't like Martin, who could amuse himself with nothing but a remote control and a flavor-of-the-month pop star on the television. Even though I had learned how to have fun with my friends in

Manhattan, I had no idea how to spend time with myself. In the past when I found myself alone, I either worked, went to the gym, or looked for a one-night stand. But I wasn't in the mood to go to the gym. As for one-night stands, hopefully, Jeremy would change that.

It occurred to me that I hadn't actively sought sex since I first saw Jeremy at the Big Cup. There had been my night of "penance" with Steve after I first saw Martin's act at Club Chaos, of course. But Blythe had forced him on me, I reasoned, so it didn't count. Regardless of how my date with Jeremy turned out, I didn't want to rely on another person for my happiness.

I pulled my cell phone from my pocket and auto-dialed Blythe.

"Adam, I'm busy," she said in lieu of a greeting. "What's up?"

"Hi, Blythe! I miss you, too!" I exclaimed sarcastically. "I need a hobby."

"A what? Adam, I don't have time for this. What the hell are you talking about?"

"What are you doing that's so important?"

"I'm having sex with Jeremy's Uncle Mario," she said. After a moment of my shocked silence, she exclaimed, "I'm *painting!* What do you take me for?"

"That's just it," I said. "You paint. Daniel is an actor. I need a hobby, too."

"I'm going to pretend you didn't call my painting a hobby," Blythe said in an even tone. "And I won't tell Daniel either when we're at dinner tonight."

"You're going to dinner with us? Yay."

"*Yay?*" she mimicked. "Is that how Martin talks? I think you've been spending too much time together. Sheila called and invited me to some dinner gathering."

"Why don't Martin and I pick you up on our way?" I suggested, knowing she didn't have cab fare. "We'll call you before we leave."

"Great. See you then. I want to work some more on this one piece. And as for your *hobby?* I think the answer is fairly obvious. It's all about porn, Adam. Bye."

"Wait, what?" I sputtered, but she had disconnected the call.

Blythe shouting, *"He writes porn on his laptop!"* during Martin's act at Club Chaos resounded through my mind. I also remembered that I'd promised to help Jeremy find a laptop to take with him to Oklahoma. Surely that wasn't what she meant. Then I realized she was talking about the story I'd been writing when we met. Even though I'd been writing to pass the time and appear busy in Café Pick Me Up, I had enjoyed myself. And writing copy for Web sites had never seemed like a chore when I was working.

It had stopped snowing, just as Martin had predicted, but my butt was cold on the concrete steps. I got up and went inside the apartment, put the bag of rock salt in the closet by the doorway, and headed for my computer.

A couple of hours later I took a break and found Martin sitting on the floor in front of the television while he gave himself a pedicure. I reached for the remote and muted an annoying show on MTV about teenagers living together. Martin gave me a questioning look.

"I need to talk to you about something," I said.

"Sounds serious," Martin said, then turned to examine several colors of nail polish.

"It's about my friend Blythe. I wanted to introduce you to her at Club Chaos when Cybeeria opened, but I got distracted by something else."

"Uh-huh," Martin said, finally settling on a teal color for his toenails.

"I told her that you and I would pick her up on the way to dinner tonight."

"And you don't want me making any jokes about Darth Wader," Martin surmised.

"I'd rather you didn't, but that's not what this is about. Blythe is—how do I describe her? She's got this tough exterior, but she's very young and in some ways fragile. She doesn't want anyone to know that. She's got a lot of pride."

"Okay," Martin said, expertly applying his nail polish as I went on to explain how I'd spent the past few months trying to take care of her by buying her groceries or making sure she was never stranded anywhere without money or a way to call me if she needed me.

"She has friends in Manhattan," I finally said, "but most of them are as young and as broke as she is. I know she and Sheila have started doing things together occasionally, which I'm happy about. Sheila has a tactful way of taking care of people. But I'd feel better about going back to Wisconsin if I was sure someone was looking after Blythe while I'm away."

"You want me to fill in for you without being obvious," Martin said with more perception than I'd expected. "I could do that. Subtlety is my middle name."

I glanced at his toenails and said, "Right."

He looked up at me and smiled, saying, "It hasn't been that long since I was her age and struggling to survive in Manhattan. You can trust me."

"I know," I said. "That's why I brought it up."

Later, while Blythe settled between us in the cab, Martin gave the driver the address, then turned to look at Blythe.

"What is that smell? Is that your perfume?"

"I blend it myself," Blythe said a little defensively. "It's got a few drops of several essential oils."

"I think it's fabulous. Very subtle," he said and cut his eyes at me for a split second. "Sometimes at the club I get nauseated smelling a crowd of gay men all wearing the same hot new cologne. Like perfumed lemmings. Or do I mean lemming? What do you call more than one lemming?"

"Call them anything; they'll all come running," Blythe said, and they both cracked up. "I know what you mean. I've been on the subway during morning rush hour and felt like I was suffocating."

"Morning rush hour," Martin mused. "Something I've never had to worry about. Elevators can be that way, too."

"Or the cosmetics section of department stores," Blythe said.

"Don't you hate that? All those people lunging at you with atomizers and scary smiles?"

"I've got this choking act I do," Blythe said, making a strangling noise as she clutched her throat and croaked, "Asthma."

"You say *asthma;* they hear lawsuit," Martin said admiringly.

"Exactly."

"I like the way you think. We have to go shopping together sometime."

By the time we reached the Renaissance Diner, they had discovered a mutual love of resale shops, *Judge Judy,* and Martin's drag show. We found Sheila, Josh, Daniel, Blaine, Andy, and Gretchen seated at a large table in the back of the restaurant.

"I'd comment on how you kept us *waiting,*" Andy said after we settled into our chairs, "but we're all *quite* familiar with Martin's need for a grand entrance."

"And to make sure his hair is perfect before he leaves the house," Daniel added.

Martin absentmindedly touched his short, blond-tipped hair and said, "Adam has more hair products than I do. He was the one who made us late, not me. He was typing away on that computer of his like there was no tomorrow."

"Did you get caught in a porn cycle?" Blaine teased.

"I wasn't looking at porn," I said. "I was writing."

Blythe looked at me and winked.

"What do *you* know about porn cycles?" Daniel asked, but Blaine merely smiled at the waiter as he came to take our orders.

Conversation was lively while we ate. Sheila said the meal couldn't hold a candle to the Thanksgiving dinner that Gretchen had prepared for them at her upstate resort, Happy Hollow, and they regaled Blythe and me with stories about their weekend. We, in turn, told them about our visit to the Caprellians', Daniel smiling intermittently, no doubt fondly recalling his previous experience with Jeremy's family, and Martin occasionally interjecting sarcastic comments and noises.

I was surprised to learn that Andy hadn't celebrated Thanksgiving with the others. He confessed that he'd spent the day working with Gay Men's Health Crisis, helping prepare and serve food at the center, then delivering meals to GMHC clients in their homes.

"The club was closed and nobody *invited* me anywhere, so it beat TV dinners at home by *myself,*" he said.

"You volunteer every holiday, Andy," Gretchen protested. "You don't fool us with your 'poor me' act."

After our empty plates were cleared and a new round of drinks was brought to our table, Sheila announced, "There was a reason I invited everyone tonight—"

"Does that mean you're picking up the check?" Gretchen interrupted, and everyone laughed. "Actually, I'm glad you did get us all together, Sheila, because I have a small announcement to make. It's been about two weeks since Cybeeria opened at Club Chaos, and after going over the books with Andy, it's clear there's been an increase in receipts."

"And over two thousand hits to the club's Web site," I interjected.

"Thanks to Adam," Gretchen said, "and his technological know-how, the way things are going, the renovation costs should be paid off in no time."

"Here's to Adam," Andy said, raising his glass.

I blushed and gulped down my wine as they toasted me.

"While that's certainly good news, I wanted to tell you about something that happened at Happy Hollow," Sheila said.

"Other than Daniel and Blaine's anniversary?" Gretchen asked.

Daniel and Blaine beamed at each other and kissed, causing another cheer and salute of raised glasses.

"That's so great," Sheila said. "But actually, I was going to say something on a more *personal* note about a big change—"

"How did you find out?" Martin interrupted. "I know you're all going to be disappointed to hear this, but Sister Mary Amanda Prophet has been assigned to a different order."

"It's true," Andy moaned. "I've lost another one."

"Martin, what are you talking about?" Daniel asked.

"Sister Mary's last performance is on New Year's Eve," Martin announced. "Then it's off to a leper colony for her to spread good cheer where it's really needed. Of course, the lepers would give their right arms for good entertainment." After we all groaned at his bad joke, he continued, "As for me, I'll be starting rehearsals as a member of the Kit Kat Club in Broadway's revival of *Cabaret.*"

Nobody could stay seated after hearing that. We all jumped up to hug Martin and give him our best wishes.

When we sat down again, Martin said, "It's a small part, but I'm so happy."

"We're happy for you, Martin," Daniel said.

"I can't believe you didn't tell me," I said. "I'm your roommate, and I have to find out with everybody else."

"You're not known for your sleuthing skills, secret Asian man," Blythe said.

"I can't believe Martin held it in as long as he did," Andy said. "He gave his notice to me last week."

"Cheers to Martin for renewing an old dream!" Daniel exclaimed.

Once we quieted down, Sheila said, "I think someone else at this table has some big news."

"That would be me," Blaine suddenly said, and Sheila buried

her face in her hands for a moment. "I've been given final casting approval for Allure Cosmetics' new Zodiac Girl."

"Blaine, don't keep them in suspense," Blythe said. "You picked me, didn't you?"

"It was so close, Blythe, but I'm afraid not."

"Oh, well," Blythe said. "Always a bridesmaid, never a—"

"Tori Spelling," Martin interjected, and Blythe threw an olive in his face. "Good shot! I love olives."

"Actually, Sheila got the Zodiac job," Blaine announced.

"Doesn't anyone care that I—" Josh started to say, but he was interrupted by Sheila.

"I got it? I got the Zodiac job!" Sheila yelled and leaped from her chair to hug Blaine. "Thank you. Thank you so much, Blaine! Oh, my god, this is fantastic!" She turned to hug Josh, who sat rigidly in his chair with a peculiar expression. "Right," Sheila said and stood behind him with her hands on his shoulders. "Since I finally have everyone's attention, Josh proposed to me at Happy Hollow after Thanksgiving dinner."

We all stared at them in rapt silence until Gretchen finally said, "I think this is where you tell us whether or not you said yes."

"Oh! Yes! I said yes."

Once again we all broke into cheers, applause, and hugs for the happy couple.

"Are you positive you wouldn't rather be a lesbian?" Gretchen asked Sheila, who only giggled and nodded. "If you're sure, then I'm glad you're the one I lost her to, Josh," she lamented and shook his hand forcefully.

"If you give me enough time, I'll do a wedding portrait," Blythe offered. "Of course, it'll be abstract."

"Martin can be the maid of honor," Daniel said as he hugged Sheila.

"And Daniel can be the flower girl," Martin shot back.

While Sheila and Josh talked about how they'd probably have the wedding in Eau Claire, I took a break to check in with Lester on my cell phone, since I had the ringer turned off. Then I decided to check my voice mail. I felt a twinge of nervousness when I heard a message from Jeremy letting me know that he'd be back in town the next day if I wanted to call him.

I spent the rest of the evening fantasizing about him, happy that everyone was so caught up in the festivities that they didn't notice how quiet I was. In all the time I'd spent with Martin, Daniel, and even at the gym with Blaine, I'd told none of them what had passed between Jeremy and me at Thanksgiving in his room and that we'd agreed to go out. It was like knowing the best news in the world and keeping it to myself. I just wasn't ready for everyone to talk about it.

When I returned his call the next day, we made small talk about his trip and I told him everyone's news. Finally, he broached the subject uppermost on my mind.

"Do you still want to do something?"

"Absolutely," I said. "If you mean a date. I know you wanted to shop for a laptop—"

"Date, I meant the date," Jeremy cut me off. "My schedule is wide open."

"I do have a plan," I said. "If you can make it a daytime thing instead of at night."

I explained that I wanted to be out of the city. I was beginning to miss the country life, and after hearing about Happy Hollow, I felt like a short romp upstate might tide me over until I left for Eau Claire. I'd searched the Internet for somewhere close but removed enough to get the sounds of honking horns, cursing pedestrians, and wailing sirens out of my head. Cold Spring, New York, looked like a nice spot by the Hudson River. There was a small village and a network of hiking trails through the hills overlooking the Hudson River Valley.

"That sounds great," Jeremy said. "You remembered that I love being outdoors and hiking."

"Uh-huh."

"Cold Spring is only an hour away by the Metro-North train," he said. "But I've never been there. I can't wait."

Martin knocked on my bedroom door as Jeremy and I finished our conversation and hung up.

"I just got the most bizarre call," he said. "You could have warned me."

"Bizarre? Warned?"

"Ethan Whitetail."

I laughed and said, "Martin, you have to start using his real name, or you're going to screw up to his face one day."

Martin shrugged and repeated, "You could have warned me."

"Did he ask you out?"

"I told him I wasn't ready to date yet. He understood."

"He's a good guy, Martin. He told me that you appeal to his sense of humor."

"Who knew he had one?" Martin asked. "I didn't close any doors. But there's too much changing in my life as it is."

"Because of leaving Club Chaos?"

"Not to mention that you've saddled me with your daughter."

"Yeah, I could tell last night that a new playmate will be a burden for you. Admit it. You're going to miss me."

"Have you been taking it's-all-about-me lessons from Daniel?"

"No, I'm being home-schooled."

"Smartass. Ethan's unrequited love for me wasn't the only shock I got."

"No?"

"He told me how much Jeremy is looking forward to *your* date."

I groaned and said, "Please don't start on me about Jeremy. Please."

"I'm sure I don't know what you're talking about. When is the big event? Should I call Liz Smith and have it put in her column? Does *Daniel* know?"

I glared at him a minute, then said, "No. Nor does he know you're sleeping with the enemy."

"I most certainly am—"

"If you don't want me telling him that, you'll keep your mouth shut. And don't be home tomorrow afternoon. Jeremy's meeting me here, and I don't want you tormenting us."

"I never knew you could be so vile. If I weren't *years* younger than you, I'd swear I spawned you myself."

The next day, Martin left the town house well before Jeremy was due to arrive. As I finished lacing up my new Timberland hiking boots, the doorbell rang, announcing Jeremy's arrival and ushering in a feeling I hadn't had in a long time. I felt the way I had when I went to pick up my prom date, only this time I had a real sense of possibility. Along with that feeling, though, heat rushed to my face, and my stomach twisted into itself like a snake around a tree.

I quickly ran to the bathroom and splashed cold water on my face. I looked at the mirror and took deep breaths. It was unlike me to be either giddy or nauseated. The feeling quickly dissipated as excitement flowed through me again. I raced to the door, hoping Jeremy hadn't vanished. But when I opened it, a harried Martin pushed his way in and past me.

"Adam, I'm sorry. I know I said I wouldn't be here, and I won't be, but I forgot my—" He stopped mid-sentence and whipped around to gaze at me. "Are you climbing a mountain or going on a date? Or just climbing Jeremy?"

"You will be leaving again, won't you?" I asked sarcastically.

"You really have been living with me too long. Yes, I'll be gone in a minute. As I was saying, before being shocked by the sight of your Grizzly Adams costume, I forgot my credit cards and only realized it after I had my new outfit at the cashier. I rushed back here hoping to catch you before you took off, because I also left my keys."

He pulled his credit cards from between the sofa cushions, then tugged his keys loose from the tangle of fringe at the end of the orange afghan draped over the arm of the recliner.

"Okay, I'm off. Before the clerk figures out that I put sale stickers over the full price on my new shirt and pants."

Martin opened the front door to a startled Jeremy standing on the stoop with one arm behind his back and one finger poised near the doorbell. His initial shock gave way to a bright smile as he locked eyes with me over Martin's shoulder. Martin looked from Jeremy to me, then back to Jeremy. He smiled as he stepped past Jeremy, then barked out a quick, gleeful laugh as he ran to the curb to wave down a cab.

After letting Jeremy inside and closing the door, my nervousness vanished. I turned to face him, and he held out a small bouquet of pink roses.

"I've heard about your ability to kill plants with a mere glance. Not to worry, these were freeze-dried and are supposed to have a longer shelf life than Carol Channing."

"They still smell great. I guess they freeze-dry the scent, too."

"I didn't know if flowers were appropriate for men. Back in the pre-boyfriend days, my dates usually consisted of frantic meetings on a dance floor, followed by a clumsy rush to the closest available apartment."

"Been there," I said. "They're beautiful. Thank you. Are you ready?"

"Definitely," he said as I gently set the roses on the end table next to Sarah Ferguson's photograph.

We made it to Grand Central in time to catch an earlier train than we'd originally planned. After having wondered for the past few months if this would ever happen, I could barely believe Jeremy was sitting beside me on a train, enjoying the sun coming in through the window.

The city quickly turned into suburbs as the train followed the path of the Hudson River north. Little by little, the population became sparse, and the hills on the opposite side of the river more preserved, the last leaves of autumn holding on to their orange glory.

"I feel like I can breathe again," Jeremy said, leaning forward to get a better view.

"Would you like to switch seats?"

"Not at all; this way I have two beautiful views."

I knew I was blushing, somewhat surprised by Jeremy's candor. Until that moment on Thanksgiving in Jeremy's boyhood bedroom, our relationship had been about subtle comments, bashful glances, and an unexpressed attraction that I could only hope was mutual.

"I'm sorry," Jeremy said, "sometimes I'm a little . . ."

"Forward," I finished for him. "I like it."

I settled back in my seat, letting the awkwardness fade away. I felt Jeremy lean closer, his body heat warming my cheek, which had been cool from a small draft. His left shoulder touched my right as the train tracks began to veer slightly east, away from the river. I turned my head to face him. Our noses all but touched. Then our bodies were pushed back by the force of the train coming to a stop. Cold Spring was announced, so we gathered our coats and day packs and exited to a chilly afternoon. The sky was impossibly blue, dotted by wispy cirrus clouds high above.

We walked through an old stone tunnel that led from the station onto a charming street. It ran up and down a hill lined with white buildings, all with black shutters. The smells of cooking reminded me that I'd been too nervous to eat more than a bite or two of a bagel that morning. Glancing down the hill, I could see a café with a porch overlooking the Hudson River.

"Why don't we stop and have a quick bite," I suggested.

"I have a better idea. Why don't we get sandwiches and drinks to go, then eat them once we find a nice spot along the trail?"

"Good idea, but I have to eat something small until then."

Jeremy took off his pack, opened it, and produced a Natural

Force bar, which he handed to me. I took a few bites. It was disgusting, but I ate it anyway. Jeremy seemed to study my face as I chewed slowly.

"You don't like it?"

"It's . . . okay," I said hesitantly.

"They're not that bad. I received a whole case because they had a product placement on the show."

"Okay, I have to admit it. It tastes like tree bark."

"They are pretty nauseating," he relented, and we both laughed.

After our brief stop at the café, we started up a moderately challenging trail that wove its way to the top of the mountain.

"Some time," Jeremy said, "you should go hiking with me around Gretchen's place at Happy Hollow. There are some fierce trails there. Since your boots look new, I'll take it easy on you today."

"It's not good to challenge me," I warned him. "I can get very competitive."

"Does common sense usually prevail, though?" Jeremy asked.

"Depends," I said. "It's possible I've mellowed a little over the years."

I hadn't realized that living in New York had been making me so tense, until the knots in my upper back began to ease. In the absence of external noise, my inner cacophony of "must do, must see, must accomplish" dissipated, yielding to peace of mind and comfort.

As the trail began to flatten out, we stumbled on a field dotted with apple trees. Jeremy stopped to pick two apples and handed one to me. They were late-season, but still crisp and sweeter than anything I'd find in a grocery store. I watched Jeremy bite down, his full lips surrounding a quarter of the apple, pushing out, tempting me to join him. He stopped chewing when he realized how intently I was watching him. His eyes narrowed; then he continued eating. I moved closer. A trickle of juice ran from the corner of his mouth to his chin and glistened in the late-autumn sun. I leaned forward. Jeremy drew back slightly. I reached out with my left hand and slid my finger through a belt loop and pulled him closer. Our noses touched. I slowly licked the juice from his face, from chin to mouth. He let out a small hum of pleasure.

I finally pulled away and said, "Come on. Let's keep going."

As we climbed, I noticed a small trail. I grabbed Jeremy by the hand and pulled him down the path. I bravely fought back the thorny tendrils of blackberry bushes, holding them aside for Jeremy to pass into a small clearing that ended at a cliff. He stood at the edge and looked out. I joined him, shocked by the view.

"Wow, you can see Manhattan from here," he said, tentatively taking my hand.

"Look down there," I pointed. "That farm reminds me of my place."

It was true. A white farmhouse was set pristinely in the middle of rolling fields. A large red barn sat close to the house. Silos shot up from the ground. It was so removed that I could barely make out a long driveway leading to a road.

"Let's eat here, with this view. This was so worth the wait," Jeremy said.

He pulled a tightly rolled blanket from his pack, then the sandwiches and two bottles of water we'd bought. Surprisingly, he also pulled out a half-size bottle of cabernet.

"What else do you have in there, Mary Poppins?" I asked.

"A spoonful of possibility," he answered.

We settled on the blanket next to each other, facing the view. I ate ravenously and was finished before Jeremy. I slowly sipped my wine and finished it just as Jeremy took the last bite of his sandwich. I moved closer, until my shoulder was touching his.

"I have to say something to you, Jeremy."

"Uh-oh," he said, a strained look on his face.

"It's not bad or too heavy. I just have to tell you that I've imagined this moment since the first time I saw you. Which was long before you ever saw me. After the Disorient XPress fiasco, I thought my chances were ruined."

"They almost were. I hadn't planned to get involved with anyone, in any capacity. Although I have to admit you made it difficult not to be attracted to you."

"I feel a 'but' coming on."

Jeremy didn't continue right away. Instead he squinted at a pair of hawks circling just below, over the farm. He pulled away slightly, straightening his back. I felt like a heavy blanket had been dropped on us. Then he turned toward me with a half smile on his face.

"I've always had a thing for cliffs." He paused, and I stayed silent, feeling like he wanted to say something else. He took a deep breath and said, "I had my most honest moment on a cliff in Oregon.

Daniel and I were in a house on a cliff overlooking the Pacific. There was one night we were together when it seemed like we would never hurt each other. At that moment, I would have laughed at anyone who told me I'd one day break Daniel's heart. The truth is, when I did that, I broke my own heart, too. I don't mean to get overly emotional or anything, but I feel like I should tell you, because I really like you, Adam."

"You can always say anything to me, no matter what happens between us."

Jeremy shifted to lie down, resting his head on my thigh. He reached his left arm around my back and gazed up at me while he talked.

"I'm done with men who make promises, then run away when you ask to spend more than an hour with them outside of a bedroom. I know it's old fashioned, but you saw where I come from. I want sex to mean something. I want it to be . . ."

"Making love," I finished, hoping that didn't sound too trite.

I pushed the lunch debris from the blanket and stretched out beside Jeremy, resting my head on his chest. Despite anything Martin had said about Jeremy being shallow, I knew he wasn't. He had a heart, and he had faults, making him perfectly human.

"There is something else," Jeremy said. "What happens if this gets serious?"

"What do you mean?"

"We're moving in different directions. I'm going to be off teaching; you'll be back and forth between Manhattan and Eau Claire. Are we setting ourselves up for this to end before it begins?"

"We'll find ways to see each other. It's my belief that if things are meant to work out, they will. That theory's gotten us this far, hasn't it?"

"I don't know. It's going to involve a lot of work."

"If you don't think it's worth working at, then it won't happen," I said, getting slightly defensive.

"That's not what I meant. I'm willing to—I mean, it's not me. I hear the things you say. That you're competitive. That you like a challenge. That you've never had a serious relationship. And it makes me—"

"I'm not going to be one of those guys," I interrupted, feeling as if I finally understood him. "I'm not going to let you get close, fuck you, then vanish. That's not what I'm about. The reason I never let anyone get close before was so no one would end up hurt. This is different. I want to be close. And nobody's going to get hurt."

"How do I know that?" Jeremy asked.

"You don't. You take a risk. So do I."

His eyes looked so vulnerable that I ached for him. I'd spent years avoiding heartbreak, while Jeremy had taken risks and paid the price. I knew I had no right to give him relationship advice. Especially when, as aloof as he'd kept himself, he'd still shared his friends, details about his life, even his family, with me. I'd done nothing similar to make him feel welcomed into my life.

"Jeremy?"

"Adam?"

"I don't want to rush this any more than you do. There's a lot to be said for anticipation."

He sat up to kiss me and said, "Are you cold?"

"Freezing. Ready to go back?"

"Up and at 'em," he said, standing up and reaching for my hand.

"Geez, my mom used to do that to me on Saturday mornings," I said, getting to my feet. "Up and at 'em, Atom Ant!"

"Cute," Jeremy said.

We were fast about repacking our stuff and heading for the trail. Jeremy stopped once and looked back, then we hugged and kept moving. Once we reached the town, Jeremy suggested we check out some of the antique shops.

As we compared our likes and dislikes over antiques, I noticed some stained glass windows and drew him to them.

"These remind me of my house," I said. "It was built in the twenties and has several windows like this. I love to see the sun come through them, casting their colors over my hardwood floors."

"You really love your home, don't you?"

"I do. I can't wait to show it to you. I mean, whenever you want to visit me."

"I'll visit you," he promised. His eye was caught by a shelf of toys and he laughed and said, "Check this out!"

He took down an Atom Ant push puppet and pressed the bottom, making it collapse while we laughed.

"I'm getting this," he said. "It's traveling with me to Oklahoma as my good luck charm."

"What should I take with me to Wisconsin?" I asked.

We surveyed the shelf and he handed me a tin windup lion.

"I'm a Leo," he explained.

"My golden-maned lion," I said, and the smile he gave me took my breath away.

We paid for our toys and went outside. The sun was setting, so we walked toward the train station, our steps seeming to get slower the farther we walked.

"Let's don't," I finally said, stopping to look at him.

"Don't what?"

I pointed to the Pig Hill Inn and said, "Feel like spontaneity?"

"It's my favorite dish," he said.

Within minutes, we were in a room with our own fireplace and a private bath that he immediately made use of, letting hot water melt the chill out of his skin while I got the fire going. We had dinner in our room, keeping the conversation casual. Later we stripped to our underwear and lay under the quilts on our four-poster bed, staring at the fire.

"Is this what you thought would happen when you woke up this morning?" Jeremy finally asked, breaking the silence.

"No. I thought we'd hike and talk, then you'd do your shy-Jeremy thing, and we'd go home," I said.

"Shy-Jeremy thing?" he repeated. "What's that?"

"You get all bashful and duck your head or drop your eyes and blush."

He started laughing and said, "You've got a lot to learn about me."

"I already figured that out," I said. "I'm starting to wonder who's been chasing whom."

"Well, first you were chasing Ethan—"

"No, I was—"

"Then you dumped that poor Harold guy at the retreat so you could sleep with Daniel."

"I certainly did—"

"The next thing I knew, you were living with Martin, and I'm afraid to even speculate about you and Wade."

"Now you've gone too far," I said, turning him over and pinning him down. "Besides, you're the one Martin calls a narcissistic slut." Jeremy merely laughed, staring into my eyes. "What's with you and Martin anyway? Is it just because of your breakup with Daniel?"

"I've got a theory, but I don't know how accurate it is," Jeremy said.

I moved over to lie next to him, and we continued to stare at each other, our heads on our separate pillows.

"What's your theory?"

"I think a long time ago Martin had a big crush on Daniel. He convinced himself the only reason he couldn't have him was because of me. By the time Daniel and I broke up, Martin was over his infatuation, but his desire had become a habit. Martin's a Daniel-junkie. I've only known two people close to Daniel who haven't been sliced to ribbons by Martin's scalpel of a tongue. One was Ken. The other is Sheila. Just wait. You'll get your turn."

"Are you a Daniel-junkie, too?" I asked, and though the question was playful, I knew he could tell it was something I'd worried about.

"Is it bad manners to talk about an ex-boyfriend when you're in bed with a potential boyfriend?" Jeremy asked.

"Hell, no," I said. "And don't forget the steamy parts."

He laughed and said, "Ken introduced us. It was one of those relationships that happens very quickly and feels so right. We laughed all the time. The world was a giant playground and it was always recess. In a million years, I couldn't have guessed how complicated Daniel is and how long it can take to find out what's really going on inside him. My first inkling came after we were already living together. We were planning a party, and I was telling my friend Kevin about it. Kevin said, 'What are the two saddest words in the English language?' 'I don't know, what?' 'What party?' "

I smiled, enjoying the expressiveness of his voice, which I supposed wasn't surprising in an actor.

"Later that night," Jeremy went on, "Daniel and I were making a guest list. I said, 'Hey, Daniel, what are the two saddest words in the English language?' Daniel looked up at me and, without even thinking, answered, 'Family only.' Then he cried for three days. I hadn't known that right before he met me, he'd lost five friends, one right after the other."

"Poor guy," I said, and Jeremy nodded.

"That was our pattern. Everything would be going great, something would force Daniel to open up, and I'd find out all kinds of stuff I was clueless about. When Ken told us that he had AIDS, Daniel shut down. Nothing I did made him talk about it. The only thing that stayed the same was sex. We never had a problem in the bedroom. That made me furious. Daniel is brilliant; I know I'm no match for him mentally. But I'm not just about physical stuff. Anyway, that's when Robert came along. Robert never treated me like a dumb blonde, which I appreciated, so we became friends. I shouldn't have slept with him. Looking back, I think I did it to force Daniel to talk to me, even if it was to fight. I went too far. For me, the two saddest words in the English language became, 'It's over.' At least we both learned something. Daniel is much better about sharing himself with Blaine than he ever was with me. Or at least Blaine knows better ways than I did to make Daniel talk. And I know that I need a lover who doesn't hide himself. A what-you-see-is-what-you-get kind of guy."

"It's funny you should say that," I remarked, "since I can never tell what's going on in your head. Sometimes you seem interested; sometimes you don't. You flirt, then you run away. Mixed signals."

"I told you; you confused me," Jeremy said. "I didn't want to waste my time playing games with someone who fucks and runs. Recess is over. I want more substance in my work life and my personal life."

"Are you still confused?" I asked.

"No. I think we've agreed to move slowly but in the same direction."

I nodded, and we stared at each other while I thought over the things he'd told me.

"Your turn," he said. "Relationship history."

"I had a couple of those 'I'll love you forever; goodbye' things in college," I said. "First love stuff. All drama, no future. Then I had a career, a lot of sex, and no emotion. Like I said, relationship stuff is new for me."

"So why me? I'd think someone like Blaine would be your type. You've got a lot more in common."

"I've asked myself that a few times," I confessed. "But from the first time I saw you—"

"Oh, yeah. You said something today about imagining us together from the first time you saw me, long before I saw you. I remember you from Wade's party."

"I'd seen you before Wade's party," I said, and told him about seeing him with Andy at the Big Cup.

"Good grief," he said. "You saw me there and still wanted to meet me?"

"Why wouldn't I have?"

"Because I'm awful there. Did you ever see *Soapdish* with Sally Field?"

"Yes," I said, confused.

"Remember whenever she was feeling low, Whoopi would take her to a mall in New Jersey and let fans fawn all over her?" I laughed and nodded. "That's what the Big Cup is for me. When my ego needs a boost, I go there. I'll bet I was all kinds of pissed that Andy showed up and held my admirers at bay with his theatrics."

"You did make a quick exit," I agreed. "Though you managed to give one fan an autograph."

"Too bad it wasn't you," he said. "Tell me, did you ever catch a single episode of *Man of the House?*"

"By the time I knew you were on it, they were showing some game show in its place."

"We started as a summer replacement. They tried to carry it into fall but yanked it midseason to revamp a couple of things. Little did they know I'd be one of those things."

"Are they still threatening you?"

"No. I'm yesterday's news. There was a time when that would have driven me crazy. Now I'm focusing on the future."

The room was getting colder, so I added more wood to the fire, then got back under the covers. Jeremy wrapped himself around me to get me warm again.

"I like this," I said. "I feel comfortable with you."

"Me, too. You sure you don't mind that we haven't—"

"It'll happen exactly when it should," I assured him, though I had to admit to myself that I was a little surprised by my patience. It certainly wasn't because I didn't want him. But I wanted it to be right for both of us.

I was quiet for a while, and he asked, "Are you asleep?"

"No, I was thinking. Friday I have to go to Weehawken and wrap up a couple of things with one of my clients. If you're free and not afraid of New Jersey, why don't you go with me? We could probably find you a laptop at a better price than you'd get in Manhattan."

"I won't be in your way?"

"Never."

"Shit. I can't. Friday is Daniel's debut on *Secret Splendor.* Blaine's taking off work, and they're making a party of it at their apartment."

"Oh, yeah," I said. "I'd forgotten about that. Maybe I should reschedule my appointment with Ray. I don't want to miss Daniel's first episode."

I lay there a few minutes, brooding about how long the specter of Daniel was going to haunt Jeremy and me.

"You know what?" Jeremy asked, breaking the silence again. "Let's go to Weehawken. I can set my VCR and watch it later. If you don't mind missing their party."

"That sounds perfect," I said. "Do you think Daniel will mind?"

"He'll get over it. I'll send him a plant and tell him something came up."

I smiled as I felt him relax against me. I couldn't remember ever feeling as intimate with anyone as I did with Jeremy. I had no doubt that when we finally made love, it was only going to make things better.

I was almost asleep when Jeremy softly said, "Adam?"

"Jeremy?"

"What are the two saddest words in the English language?"

"Checkout time," I said and heard him laugh softly.

SIXTEEN

When I picked up Jeremy in my rented Ford Expedition, he leaned across the seat to kiss my cheek, then said, "You're much better at this than I am."

"Kissing?"

"Renting cars."

"They were all out of Volkswagens," I said. "I tried to tell them a big car wouldn't impress you, but—"

"Yes, it does," he said. "If I'd been driving this monster on that fateful night—"

"You wouldn't have gotten a run in your pantyhose?"

He laughed and buckled his seat belt, saying, "What's all that stuff back there?"

"Computer equipment for Ray," I explained. "I had it shipped to me, so I could test it and set up a few things. Now it all gets installed at his office."

"Will that take a long time? Are you sure I won't be in your way?"

"I'm not installing it. I'm handing it over to my assistant, Lester. All I have to do is pick up my nice, fat paycheck; then I'm yours for the day."

He smiled, then flinched as I whipped around a bus, cutting off a Mercedes, which responded with angry honks.

"I haven't driven much in Manhattan," I said, "but I've learned you have to be fearless."

"Must be why I don't drive," he said, cringing at another of my traffic feats. "If your computer gig ever fails you, you can always fall back on a career as a cab driver."

Once we were in the Lincoln Tunnel, I heard him exhale, probably because I couldn't change lanes anymore. I managed not to scare him too much before I finally parked in the loading zone at Ray's building, convincing the security guy that I was authorized. Jeremy helped me take the boxes to Ray's suite.

Lester was there before me and immediately took charge of the boxes. Ray took his time giving me my check, obviously curious about Jeremy. I finally got us out of there after Ray thanked me again for all my hard work and talked me up to Jeremy one last time.

"Your marriage broker?" Jeremy asked as we made it to the elevator.

"You'd think," I said, grinning at him.

"Sold!" Jeremy said.

"You're just after my paycheck," I said, tucking it into my pocket.

"Reliable, hardworking, and smart, too," he said in a perfect imitation of Ray's accent.

"If your stand-up gig ever fails you, you can always fall back on a career in acting," I mimicked his earlier remark.

"Nah, I'd never be any good at that."

"I can't believe I never got to see you act," I complained.

"Go see Stella. She has tapes."

"I'll bet she does."

Once we were at Best Buy, I steered him from the CDs to the computer section, trying not to be too technical as we examined the available laptops.

"How come little computers cost more than big ones?" he asked.

"Good things come in small packages."

"Hmmm," he said, letting his eyes range up and down my six-feet-two frame. "Food for thought."

"*Great* things come in large packages," I said and motioned to a hovering sales associate to let him know that we were ready to make our selection.

Once the paperwork was out of the way, Jeremy said, "Now can I look at CDs?"

"You do that. I want to look in their software section."

As we started to separate at the aisle, Jeremy glanced at his watch and said, "Wait! Come with me."

I followed him to the bank of television screens, unsure what we were doing, until the opening of *Secret Splendor* suddenly filled every screen from five to sixty-five inches. Violin and flute music began to play a sickeningly sweet song. The picture faded from gray to color and the title screen emerged, followed by short scenes including a drink thrown in a man's face, a woman smiling in ecstasy with a pillow beneath her head, and a woman's hand holding a smoking gun, which made both of us laugh. The opening faded to an innocent scene of a sign near a small waterfall that read *Splendor Falls, Pop. 25,650.*

"Oh, that's my story," a woman in a bright-red coat said as she joined us. "My daily half hour of splendor!"

She didn't even notice as her husband rolled his eyes and wandered away, to be quickly replaced by a Best Buy employee.

"This is where I always take my lunch break," she said. "That Gayle has the only hair on television that literally can fill up a big screen."

"Isn't it the truth? Do you think they'll ever figure out who her baby's real father is?" Red Coat asked.

"Is that child still alive?" a stocky man asked as he nudged himself between the two women. "He went upstairs to play a couple of years ago, and no one's seen him since."

Everyone settled down as they became engrossed in the story line, which proved complicated for me, since I'd never watched the show. As the minutes passed, our little group was joined by several others, all of whom felt compelled during commercials to argue about old plot lines and critique the show's flaws. A couple of times the name Angus Remington came up, but it was obvious none of our fellow watchers had any idea that he was about to make his return to Splendor Falls. I could tell that Jeremy, like me, was eager to see the crowd's reaction.

He excitedly clutched my arm as the show returned from a commercial break to focus on silver letters fastened to an oak wall that spelled out *Remington Industries.*

"This is going to be it," Jeremy said softly. The camera panned to a large, opulently decorated office, where a rail-thin woman stood staring into space with haunted eyes. "That's Brianna. The sister."

"Poor Brianna," Red Coat moaned. "She's been through so much in her young life."

"Remember when she was locked in the mausoleum?" Stocky Guy asked.

"Two weeks," Best Buy commented, "with never a hair out of place."

"It was only two nights in soap time," Red Coat said defensively.

We watched as Brianna picked up a package from her desk, tearing it open to find an unlabeled videotape. She pushed a button, and the wall moved to reveal a TV and VCR.

"I want a moving wall," I said.

"Hush," Jeremy hissed.

Brianna slid the cassette into the machine and pressed *play*. After a few seconds, the screen was filled with Daniel's face, and he began to speak in a voice that was Daniel's yet not his.

"Hello, Brianna. You don't recognize me, do you?"

The camera showed Brianna, her eyes squinting as she stared in front of her. Then they widened in surprise, and her expression went from disbelief to horror. The camera cut back to the video.

"Think back a few years, when someone cut my brake lines." Daniel/Angus laughed eerily. "Too bad I wasn't driving. Too bad for you. Yes, dear, sweet, murderous sister, big brother Angus Remington is back from the dead. I know my face is different, but don't worry. Soon you'll be seeing me in all the old familiar places."

"Oh, my god!" Red Coat shrieked, while the rest of the onlookers stared in rapt silence.

The video stopped, the violins began, and we saw a stricken Brianna slowly lift her pink fingernails to her lips as a few tears of terror rolled down her cheek. And suddenly, we were being asked to use nature's little helper, Fiberforth.

"That's not Angus. Angus was ugly! This guy's gorgeous!" Best Buy complained.

"Plastic surgery. Happens all the time," Stocky Guy argued.

The crowd began to dissipate, except for Red Coat, who continued to stare at the bank of televisions with dazed eyes.

"Wait," I said. "It's over? That's all we get?"

"Tune in next time," Jeremy intoned in a melodramatic voice. "Oh, my god, that was great. What a perfect reintroduction to an old villain. Wasn't Daniel fantastic? In just a few seconds, that whole show became his."

I looked at him and frowned as I noticed his thrilled expression.

"What?" Jeremy asked.

"I'm not sure," I said.

"You didn't like it? I mean, I know you don't watch much TV, so I guess you've never seen a soap, but—"

"It's not that," I said.

"Then what?"

I shook my head, still staring at him. He stared back.

"Adam?"

"Jeremy?"

"You're not by any chance . . . jealous?"

"Jealous? Of what?" I asked, glancing back at the television screens.

"I," Jeremy said, moving my chin with his hand so that I had to look at him, "am long over Daniel."

"Are you sure?" I asked, realizing that I was, in fact, suddenly brimming with insecurity.

Instead of answering me, Jeremy placed a hand on the back of my neck, pulling me to him to give me a breathtaking kiss.

"Well," I said, a bit stunned, then glanced at Red Coat to see that she looked thunderstruck as she stared at us. I felt sorry for her, deciding that the shock of seeing two men kiss had pushed her over the edge. I gave her a sympathetic smile.

She grabbed my arm and said, "It's not true, is it? That wasn't really . . . *Angus Remington?*"

Jeremy turned away with silent laughter as I patted her hand and said, "I think your husband is in the stereo section."

As she tottered away, Jeremy could no longer control his laughter.

"Poor woman," I said. "How long do you think it will be before she remembers seeing that kiss?"

"How long before you forget it?" he asked.

"Never."

"Good. You can savor the memory every time you get foolish notions about Daniel and me."

I silently followed him from the store after his credit was approved and he was presented with his expensive new toy. When we were all tucked into the Expedition, he grabbed my hand before I could put the key in the ignition.

"Tell me you believe me about Daniel," he said. "It's the kind of thing you shouldn't brood about."

"I'm not much of a brooder. Sometimes it does seem like you're preoccupied by him."

"No. Not by him. By how badly I screwed up, so I don't make the same mistake in the future. As for Daniel, he'll always have a special place in my heart and my life as a friend who shares memories with me."

I nodded and started the car, forcing myself to talk about his new computer and how, by making him part of Adam AdVentures' network, I could save him money on software. I was relieved when we arrived at the town house to find it empty. I'd endured enough commentary from Martin about how my first date with Jeremy had extended into the next day. Seeing us together would only set him off again.

After I stripped unnecessary programs from Jeremy's laptop and installed the ones I thought would be useful to him, I spent a few hours giving him quick lessons on everything. He'd learned that many of his friends had AOL accounts, so I helped him set one up and gave him a quick tour of AOL's features, including chat rooms. Then I helped him make a buddy list so he'd always be able to tell when I was using my AOL account, adding my parents' screen names to those of his friends.

After we ate sandwiches, I lay on my bed, staring into my office as Jeremy sent e-mails to let people know that he'd finally caught up with the computer age. I was still surprised by my behavior at Best Buy. I thought it was a good idea to leave Jeremy alone to write his friends, so he wouldn't think I was one of those possessive guys who felt threatened by the other people in his life. I'd always freely admitted to being competitive, but I'd never felt jealous before, and it wasn't pleasant.

I watched him type, drinking in the sight of him when he paused to think, a slight frown on his face, or unconsciously ran his hands through his hair, which was why it was always a little messy. I liked the way he stretched out his legs, sometimes putting one foot over the other and tapping his feet as if to some interior rhythm. When he got really intent on what he was writing, his typing got faster and he leaned forward with a grin. I thought about sketching him, but I didn't want to make him self-conscious. Instead, I made mental snapshots to review later, when we were apart.

The thought of being hundreds of miles away from him squeezed my heart, and I turned over so he couldn't see my face if he glanced into the bedroom. My old fantasies of Jeremy had been fun, but having the real man in front of me created an overwhelming and unfamiliar sensation with much more power to disturb me than jealousy had.

I was thoroughly and hopelessly in love with Jeremy Caprellian. The thorough part didn't bother me so much. It was, after all, what I'd been longing for during those lonely evenings in Eau Claire. It was the hopeless part I worried about. In spite of my reassurances to Jeremy, how did two men living in different states sustain a relationship?

"Hey," Jeremy said, sitting on the bed behind me.

I turned over and opened my arms without a word. He settled down next to me, and we lay there a while in silence, lost in our separate thoughts.

"I guess I should return my rental car," I said. "I can take you home first."

"Traffic will suck. I can get myself home."

"As far as I'm concerned, you never have to leave my bedroom."

He smiled and said, "That might be nice. Unless Martin boards up your bedroom door."

"That might be nice, too." I smoothed his hair down. "Under those circumstances, I can't promise I'd still be patient."

He laughed, and we got up. I helped him pack his new laptop in its case, and we left the town house together. After a final kiss, I climbed into the Expedition and watched in my mirror as he walked away from me.

When I got back from returning the car, I shaved and took a shower because Blythe and I were supposed to go out. I decided to check my e-mail one last time, in case Lester had sent any messages from Patel, Inc., and grinned as I saw that I had mail from JCNYC, Jeremy's AOL screen name. I opened it and found a one-line message that read, "Who said I wanted you to still be patient?"

"Now you tell me," I grumbled, but smiled in spite of myself. Since he'd made me wait, I decided to let him wonder about it for a while. Not too long, though; I'd call him later and set up another date.

When Blythe answered my call, I said, "What should we do tonight?"

"Something neither of us has ever done before," she said.

"Go to an opera? Commit grand larceny? Sleep with a woman?"

"Nice try, Columbo. Something we can do *together.*"

"Get a tattoo?" I suggested.

"I promised my parents that if I ever decided to get a tattoo, I'd wait one month before going through with it. Just in case I changed my mind."

"Disorient XPress has changed karaoke night to Friday," I said. "I've never sung karaoke. Have you?"

"No," she said falteringly. "But does it have to be *there?*"

"I need to thank Brenda Li for her help with my disks. Besides, although I know it wouldn't go over big with some of the Club Chaos crowd, I kind of like Disorient XPress."

"Okay. Fine. If it's karaoke you want, so be it. What do you feel like? Just us? Or do you want to invite someone else along?"

"Let's discuss it over dinner."

On Blythe's recommendation, I met her at a diner in her neighborhood that served Russian food. I expected nothing but cabbage and boiled potatoes, but of course the food turned out to be tasty and healthy. The diner was crowded, but the noise level was perfect for an intimate conversation. I told her about my day with Jeremy, leaving out my realization that I was in love and that we might be about to take things to the next level.

She smiled and said, "We missed you at Daniel's today."

"Did you have a good time?" I asked.

"Yes. Martin and I kept your secret."

"What secret?"

"That you and Jeremy were together today. And that you had your first official date in Cold Spring."

"Martin managed to keep that to himself? I'm shocked. But I'm not surprised that you did. You're good at keeping secrets."

"Is that a crack about Wade?" When I merely laughed, she said, "I'm not sure you deserve me."

She opened her purse and brought out her cell phone. She flipped it open with a mischievous glint in her eyes and pressed a button.

"Hi, Daniel, it's Blythe," she said, still staring at me with a wicked grin. "Are you busy tonight? Oh, good. Adam and I were wondering if you and Blaine would like to join us for karaoke at Disorient XPress? I guess in an hour or so. You will? Cool. Would you mind calling everyone else for us? We're in the middle of dinner. Thanks! Say, guess what I found out? Did you know Adam's middle name is—"

"No!" I yelled and lunged for the cell phone, wresting it from her hands.

"Filbert!" she exclaimed and cackled with laughter while I frantically pushed the *End Call* button.

"You are evil and must be stopped," I said to Blythe.

"Never! Adam *F*-is-for-*Filbert* Wilson."

"How did you find out?"

"Wade, of course. Filbert was your password on those disks."

"Geez. If there's one person you cannot tell what the *F* stands for, it's Martin."

"Okay," she said with a sigh.

Somehow I had the feeling that she had her fingers crossed when she said it, but at least I knew he wouldn't be joining us, since he had to perform at Club Chaos.

"I have something for you, but now I'm not sure *you* deserve *me*," I said.

"My cell phone? Give it back!"

I handed her the cell phone and said, "No, something else."

"You've given me too much already, Adam."

"This is as much for me as it is for you," I said, reaching into my coat pocket. "It's an open-ended plane ticket to Wisconsin. If you ever want to come see me or just get out of the city for a while, you're always welcome."

"It's the perfect gift, but I can't take it. Besides, you'll be back soon enough."

"Not another word. I want you to take it, for my sake if not for yours. If it hadn't been for you, I might never have grown to love this city, met Jeremy, or opened my eyes to all the potential around me. Besides, I would love to show you my world."

"Would I have to dress like a farm girl?"

"Yes, overalls and flannel only. Be ready to milk cows at five every morning."

Blythe looked at me with mock disdain, then smiled as she looked at the time on her cell phone, letting me know it was time for us to go.

Brenda Li greeted us with joy when Blythe and I walked into Disorient XPress.

"Did you get into any trouble with Wade after the disk-recovery operation?" I asked, extricating myself from a bone-crushing hug.

"Not after this one got done with him," Brenda said, giving Blythe a slightly less passionate embrace.

Blythe shrugged and nonchalantly lit a cigarette.

"Not so close to the hair, doll," Brenda said, backing away from Blythe's flaming Zippo. "This wig holds several ounces of industrial-strength hair glue. Also, be warned: Daddy Warbucks is here tonight with his faithful sidekick, Tonto."

"Any other fantasy characters you want to throw into that mix?" Blythe asked.

"Just Superman here," Brenda said, running a hand over my biceps.

I was nonplussed for a moment, remembering that Sam69wu had called me the same thing; then I said, "Me? I'm Atom Ant."

"Never heard of him," Blythe said, blowing smoke my way. "Who does that make me?"

"Velma from *Scooby Doo,*" I suggested.

"The lesbian?" Brenda Li asked and gave Blythe a piercing look.

"See what you started?" Blythe asked.

She noticed, just as I did, that Brenda was no longer listening to us, her attention apparently riveted by a new arrival. The two of us turned around to see what celebrity was causing her to stare open-mouthed toward the door.

"Daniel?" Blythe asked, since only he and Blaine were standing in the doorway while their eyes adjusted to the dim light of the bar.

But Daniel might as well have been invisible, since Brenda abandoned us and bypassed him for Blaine.

I laughed and said, "This should be fun. Blaine's no fan of drag. I'm surprised Daniel even convinced him to come here."

"Maybe he's a big karaoke buff," Blythe conjectured. We laughed out loud at the thought, finding it hard to picture Blaine comfortable in front of any audience other than in the gym or the boardroom.

Brenda led them to us after a moment or two. Blythe asked Daniel if he'd invited any of the rest of the gang to join us.

"Sheila and Josh said they'd be here in a little bit. Martin's performing, of course. Oh, and I called Jeremy. He said he wouldn't miss it."

I felt a rush of pleasure that Jeremy, after sending his suggestive e-mail, wasn't waiting for me to e-mail or call. Unless I was misreading him altogether, he was going on the offensive. And I was more than willing to let him.

"Sorry I had to miss your party today," I said to Daniel. "But I saw the show. Very dramatic. It won't be long before you'll be unable to show your face in this place without being inundated by *Secret Splendor* fans."

"Thank you," Daniel said.

"Wasn't he great?" Blaine asked proudly.

"I've decided to make a point of seeing the show," I said. "It will be my only TV addiction other than sports."

"My god, you *are* a friend," Daniel said and gave me a little hug.

Brenda guided us to a table with enough seating for us, as well as room to expand if we needed it. I picked up the karaoke list and leaned over to share it with Blythe, each of us giggling at the thought of doing some big production number with everyone there. I decided "New York, New York" would be too predictable. In spite of how I'd grown to love the city, I couldn't bring myself to sing about it.

Brenda brought drinks that must have been ordered by either Daniel or Blaine, as neither Blythe nor I had been asked. When I glanced at them to say thank you, they looked as surprised as I did. We all shrugged and began drinking.

Blaine leaned over and said, "I didn't ask you the last time we saw each other. Did you catch that Lions–Steelers game on Thanksgiving?"

"No, but I read the play-by-play online."

"Oh, man," he rolled his eyes. "The refs sucked so bad."

"You know, anytime you're in Eau Claire, you and Daniel are always welcome at my place. To watch games or hang out."

"Thanks," Blaine said. "It's more likely that Daniel will be relieved if I have somewhere to go and he won't be forced to watch sports."

I heard Blythe groan and looked up to see Wade crossing the room toward us, with Ethan following close behind.

"Hello!" Wade said jovially. "I see you got your drinks? Good. How is everyone tonight?" His eyes went from Blaine to Daniel, skimmed over me, and finally rested on Blythe.

"Hello, Wade," Blythe answered for us all in a strained but civil voice. "Thanks for the drinks. We're all doing well. And you?"

"Good, good." He nodded uncomfortably and stuck one hand in his pocket, the other holding what could have been water but I suspected was vodka on the rocks.

I saw a turban emerge from the darkness of the room and appear over Wade's shoulder.

"Hello, Daniel," Bonnie Seaforth-Wilkes said. "Wonderful show today. Now, do tell me, Ethan, which of these gentlemen did you say is Adam Wilson?"

She was looking hopefully toward Blaine, but when Ethan redirected her attention my way, she turned a barracudalike grin on me. I stood so Ethan could introduce us.

"Mr. Wilson—"

"Adam, please," I insisted.

"Adam, here's my card. Call me after the holidays." Even she must have realized how imperious she sounded, so she quickly added, "Please. One of my directors at Seaforth Chemicals showed me the marvelous Web site you made for Club Chaos."

Wade frowned, and I saw Ethan turn away to hide a smile.

"I'm glad you like it," I said.

"Like it? It's fantastic. Our marketing team is even interested in buying into the site and decreasing funding to some of our other venues." The glance she threw in Wade's direction seemed to hold something of a warning. "My company's Web address is on my card. Our site is terminally boring. Why don't you and I have a little tête-à-tête in January and discuss how you can resuscitate it?"

Wade definitely had an ashen color now, no doubt feeling one-upped by Andy. Without wasting a second, except to lustily widen his eyes at the approach of Josh, he scurried after Bonnie with obvious desperation. If I'd ever wanted revenge for what Wade had done, not only to me but to Blythe, fate had done my dirty work for me.

"Sheila's at the bar getting our drinks," Josh said looking around the table. "Did I miss something?"

"Only a visit from Adam's avenging angel in the shape of a turban-wearing septuagenarian," Blythe said.

Josh shrugged his shoulders and took a seat next to Daniel.

"All right," I said, looking from Daniel to Ethan. "Which one of you used your connection to Bonnie on my behalf?"

Their faces were convincing in their innocence, and I frowned.

Maybe Bonnie had been telling the truth, and someone who knew me only through my work had recommended me to her.

As Sheila greeted us and gave Josh his drink, I noticed Daniel talking to Lu Pi Ho, the drag queen hosting karaoke night. He pointed at a list of songs and she nodded, writing notes on a clipboard.

"I made my selection," Daniel announced when he came back to our table. "Who's next?"

"Come on," Sheila exclaimed, downing her drink and grabbing Blythe's hand. Blythe looked at me in horror but allowed herself to be led away.

"What song did you pick?" Josh asked Daniel.

"My lips are sealed," Daniel said.

"Oh? The Go-Go's song?"

"No," Daniel said with a laugh. "That's 'Our Lips Are Sealed.' Hey, there's Jeremy."

As I stood to get Jeremy's attention, Lu Pi Ho strode onstage and picked up the microphone.

"Thank you for coming tonight, everybody. We've got a long list of performers, so let's get right to it. Our first crooner is visiting the Big Apple from Wisconsin. From what I can see, I wish he'd take a bite out of my big apple. Give a warm welcome to Adam Filbert Wilson!"

"Filbert!" Daniel, Josh, Sheila, and Blythe all screamed at the same time.

I was frozen in place, with probably the world's worst case of stage fright magnified by the horror of hearing my middle name shrieked at me. I was dimly aware of Jeremy walking toward our table, ignoring Ethan's welcome and Daniel's smile, his eyes fixed on me. When he reached me after the longest five seconds of my life, he took my hand and said, "Nothing to be afraid of. I'm a trained professional, and I'll be right beside you."

I forgot there was anyone else in the bar as Jeremy led me to the stage. We both broke up with laughter as the karaoke machine began playing "Beauty School Dropout." The audience cheered as we finished our rendition, and we took a few bows before we left the stage.

"That was awful," Sheila said with the brightest of smiles. "Promise me you won't sing at my wedding."

"Simply terrible," Daniel agreed, but he was looking at Jeremy and me with a knowing glance. I realized our secret was no longer much of a secret.

"Swear you'll never do it again," Blythe pleaded.

"Don't hold back," I implored my friends. "Tell me how you really feel."

"Jeremy was great," Josh said, and the others quickly agreed. As competitive as I could be, I knew better than to attempt a sing-off. My vocal chords were meant for hearing-impaired listeners and weimaraners only.

"Jeremy," Ethan said, "I was going to call you later. May I have a word with you?"

After a quick glance at me, Jeremy nodded. They walked away, and I sat down as Lu Pi Ho called Daniel and Blaine to the stage. Blythe and I shared a moment of wide-eyed anticipation, sure that Blaine wouldn't go through with it. We were quickly proved wrong as Daniel and Blaine launched into a duet of "I've Had the Time of My Life" from the movie *Dirty Dancing*. Remembering Daniel's past as a performer, his dead-on tenor version of the Jennifer Warnes part wasn't a big surprise. But Blaine's turning out to be a karaoke god had our whole table in shock. Even Sheila was agog at his perfect pitch and timing as he sang Bill Medley's part.

"I had no idea he could sing like that," she said as she watched Blaine and Daniel stare into each other's eyes and sing their hearts out.

"If he lands in the audience and lifts Daniel in his arms over his head, I'm gonna have to go home and touch myself," Blythe said.

"Oh, no you don't," Sheila said and finished her gin and tonic. "We're next. You're coming with me."

"Wouldn't you rather sing with Josh?" Blythe begged.

"I'm going to marry him," Sheila said with a snort. "We've got the rest of our lives to sing together. Now move!"

Blythe looked to me for help, but I shook my head and laughed. I'd had to humiliate myself onstage; as far as I was concerned, it was her turn. Blythe finished her martini, groaned in despair, and once again allowed herself to be led away by Sheila. Daniel and Blaine finished their duet with a kiss and brought the house down.

"All right, you two, break it up," Lu Pi Ho said into her microphone, pushing Daniel and Blaine apart. "It's not that kind of show. If you want to come back to my place later tonight, though, I'll make the popcorn. You bring the oil! Okay. Please welcome our next songbirds, Blythe and Sheila."

Jeremy looked preoccupied as he took his seat next to me.

"What did Ethan want?" I asked.

"I'll tell you after they're finished singing," Jeremy said.

I noticed that Daniel was watching us again. I returned his gaze, wondering what he was thinking. He raised his glass in a little toast; his blue eyes smiled their approval; then he turned to watch the show. At any other time of my life, I might have felt like whatever was happening between someone and me was none of his ex-boyfriend's business. But these two had managed to remain part of a family, and I realized that all I wanted was to be included.

I took a deep breath and released it to get rid of my last bit of anxiety, then followed Daniel's example and shifted to watch as Blythe and Sheila stepped onto the stage from different sides. They met at the center, looked each other up and down, then turned to face the audience as the music for "The Lady Is a Tramp" began playing.

Sheila sang the first line, Blythe followed suit on the second, and they continued trading lyrics and gesturing at each other through the entire song. I couldn't stop laughing, and neither could the rest of the audience. By the end of the song, they were shoving each other aside and vying for the center-stage position, but they finished in unison to thunderous applause.

I glanced at Jeremy, realized he wasn't clapping, and put my mouth close to his ear.

"What's wrong?"

"Can we find somewhere less noisy to talk?"

We stood up together; then he followed me to the bar, where Brenda Li was covertly sharing a cigarette with a customer.

"Where's Wade?" I asked.

She gave Jeremy the once-over and said, "Upstairs with Tonto and Bonnie Blueblood."

"Is his office unlocked?"

"You know the way, doll. I can run interference if it's needed."

"You always do." I winked at her and led Jeremy to the office, closing the door behind us. "What the hell did Ethan say to you?" I asked Jeremy, who was obviously upset.

"He didn't say anything. I mean, he did, but not the way you mean. He found someone to help fund our program in Oklahoma. He wants me to go with him to Tulsa tomorrow to talk to them."

"That's good, isn't it? To get your program funded?"

"You'll be gone to Wisconsin before I come back for Christmas in Brooklyn. I don't know when I'll see you again. I've dreaded this since Thanksgiving, and now I'm facing it too soon. But I have to go."

"Of course you do," I said. "Hey, listen. I don't want to say good-bye to you either, but after everyone does what they're supposed to for the holidays, there's no reason I can't come to Oklahoma. Or you could visit me in Wisconsin. This is not the end of anything. It's the beginning."

"I know." He took a deep breath. "I pictured this working out a little differently. If I'd known I was leaving town, I wouldn't have spent our last day together watching Daniel on that soap opera or sending e-mails or singing karaoke—"

"Come on. I'm taking you home."

"I don't want to deal with Martin."

"We'll go to your place," I said. "Just give me one second."

I pulled out my cell phone and speed-dialed Blythe, hoping she could hear her phone over the noise in the bar.

"Adam?" she answered, sounding bewildered.

"Remember that night you ditched me at Wade's party?"

"Uh-huh," she said.

"Please forgive me for doing the same to you. Do you have cab fare? Because I really need to get out of here. With Jeremy. Without drama."

"Go," she said. "I'm well taken care of."

"I love you."

"I love you, too. Call me tomorrow?"

"Count on it," I promised. I snapped the phone shut, turned to Jeremy, and said, "Let's go. Unless you feel like you should tell them—"

"Please let's go," Jeremy begged.

The events of the evening were taking their toll on us. We rode in the cab in silence, Jeremy's head on my shoulder. I placed my arm protectively around him, occasionally moving my thumb just the slightest bit, feeling the smooth skin of his chest underneath his shirt. I couldn't tell if his eyes were open or closed, but he let out a small sigh of contentment.

Jeremy fumbled with his keys before finding the right one, and we stepped into his apartment. It was nicely furnished, with a beautiful antique love seat as the centerpiece. He took my hand and led me to his room.

"Don't you have a roommate?" I asked as we walked down the hall.

"Yes, but he won't be home tonight. Robert's been dating someone and hasn't really been around a lot."

"That's good," I answered.

Jeremy flicked a light switch, and his bedroom was bathed in the warm glow of a Tiffany lamp, which cast various colors and shadows across the walls. His bedroom was a lot like his old room at his parents' house, except this one was messier. Several pairs of pants on hangers were draped over the arm of an overstuffed chair. A four-poster mahogany bed sat in the center of the room with a down comforter so thick that if you dove on it, you might never be found. However, diving would be impossible because of the piles of folded clothes that covered the bed.

"Believe it or not, I cleaned my room after our trip to New Jersey today," Jeremy said sheepishly and began moving the clothes off the bed.

"It's fine," I said. "Don't worry about it." When he was finished clearing the bed, I handed him my coat, which he laid with his on top of a chair. Then I stood behind him and wrapped my arms around his chest, saying, "Are you feeling better?"

"I'm disappointed. I wanted to spend more time with you."

I turned him around so he could see me smile, then kissed him softly on his lips.

"What was that for?" he asked. "What are you grinning about?"

"Because I feel the same way," I answered. "And just knowing you want to be with me makes me happy. Besides, we're both leaving town. We thought I'd be going first, but now you are. It doesn't matter, as long as I know we're on the same page."

"I know we are," he said and moved forward in my arms so he could rest his head on my shoulder. "But what happens after I leave?"

"I don't know," I said tentatively and honestly. "All I can say is that I've never felt this way about anybody. It's not going to stop just because we're apart for a while."

"Adam, I—" Jeremy began but stopped. He lifted his head and looked into my eyes, then said, "I hope you're right."

He turned and placed his hand on my chest, slipping his other hand around my back and pulling my hips against his. He looked at me with a sexy, silly smile on his face. I leaned in and wrapped my arms around him, holding him tightly and smelling the skin on his neck. Our relationship was relying heavily on fate, and I wanted to hold a part of him in each of my senses so that I'd never forget this night. I gently held his face in my hands and kissed him, parting our lips and tasting his tongue.

We took our time undressing, watching each other. I was fascinated by the way his skin glowed and moved as he removed his shirt, so I reached out and ran my fingertips over the muscles of his stomach. My fingers stopped just under the waist of his jeans, and I used my other hand to undo the buckle of his belt. Once it was undone, I opened the top button of his jeans and stopped to pull my sweater over my head.

As I freed my arms from the sweater and threw it aside, Jeremy turned me around and removed my T-shirt. He kissed me between my shoulder blades and ran his hands down my arms until he held my hands in his. He wrapped our arms around me from behind and pressed his body tightly against me as he whispered, "Your skin feels like electricity next to mine."

"Yes," I agreed and let go of his hands as they ran down my chest to unbutton my pants. I kicked off my shoes and turned around, needing to taste his mouth again.

He traced my lips with the tip of his nose, his eyes closed, and kissed my chin. I tilted my head back, felt his tongue run down my neck, and let out an audible moan of pleasure. I finished unbuttoning his jeans and slid them down his legs, taking the time to crouch at his feet so he could step out of them. I kissed his thighs, then stood up so I could take off my pants.

I savored the sight of him as we got completely undressed. Jeremy took my hand, leading me to his bed. He pulled me down next to him on top of the comforter and we lay side by side. I placed my hand on his hip, lightly stroking the back of his thigh as he traced his fingertips from my temple to my lips. I stared deeply into his eyes, wordlessly asking if this was what he wanted. He answered by taking a condom from his bedside table before rolling over and covering my body with his own.

We made love with him on top, straddling my hips as I moved mine from below. I kept one hand on his hip, the other clasped firmly in his until we collapsed in a tangle of panting, sticky bodies. Jeremy remained wrapped around me as he kissed me sweetly on the lips.

"You're still kissing me," I said and smiled.

"I can't seem to stop," he said. "I feel so alive right now."

I grabbed him and started rolling back and forth while he laughed. I stopped and pressed my forehead against his and said, "This is my favorite moment. Right now."

"Mine, too," Jeremy agreed. "There's nothing going on anywhere in the world, except for us and what's happening in this room. I'm so glad you're with me. I don't want to stop."

"Then we won't," I said. I rolled on top of him, my face over his, and kissed him passionately. Our hands roamed over each other, and once again our lovemaking was explosive and beautiful.

I shuddered with sheer joy when we finished. I'd been so wrapped up in our pleasure that time had lost all importance. I looked up to realize the sun was invading the bedroom, and I smiled at how brilliant and clear everything was. Jeremy pulled me closer and hugged me, his arms shaky and exhausted from sex.

"It's tomorrow," he sighed.

"Already?" I said. "I was just getting started."

"Right," Jeremy said. "I don't know about you, but I'm exhausted. But I'm definitely not complaining."

"I hate to ask, but what time do you have to go?"

Jeremy buried his face in my neck and groaned with exasperation before saying, "A car is picking me up at nine."

We lay in silence. I felt like we had spent the night making love in a bubble, and if either one of us moved, the bubble would burst. Jeremy finally sat up and said, "Don't make me do this alone. I need your help."

We got out of bed, and I held open his duffel bags while he piled clothes inside. Then we went into the bathroom, and I watched while he shaved. We took a shower together, washing away our sweat and giving each other bittersweet kisses under the spray of water. Afterward, I donned my clothes from the night before and watched as Jeremy dressed in black jeans and a dark pullover.

"I'm in mourning," he joked. "What time is it?"

I looked at my watch. It was eight-thirty.

"Checkout time," I answered.

"The two saddest words in the English language? How dare you?" he said with a rueful laugh and threw a pillow at me from across the room.

We gathered up his bags and went down to the street to wait for the car. I sat beside him on the stoop with my arm around him, willing the car to get a flat tire or run out of gas before it ever reached his block.

"I'll call you when I land," he said, "so you'll know I got there safely."

"Okay," I said.

"I have my laptop, too. So I can send you e-mails."

"Okay. I'll answer them," I said. "Just to warn you, my e-mails tend to get lengthy."

"I'm looking forward to them," he said.

A black car rounded the corner and pulled up in front of us. Jeremy warily stood, and I helped him put his bags in the trunk. We stood next to the car, staring helplessly at each other. Jeremy put his hand on my arm, and I pulled him into an embrace.

"I'm going to miss you so much," he said, and I felt his body start to shake against mine.

"Jeremy, I love you," I said and kissed the top of his head. He pulled back and looked into my eyes, so I said again, "I love you."

"Adam, don't make this harder for me," he pleaded.

"I'm not trying to," I said. "I have to be honest with you. And with myself. I love you. I want you to know that." Tears ran down his face, but he smiled at me. I wiped his cheek with my fingertips and kissed him tenderly, not knowing if it would be the last time. After a long moment, I broke away and said, "You'd better go."

The car passed me as I made my way down the street. Jeremy was staring balefully at me from the rear window as the car started around the corner. I lifted my hand to wave goodbye. When the car slid out of sight, I brought my hand to my face to wipe away my own tears.

I felt a sudden, sharp need to be home in Eau Claire. I wanted to see my parents. I wanted someone to reassure me that I'd done the right thing by declaring my feelings for Jeremy. I couldn't tell my family about this in an e-mail or on the phone. Until I was with them, it would all remain my secret.

It was my last full day in New York, and I chose to spend it alone. I knew packing wouldn't take long, so after a morning nap and another shower, I bundled myself against the cold and went to Central Park. I was walking around Bethesda Fountain, reliving memories, when Jeremy called to let me know he'd arrived safely in Tulsa. Our call was a little hurried, but I understood that he was there on business. Once I got to Wisconsin and his life resumed some normalcy, we assured each other that we'd have plenty of time for long phone calls and e-mails.

After I went home and packed, I met Blythe in front of her building; then we walked to a nearby bistro for dinner. Our conversation, usually lively and jumping from one topic to the next, was stilted and filled with lulls. She'd catch me staring into my glass of wine and we'd smile, both of us knowing the other was feeling depressed about my imminent departure. After dinner, we walked through the streets with no particular destination in mind, arms folded against the cold.

"Now what?" Blythe asked.

"You're the one who always tells me where we're going," I stated.

"You've been here for months, Adam. It's your last night in Manhattan," she said. "You decide. I'm tired of being the one in control."

"Okay, Miss Jackson," I said and flagged down a cab. "Get in."

A short while later, we settled onto a red sofa in the Big Cup with mugs of cocoa warming our hands.

"Why'd we end up here?" Blythe asked. "Are you looking for someone who'll give you one last wild night in the big city?"

I quickly scanned the room, meeting admiring glances, quick appraisals, and lingering looks, then turned my attention back to Blythe.

"Not at all. Besides, I'm here with you," I said. "Maybe I wanted to return to the scene of the crime. This is where I first saw Jeremy. I miss him."

"Already?"

"Yes. Is that so hard to believe?"

Blythe's eyes bored into mine from over the rim of her cup as she sipped her hot chocolate. She swallowed, licked her lips, then said, "Oh. Now I get it."

"Get what?"

"To be more precise, you got it."

"You should have been a mind reader, not an artist. You missed your calling," I said, and she laughed, nearly spilling hot chocolate on her coat. "How do you know these things?"

"I pick up on emotions, vibes, and expressions, then combine them with an educated guess. Or maybe I'm full of shit. Was it everything you dreamed it would be and more?"

"Stop teasing me, or I'll tell you nothing," I muttered.

But I told her everything, minus a few of the more graphic details. When I described how wonderful it felt to hold Jeremy in my arms, she closed her eyes for a moment and nodded.

"That sounds nice," she said softly. She opened her eyes and asked, "When do you think you'll see him again?"

"I don't know," I answered and frowned into my half-empty cup.

"Do you want to see him again? Or is it over now that you had sex and he's gone?"

"I want to see him again. I don't want it to be over. Not by a long shot. But I don't know how long his Oklahoma job will last or what he'll do afterward. And I'll be going back and forth from here to Wisconsin, so I don't know how this is going to work."

"Talk about a rock and a hard place," Blythe mused, and we both sat in silence for a moment. "You're in love with him, aren't you?"

"Yes," I said and downed the rest of my hot chocolate. I set the empty mug on the table in front of our sofa and said, "He's completely under my skin."

Blythe finished her drink and confessed that she didn't want to go home. I wasn't ready to give up her company either, so I suggested she spend the night at the town house. We lay on my bed and talked until we both fell asleep.

I woke up at two in the morning and crept into the living room when I heard Martin come home. He was dropping into a chair with a weary sigh when I joined him.

"What are you doing up?" he asked. "Don't you have a flight in the morning?"

"At ten. Blythe's here. She's asleep, so keep quiet. I heard you come in and thought I'd say hi."

"Hi," Martin said. He took off his boots and threw them into a corner with a loud thud. "It's a good thing I'm kicking the habit, so to speak. These audiences are getting worse every day. Or maybe it's me. Let's see if you get this joke. What do you say to a pregnant nun?"

"What?"

"Gotcha!" he exclaimed, waited through my silence, then said, "Nobody got it tonight, either."

"When's your last show? New Year's Eve?"

"Yes," he said and stood to hang up his coat. "You're lucky you're leaving now, because I'll be a beast until this is over. I'll be in rehearsals for *Cabaret* in the afternoons during the same time I'm finishing my stint at Club Chaos."

"Why don't you just stop working for Andy now?"

"Because he needs time to find my replacement. Or to groom one of the other performers to take the headlining spot. Regardless, Andy's an old friend, and I'm not going to leave him high and dry."

"Speaking of which, what did you decide to do for Christmas?"

"I don't know," Martin said airily. "Maybe I'll wander around a desert, find a manger, and wait for three wise men to come along. Or even three stupid men. I'm not picky."

"The invitation is still open if you want to join me," I offered.

"In your little house on the prairie? I don't think so. I'm no pioneer. Thanks anyway. I'll be okay on my own. Besides, like I told you, I'll be busy with rehearsals and shows," Martin said offhandedly. "What about Jeremy? Won't he spend the holidays in Old Claire?"

"Eau Claire," I corrected him halfheartedly. I was going to miss his habitual assault on names. "He promised to spend Christmas with his family."

Martin sank onto the sofa and I joined him on the other end. He propped his feet on my thighs and said, "Are you excited to go home?"

"This place feels like home to me now, but yeah, I am. I'm not thrilled about the flying part, but I really miss my family. Do you miss yours?"

"It's been so long since I've spoken to them," Martin said and suddenly became interested in a hangnail. "Besides, my family is here now. If Gretchen and I don't join Andy at Gay Men's Health Crisis, *he'll* have a crisis, and we won't hear the end of it. I feel like I owe it to Ken to be there. Last year we performed at a pediatric AIDS unit."

"What did you do?" I asked.

"Bernice, the sound technician at Club Chaos, burned a CD of Christmas songs by the Supremes. We got decked out in our flashiest frocks and put on quite a show. We even let Gretchen be Diana Ross. The kids ate it up. Later, Ken changed and did a few Judy numbers for them; then we all watched *The Wizard of Oz.* It wasn't exactly a traditional Christmas, but the kids had so much fun. It was also Ken's last performance as Judy. He went into the hospital for the first time shortly after that. So you see, it's going to take a while for me to thoroughly enjoy the holidays again."

"I understand," I said and started massaging his feet. "Call me if you need to, okay?"

"I know you're going to miss me, and that's the real reason you want me to call," Martin joked. "You can always log onto the Cybeeria Web site and watch my last shows. And yes, I plan on spending lots of time with Blythe. I wonder what she got me for Christmas?"

"I'm glad you plan on spending time with Blythe, but she'll be in Vermont for two weeks with her parents."

"What? She's not roasting chestnuts at Wade's house? What a shame," Martin said, then took notice of the time. "Hey. You have to be up in a few hours. You need your beauty sleep. A week's worth, by the look of things."

I playfully threw Martin's feet off my lap and went back to bed. I woke up much later from a dream about a parade. The last thing I saw was Brenda Li perched on a candied-apple red Volkswagen convertible, tossing samples of Fiberforth to the cast of *Friends,* with Martin on the sidewalk screaming, "Don't use it, Monica, you're too skinny already!"

"Good grief," I said, turning over to look at the clock. "Did I oversleep?"

"No. You have plenty of time," Blythe said. She was sitting at the foot of the bed with my sketchbook in her lap and a pencil in her hand. "By the way, the painting I gave you looks good over your dresser. But why'd you hang it upside down?"

"I did not," I said.

"I know," she admitted. "I just wondered if I could shake your confidence."

"I was studying art before you were born," I said.

"What were you dreaming?"

"I don't know. Something about a parade and Brenda Li."

"You sort of weren't dreaming then," she said. "Brenda was in here with Martin, and they just had to look in on you, Brenda being so smitten and all. You probably heard them talking."

After yawning and stretching, I started to feel awake. It finally registered that Blythe was drawing something in my sketchbook.

"What are you doing?" I asked.

She smiled without looking up and said, "I'm drawing, Einstein."

"I can see that, Picasso. *What* are you drawing?"

She sighed and flipped the sketchbook over in her lap so I couldn't see it, saying, "Go shower, get dressed, and have some breakfast. I should be done by then."

Instead of yanking the pad from her hands like I wanted to do, I did as she asked and got cleaned up. Later I went into the kitchen and found Martin and a stranger seated at the kitchen table, sipping coffee.

"Are you all packed and ready?" Martin asked.

His companion, a sandy-haired older man with hazel eyes, broad shoulders, and hands like a bricklayer's, smiled at me and said in Brenda Li's gravelly voice, "Would you like some pancakes, doll?"

"Brenda Li? Is that you?" I asked.

"It's actually Joseph Stoyanovich. But you can call me Joe. Or Brenda Joe, if you must. I don't mind. But eat something, doll. Ya got a big day ahead of you." He got up from the table and started pouring orange juice into a glass. "Here's some juice. Now what can I getcha? My world-famous pancakes? Do ya like bacon? Sausage? Bagel and schmear?"

Afraid to offend Brenda Joe, I sat down to a plate heaped with food and tried to forget my stomach, which was already queasy because of my fear of flying. Blythe walked in, sketchbook in hand, and looked at my plate in horror.

"Good grief, Adam. What's that, the Last Supper?"

Martin laughed and said, "Don't say it like that, Blythe. You know he's afraid of flying."

"Sorry, I forgot," she said. "You'll be fine. Here. This is for you."

She tore a page from the sketchbook and passed it across the table to me. It was a drawing of me, asleep in bed with the sheets half-covering my chest and my arm tucked under my head. After months of exposure to Blythe's abstract paintings, I was startled by the realism of the pencil drawing.

"Let me see," Martin said, snatching it from my hand so he and Brenda Joe could look at it.

"You drew that this morning?" I asked.

"I woke up early and saw your sketchbook. Before I knew what I was doing, I was drawing you."

"Can I have this?" Brenda Joe asked with a salacious gleam in his eye.

"It's for Adam," Blythe said with a laugh. "I was thinking you could send it to Jeremy as a reminder of what he's missing."

"You're what I'll be missing," I said to Blythe and got up to hug her.

"This is good, Blythe," Martin said, handing the drawing back to me. "I had no idea you could draw like this."

"I can do anything," she said.

"That's my motto, too!" Martin exclaimed. "Yikes, Adam, look at the time. You have to get out of here."

Outside the town house, I hugged Martin goodbye while Brenda Joe loaded my bags into the back of a cab.

"I'll see you in a couple of months," I said to Martin.

"I'll e-mail you from Cybeeria," he promised.

I turned to Blythe and said, "I think I'll miss you most of all."

"Don't do it," she said. "I know I act like a hard-ass, but don't say bye to me. I'll start crying."

I gave her a little squeeze and let her go, only to be whirled into Brenda Joe's embrace.

"See ya later, dollface," he wheezed, nearly crushing my ribs. "I'm gonna miss your sweet mug around here. Now get goin' before you miss your flight."

When my plane taxied down the runway and took off, I didn't even think about controlling gravity with my mind or steering with my armrests. Instead, I took Blythe's drawing from my briefcase and thought about Jeremy. I imagined him lying next to me in the sketch and smiled. I decided to follow Blythe's suggestion and mail him the drawing when I got home.

I turned my gaze to the window as the city grew smaller, thinking about my friends who were still on the ground. I didn't feel sad. I knew I would return and see them again. Instead I felt exhilarated, because I was in love. With Jeremy and with New York City.

"Look around at what your life has brought you," I whispered the words of the limo driver who'd given me my first sense of New York all those months before. I pressed my forehead against the window in a silent goodbye to my adopted home.

SEVENTEEN

I hadn't told my parents the exact time of my arrival because I needed a quiet homecoming at my farmhouse. I wanted to walk through my front door and fantasize about being there with Jeremy, trying to see everything through his eyes. Once the driver left my bags on the porch and took my money, I waited until he'd pulled away before I put my key in the lock and opened the front door.

I was overwhelmed by the sentimental feeling that swept through me as I walked from room to room and saw evidence of how my mother and Tracy had prepared everything for my return. The kitchen was well stocked. The house was spotless. Everything lay in readiness for my comfort. Even the fireplace had a good bundle of kindling resting under the stack of logs.

I lit the fire and stood in the living room a while, imagining Jeremy in the recliner or lying on the couch in his sock-clad feet. I saw us sitting cross-legged on the floor next to the hearth, eating popcorn while we watched a movie. I saw him walking out the little side door to bring in more wood from the stack that was always neatly piled alongside the house. I saw him until my eyes stung and my throat hurt with all the promises I hadn't made because he wasn't ready to hear them.

I finally put the computer bags in my office, then took my luggage upstairs, my feet heavier on each step, so that by the time I walked into my bedroom, I felt like I weighed a thousand pounds.

"Isn't love supposed to make you happy?" I asked out loud, but no one answered.

I was home. It still smelled and looked like home. But why did it feel so empty when it never had before?

I thought about all the things I would miss. Martin singing along to a Madonna-thon on VH-1. Blythe's noisy laugh. Daniel calling to fill an hour with gossip about *Secret Splendor*. Working out with Blaine. Sheila and Josh's enthusiastic discussion of any random topic. Gretchen's practical approach to solving problems. Lester's cocky conversation, Ray's melodious accent, and even Andy's annoying habit of overemphasizing half his words. In mere hours, I felt like a huge chunk of my life had been taken from me.

Most of all, I missed the idea that Jeremy might be around any corner, up any street, in any restaurant or coffee shop. If I couldn't have New York, I wanted Jeremy. In my house, in my bed, in my life.

The sound of someone knocking on my front door startled me out of my reverie. Though I'd thought I wanted quiet solitude, I ran down the stairs, eager for any human voice that would make me stop feeling like a stranger in my own home. I opened the door and felt like I'd stepped back a dozen years in time.

"Lars?"

Lars laughed and said, "I was hoping you'd be home. I had to pick up a tree for my parents, and I figured you wouldn't have had time to get one yet."

He gestured toward a Christmas tree leaning against his pickup truck. I looked from the tree back to him, unable to believe my eyes.

"You look great!" I burst out. "For a minute there I thought we were back in high school."

"I'm not quite to that point and probably never will be. But I sure do feel better." He came in and took off his coat, smiling at me. "I weigh about sixty pounds less than I did the last time you saw me. I've been working out and running. Plus I cut out some of that Midwestern cooking."

"You look ten years younger," I said.

While Lars warmed himself in front of the fire, I brought beers from the kitchen and stood admiring him. His hair had been cut to about an inch in length, with his bangs styled into a spiky look. His face was as trim and handsome as when we'd been in high school; the weathering only made him look more interesting. It was as if he'd leaped from boyish good looks to handsome man with none of the intervening bad years.

"That tree is a little thank-you," Lars said.

"For what?"

"For sticking by me all these years when I was so screwed up. When you left for New York last summer, I decided it was time to do something about my life. Just like you did."

"Lars, you've always been successful," I said. "Are you leaving the insurance business?"

"No, business is fine. It was my personal life that was a mess." He took a swallow of his beer. "I'm not ready to march in any parades or make any headlines in the *Leader-Telegram,* but I got tired of being unhappy and alone. I've been dating a guy from Madison. Who knows what will come of it? I'm taking it slow. Where's your tree stand?"

"In the attic with my Christmas stuff. If you can stick around and help me decorate, I'll thaw a couple of steaks for dinner, and we can catch up."

"Sounds great," Lars said.

After I found the stand, Lars went outside to take care of the tree while I brought the rest of the decorations from the attic. By the time he finished stringing lights, I had dinner ready. We talked about Eau Claire friends while we ate. After he helped me load the dishwasher, I put on one of my parents' old Andy Williams Christmas albums while we finished decorating the tree. He told me about his potential boyfriend, Tyler, who owned his own real estate firm in Madison.

"What about you?" he finally asked. "Did you find all those hot guys I've heard about in New York?"

"I found one," I said. "But first I have to tell you about somebody else. Do you remember Daniel Stephenson?"

Lars frowned for a few seconds; then he said, "You mean Danny? Bill Hamilton's buddy? The one who was in all the school plays?"

"That's the one. Now he's Daniel. He's still an actor. We ran into each other in Central Park."

I told him about how I'd had to mend fences with Daniel and what he'd been doing over the years. I included his new job on the soap but left out any mention of Blaine, remembering that the Dunhills were still unaware of too much about Blaine's life. I trusted Lars, but I felt like Blaine had a right to his privacy. I finished my stories with enough details about the Disorient XPress caper to have him roaring with laughter.

"That's my man," he said when I told him about putting my football moves on Ethan. "I never had to worry when you ran with the ball." We grew quiet for a few minutes, staring at the lights twinkling on the tree while we drank the brandy I'd poured. "Adam, do you ever wonder how things might have been? If I'd had the guts you did?"

"I used to. I was so crazy about you."

"Everything about you scared me. The way I felt. The way I wondered about what you felt. Most of all how fucking honest you were. I was too scared to even be friends with you."

"Those days are over," I said. "We've been friends a long time."

"So tell me about this guy. It's not Danny Stephenson, is it?"

"It's about as strange. His name is Jeremy, and he's Daniel's exboyfriend."

As I talked about Jeremy, I realized that I was expressing some of the things I'd only hinted about to Blythe. It felt liberating to admit how much in love I was with Jeremy and how he dominated my thoughts. It occurred to me how hard it had been not to talk about my feelings to Daniel, Blaine, or Martin, because their perspective of Jeremy was colored by too much history.

"I'm sorry; am I babbling?" I finally asked. "It's a relief to have somebody to talk to who knows me and not Jeremy."

"I think Jeremy is a lucky man. It's all going to work out."

"I wish I had your confidence."

"Adam, any man would be a fool not to take what you have to offer. I should know. Not that you ever offered."

"I remember one night—"

"Good old Rachel Monroe," he said. "Was she a bitch or what?"

"Totally. But I've never been sorry about what happened. It clarified things for me."

"It confused the hell out of me. But you know what? I've never been sorry either. Now I'm getting out of here before you say—"

"Shut up and kiss me."

We laughed, and I walked him to the door. He put on his coat, then turned to embrace me.

"Be patient," he said. "I'm proof that miracles happen."

We hugged good night, then I leaned against the door after I closed it, listening as his truck went down my driveway. Though he'd been the last person I expected to see, somehow Lars had managed to return my feeling of home to me.

I realized over the next few days that he'd also returned a sense of balance to my attitude. Though I missed Jeremy and told him so frequently in our e-mails and phone calls, I gradually readjusted to life in Eau Claire. I'd lost my sense of urgency to talk to my parents about everything that I was thinking and feeling. I could tell they knew something was on my mind, but they waited, as they always had, for me to come to them.

Jeremy was delighted when I had Blythe's sketch of me matted and framed and sent it to him. He'd caught me on the farmhouse Webcam Christmas Day, playing in the front yard with my nephews and the weimaraners. I complained because I had no pictures of him. A few days later, I got a package from Stella with an array of photographs of Jeremy at all ages and a note asking me when I was coming back to Brooklyn.

As I'd promised Daniel, I taped *Secret Splendor* every day and watched it at night while I ate dinner. I found myself getting caught up in the story, especially the wicked deeds of Angus Remington, but I really liked our occasional phone calls when Daniel gave me off-screen gossip about the cast.

I flew to Chicago to meet with Bonnie Seaforth-Wilkes and a couple of her directors at Seaforth Chemicals. As she had implied they might, Seaforth bought a big chunk of advertising on the Club Chaos site, not for Fiberforth, which Wade was managing to hold on to with his *Secret Splendor* Saturdays, but for an upscale line of pet foods. The directors were convinced that if anyone would pay their high prices, it was gay men, and the site was continuing to get a lot of hits. They also put me on retainer to present them with some ideas for their main Web site. I was sure I could get the account.

Jeremy told me that Blythe and Uncle Mario had settled into an occasional lunch routine, which tickled the entire family, who felt her friendship was giving him a new purpose in life. It was Blythe herself who called me with the big news there. Uncle Mario had visited her loft to look at her paintings. Though he freely admitted to knowing nothing about art, he said he recognized "moxie" when he saw it and believed Blythe was loaded with it. He offered to back her first showing at a gallery in Brooklyn, and Blythe accepted. When I expressed surprise, she explained that she knew exactly what she was getting with Mario Caprellian, who, in spite of his flirtatious ways, was a perfect gentleman. The exhibit would take place in the summer, and we agreed that I would help put things together, including tying it into her Web site.

Once my classes started, I kept myself busy enough to take the edge off missing Jeremy. But he was never far from my thoughts, especially at night, when my need of him often drove me out of bed to my computer, where I continued to write about my adventures in New York. He had settled into his new life in Oklahoma, and his conversations and e-mails reflected his pleasure in what he was doing. He had no regrets about having quit the sitcom, which was canceled in mid-January.

I tried not to wonder too much about what his contentment meant to us. Though our conversations, particularly the late-night ones, were flirtatious and sexy, neither of us mentioned my declaration of love, nor did I repeat it. I didn't want him to feel pressured. I certainly didn't want him to make a similar confession just because he thought I wanted to hear it. A couple of times we tried to make plans to see each other, but the timing was never right.

I finally decided the snow that covered my land was the perfect analogy for this interlude in our relationship. It was beautiful to contemplate, and beneath what was frozen, life was preparing to burst forth in spring. Just as there was a rhythm and meaning to the seasons, things would develop with Jeremy as they should. When it was time, we would progress to the next phase of our life together.

Lars and I began working out together a couple of times a week. I met Tyler, his potential boyfriend, and found him completely different from what I'd envisioned. I'd thought Lars might try to reclaim the youth he'd cheated himself out of, but Tyler was a forty-year-old man with a great attitude. He was clean-shaven, including his head, which he said he'd started shaving once it was obvious that he was losing his hair. His twinkling green eyes seemed to take in everything around him with enjoyment, and they often rested on Lars with deep affection. He also had a passion for sports. I couldn't have picked a better man for my old friend.

As for Martin, he was obviously enjoying his part in *Cabaret*. Though he did manage to send me an e-mail from Cybeeria now and then, I got most of my news about him from Blythe and Daniel. Until one afternoon when an e-mail showed up in my inbox from Ethan.

Hi, Adam, I hope you don't mind that Jeremy gave me your e-mail address, as I'd lost it. I wanted to write and say thanks. I was in Manhattan last Saturday and met Martin for lunch. I can't remember the last time I laughed so much. He's like a breath of fresh air.

We enjoyed rehashing our first meeting, when I was nearly tackled by Miss Saigon and manhandled by the rest of her team. But what touched me, and compelled me to write you, was that Martin told me you'd never had anything but kind words to say about me. I don't know if a romance will come of this, but I do appreciate that you didn't allow some of our misunderstandings to sabotage a possible courtship.

Even if the end result is a friendship with Martin, he is someone I've needed in my life a long time. He and I have an amazing amount in common, which may surprise you, but especially because of our family backgrounds. I was able to talk to him about things I haven't wanted to think about in years. Again, thanks.

However, I do have a bone to pick with you. Why are you delaying taking action about my lovesick colleague? He is happy with his work. But work is only a part of life. What did you learn at the Spirit Matters retreat? My best, Ethan.

I stared at my screen, trying to decipher Ethan's e-mail. Was he telling me that Jeremy was unhappy? If so, it wasn't something I'd ever picked up from Jeremy. Then again, hadn't I often accused Jeremy of being inscrutable? If I'd had trouble reading him in person, it was entirely possible that I was missing something now. But what?

As for what I'd learned at the retreat, I assumed Ethan was referring to his talk, which had been about integrating the different parts of our lives to achieve balance. But I'd done that. Emotionally, I had deeper friendships than I'd ever had. If the most significant one happened to be long-distance, that was helping me develop patience. I was still taking good physical care of myself. I had two little totems sitting next to my computer—a plush zebra toy and my windup lion—to simultaneously remind me to develop myself spiritually but keep things light. As for my cerebral side, my students provided plenty of challenges to keep me on my toes.

I closed the e-mail and frowned, wondering what I was missing. I wound the tin lion and watched it walk across my desk, thinking about the day in Cold Spring when Jeremy had picked it out from among the toys.

It dawned on me that Ethan's hints were about Jeremy, not me. Maybe he meant that Jeremy was unhappy because his focus on work was throwing his life out of balance. But if that was true, wasn't it Jeremy's responsibility to correct it?

I was so lost in thought that I was caught completely off guard when Sadie and Marnie came bursting into the office. Sadie knocked over the trash can, and Marnie immediately investigated each piece of rubbish that tumbled onto the floor. I heard my mother opening and shutting cabinets in the kitchen.

I laughed as I realized who she reminded me of. Apparently, my desire to stock Blythe's cupboards came naturally to me. I got up from my desk to join my mother in the kitchen.

"Aggie, thank god you got here in time," I said, kissing her cheek. "Computer geeks worldwide were planning to broadcast Adam Aid over the Internet before I starved to death."

"Your sarcasm's out of season, and I don't think you have a permit," she said.

"You wouldn't have such snappy comebacks if it weren't for those folks at PFLAG," I said, opening a bag of cookies and biting into one after offering it to her.

She stopped in the act of opening the refrigerator door to stare at a picture of Jeremy held there by a magnet. After a brief glance at me, she opened the door to put in another carton of orange juice, bringing my total to three.

"Just ask. I know you're dying to."

"After hearing about him for months, I assume that's Jeremy," she said.

"Yes."

"He sent me an instant message last night. His mother wanted my stroganoff recipe, and he correctly assumed that I was the one who showed you how to make it."

"Have I taught you nothing about talking to strangers online?"

"When someone begins by telling me he's your friend—"

"He could just as easily be my psycho stalker," I pointed out.

"Then why would you have a picture of him on your refrigerator?"

I gave up trying to follow her logic and asked, "Is that all you talked about?"

She began unloading fruit into a bowl and said, "Here, have a banana."

"Mom, I don't want a banana. What else did you and Jeremy talk about?"

"His work," Aggie said. "Pick up that bag for me. It's heavy."

I hefted a brown paper bag onto the butcher-block island, and she rewarded me with a banana for my efforts.

"Just eat it," she said and started stacking cans of soup on the counter. "It sounds like he's enjoying working with those kids. It's very admirable what he's doing."

"I agree," I said and threw away the banana peel. "How much cream of mushroom soup do I need?"

She looked at the small pyramid of soup cans, which made my kitchen look like aisle five of Randall's supermarket, and said, "They were on sale. Please put them away for me. Jeremy seems like a nice young man."

"He is. I just wish he worked closer to home," I said, moving the cans to a cupboard.

"Even if he weren't in Oklahoma, his home is in New York."

"Yes, but I'll be going there a lot on business. If he was there, I could see him. I have no reason to go to Oklahoma."

Aggie had started folding paper bags, but she stopped and said, "Wouldn't you rather have him *here?*"

"Of course I would, Mom, but I can't force him to be here if he doesn't want to be," I said, loudly banging the cupboard door shut. "There are laws against that."

"What if he wants to be here with you?" she asked.

"What? Did he say something to you?"

"Hold your horses," she said, dropping a paper bag like it was a penalty flag. "No, he didn't say anything to me. I only asked him about his job. He talked about his holidays. I told him that it sounded as if you enjoyed Thanksgiving with his family, and I gave him an open invitation to visit us."

"Aggie!" I was taken aback. "What did he say?"

"He thanked me, Adam. Like a polite boy should do, instead of calling his mother Aggie."

My father came in with bundles of kindling and said, "I think the thermometer dropped ten degrees in five minutes. The weather gets crazier every year." When this was met with silence, he looked from my mother to me and said, "I'll put these next to your fire-place, Adam."

"Thanks, Dad." I watched as my mother took coffee and filters from my cupboard, then asked, "What's going on here?"

"Your father and I want to have a talk with you," my mother said.

"Is it as serious as it sounds?"

She laughed and said, "You act like a kid whose darkest secret has been found out. Relax."

I went to help my father with the fire. When the coffee was done, Aggie brought it to us on a tray, and I poured, remembering out of long habit how each of them liked it.

"All right, out with it," I said, nudging Marnie out of my way so I could sit down.

"It's not a big deal," my father said. "Has anyone said anything to you about me running for the school board?"

"No," I said. "But if you want my opinion, you should do it if you're interested. What do Mike and Julie think?"

"They're all for it. I'd like to give it a shot. Of course, it should be your mother running. She's the political one."

Just as I began feeling relieved that this talk had been about them and not me, my mother said, "Adam, you know I don't meddle, but I'd like to continue our earlier conversation. Ever since you came back from New York, you've been in a strange mood. You don't have to tell us why, but—"

"We've been wondering if you're unhappy because you want to move to New York," my father cut in, obviously having decided not to beat around the bush. "We don't want to be the reason why you don't. Of course, we'd miss you, but we've never tried to live through our kids. We'd never hold you back."

I had a lump in my throat as I said, "I'm sorry. I should have talked to you about all this as soon as I got home. The truth is, I've fallen in love with someone who's given me no reason to believe that's a decision I have to make."

"Have you told him how you feel?" my mother asked.

"I told him I love him. I haven't said anything about either of us moving. It hasn't gotten that far. Besides, I'm not sure I'm ready to make that kind of change."

"Could he move here?" my father asked.

"I don't think so," I said. "He's starting a new job, and he seems happy. I can't ask him to give it up."

"I'm sure you two will work it out," my father said. "You need to tell him what's in your heart, son. Or you may never know what you missed."

"I wish every gay person I know could have you two as parents," I said. "I'm so lucky."

"Like Lars," my mother agreed. "How many years has he wasted just to please his parents and keep his secret?"

"You know about Lars?" I asked, shocked, because I'd certainly never told her.

"I knew about Lars before I knew about you," she said with a laugh.

"You're scary."

"She's a pistol," my father agreed.

After they were gone, I sat in front of the fire for a long time, contemplating what they'd said and trying to apply their wisdom to Ethan's e-mail. Finally, I went back to my computer, hoping for an e-mail from Jeremy, but nothing was there. Nor was he online under his AOL screen name.

I took a deep breath and started composing one to him.

Hello, Golden Boy, you've been very much in my thoughts today. What's new, huh? But I was thinking particularly about Cold Spring. Weren't we there when you told me you didn't want someone who'd fuck and run?

In a way, that's what I've done all along. You asked how we would manage a long-distance relationship, and I told you it would work out. You asked how you could know I wouldn't hurt you, and I told you to take a risk. Then I had the gall to say "I love you" as you were leaving, never to broach the subject again. I've been telling myself I didn't want to put pressure on you. I've convinced myself that I'm being fair by not saddling you with my emotions and expectations while you're trying to start a new career. That's partly true, but it's not the whole truth.

What I haven't been telling you is that I don't just miss you, I'm miserable because we're not together. After all I thought I learned during my months in New York, I came home and started doing the same thing I've always done. Kept myself busy so I wouldn't have to think about how lonely I am. Assured myself that just because I have new and deeper friendships, I've finally started to risk myself emotionally. Told myself that because I said "I love you," I did my part. As if it doesn't take actions to give meaning to words.

Jeremy, if you're willing, together we can find a solution to this long-distance bullshit. I'll do whatever it takes to make this work, because I do love you and I want us to be together. If you don't feel the same way, then you don't. I'll have to accept that. But I'll never be sorry for loving you because, to use a phrase of yours from Cold Spring, you showed me that a "spoonful of possibility" is more nourishing than a feast of not enough.

Call me when you get this, and don't be afraid to be totally honest. I'm still willing to be as patient as I need to be. But if all my feelings and hopes are just pressure that you don't need, I won't keep forcing you to deal with it. I love you. Adam.

Periodically throughout the evening, I checked to see the status of the e-mail, but it remained unread. I finally went to bed, making sure the phone next to me had the ringer up as loud as it would go.

When I woke up the next morning, it took me a minute to remember why I was feeling such intense anxiety. Jeremy hadn't called. I hurried downstairs and checked the e-mail status again. It was still unread. I tried to call him, but he didn't answer. I took a chance and called his apartment in New York, but all I got was Robert's message on the machine, which told me nothing. For a moment I considered unsending the e-mail, but reminded myself that Jeremy had my cell phone number. He could reach me anytime.

It was probably not my most brilliant day in the classroom, but my students didn't seem to notice anything amiss. I wasn't sure what that indicated about my usual teaching technique. Though I accessed AOL several times through the school's server, I still didn't hear from him. I checked in with Tracy periodically, but all my messages were business-related. By the time I left campus to meet Lars at the gym, my feelings were swinging between anger and raging insecurity.

Lars was full of details about a cruise he and Tyler were discussing. I managed to grunt out appropriate responses in spite of the brutal workout I put myself through. As soon as I left the gym, I called Jeremy at his Oklahoma number, but he still didn't answer. I was disgusted with myself for behaving like a teenager enduring his first crush. Of course Jeremy would call me as soon as he read the e-mail. He'd never purposely torment me.

Except that when I got home and checked the e-mail status again, it had been read. Yet my cell phone hadn't rung. I had no messages on either phone. And I had no reply.

I trudged up the stairs, threw my gym bag across the room, and climbed into the shower, trying to wash away the day's emotions. When I went downstairs, I pointedly ignored the computer and busied myself with dinner. While I ate, I realized just how angry I was when I told Angus Remington to "off the bitch" as he toyed with his sister Brianna's emotions.

"This is ridiculous," I muttered, pushing my plate aside and walking back to my office. I signed onto AOL and found a response from JCNYC.

> *Greetings, Atom Ant. Not only are you a better writer than I am, but you're much better at expressing your emotions. After reading your email, I'll try to follow your example.*

> *You've been on my mind a lot lately, too. In fact, I often think about that day in Cold Spring and, as you know, look at your house on your webcam. You described it to me perfectly. However, I'm still looking for that stained glass window. Maybe it's on the other side of the house?*

> *But what I'm constantly thinking about is our last day together. Our last night was amazing, but I keep replaying the following morning over and over in my head. I wish things had turned out differently. Yes, I said I didn't want somebody who would fuck and run, but I felt like I was the one who was running. Or being forced to run. But then I did the same thing that you did. I threw myself into my work so I wouldn't have to deal with the pressure of our relationship. Our program has gotten an incredible response from the community and it looks like we're on the verge of getting Federal grant funding. Ethan is dealing with all that and I've been assigned to draft a curriculum for AFNAT's drama program. Not only for future instructors to use, but for Ethan to submit for the grant applications. I'm glad the program is getting recognition, but my time is slowly being taken away from the kids, which is why I did this in the first place.*

> *And my time is being taken away from you. I didn't lie, though. I have been thinking about us, but maybe you've been feeling my energy being diverted into my work. Maybe I've been hanging out with Ethan too much. But I'm glad I made the decisions I did. And that I took the path that led me to where I am right now. But I should follow your lead and do what I have to do to make this work. All I need is a little more time and trust that I care for you deeply. Jeremy.*

"I did say I'd be patient, didn't I?" I asked. I then proceeded to do something I hadn't done in years.

The next morning I awoke with a well-deserved hangover. Though it wasn't a school day for me, I forced myself to take a shower and leave the house before Tracy got there. I put a copy of Jeremy's e-mail, my laptop, and my sketchbook in my shoulder bag and drove my truck to Madison. I wasn't interested in running into anyone I knew in Eau Claire. For the same reason, I avoided my favorite hangouts in Madison, pulling into a Starbucks, though the ambience was a sad imitation of the quirky coffee shops in Manhattan that I missed. Then again, maybe it was the perfect match for my less-than-perfect mood. By my second cup of coffee, I was ready to read Jeremy's e-mail again. Maybe I'd missed something the night before.

It hadn't magically improved during the night, however. I tried to break it down and understand just what it was that annoyed me so much. Was it the frivolous salutation to "Atom Ant?" I had, after all, called Jeremy "Golden Boy," but I'd thought that was romantic, even a little sad, considering how much I ached for him. Still, maybe I was misreading him. Maybe it was not only a term of endearment, but a way of calling me his superhero. Whatever.

Was it the way a discussion of our last day together had suddenly morphed into information about his work? I wanted to talk about spending the rest of our lives with each other, and he talked about what was keeping him busy. I conceded that might be his way of letting me off the hook for using my work to neglect my emotions. Maybe he was just being empathetic. But did I really have to know how closely he was working with Ethan? Had I mentioned other men in my e-mail? I had not.

"Maybe I've been hanging out with Ethan too much." What the hell did that mean? Was it just because he'd talked about "energy?" Or was there a more subtle message there? Or was I once again being stupidly jealous, just like with Daniel?

"Why am I doing this to myself?" I muttered.

"What?" a woman sitting at an adjoining table asked. When I stared at her, she said, "Sorry, I thought you asked me a question."

I shook my head and returned my attention to the e-mail. Maybe

I was being unfair, because all I'd wanted was a phone call from Jeremy in which he would tell me he loved me. Then I could make my grand gesture, vowing to give up hearth and home to be by his side. But he wasn't asking for grand gestures. He was asking for time and trust.

I'd give him time. All the time he needed. But I'd be willing to bet he wasn't running around like an idiot today, checking his e-mail or voice mail every few minutes for a response from me. He was too wrapped up in his work to do that. Ethan would probably say that was the universe's way of showing me what it felt like to be on the receiving end of my workaholic behavior.

I put the e-mail back in my bag, taking out my sketchbook and idly flipping through the pages. I looked up as the door opened and a blast of cold air filled Starbucks. My heart skipped a beat.

If I'd occasionally suspected I was fulfilling some guy's jock fantasy, the man who walked to the counter could easily have been the central figure in someone's construction worker fantasy. He was several inches shorter than I was, dressed in jeans and work boots. I could see the collar of his thermal underwear under his dark-blue shirt. His jacket was short so it wouldn't obstruct his tool belt, which hung low under his long waist.

I glanced outside, saw the phone company van that had to be his, then turned my eyes back to him. He had a ruddy complexion, short ash blonde hair, and great blue eyes. After his order was filled, I checked out his perfectly shaped ass and powerful thighs as he walked to the far counter to add cream to his coffee. Just before he turned around, I looked at the woman who had earlier thought I was asking her a question. Her eyes were riveted to Phone Guy; obviously, gay men weren't the only one with that fantasy.

He turned and walked toward us, scanning the area for the table he wanted. I waited, wondering who his eyes would connect with, if either of us. His gaze went right over the woman and locked on mine. He tilted his head back in quick acknowledgment; then he took a seat by the window, where he and I would have an unobstructed view of each other. I glanced at the woman, who had resumed reading her book.

I let my mind consider the possibilities. The men's room at Starbucks? The cab of my truck? The back of his van? A motel down the street? When I'd made my decision, I put the sketchbook back in my bag, stood up, shrugged into my coat, and walked outside. I climbed in my truck and sat still for a minute, lightly banging my head on the steering wheel while I laughed helplessly. The words I'd spoken to Blythe had never seemed truer. Jeremy was under my skin. I drove off alone.

By the time I left Madison that afternoon, I had three new accounts, two of whom I'd stolen from one of Madison's preeminent Web designers. There was nothing like sublimating sexual desire with work to make a man ruthless.

When I got home, Tracy was just closing up shop. She handed me several phone messages; two of them were from Jeremy. Then she warily took my notes from me so she could type up my three new contracts the following day.

"What's wrong with you?" I asked, frowning at her.

"I can see you're the evil twin today," she said. "I'm just laying low."

"If I am, it's not your fault," I said. "Have I ever taken out my moods on you guys?"

"So that's why you stayed away today. Which reminds me: next Sunday is Valentine's Day."

"Perfect," I grumbled.

"What?"

"Yes, it's Valentine's Day, and?"

"J. B. and the guys have arranged a weekend in the Twin Cities. They found this sweetheart package deal and—"

"By the guys, I'm assuming you mean Scott and Pete?" I asked, referring to my other two employees.

"And their wives, yes," she said. "We'd like to leave early Friday morning, making a long weekend of it. Will it be a big deal if all three of us aren't here next Friday?"

"I'll manage," I said. She looked a little injured, so I added, "I'm sorry. It really isn't your fault I'm in a bad mood. You should all go. Have fun. Don't get pregnant."

"I'll do my best," she said, laughing.

After she was gone, I picked up my cordless and dialed Jeremy's number while I started checking e-mail. When he didn't answer, I threw the phone across the desk. What was the point of returning his calls if he was never at his damn phone?

I finally reached him late that night, but he was exhausted and our conversation was short. Neither of us mentioned our e-mail exchange. That proved to remain the case throughout the next week.

We went back to talking about work, weather, and how we missed each other. At times I felt as though he was on the verge of telling me something, but I never pushed him, and the opportunities slipped by.

On the Friday before Valentine's Day, I sat at my desk with Seaforth Chemicals' Web site open on my screen, trying to think of ways to make it look innovative and fresh. At ten in the morning, I remembered that I had given my employees the day off. I put my head in my hands and massaged my temples, thinking about how excited they probably were about their weekend plans. Happy couples on a romantic, carefree weekend, with the world as their oyster. Perhaps even eating oysters before retiring to their rooms to make love. The fact that I wasn't invited—wasn't even asked by Tracy if I had somebody in my life—raced through my mind. I felt jealous and upset, but most of all, I was angry at myself for allowing my emotions to get the better of me.

The phone rang, and I picked it up and barked, "Yes?"

"Geez, I haven't talked to you in over a week and that's the greeting I get?" Blythe complained.

"I'm sorry. How are you?" I asked.

"Great," she answered. "What's up your ass? Should I call back later?"

"My friends are all away for the weekend celebrating their perfect relationships."

"I see. And you're not."

"No. I'm here in my house. Alone. Pretending to work, but I'm really staring at my buddy list and waiting for a screen name that will never appear."

"I assume you mean Jeremy. I don't have unlimited cell phone minutes, so why don't you give me the Cliff's Notes version of what's been going on?"

I told her about my conversation with my parents, the e-mail from Jeremy, and how we had been avoiding the million-dollar question: *Now what do we do?*

"If you've told him how you feel and he hasn't responded, I guess it's time to move on," Blythe suggested, saying exactly what I hadn't wanted to admit to myself. "Which really sucks, because I thought he was great."

"So did I. Do! I do think he's great. I'm not ready to give up yet," I insisted.

"I want to fly to Oklahoma and kick his ass," Blythe said, which made me laugh. "Of course, he'd have to kneel down so I could reach it. Wait; that's an image you shouldn't have in your head. I really think you should think about moving on, Adam. If he's not willing to make you a priority in his life or recognize you for the wonderful man you are, what's the point? You should be with someone who supports you and gives you what you need."

"He said he needs me to give him time and trust," I said.

"It seems like you've done that, but it's not working. For either one of you."

"That's the thing. I don't know if it's working for him, because he's not telling me anything. I'm going to grow old alone and end up being one of those people who never leaves their house. People will go by my house and point, saying, 'Old Man Wilson lives there. He went crazy back in nineteen ninety-nine.' "

"At least you'll be guaranteed a good time every Halloween," Blythe cracked. "And you won't have Jehovah's Witnesses knocking on your door. Weren't you supposed to come back to New York this month?"

"Next week. I have to go to Chicago on Monday to present a proposal to Seaforth's board of directors for their Web site," I said, grateful that she'd changed the topic.

"How does that get you to New York?"

"Seaforth is in Chicago, but Bonnie will be in New York attending a divination workshop."

"What's that?" Blythe asked.

"I have no idea, but apparently, she can't leave New York because some planet is ascending on her chart."

"I hate it when that happens."

"I'll have to make the same pitch in two locations. The upside is that I'll be in Manhattan and can touch base with my other projects while I'm there. Not to mention seeing my friends. And you," I added.

"Now I know how Y feels when used as a vowel," Blythe said. "And sometimes Blythe. So you'll be here when?"

"Thursday or Friday, I think. The problem is that I haven't gotten any work done on this stupid Web site, because I've been spending most of my time pining for Jeremy. Why don't you use the ticket I gave you and help me through this?"

"No offense, but I'd rather save it for when it's warmer there,"

Blythe said. "I have way too much to do getting ready for this show-ing."

"It's four months away!"

"You know how I operate, Adam. I have to figure out what I want to include, how I want everything hung, in what order, yadda yadda yadda. Everyone's been really cool, though. Josh has had showings of his photographs, so he's told me what to expect. Sheila keeps bringing casseroles by, like food will solve anything. Martin keeps me laughing when I get insane, and Blaine's been helping me frame my paintings."

"That's great," I said, happy that our friends were taking care of her.

"I gotta go," Blythe said. "Mario's taking me out to lunch. I love you."

"I love you, too. See you soon."

As I hung up the phone, loneliness crept over me, and my office felt like it was shrinking. Jeremy's screen name still hadn't ap-peared on my buddy list. My house was so quiet that I could hear the walls creak every time a gust of wind blew outside.

I pushed all my anxiety aside, and the hours flew by as I worked on the Seaforth site. I mapped out all my ideas on paper and began pulling information from the old site, saving it on several Zip disks, laughing because they reminded me of breaking into Wade's office at Disorient XPress. I began to feel creative again as I made a Shockwave movie using the Seaforth Chemicals logo and images of products manufactured by their various subsidiaries. By ten PM, I was nodding off in my computer chair, but I knew that a position as Seaforth Chemicals' Webmaster would soon be mine.

I spent Saturday at my parents' house and told them about Blythe's advice regarding Jeremy.

"Move on?" my father said slowly, as if thinking it over.

"It's never been like you to give up, Adam," my mother com-mented.

"I'm not giving up, Mom," I said. We were seated at the dining room table stuffing envelopes for her mailing list, so her PFLAG chapter's members would know about a conference being held in Chicago. "I let him know how I felt about him, and he's done noth-ing to reciprocate. I think maybe Blythe's right, and I should think about moving on."

"There's no shame in admitting defeat, son," my father said, totally missing the point.

"Yes, there is," my mother said emphatically. "I know that boy loves you, too."

"He told you in an instant message? An e-mail?" I asked sarcastically. "That's great if he did, Mom, because it's more than I can get out of him. But if he did tell you, it doesn't change anything, because he didn't tell me."

"Don't get impertinent. You know I don't meddle. Here, lick these."

"Why can't you just e-mail everybody so we don't have to do this?" I complained while taking a stack of envelopes from her.

"Because not all the members are online," she said. "Here's a sponge. Save your tongue so you can keep being a smartass."

"You two are driving me nuts," my father said. "You," he said, pointing at Aggie, "need to remember that our son is a grown man and has to make his own decisions. And you, son, need to stop being such a baby and take care of yourself. I think your friend is right. If Jeremy's not meeting your needs, you should kick him to the curb."

"Kick him to the curb?" I questioned. "Where did you get that?"

"Your father's been watching Ricki Lake and other talk shows so he can get in touch with the issues kids are facing today," my mother explained. "Hank, I need to show you that thing in the kitchen that I need you to fix."

"Real smooth, Mom," I said as they went into the kitchen.

While they were gone, I kept sealing envelopes but thought about Jeremy. Blythe was right. I deserved someone whose focus was on me. Even though I respected Jeremy's job and his work with teenagers, the distance between us was too much for me to bear. Not only the physical distance, but the emotional distance. I had put my heart on my sleeve, and he didn't respond. The only sensible thing to do was move on.

My parents came back into the dining room and sat down again.

"Son," my father began, "I think I spoke too hastily. Why don't you talk to Jeremy one last time and tell him how you feel?"

"No, Dad. I've done that a few times and it didn't work," I said emphatically. "Mom, I know you mean well, but I really think Blythe and Dad are right."

"Fine," Aggie said, holding up her hands as if repelling the topic to another room of the house. "You win. I won't bring it up again. Not that I brought this up. You did. But that's okay. I love you and support you in whatever you choose to do."

"Thank you, Mom," I said.

"Even if I don't agree and think you're wrong," she finished. "Are you staying for dinner? I made pot roast. Tomorrow I need to come by your place and use your photocopier to make more flyers."

"Why don't you just print them out from your computer?" I asked.

"The printer's on the fritz again," she said.

"I could take a look at it," I offered.

"No, son. I looked at it and it's kaput. I think it's time for a new one," my father said. "You've got enough to worry about with that Soul Force project."

"Seaforth," I said, correcting him, and was reminded of Martin, which made me laugh.

On Valentine's Day I put the finishing touches on my Web site for Seaforth Chemicals. It wasn't a complete site, because I didn't have up-to-date information on their figures, products, and future projects. But as a revamped version of their old site, it still looked impressive. I honestly didn't care if I got the job or not, since I had little interest in working for a large corporation. But I liked Bonnie Seaforth-Wilkes. Not only did I look forward to seeing her again, but meeting her in Manhattan meant I could reconnect with my old friends and avoid brooding about Jeremy.

After I packed up my PC laptop, my PowerBook, and various disks that I'd need for my presentation, I went online and booked a flight to Chicago that left the next morning.

With that out of the way, I bundled up in my coat and scarf and took my sketchbook and pencils outside. I walked down a path that I kept clear from my barn to the woods. As I walked through the trees, the path narrowed and led to a pond in a clearing. Rocky and surrounded by tall, reedy grass, it provided a safe haven where I could sit and think without being disturbed.

I sat down on a flat rock and opened my sketchbook. Poising my pencil over the paper, I cleared my mind. My hand seemed to move of its own accord, shading and scraping lines across the page. I recreated Blythe's drawing of me sleeping in my bed at Martin's town house. In my version, Jeremy was lying next to me with my arm around him, his eyes closed in slumber, his head on my chest.

I heard something crashing through the woods toward me but didn't lift my head until it was too late. Sadie and Marnie jumped on me, knocking the sketchbook off my lap and into the pond.

"Fuck!" I yelled, trying to get the hyper dogs off me. "Get off me!"

The dogs, having done their duty by greeting me, bounded back through the woods on their way to the house, where my mother was probably using my copier.

I peered over the rock and tried to find my sketchbook. The pond was shallow, and I reached into the frigid water to retrieve it. My drawing of Jeremy and me was intact, but soaked through and smudged.

"Stupid pond," I muttered. "Why couldn't you have been frozen over?"

I went back to the house to yell at my mother about her crazy dogs and found her in my office.

"Your dogs ruined my sketch," I said, holding up my wet sketchbook like it was a smoking pistol.

"Adam, I don't have time for your nonsense," Aggie said. "I'm sure the dogs didn't maliciously ruin your sketch. I had enough to do today with running to the airport and coming here to copy flyers. Now I have to get these in envelopes and coach your father on district school policies."

"What were you doing at the airport?" I asked, dropping my wet sketchbook on the desk.

"Before you say anything," she began, "I wasn't meddling. Jeremy needed someone to pick him up, and I offered. Now it's up to you. I'll call you later."

I was too shocked to move or vocalize even one of the hundred comments or questions that raced through my head. Before I knew what she was doing, she'd kissed me on the cheek, and the next thing I knew, she was outside yelling, "Girls! We're leaving!"

"Wait. Where?" I asked, unsure if she was telling me Jeremy was at her house or mine. I heard the sound of footsteps over my head and said, "Jeremy? *Jeremy?*"

He must have heard me because the footsteps moved toward the stairs. By the time he was halfway down, I was in the living room, reaching him just as he made it to the bottom step. He practically leaped into my arms, wrapping his legs around me as I kissed his mouth, then his eyes, then his mouth again.

"Surprise! Happy Valentine's Day," he said. "I've missed you so much."

"Wait. I can't—I have to think," I said.

"Okay," Jeremy said agreeably. "You think. I'll be busy doing this." He unbuttoned my shirt and pressed his lips against my throat. "And this."

I felt like I was moving in a dream as he led me up the stairs to my bedroom and eased me to the bed.

"Jeremy—"

"Keep thinking. I spent a flight, a layover, another flight, and a car ride fantasizing about this. The car ride part wasn't easy, either. Your mother's wonderful, but it's hard to talk to someone when all you can think about is doing this to her son."

His tongue made its way down my body and I lay back, too weak with desire to do anything but surrender to him.

"Jesus," I said after he'd finished and moved up to rest his head next to mine on the pillow. "Is there no end to your talents?"

"You'll just have to keep me around to find out, won't you?"

"Don't joke about that," I said. "There's still an angry man inside me who's taken quite an emotional beating from you the last couple of weeks."

"Ethan told me Gemini men are great communicators," Jeremy said. "But no one told me you'd communicate with me through someone else. Instead of telling me how much my e-mail upset you and what you were thinking, you told Blythe. Who talked to Sheila. Who told Daniel. Who made a searing phone call that reminded me that his years hanging out with drag queens trained him in the art of shredding my character and good intentions."

"What good intentions?"

"All I wanted was time to wrap up loose ends. To fulfill certain commitments I'd made to Ethan and help him through a busy period. I made it perfectly clear in my e-mail that I wanted to be more involved with the kids than I could be in Oklahoma. I also told you I'd been replaying our night together, and the morning I left, and that I wished things had gone differently. I wanted so much to tell you that I loved you that night, but I didn't want to scare you off. The next morning you told me, and I wasn't sure if it was just the emotion of the moment or if you meant it. You never said it again, and I was afraid you regretted your words."

"If you had just told me—"

"Let me finish. You'll get your chance. I started falling for you at the retreat in that chakra class. After we got the disks from Disorient XPress, I understood how much I cared, because I was so disappointed when I thought that you and Ethan were dating."

"There was never anything like that between Ethan and me."

"I was pretty sure of that by the night I went with Daniel and Blaine to the Screening Room. That's the first time I understood what it is you do, and I was impressed. Not only did I think you were talented, but you were using your talent to help Andy. Your work was more than just a job to you. When you stood up to Daniel on my behalf, I felt like you understood that I wanted to do the same thing. Help people. By the time we danced at Club Chaos, I had no doubts about my feelings. I wanted to take things slowly to give us *both* time to be sure."

"I was sure. But I didn't mind waiting, Jeremy. After you went to Oklahoma, I didn't talk to you again about my feelings because I didn't want to pressure you. And you seemed so absorbed by your work."

"I did love what I was doing, and it kept me from dwelling on how much I wanted to come here. But you never asked me. You made a couple of halfhearted attempts to arrange something, but the slightest obstacle stopped our plans. You said you missed me, but it was obvious you were content to be back home and wrapped up in all that was going on here. And that damn Lars person kept showing up in your e-mails and our conversations. If you knew how many hours I kept your Web site up on my computer, staring at your house like I could magically transport myself here . . . It wasn't until I got your e-mail that I was sure about your feelings. Then all I asked for was time and trust. There was no way I was going to tell you I loved you on the phone or online. I had no idea you were angry with me, because you never said so. I'm done."

"I don't think you are."

"I love you. I don't want you to give up your home for me."

"My mother—"

"Is a wonderful woman or you wouldn't have told her the things you didn't tell me."

". . . talks too much," I finished.

"I have a degree from Juilliard. I've looked into the school sys-tems here, and I can easily get my teaching credential if I decide that's what I want to do. I don't have to be with Ethan to help him design programs or write grants. AFNAT will pay me a salary wherever I am. And where I want to be is right here. Now ask me to stay."

"It's apparent that you intend to, whether or not I ask," I teased him.

"Ask or you may never experience the rest of my talents."

"Jeremy, will you please move in with me so that we never have to talk through e-mails again, unless one of us is traveling? Oh, shit, I'm supposed to go to Chicago tomorrow to meet with Seaforth Chemicals. I'll see if I can reschedule—"

"I haven't answered yet."

I gave him an exasperated look and said, "Well?"

"Are you always this cranky after you've been given a world-class—"

I clapped my hand over his mouth and said, "Say it!"

He pulled away and said, "I can't talk through your hand. Yes. I will move in with you. And you will not reschedule your trip. One of us has to earn money. Government work and teaching won't make me rich. I can be very high-maintenance. In fact, why don't I have a present for Valentine's Day?"

"Did you check your e-mail this morning?"

"No."

"I sent your present electronically," I said. "Fortunately for you, I just happen to have a hard copy."

"A hard what?"

"Will you be serious?" I reached into my drawer and pulled out a notebook.

"A love letter?" he guessed.

"No. A story. The one I sent you is illustrated, but you'll have to settle for the narrative right now."

"You wrote me a story?" he asked, his eyes filling with tears even though he was smiling.

"And illustrated it. It's called 'The Lost Lion,' " I said, then began reading. "One time, in a land covered with snow, a very brave lion found himself lost and alone."

"This better have a happy ending."

"Jeremy, I promise you, I will always give you a happy ending."

He nestled next to me under the covers as I continued reading the story of the lion who found his way home.

Please turn the page for an exciting sneak peek
of Timothy James Beck's next novel
I'M YOUR MAN
coming in trade paperback from
Kensington Publishing in December 2004!

After pushing my way through the lobby doors, I consciously kept my pace slow and steady. I was in Baltimore, not Manhattan, so there was no reason to rush. I heard a dog barking when I rounded a corner, and I wondered how Rowdy would like living in the Big Apple. I couldn't imagine Frank turning his dog over to one of the dog-walkers who strode down the sidewalks clutching a dozen leashes being pulled in different directions like a willful balloon bouquet. Rowdy rarely left Frank's side, and I was sure that wouldn't change in Manhattan.

A pair of men, obviously a couple, walked toward me. They weren't holding hands, or walking with their arms around each other, but the close proximity they kept, as well as the affectionate eye contact they maintained as they spoke, indicated that they were a couple. Both men were in their late thirties and were dressed similarly in khakis, sweaters, and light jackets. I imagined the two of them in a Dockers ad in *Advocate* magazine, with their hands in each other's back pockets and grins on their faces.

When they passed me, I could see how attractive they were. One of the men returned my appraisal with a quick wink. I smiled, and I could see his partner give him a playful jab in the ribs to get his attention back where it belonged. After a few paces, I couldn't help but turn around to look at them. I caught them looking back as well, and they laughed and waved. I waved back.

I remembered taking long walks through Central Park with

Daniel when we were still together. We'd buy coffee and doughnuts to take with us as we meandered through the winding paths in the park. Daniel would point out certain plants and trees to me, explaining their growth habits and blooming periods. I'd listen and nod, but Daniel knew I'd never remember what he told me. To me, horticulture was like quantum physics; I appreciated it, but knew I'd never use it.

We'd have our coffee and doughnuts on the terrace of Bethesda Fountain. Oftentimes we'd tell each other stories and people-watch, since the terrace was a popular tourist stop. Then we'd follow paths deep into the heart of Central Park, walking hand in hand, oblivious to anyone but each other. When we reached the Reservoir, we'd walk along the running trail, mindful of the joggers while we loped along, talking the whole way, until we'd walked the entire distance around the basin of water. Then we'd go home, to his apartment or mine, it didn't matter, and lie together on the sofa, holding each other until our breathing matched.

As I watched the khaki couple walk away, I felt a stab of jealousy deep within me. I missed being part of a couple. Standing on a sidewalk in the middle of Baltimore at night, I suddenly felt very lonely.

I noticed that I was in front of a bar that had several signs with rainbow strips of buzzing neon underneath, around, or unfurling from the names of domestic beers in the darkly tinted windows. An imposing man with several tattoos, who was dressed in camouflage pants, a black T-shirt that looked a few sizes too small for his muscular build, and heavy black boots, stood to one side of the door. I glanced at him, looking for any sign that indicated a cover, and found none. He said nothing to me, but simply raised his eyebrows once in acknowledgment of my presence. I nodded my head in response and stepped inside.

There were televisions mounted throughout the bar, playing everything from soundless performances of music videos, clips from MGM musicals, and *Saturday Night Live* skits, none of which matched the music I heard from the jukebox across the room. Through a doorway to the right, I could see two well-built men, one leaning against a wall with a beer poised phallically on his groin, the other stretching over a pool table, carefully lining up his shot. There must have been several tables in the second room; although he hadn't shot, I could hear the clacking of billiard balls from other directions and the "thunk" of an occasional ball dropping into a pocket.

I walked to the bar. The bartender, a shorter version of Michael Jordan, greeted me with a smile and said, "What can I get you?"

"Sam Adams," I answered.

"You got it." He popped the top. "Glass?"

"No, thank you."

"No, thank *you,*" he said, as he put the change I left with the rest of his tips. "You're obviously not from here."

"People from Baltimore don't tip?"

"Not *that* much. I'd welcome you to Charm City, but I'm sure someone as cute as you has already been welcomed." That removed all doubts. I was definitely in a gay bar. He went on, "I can at least be the first to welcome you to Shenanigans."

I stopped mid-turn and said, "Shenanigans? That name sounds familiar. Are you famous for something?"

"Do you watch soaps?"

"No," I answered. Which was honest enough; I hadn't watched *Secret Splendor* since Daniel and I broke up.

"Our owner is a big *Days of Our Lives* fan and named this place after a bar they wrote out of their storyline in the '80s. His little homage to days of our lives gone by."

"Good times," I said, and heard him laugh as I made my way to a table. At least I could be sure *Secret Splendor* tapes wouldn't be popping up on Shenanigans' TVs, the way they did in a couple of bars in Manhattan.

I decided to put my people-watching skills to better use than nostalgia over Daniel, settling in to check out the bar's patrons. I was reminded of those beer commercials with young, vibrant, beautiful people having fun and laughing. Shenanigans was nothing like that. Everyone I saw struck me as ordinary. Perhaps I was used to Manhattan bars, the majority of which were designed to be featured in magazines as the next hot spot, only to be shut down and renamed a month later. I liked the idea of a bar that stayed around long enough to have a floor that felt a little gritty, lighting dimmed by a few burned-out bulbs, and regulars who knew I wasn't one of them but still gave off no attitude.

I saw a man come out of the poolroom and sit at a table across the room. He saw me squinting at him and raised his glass in my direction. I realized that I'd started an exchange I hadn't intended. He picked up his napkin and wrapped it around his drink, then crossed the room toward me. As he got closer, I thought of how Lillith always said, *There are no accidents.* Maybe I did mean to start an exchange with him. He was attractive, with shaggy blond hair, brown eyes, and a five o'clock shadow.

"Hey," he said. "May I join you?"

"Have a seat. I'm Blaine."

"Todd. You come here a lot?" he asked.

"No. I'm in town on business. Do you?"

"No, I'm here for work, too. Where are you from?"

"I live in Manhattan, but I'm from the Midwest," I answered. "How about you?"

"Miami. I work for an import/export company. What do you do?"

"I'm in advertising."

"How long are you staying?" Todd asked.

This was the part I hated. Until Daniel and I split up, he'd been the only man I slept with. After we broke up, I made up for lost time, feeling like I'd spent my twenties in two dead-end relationships. I'd married Sydney because I thought it was the right thing to do. I'd been with Daniel for love. I'd quickly learned that one-night stands were about instant gratification, so I didn't see the point of forced conversations or shared histories.

"Long enough to fuck you," I answered.

He started toward my side of the table, and I turned on my barstool to face him. He nudged his way between my legs and put his arms around my waist. Without another word, we tilted our heads and pressed our lips together as I put my arms around him, bringing him closer to me.

When I opened my eyes the next morning, it took me a minute to recognize the hotel room and another minute to realize that I wasn't alone, although I couldn't remember his name. I ran through the alphabet until I got to *T.* Todd. That was it.

I did remember the previous night and how removed I felt when Todd gripped the railing on the balcony overlooking the harbor until his knuckles turned white. Physically, it had been exciting to discover a new body, and a rather nice body at that. Something was missing though. Or maybe it just felt wrong because I'd let him spend the night. Sleeping together in the same bed implied an intimacy that I didn't feel.

I rubbed my eyes and decided to take a shower to rid myself of the smell of Todd. I got up without causing him to stir, then looked back at him. I feared that in daylight, I would discover that I'd brought home a monster whose imperfections had been hidden by shadow and the dim lighting of the bar.

The blinds cast vertical lines up and down his firm body. In the slats of light, I could see that my first impression had been right. He was handsome. But I felt a shocking rush of discomfort when I realized something else. He reminded me of Daniel. A rougher and less put together version of him, but a resemblance nonetheless. Maybe I was looking for similarities, but the end result was the same. I wanted to get him out of my bed and my life and get in the shower to wash away the night before. I almost sprinted toward the bathroom, but something squished between my toes. I looked down and saw a hastily discarded condom.

"Yuck!" I exclaimed, not meaning to say it out loud.

"What?" a sleepy voice asked from the bed.

I turned my back to him as I spoke. "Nothing. I'm just going to hop in the shower."

Todd didn't respond, and I shut the door to the bathroom and turned on the shower. As the water ran over me, I became conscious of the sore muscles in my back, neck, and legs. Gavin's warning had come true. I felt as if I'd had a brutal workout rather than a soothing massage. I twisted the nozzle to turn the spray to a pounding stream, centering my sorest muscles beneath the water. I felt like I was trying to beat out more than the stiffness.

When the soreness eased, I turned off the shower and got out quickly to towel dry. Hopefully, I would have the day to myself and not feel obligated to spend it with Todd. I wrapped the towel around my waist and stepped out of the bathroom.

My gaze fell on the bed, empty except for a hastily scribbled note lying on top of Todd's pillow. I walked over and picked it up.

Dear Brad,
You've definitely made my top-ten best-tricks list. Sorry I had to run. I forgot I have a meeting today. Maybe some other time.
Todd

Brad. I rolled my eyes, offended that he couldn't even remember my name. I whipped the towel from my waist, and it fell limply on the back of the oak desk chair.

After I dressed, I did a quick sweep of the room, looking under the bed for any misplaced items or stray socks. I picked up the used condoms from the floor and flushed them down the toilet, then grabbed the garment bag and strode to the elevator.

The lobby bustled with tourists and businessmen rushing to their destinations. A slight man behind the desk smiled at me as I approached.

"Was everything satisfactory, sir?" he asked, quickly typing something into the computer after I gave him my room number.

"The suite was fine," I said.

"Do you have the Amex that was used to hold the room?"

"Yes," I said, pulling my wallet from my back pocket. As I opened it, I flushed. The five hundred dollars in cash I'd had was missing. "This is not happening," I said, clenching my wallet in my fist and trying with all my might not to launch it across the lobby.

"Is the card misplaced, sir?"

I opened my wallet and pulled out the card. "No, it's right here."

I handed him my Amex and waited while he printed out my bill, silently cursing myself for bringing a stranger into my life and leaving him alone with my wallet. Everything he'd said to me was most likely a lie. Probably even his name.

I decided there was no point in calling the police or trying to get back the money. I'd only embarrass myself in the process. I chalked it up to a five-hundred-dollar lesson and asked the hotel clerk for the name of a car service to take me to the airport. Preferably one that would accept credit cards.

When my plane touched down at LaGuardia, I finally felt at ease and indifferent about Todd, the thieving trick from hell, but I was still bitter about losing five hundred dollars. I felt stupid for carrying that much cash in my wallet. Because of my size, I'd never felt threatened or worried about being attacked on the street. However, realizing that I'd invited a thief into my bed made me think that my mind wasn't as developed as my body.

I shrugged that off and found an ATM machine to get some cash. My cell phone rang while I stood in line outside the airport, waiting for a cab.

"Hello, Mr. Dunhill."

"Hello, Ms. Medina," I said to Violet. "I trust you've—"

"Cleared your schedule for today?" she asked. "Yes, I did. You only had one appointment. It was nothing that couldn't wait until Monday, so I went ahead and postponed it."

"That wasn't what I was going to ask, Violet."

"Oh. I fed Dexter this morning. Though I needn't have bothered, since he helped himself to a loaf of bread that was on top of the refrigerator."

"That's his way of telling me to back off from carbohydrates."

"I saw a dry cleaning stub on your counter, so I took the liberty of picking that up for you, since it was ready."

"You didn't have to do that."

"I know. You owe me fifty dollars."

"My dry cleaning bill was fifty dollars?"

"No. Your dry cleaning bill was forty dollars. You were out of cat food."

"What kind of food did you—"

"And litter."

"What did I do to deserve you? Manhattan, please. Forty-sixth Street and Ninth Avenue."

"Sounds like somebody just got a cab. You're not coming to the office today?"

"No. I'm going home."

"Good. I can cut out early and go to Barneys. I mean, I can finish typing these reports," she said, as if I would ever reprimand her for taking an afternoon off to go shopping.

The first time Violet ever took a sick day was the previous November, when she literally had to be carried out of the office on a stretcher because of stomach cramps. The pain had gotten so bad she was doubled up on the floor, clutching the itinerary for an upcoming location shoot and trying to crawl to the photocopy room. An ambulance had been called after Violet screamed out in pain when Evelyn, our office manager, tried to help her walk down the hallway to copy the itineraries so they'd go out on time. Two days after her appendix was removed, Violet called me, begging me to help bust her out of the hospital so she could get back to work.

"You're taking an afternoon off? There must be a full moon," I joked.

"You sound like Lillith," Violet said, hitting me where it hurt. "Speaking of Lillith, I suspect the reason you're not coming in today is so you can have a weekend to figure out what you're going to say to the boys upstairs about your resignation."

"If there's a Cuban version of Miss Marple, you'd be her," I stated wryly. "Which brings me back to what I was originally going to ask you. Have you typed your resignation yet?"

"If that's your clever way of asking me to jump ship and work for you at Lillith Allure, Mr. Dunhill—"

"Which it is. Yes."

"I'm not sure I can—"

"Take the bridge. Don't take the tunnel," I said to the driver. "I'm sorry, Violet. You were saying?"

"That's okay. If you had given me a little more time, I might have—"

"Do I need to give you money for the toll now? Or do I give you that at the end of the trip?" I asked the driver, who eyed me curiously, as we hadn't reached the bridge yet.

"You give it to me now. You give it to me later. It makes no difference," he said.

"Okay. I'll give it to you later," I said.

"If you interrupt me one more time, *I'm* gonna give it to you later," Violet said.

"I'm sorry, Violet. It won't happen again. What were you saying?"

"Stop playing games with me. I'm not turning you down," she said.

"Good," I said, breathing a sigh of relief. "I was running out of ways to interrupt you."

"I need more information before I can give you an answer," Violet said. "Plus I want to be wooed. Take me out to dinner, and we'll talk it over."

"Wooed? You want to be wooed? All right. Why don't we—"

"Sunday night? Eight? At Firebird? I'd love to," Violet interrupted.

"You've already made the reservations, haven't you?"

Violet confirmed my suspicions by not answering. Instead she asked, "I don't suppose you've seen the papers this morning? One paper in particular, I should say."

"No," I answered tentatively, hoping that any news about Lillith Allure hadn't been given to the press yet.

"Pick up the *Manhattan Star-Gazette* when you get home," Violet instructed.

"No," I begged. Violet knew that I only read the *New York Times* if I wanted news. The *Star-Gazette* was for entertainment news or, worse yet, when my friends and clients were hit hard in Lola Listeria's gossip column. "Maybe you should read me the highlights."

"Okay," Violet answered, and I heard the rustling of newspaper pages as she found the column. I calmed myself by looking at Manhattan's skyline as the taxi cab went over the Triboro Bridge. I was almost home.

"Ready?" Violet asked. "There's a whole section about an actress whose foot had to be cut out of a boot at a department store. I was going shoe shopping today, but now I don't think I want to."

"Just skip to whatever's relevant, please."

"If you want relevance, read the *Times*. Okay, here it is. 'Fashionista's Flight of Fury.' "

"Oh, no," I said.

Violet read on, "Saturn must have been lodged in Uranus during a flight to Baltimore when a certain model learned her agent turned down a booking for Claude Martrand's fashion show. Perhaps she was more furious because she hoped the designer would give her a free wedding dress? Or is it because our girl is too busy to get married? Lola's looking into her crystal ball, readers, and the future seems mighty cloudy. Not only for our star-crossed model, but for Metropole, too."

"Sheila will have a fit," I predicted.

"A fit has been had," Violet said. "Sheila's moved on to rage. She called me an hour ago."

"Maybe I should go see her," I mused.

"Let her cool down first," Violet advised. "She's working out her aggression in a kick-boxing class. Do you really want to see her right after that?"

"You're right, as usual. I don't. I'll call her later. We're pulling up to my building. I'll see you Sunday night, Ms. Medina."

"Good day, Mr. Dunhill."

My apartment was on the fifth floor of an old tenement building in midtown Manhattan. The neighborhood was affectionately named Hell's Kitchen. Though I'd lived there for three years, I still hadn't figured out how its name originated. I'd heard several theories from my neighbors, all of them confirming that the name had been around since the late 1800s. A woman who lived downstairs said there used to be a German restaurant named Heil's Kitchen a few blocks down from where we lived. The man who owned the dry cleaners on the corner said a *New York Times* article named a building in the west Thirties "Hell's Kitchen" because of a multiple murder that happened inside; the name spread to the area around it. For more than a century, the west side of Manhattan was home to the mob and street gangs. I personally thought my neighborhood got its name because there were so many restaurants in the area.

If Hell's Kitchen was still fraught with crime, I would never know it. When I first moved into my building, it was because the apartment was affordable. Now I appreciated everything about my neighborhood. I loved stopping into St. Famous Bread to grab a muffin and hear a cheery hello from the owner every morning on my way to work. I loved my deli, where I was always greeted like a cherished friend. I liked seeing familiar faces among the people on the sidewalks, even if I'd never have names or histories to go with them. If I wanted to bring work home with me, I could do it on my own terms. Everyone I knew from the world of advertising lived on the Upper East Side, out of town on Long Island, or in New Jersey, so it was rare to run into someone from the office in my part of the city.

The minute I let myself into my apartment, Dexter was underfoot, meowing to be fed. I stepped to the left, trying to avoid trampling him, and knocked over a small table, sending several days worth of mail, my keys, and a telephone tumbling to the floor.

"Damn you, Dexter!" I shouted, and he ran through the apartment to the safety of the bathroom. He didn't fool me. I knew in five minutes he'd forget all about my temper and would come back to let me know he could see the bottom of his food dish.

I was surprised to notice that my answering machine showed no messages, until I saw that Violet had screened them all and transcribed them onto a small notepad, which I found amid the clutter of stuff that I'd knocked to the floor. The majority of the calls were business related. Except for a call from Gretchen. Figuring she was most likely working, and not wanting to go through her office's convoluted voice-mail system, I dialed her cell phone, intending to leave a message to let her know that I was back in town.

"Hi!" Gretchen exclaimed, surprising me. Before I could say a word, she said, "Hey, I have to take this. Give me a few minutes."

I could hear voices in the background when she answered my call, then I heard her walk away until the sounds of New York's white noise replaced the voices. She must have stepped outside.

"Okay, I can talk now," she said. "Sorry about that."

"Are you at work? It sounds like you're outside. What did you do, step out on a ledge? Don't do it, Gretchen!"

"Accountant and window ledge jokes are about as tired as postal workers and pistols, Blaine. Besides, the market is quite bullish today. And so am I. But no, I'm not at work."

"I have a message that you called me. What's going on?" I asked.

"I saw Lola Listeria's column in the *Star-Gazette*. I tried to call Sheila, but she was at the gym or something, according to Josh. He didn't say anything about the column, and I didn't ask."

"Smart move," I commented, filling Dexter's bowl with food. He immediately came out of hiding to eat, not bothering to thank me. "I haven't talked to her yet. I'm not looking forward to it."

"I don't want to see her blow a good thing by flipping her lid. That's all," Gretchen said. "She's very lucky to be successful. Especially in a career where everything could end as quickly as it began. So I wanted to see if there's anything I could do."

"Sheila's no fool. She knows she has a good thing. One little argument with her agent won't send her life falling down like a house of cards."

Gretchen suddenly became quiet, and I could hear someone speaking to her in the background. Then she said, "I have to go, hon."

"*Hon?* You never call me that. Or anyone, for that matter. Gretchen, where are you, anyway?"

"Okay, 'bye," she said quickly and disconnected our call.

Still holding my cordless phone, I stood in the middle of my apartment, wondering why Gretchen had acted so oddly. It was almost as if she was keeping our conversation a secret from someone. She'd said she wasn't at work, where it might make sense to disguise a personal call. But since she wasn't, why would she take the call outside? Away from whomever—

Suddenly it was all too clear to me. I strode across my apartment to one of the two windows and looked down at Daniel's patio garden. There, talking with Martin and gesticulating, her cell phone still in her hand, was Gretchen. I turned on my cordless phone and started punching in numbers. When she answered, I said, "Gretchen, *hon,* when you're done down there, could you stop by my place for a minute? I've been thinking of investing in a new home. The view here sucks."

I hung up without waiting for an answer. She looked up at my window, as did Martin, who blew me a kiss. I waved, then stepped away from the window. If the only word for my reaction was petulant, the best description of my mood was pissed off. Which I knew was ridiculous. Gretchen and Martin had been friends for a long time. Even if he'd been part of my breakup with Daniel, I couldn't expect everyone else to be mad at him, too.

I supposed what was really bothering me was how seeing them at Daniel's made me feel excluded. It reminded me of the time when I'd first noticed him and tormented myself trying to figure out who he was, who his friends were and what they talked about, and what the details of his life were. It was as if Daniel was a stranger again, and I was on the outside.

The phone rang, and I took a deep breath before I answered.

"You sound strange," Violet said. "I forgot to tell you something. You received a fax today from Gavin Lewis. The massage therapist I found for you in Baltimore. What should I do with it?"

"We'll talk about it on Sunday night. Stop working!"

"Not to worry. I'm already checking out a sexy sales associate at Barneys."

"He's gay. Or in a committed relationship. Or both."

"How do you know?"

"Because I don't need for you to fall in love, get married, and leave me."

"I'll keep that in mind. Good-bye again, Mr. Dunhill."

The phone rang again as soon as I clicked off. I sighed and answered it in a more polite tone.

"Lunch tomorrow at one," Gretchen said briskly. "The Vinyl Diner."

"I'll see you then," I agreed.

Gretchen was at the restaurant before me the next day. "Hi," she said, but didn't stand to hug me. I could tell by her guarded expression that she was trying to gauge my mood.

"I apologize for being rude to you on the phone yesterday," I said. "I'm still not exactly in the best space when it comes to Daniel."

"Figuratively, or are we back to discussing apartment locations?"

"Both," I said, then paused while she considered her ordering options with the waiter. After he left, I said, "Why do I get the feeling this is not one of our regular get-togethers? What's on your mind?"

The clattering of plates made her wince, and she looked around. "I probably could have chosen a quieter place. I don't know how I feel about yelling private things about my life for an audience."

"We could walk back to my apartment after we eat," I suggested. "I'm sure Dexter would be thrilled by the possibility of another pair of hands to feed him."

Gretchen laughed, and we talked for a while about Dexter, then Sheila and Josh. I noticed the shadows under her eyes and wondered if she'd been working longer hours now that we were entering tax season, or if something was bothering her. I felt a guilty relief that someone other than me might have problems that led to sleepless nights.

After lunch, we strolled back to my apartment. There was a chill in the air, but Gretchen seemed to be in no hurry. That made me curious. It was obvious she had something she wanted to talk about, but equally apparent that she dreaded it.

While she petted Dexter and caught her breath from the five flights up, I poured glasses of wine for us, hoping that would help relax her. I didn't mind if it turned into a lazy Saturday afternoon that stretched into the evening. It seemed both of us needed a break from something in our lives.

"Where would you move?" she asked, sipping her wine as she looked around. "The rent here is great. You've got two bedrooms. You could convert Sheila's old room into an office."

"I like the apartment. I like the rent. I like the neighborhood. But it's impractical now that Daniel and I broke up. My gym is in Chelsea. My office is even farther. It would make sense to be closer to both."

"I guess. Except for the whole ordeal of finding another place, moving—"

"I may have that covered," I said, then told her about Gavin and my idea to hire him as my personal assistant.

"Are you sure?" Gretchen asked skeptically. "He's a total stranger. There are a lot of unscrupulous people out there."

"You're telling me," I said, thinking of Todd the thieving trick. "But if Gavin's references check out, why not?"

"For one thing, it sounds like his most important reference is dead," Gretchen said. "Although I probably have some clients who knew Lowell Davenport. Would you mind if I asked around about this Gavin guy?"

"Gavin Lewis. Not at all," I said, liking it that Gretchen felt protective of me. "I think moving is a good idea for several reasons. Yesterday, for example. I don't need to know when you're with Daniel."

"He's not back in town," Gretchen said quickly. "Martin and I were there to water his plants."

"He'll be back eventually. You don't need to be caught in the middle. We have other friends in the same predicament. Sheila. Josh. Adam."

Gretchen smiled and said, "Aren't you forgetting a few names?"

"No," I said. "You're the ones I want joint custody of."

"Maybe I should make you fight for me in court," she said, running her fingers through her hair. When Sheila made the same gesture, she looked girlish and flirtatious. Gretchen looked tired and exasperated.

"What's wrong?" I prodded. "What's this all about?"

"I don't know how to explain it," she admitted. "Without sounding really weird and freaking you out."

"You're usually blunt," I said. "That works for you, doesn't it?"

She narrowed her eyes, inhaled, squared her shoulders, and asked, "Have you had sex with anyone other than Daniel since you broke up?"

I nearly spewed my wine, but managed to merely choke. Gretchen thumped my back a couple of times, and I looked at her warily.

"Why would you ask me that?"

"Maybe I should back up. I'm not asking from a moral standpoint, or as Daniel's friend. But it's not idle curiosity, either. See, I want your sperm."